Under the E
of the World

Book Four of the Surface and the Deep

Story of Anna of Cleves

By G. Lawrence

Copyright © Gemma Lawrence 2025
All Rights Reserved.
No part of this manuscript may be reproduced without Gemma Lawrence's express consent.

**Dedicated to Fe
And all her bees**

Prologue

July 1557

Chelsea Manor

England

There is a sound of weeping. Soft tears fall on soft cheeks, and ruddy ones. I wish I had the strength to tell my people not to cry so for me, but barely can I lift my head. I am so weak. Yet if I could I would tell them not to sorrow. I see the end; it is not to be feared. There is no mouth of darkness waiting to swallow me. There is a darkness yes, but within its folds there are hands, ones so familiar, and to me they reach, in love.

People will say I died alone, yet I am surrounded by people. They will say I could have lived longer, and that is indeed true, that I could have done more, which is true also, although a pointless observation. All people could do more if they had more time, and some do nothing with the time they are given but waste it. I have done enough, and the hands reaching for me are proof of that. The Almighty has sent a guide to lead me to the next adventure, a guide I know well and trust, and in this last service done to me, sending a friend in a time of uncertainty and fear, I know God is at peace with all I have done, and not done, with this cherished life granted to me.

What more will friends gathered here, at my sickbed and those far away, wish I might have done? What are the things of which we should be proud in our lives? I was born a Duchess and once was a Queen. People will tell you titles are something to be proud of, that I did well to achieve the highest of positions, save Empress, to which a woman might aspire.

Yet when I look back on my life, that short time as Queen is not what I hold dearest to my heart, it is not what I clasp against me, a reminder of the goodness in my soul, of the worth of my life. The times I hold most dear are brief, fleeting moments, times when I managed not to respond with fury when someone angered me, times when I was calm whilst someone tried to treat me as if I was less than human, times I helped a friend or a stranger, when that act might well have put me in danger. Times of courage, small deeds which might never be remembered, these are what I remember, not the crown, a gaudy diadem intended to impress the credulous, that I briefly wore, not the title I was born into, a gift of luck and not of worth.

It is not the worth the world recognises which denotes our value as a person. The world is a fool, blind to the goodness and purity of a soul as it gazes instead, its feeble sight bedazzled by glitter of gold and temptation of silver, by softness of fur, upon the rulers we have accepted and bowed to out of fear. The world is a gadding, sycophantic servant of the rich, for it is they who have moulded it and shaped it over eons, fooled it into thinking that in affluence is the measure of a soul found. The world is made of our minds, our eyes, and they have become deceived. We have forgotten what is good, under the glamour of gold, mistaken what is pure when upon pearls we gaze.

A glittering show bedazzles us, so we stare in one direction alone, confused, not understanding we see not light, but the mere reflection of light cast on a diamond's carved surface.

There comes a time in life where we all must turn from this false show, decide to act as our morals and heart and soul dictate, to stand for what we believe is worth standing for, to let go what we believe is not. As we make that choice, we decide who we truly are. There are things worth dying for, there are people worth surviving for, the choice that must be made is ours and it is the most precious thing we can do with this one life we are granted.

So many people only behave well when the eyes of the world are trained upon them, but it is not those eyes we should worry on. It should be the inner eye of our own conscience we have a care for, aiming to make that eye content when on our deeds it settles.

So, when it comes to the end, as the end comes for me now, it is not crowns and riches I remember. It is friends, family, those I love and have loved me, and what I remember is how I treated them.

That is why I may stare into the end with clear eyes, never fearing what will come. I may become only a footnote to history, a scrap of a life barely noted except to say that once I married a king, but to those whose lives I aided, I meant something. To them, at times, I was everything. That is enough for me.

Should it matter that history, that inconstant, wealth-worshipping creature remember us, or should it be we place more worth in remaining constant in the minds and hearts of those we did acts of goodness for, no matter if those deeds are never known or recorded?

A swan glides on the surface of waters deep, no one noting the grace we all see is granted by her legs paddling hard and suffering long underneath. Such is the same of life. People see what is obvious and miss what is not. They see the surface, for it is under the eyes of the world, but the truth of us, of our souls, lies in the deep.

Chapter One

February – March 1542

Richmond Palace

"Yes, Madame de Cleves."

The voice muttered so low I had to squint my eyes, as if such would help me to hear better.

Head bowed, eyes down, Kitty scurried away, a shell of her former self. She had been like this since men of the King, who had taken her for questioning over her incautious remarks about the King's marriages, had released her back into my house. Jane Rattsey had gone home, at her request, and seeing her, too, transformed into a hollow woman I had released Jane out of pity, telling her she could return to my service whenever she liked.

Quiet, subdued, scared, Kitty knew how close she had come to greater punishment, punishment that came with blood. The axe had swung close, grazed skin upon her neck. Now my formerly bright, outspoken maid was meek, obedient, a model servant in many ways, yet though many times I had told Kitty to watch her mouth's proclivity for loose gossip, I missed now the words that once had come tumbling from her lips with such abandon. She was probably safer now that she was scared but she had become less than she had been before. The King in his *greatness* had made her smaller. The fear his men had inspired in my servant had sucked at the essence of her soul, left her a ghost of herself. Kitty haunted her own life now.

Was this what the King would do to all of us in the end? That even if he did not kill us as he had two wives and so many friends, he would make his subjects ghosts, make us so afraid of death and pain we ceased to live whilst still alive? Would we all end up hollow, staring things, portraits upon his walls, glassy eyes and empty minds? Soon people would not dare to think in case that thought became treason, since the King now changed his laws to kill anyone he wished. It seemed Bluff Hal was surrounded by people, yet soon not one of those faces would have a soul or spirit or heart behind it. Would we end up walking through this life alive with nothing worth living to call our own, no opinions, no beliefs, no other will but his?

The one who had tried to live by that maxim was dead now, a true ghost, so even absolute obedience would not save us.

Yet in the short life she lived, Catherine Howard had been a quiet rebel. That much was true. Even though I believed her innocent, it was true she had deceived the King in certain ways. Not the ways men said, not what she was accused of, but she had given her heart to another, she had considered a time the King did not hold her liberty in his hands. I did not believe charges of adultery or treason, but I did believe the young girl had been planning, had dared to hope, for a life all her own.

Had Catherine Howard perhaps lived more than any of us would? The King, his temper capricious and cruel when unleashed, was bent on quashing all who did not agree with him, his boot merciless and resentful, relentless as it pressed on the neck of his country choking air from the windpipe of his people. With sad eyes I watched Kitty depart the chamber. I doubted she would ever say another word out of turn after the fright she had experienced. Her body had survived arrest and questioning, but a part of her had died.

I wished I could in some ways act as the King did. I did not wish to drain the life out of people, but I would have wished I could kill certain ideas that people formed. My brother was still sending ambassadors to meet with members of the council, trying to persuade the English King that now Catherine Howard was dead he should take me back as Queen. To Ambassador Olisleger I had said that if the King decided to take me back, then for the sake of my country I would again step into the flames and become his Queen, yet with all my heart I hoped the King did not want me any more than he had two years ago when first I stepped on the shores of England.

If I became his Queen again, would I become as Kitty was now, a broken fragment of a person scuttling around, trying to be quiet so no one noticed me? Trying to be meek so no one thought me bold enough to behead? Trying to be in all outward ways obedient so no one thought me a traitor and locked me away in that Tower so full now of ghosts of all the people who the King once loved and who had loved him, where echoes of past loves had become haunted screams?

If I became his wife again, would I become Queen of a nation of the living or dead? Would I be able to exert any form of influence upon my husband to help save my people from war with the Emperor? And if I could have no influence, as I thought would be the case, what was the use of this sacrifice of my freedom, happiness, my liberty and quite possibly my life? Every one of his wives he had destroyed in one way or another. Why would I be any different?

There are some battles which cannot be won, and to throw oneself into the fray is not bravery but suicide. Would I give up my life for my people? I had already sworn to, if the King wanted me. Did I think this sacrifice worthy of my life? No, I did not.

The King had proved what he wanted of a wife now, he wanted a mirror reflecting only the best of him, his glory, his magnificence. He wanted not a wife who would influence him. Those days were dead, long buried and rotting in the ground. He wanted Jane Seymour, or the woman she had pretended to be whilst his wife, in the body of young Catherine Howard. No more Katherines of Spain, no more Anne Boleyns. My brother thought I could marry the King and convince him to enter war alongside Cleves against the Emperor. If I married the King, I knew I would not dare open my mouth.

I alone appeared to know this, everyone else was lost in a delusion.

Even people close to me thought I should be eager to be Queen again. Ambassador Harst had always believed it was my destiny and was in a flurry, running about court, trying to gain supporters for me. Olisleger was well aware I was afraid, yet since my brother had pressed him to convince me to become Queen again, Olisleger seemed to have convinced his troubled conscience that truly I *did* want to be Queen and was simply afraid of rejection.

I was more afraid of acceptance.

The only one who seemed to truly understand was Katherine Willoughby, Duchess of Suffolk. She understood because, as was clear to me and all people, if she had not a husband living, the King might well have looked her way for a new wife.

"If you were to wed the King anew, there would be many to support you," my friend mentioned as we sat with spiced, warm wine at my fireside.

"And just as many to not." I stared into the flames. "You know as well as I do, my friend, the court of England has fangs and claws, eager things ready to rip a woman to shreds." *As we have just witnessed*; I thought of young Catherine, cold and decaying in her bloody grave.

"Much as I know you are nervous, you should know, there are people saying you are, in fact, already married to the King now." Katherine sipped her wine, hot vapour puffing over her words.

"How so?"

She cocked her head. "It is a little technical and not at all clear, but some say that because of the accusations against Mistress Howard of bigamy, which never were fully proved, as well as the charges of treason, her marriage to the King was not valid."

"But the King's Act upon marriage to Catherine stated that a previously unconsummated marriage was made void by a consummated one," I objected. "So my marriage was rendered void by hers to the King."

"But if she was wed, as some believe, to Dereham, then her marriage to the King was not lawful, and the consummation of her marriage to the King therefore did not render your marriage to him void. Do you see?"

I would have laughed, had there been any mirth in me. "The King will choose a new wife, of that I am sure. I am also sure it will not be me."

Others were not so certain. In fact, much of England appeared to be under the impression that I was fair in love with the King. Largely this was due to that infamous book, the letter apparently penned by me in which I lamented the loss of the King's love and wished again for marriage with him.

The book "written" by me was still circulating. The King of France, another who was encouraging the King to wed me again, largely because he was allied to Cleves and wanted England as a companion in war, had sent people to find the printer and stop them after the King's ambassador, William Paget, pressed him on the matter, but evidently enough copies had leaked out for people to trade with one another. In many circles the book was gaining me sympathy. People thought I had written it and was denying authorship in case the King came to my door threatening to arrest me for treason. They said I had penned it as a way to gain back the attention of the King, so long turned from me, towards a younger woman. Limited though my experience with men was, I thought shaming the King in front of his peers as well as his people was hardly the way to his heart. To death, it might well be the way, but not to love. The King did not like people feeling sorry for anyone but him, after all, and this pitiable text had brought me once more to the fore of people's sympathies, pitting me in many ways against the King, who according to the letter was my wrongdoer, denying me the love I so cherished for him.

"Whoever wrote that book is no friend to me, more likely enemy," I had told Katherine.

She nodded in thought. "I understand," she agreed. "It has put you in a perilous position."

"And the worst of it is, the people believe I am this lamenting, howling woman!" I threw my hands in the air. "It is so easy to believe, is it not, that a woman rejected must always be pining for the one who rejected her? No one can quite bring themselves to believe I might have been relieved by the rejection. Every cast-off woman *must* be a pitiable figure, pining away for lack of love."

"Well, you know you cannot *possibly* be happy without a man." Katherine's eyes sparkled with mischief as her tongue dripped with sarcasm. "Such a thought would upend the world. Even nuns and abbesses have Christ as their husband."

I managed to laugh a little.

In response to this outburst of support and sympathy for me, I had maintained the late fiction of my illness so I could avoid people. The fever which had apparently recurred in my blood for months, keeping me away from court and the King, was here again, holding me in bed. When a doctor sent by the King had come to my bedside, I had been forced to douse myself in warm water and affect spasms of the body. Telling him the fever did not fall on me every day, but came back every three and listing more of what I could remember from my mother's herbals, I convinced the foolish man I was indeed sick. That my "sickness" did not come upon me every day was useful, as plenty of people had seen me out of bed.

After he had examined my urine – which, although perfectly healthy in colour he *tsked* at with a dour brow – he announced to the King I was suffering a tertian fever. I had been rather pleased with my abilities as a player. I should have been on the stage.

More remedies, the King's personal recipes, had been sent from court, leading to even more fools saying it was clear the King would take me back for look how deeply concerned he was for the welfare of the Lady of Cleves. I had been stuffed full of these remedies of the English, some good and some bewildering, as well as being vigorously bled which had the effect of making me weak and shivery the next time a doctor came to inspect me, which I supposed was to my benefit.

I had my people dispose of the King's herbs and remedies after that and took my own to restore myself. Some physicians of England knew much, I will grant that, but some I was more knowledgeable than, something I became painfully aware of as they rattled on, speaking on subjects of which they knew little yet affected to know much. Some were dullards entirely reliant on magic to impress patients and glean money from purses. Some were *kwaksalvers*, or quacks as the English charmingly called them, hawkers of fraud and fakeries. The King, who despite all evidence to the contrary thought himself an expert, employed both, not knowing the difference between them. I, trained in herb lore and remedies as a child, who had continued to educate myself as a woman, could see vast disparities.

I supposed some of this willingness to believe in such men was desperation, and the rest arrogance on the part of the King. He believed himself, on the basis of but small evidence, to be an expert in medicine, just as he was in almost everything else. He was a philosopher, athlete, doctor, physician, midwife, scholar, king and pope. No man is all these things, and the King certainly fell short of many of the titles he awarded himself.

That he believed men who knew nothing yet spoke with confidence, a key aspect of any trickster, demonstrated the King's lack of true knowledge. He deceived himself about the depths of his knowledge just as he deceived himself about the depths of his heart. He wanted to believe in magical cures. His leg assailed him, headaches too. When one is sick and broken, magic becomes most attractive, the idea someone could just drink a potion, and spirits of sickness would retreat is enticing. The King had money and would pay a great deal for a simple potion which immediately cured everything. It did not, of course, exist.

I nodded to my man Diaceto – one of my household who had come with me from Cleves and never returned – as he entered with a missive. He had started as a page and become a gentleman server. He was also becoming one of my best links to gain information.

The message in his hand was not as interesting as the one he had memorized. In a low voice, so if Wymond Carew was listening at my door again, trying to get me or more of my household into trouble with the King, he would hear nothing, Diaceto murmured, "Vice-Chancellor Olisleger sends word, Highness. The Emperor is to go to Castile, leaving his sister Maria of Hungary in charge of the Low Countries. There is word he is mobilizing for war with France and Cleves."

I breathed in. "And my brother?"

"Is doing the same, Highness, in terms of preparation. Chancellor Olisleger is sending someone now to check on the progress of the matter, but he sends word there is a good chance he may be recalled to Cleves at this delicate time. Your brother the Duke will need his best advisors."

"Of course. I hope Olisleger will have a moment to see me before he leaves?"

"He says if it is a swift journey, there and back, he may simply go, my lady. If it is a longer time he will be away, he will come to you first, of course."

I inclined my head. Olisleger had frequently had to run back and forth from our country to England when my brother had need of him. "You will need a reply to this." I indicated to the paper he had carried which held news of the numbers of deer in my parks, a cover for the true news of course.

"Otherwise that odious Carew, no doubt listening at the door, will grow suspicious. He may ask to read it, hand it to him without argument if he does."

Carew was still checking my correspondence. I wanted no tales of me talking of anything of importance getting to the King. The King kept me in ignorance, as far as he knew, and that was how I would officially stay. Little was written down anymore by any of us. It was safer that way.

"You have been at court?" I asked Diaceto as I wrote. He inclined his dark head. "Tell me, how does the King?"

"Merry and well, so says everyone, Highness. He is inviting many ladies to feasts; people say he will choose a new wife soon from amongst those at court."

"Does he still send many presents to Mistress Anne Bassett?"

"That affair appears to have become a little less enthusiastic since her sister, your servant Kitty, was arrested, Highness," my man said. "But there are many others he may choose from. It is said the sister of Master Cobham was greatly favoured by the King at one event, she who is married to Thomas Wyatt, though not happily, and the daughter of Madame Albart at another. Many people speak highly of you, Highness, as well, putting you forth. The King has not said yea or nay to any proposal."

That was what worried me.

The King's reaction to his wife's death chilled me. Although he had been enraged at first when he heard Catherine had been with other men before him, although he had been sad when she was in prison at Syon, now she was gone of this world he was straight away getting down to business again. These feasts where women of court were invited, they were like a man interviewing for a post in his household, or as if the King was to go to market to pick a new horse. The suggestion, after Jane Seymour had died, that the French King send his womenfolk to Calais so the King could pick whichever he liked the most, had been shamed out of coming to reality as French ambassadors roundly informed the King he could not choose a French wife thus, like a man in a brothel picking his mount for the night, yet now he was using the same method to find a new English wife.

Or an old one of Cleves.

If you had told Olisleger no, and stuck to it, you would not be in this position, said the dry voice of the long-dead Queen in my mind.

You could not understand, I replied in the stillness of my echoing thoughts. *You, you he took for love, when he still had a heart which beat inside him. I came here for my people, I knew it was a risk to my life then, when first I was sent.*

How many times will it be acceptable for your brother to send you to stand before Death, Anna? asked the voice. *Your people do not ask this of you, he does. Would he risk himself for them, as you are willing to? Men ask much of us which never are they willing to do themselves.*

If there is war, he will fight alongside his men.

Will he? Many generals do not into the fray go, they stand aside, letting others bleed for them. Every marriage risks a woman's life in childbed, so always it is a sacrifice, but in this match, child or no child, your blood could well spill. He would send you into the fray, but would he go there himself?

In truth, I was not sure.

Chapter Two

April 1542

Richmond Palace

"You have come in person," I said sadly to Olisleger.

"I have, my lady." He kissed my hand.

"You think therefore you will be away some time?"

He inclined his head, glancing around before he whispered into my ear. "The Emperor has asked your brother to support him against the threat of the Turks, but Duke Wilhelm retorted he only would on one condition, that the Emperor not attack or harry him for twenty years. Charles V would make no such promise, so the last chance to make friends between them is dead."

I sighed. Sometimes I did not comprehend my brother. Goading the Emperor as if he had as many resources and men as the most powerful ruler on earth? "Keep my brother safe, Olisleger, from himself if no one else."

Olisleger stood back, smiling sadly. "It is not in the nature of princes to listen to mere servants, sadly, my lady, but for your sake I shall do my best. Your brother recalls me home, but I hope I will be able to visit again soon. I am still a named ambassador to England, after all."

"I shall pray for you, and for your return."

"You still have Harst, my lady, and many friends here in England."

"Not as many as I would like."

He clasped my hand. "No man, or woman, my lady, can be friends with all people. It is a thing impossible, for even were you to be loved by many there would be some who would hate you for that very reason."

"How true, and how sad are those words, my friend."

He leaned in as if to kiss my cheek and there came another whisper. "There is word, most secret, Highness, that your former husband intends to ally England to the Emperor, rather than with François and your brother. If this happens, Highness, you will be in a situation most delicate here in England. We will try to extract you."

As Olisleger stood back I caught fear in his eyes. He knew such thoughts were futile. My brother, my people, they might try to extract me, but it would not work. The King was never going to let me go now. If he joined with the Emperor, I would be left, stuck, a prisoner in a country officially at war with my homeland. I would be one of the enemy, standing unarmed on the wrong side of the field. My position was already delicate. This could make it untenable.

"This means he does not want to wed me again," I whispered to myself when Olisleger left, but this news, which should have sent my heart surging, did not bring much comfort.

Out of one danger I might be, as long as the King kept to his present course and that was by no means certain since he was changeable as the English weather, but even if removed from this one danger, I was now facing another.

"Do you think some people are ever destined to be in the wrong place at the wrong time?" I asked my friend of Suffolk.

She smiled. I had explained my new, worrisome situation so she knew what I was asking. "I sometimes wonder on the will of God." She linked her arm with mine as we walked in the frosty spring gardens, her hand meeting mine in the curve of our arms. The air was icy, our breath emerging as clouds of silvered mist. "And yet I have to believe there is to all things a purpose, whether we can see it or not."

"You do not think, then, that some end up not where they are supposed to be?"

"I think we all end up where God believes we may be of use, my friend. Sometimes that may well not be a good or painless place, but we are set there for a purpose, that I do believe. Sometimes our role is to help another, perhaps in a way we never will know or understand, and sometimes our role is to help ourselves. I do believe that God delivers us into a position where we may do *something*, little or great, for the betterment of the world, and if we do not do this, we do not carry out His plan. But if we do all we can, we work for the Almighty."

I put my other hand on hers as well, covering her cold hand with both of mine. "So, I am meant to be here, for some purpose, though sometimes it feels I am adrift?"

"We are all adrift at times, my friend. The secret is to catch on to one another in this furious sea we have been thrown into and hold on. I think you were meant to come to England."

"For what purpose?"

Katherine smiled. "If for nothing else, to be my good friend and comfort in this world."

I laughed as we walked on, clasping the hand of my friend tighter, warming her skin with mine.

Chapter Three

July – October 1542

Hever Castle

Kent

I moved my household to Hever that summer. It was safer to get away from London in the heated months in case of plague, and at times, when strolling the gardens of Hever, planning additions to the house or hunting in the marshlands, I could for a moment forget the horrors about to fall upon my country, the fear inherent in my own position in England, what would become of me. Then, when I achieved a moment of peace, I would suffer guilt for having the licence to forget the troubles of others for a while. It was a freedom others did not have, particularly those who would feel the brunt of this coming war the most, such as the poor. I, here in England, might be in danger if my new brother went to war with my homeland, but I would not witness what those at the sheer, brutal face of war would. My position in title and location offered me this concession. I was aware how fortunate I was.

That summer the Schmalkaldic League seized the duchy of Brunswick, last of the Catholic territories in the northern Germanic states. Brunswick's leader was captured and taken to Hesse, where he stayed for several years as a prisoner. Swiftly, reformation was spreading in states affiliated with the League, and to the intense consternation of the Emperor the mint started to circulate coins bearing the likeness of my brother-in-law Johann Friedrich on one side and Phillip, Landgrave of Hesse, his fellow leader of the League, on the other. In many ways, this minting of coinage was an even more direct threat to the power of the Emperor than invasion or battle. Coins were the way most people saw the face of their ruler every day; it was a scream of defiance against the Empire and a sign the Emperor was being removed.

We had heard in June, through Harst, that the word amongst ambassadors was that my former husband was now close to making a formal alliance with the Emperor but had expressed some concern about the Emperor's intentions towards Guelders, and therefore Wilhelm and my people. Although this concern had been expressed, which showed the King was thinking of someone other than himself, a remarkable thing in itself, it had not stopped any plans of alliance with the Emperor.

Talks were still going on and the word was the King would offer support to Charles. They would make war on France together, which was, of course, the sweetest segment of this tempting fruit to my former husband, and once that land was theirs, they would carve it up between them. The King would emerge from his reign victorious, with a male heir waiting in the wings and having restored the once great empire of England. All else he had done for which men might name him a tyrant or a monster would be forgotten, for it would be whispered by the dusty breath of history that he had done his duty, done as much if not more than his father, had done as a king should. He had always wanted to be as Henry V, the warrior-king who had marched out to claim back England's empire, and if a campaign in France went well, Henry VIII would be remembered for the same thing.

The King was relying on the breath of history speaking his name, and on the memory of history being ever a patchy and inconstant record. It was not too much to hope for. The remembrance of history *is* an ever-unreliable creature, accustomed to pandering to the whims of fickle kings and men with blood on their hands, used to omitting much and recalling but small detail. If he could win this war, he could make all his dreams come true and history would dance at his side, fawning on his name forever more.

"I have heard, Highness, the King is suggesting that Duke Wilhelm repudiate his match with Jeanne of Navarre and join the alliance *against* France. In such a deal he would be given either Lady Mary or Lady Elizabeth as his wife and would retain Guelders for his lifetime." A breathless Ambassador Harst still had his cap in his hands and his travelling cloak on his shoulders as he gave me this news, so eager was he to impart it. "The King appears to be negotiating with Ambassador Chapuys, trying to find a way to persuade your brother to join with England and the Empire, rather than France."

As a silent prayer I touched a jewel upon my girdle, a chain which held a pendant showing Jacob's Ladder, picked out in enamel, demonstrating God's wish to reunite Heaven with Earth. "Would the Emperor agree? Has it not already gone too far for this?"

Harst scratched his nose. "I have heard, Highness, the King is quite adamant that out of respect and friendship for you, he will not aid the Emperor in doing anything against Cleves."

I doubted this was true. The King thought of me at times as a friend, but such emotions meant little to my brother of England. If he was saying this in talks it was either to extract something of worth for himself from the deal, or it was to settle that ever-unpredictable conscience of his so that if the Emperor did march on my people, he was not to blame for it.

I smoothed my dress, more to give myself command over my racing thoughts than to erase any creases from the crimson velvet. "But in other ways he will act, against France he will, so whilst he would not attack Cleves with English troops, he would weaken my brother by attacking his allies. Then the Emperor will come for my brother, for our people, Harst, and you know what will happen. We are too small a country to withstand the wrath of the forces the Emperor may unleash. Cleves breeds men of courage, but we are too few and they too many."

"The King has always wanted France, and no friendship with any person or alliance would get in the way of that."

I tapped a fingernail on my armrest. "Would Wilhelm do this? Enter into a pact with England and the Empire?"

Harst appeared dubious. "I am not even sure the Emperor would support the notion, Highness. Were your brother to annul his present marriage and be promised to another bride in order to retain Guelders, the Emperor would want him, surely, wed to a woman of his own family, not one of the daughters of the King of England, in order to ensure your brother remained loyal to the Emperor. The Emperor is unlikely to trust that an alliance between Wilhelm and Henry of England would continue to be loyal to his interests indefinitely, he does not trust the King that much and for good reason. Promises between princes are fragile things and both the Emperor and the King have made many an oath most sacred and eternal to one another in the past and gone back on them the moment a better deal came along."

"I doubt Wilhelm would agree either, in any case." I chewed my lip. "It is clear this is about more than Guelders, but about pride for my brother. He desires to face the Emperor, to show Charles V that he is equal to him. The trouble is, he risks Cleves in the process. Our father kept our country safe, always. He negotiated, used politics, for he understood the strengths of Cleves but also our limitations. I wish my brother would demonstrate more care for our country."

"At least it appears the King has concern for our country, my lady."

"Concern is easy to express, without action it is meaningless."

"Imperial ambassadors are saying it would be better for the Emperor to hold Guelders."

I chuckled darkly. "Of course they are. What are they supposed to say, it would be better their master did not hold a land he so clearly wants? They would lose their posts and their lives."

I breathed out slowly, staring at the window and seeing nothing there. In my mind's eye, I saw Cleves on fire.

*

In the first days of July, we received word that a league had been created between France, Sweden, Cleves and Guelders which also included the Duke of Prussia and the Kings of Scotland and Denmark. At least Wilhelm had a few more allies, and ones who would fight on many fronts against the Emperor. If he was to be defeated, there would have to be a coordinated attack from many sides, that was clear even to me, and I had no experience of war. There was news too that since Johann Friedrich had captured the Duke of Brunswick, an ally of the Emperor who had been helping to defend the Hungarian front against the Turkish threat, that area was now at risk. If the Ottomans attacked the Emperor at the same time as this new league, even his vast armies and resources would be stretched thin.

This new alliance left me in a quandary, however. If my new brother was allied with Charles V, and Charles lost against France and Cleves, would England be invaded? Would the people and country I had come to love come under attack from my brother and his allies?

If Charles V was not beaten back, he would in all likelihood attack my country with resentful anger, claiming the lives of thousands of my people, spilling the blood and shattering the bone I shared in this world. And would he not go for Cleves first, before France, seeing it as the feebler target and if destroyed it would make France, the stronger dog, all the weaker for having lost his little yapping hound at his heel? My brother was that hound, and Charles would snap his neck, I was sure, before heading into battle against his true foe of France.

There was no way for this to turn out well for me. Either my people of Cleves would be slaughtered, or my people of England.

"Why cannot men make peace and keep it?" I asked myself as I sat at my fire that night. There were no flames, since it was summer, but roses picked from the gardens were there, red as blood in the flickering candlelight.

My father had been famed for the peace he had maintained. He had been a pragmatist, Wilhelm was not. If anything, he was a fantasist. My brother was to march into war, supposing he would be victorious, France on his side as well as other countries, but I did not trust this action would keep Cleves safe. My country and my brother, they were being played with, pawns in the games of greater countries with more men and more resources, and Wilhelm could not see it.

Did men of power never feel any pang of conscience about the thousands they would send to die on their behalf, just for greed? Did they never wonder what a heaven we could make of this Earth if we did not set Hell loose upon it so often?

Was it a thing so impossible that men could promise peace and maintain it? What was more land to these men who already had so much coin they could barely spend it? The King was fat and rich on the money of the monasteries, a glut of gold he could hardly contain, so why did he need France too? Why did the Emperor need Guelders? Why could Wilhelm not negotiate with Charles V rather than taking our people into a war which would endanger so many? Was it that all rulers were like Wilhelm, their pride more important to them than their people? Was it the nature of a king to care for nothing but himself? Was that how kings became kings? We once had a King of kings, and he owned not a scrap of land, nor a piece of gold. We were all supposed to emulate him, but who truly did?

Then news came, my answer too, I suppose, on what was most important to men. In July, Wilhelm and François declared war on Charles V.

Diaceto gathered information for me. "Thus far, it goes in their favour. Your brother and his allies have waged separate attacks on the Low Countries, which the Emperor is absent from. His sister Maria of Hungary being in charge instead, it is thought she will be easier to overcome."

"Easier because a woman is in charge?" I asked, acid in my tone.

"Indeed, my lady." Seeing my face, he hurried on. "That is only what *they* think, Highness, of course."

"Of course."

By August it seemed much was going the way of my brother and his allies. The Duc D'Orléans was laying siege to Danville, and my brother's commanders had marched into Brabant by the 15th, setting the country surrounding to fire and sword. By the 28th they were at Antwerp and word reached England swiftly that my brother's men were laying siege to that great city.

"They lay siege to Antwerp which is posing a serious threat to the city and to the Emperor's plans, but I fear, my lady, it makes their cause unpopular here, for the city is vital to English trade, and this disrupts it." Harst looked unsure as to whether this was good or not. For my brother, it was. For me, it was not.

"Antwerp is the chief city of the Low Countries," I said. "The Emperor will not stand it to be taken."

"The men of England may not either, Highness. They are petitioning the King to take a stand for the city."

"What does the King say?"

"He seems to have small sympathy with his merchants. He told men who came from the city of London to petition him that they had known war was coming a long time and should have put their affairs in order so as to not be affected by it. He will take no stand for Antwerp, he says, but at the same time he has, however, refused another invitation to join the league put together by François and your brother against the Emperor."

I frowned. "The King hedges his bets."

"And yet there is word he has signed a treaty with the Emperor."

"I would wager that treaty is over the attack on France. The King cares about his glory and lands, not those of the Emperor. Risk men in Antwerp, far from supplies and his own lands, and he risks much, possibly for no return. He will save his men for France." I thought a while. "How many do we have, Cleves, I mean?"

"About 20,000, about 4,000 of them horsemen. I have heard the Marshal of Guelders, Maarten van Rossum, has taken perhaps 10,000 foot soldiers and 1,000 horse into the Low Countries. Another 2,000 horse and 10,000 infantry have gone to Imperial Luxembourg to aid the Duke of Orléans and the Duke of Guise. Your brother has chased the Prince of Orange from Brabant and has a hold in Friesland. He has sent orders that English merchants are to be left unmolested, their goods and families untouched, but otherwise has allowed his men to pillage."

"To attack as they will?"

"Such is common in war, my lady. Men fight for small pay, but there are other ways to gain reward."

"Just because something is common, Harst, does not mean it is right."

"I understand, my lady, but such is the way of the world."

"When people say that, my lord, it simply means they will do nothing to alter the ways of the world."

Harst lifted his eyebrows. "When people say that, Highness, it means they have small power to alter it. I do not command troops."

I sighed. "I know, my friend." I paused a moment. "It sounds hopeful so far, though? The war?"

"There has been much noise and smoke. Maria of Hungary appears isolated for now, her brother the Emperor cannot get his troops to her unless he is willing to march them over the Pyrenees, for to take them any other way out of Spain marches them straight past France, and they will be engaged, which would possibly cause the Emperor to lose too many. Her brother Ferdinand may be able to help but it would appear he is reluctant to send troops away from Bohemia and Hungary in case the Ottomans attack in stronger numbers."

"It sounds as if this was a well-thought-out plan, then?"

"Yet it appears all this attack has done to the Emperor's peace of mind is for him to worry a little this will give the Turks an opening to attack," Harst told me.

"You mean, the invasion of the Low Countries, concerns him little? He still thinks his true foes the Ottomans?" If he considered war on his territories but the buzzing of flies, this was not good.

"Indeed, my lady. It could be bravado, of course, but it is troubling that he does not seem overly concerned."

By October, the news was dire. Allies of Cleves had taken great losses and were falling back. My countrymen were not doing well. Many in fact had rebelled.

"Men of Cleves sent to aid French troops have turned mutinous, some turning back and marching for home and some going to Vendome. A few have stayed with D'Orléans, but they are not many. The French are saying they cannot trust the men of Cleves." Harst rubbed his temple. "Luxembourg has been retaken by forces of the Emperor, and the campaign by Maria of Hungary is proving most effective, it is now said the Duc D'Orléans has lost in eight days that which it took him three months to gain." Harst looked weary and worried. "The Burgundians have captured money, some 50,000 crowns which François sent to your brother to support his war against the Emperor. He is now in financial problems, my lady. "

"What of England?"

"It is said, Highness, the King made a secret pact with Charles of Spain to invade France in two years' time. This gives the Emperor these two years to weed out the allies of the French, so he and the King can invade together a much-weakened France."

I looked away, shaking my head. The King was a fool if he thought for a moment Charles V would give him what he wanted from France. Charles would simply hand over France to the King of England when he was the one who had done all the additional work of setting down his enemies? I thought not. The trouble with Henry of England was, he thought he was more important than he was. Mistake me not, over his own people, over me, he held the power of life and death and that might well make a man feel mighty, but to other kings, he was not as impressive as he thought himself. His arrogance was matched only by his self-delusion, and that stark truth he might finally understand at the conclusion of this war, which had already cost so many lives.

Although perhaps not. The King had a remarkable talent for deceiving himself.

"My brother is the same animal," I whispered to myself. The same false pride, the same need to display might, was in Wilhelm too, and our people were paying the price for it.

That was made only clearer to me when, that October, Imperial forces marched into Julich, into the lands of my mother.

"Duren surrendered first." Harst looked as sick as I felt. "Then the City of Julich was taken. Our people held out a while but were forced to surrender on the 10th. On the 22nd, my lady, the last town of your mother's duchy was claimed. It is said the Emperor's forces saw little resistance in the field."

"Because all our men are elsewhere." I felt helpless, weak. Troops of the Emperor were so close to my family. I could feel the terror of my own blood on the wind, and I could do nothing. Never had I felt more pointless.

"Winter is almost upon us," Harst said, trying to reassure me. "The time for waging war is coming to an end. Your brother will have time to regroup."

"But the Emperor's troops, sent by this woman all of you underestimated, are at our very gates, Harst. Already they have half the duchy in their possession, half the people."

I sank into a chair, feeling as if I might faint. I was almost disappointed when I did not, since it might have afforded me some relief. Oblivion is better than reality, at times. Sadly, it seemed I was not a woman to faint when trouble came. I wondered in truth if any women were, or if it was a device put about by men to make it seem we were fragile and incompetent, too troubled in mind by war to stand even the idea of it. If anyone wanted proof to the contrary, one only had to look at the woman my brother and his allies had attacked, Maria of Hungary. They had thought her weak, isolated, alone. She had proved it mattered not if she was alone, still her men fought for her and their country, and weak she certainly was not.

Of course, her victories would in time become those of the Emperor, that was how history would remember them.

"What is my mother thinking, at this time so horrible?" I asked, almost not to Harst but to the air about me, where smoke from candles wafted as white snakes in warm air. My heart twisted, wrenching inside me it squirmed. "I should have gone home, Harst, years ago, when first the King repudiated our match. I should have gone home. I was selfish."

"Highness, your mother is a woman of valour, and I have no doubt she mourns for her homeland, but she is strong, as are all the women of your family, including you. When you stayed, you did not in truth have a choice. The King made demands of you, and we all agreed to them, even your brother, hoping it would keep you safe."

"But I wanted to stay, so I put no fight against his wishes. I should have gone home, should have found a way, then I could be there with my family at this time."

"Then there would be another member of our royal house in possible danger, my lady. At least with you here, we know one member of the ducal line is not within the war."

"Not within the war, but not safe, friend. Still not safe."

"Safer, from this threat at least, my lady, and now, as winter dawns your brother has time to regroup, to get money from his allies and bolster our numbers. There is word he will gain another 30,000 foot soldiers and 4,000 horse. The fight is not yet over, my lady."

I stared bleakly at the Ambassador. In my ears I could hear the people of Julich screaming. "Indeed, friend," I said. "That is what scares me."

Chapter Four

December 1542 – Summer 1543

Bletchingley Place,

Richmond Palace and

Hampton Court

"The King of Scots refused to cross the border for talks, again?"

"He did indeed, Highness."

"And how has the King responded?"

"The Duke of Norfolk has been sent to wreak devastation and raid into Scotland. They hope that by such means King James will be brought to reason by his uncle the King."

I must have looked highly sceptical and Harst clearly did not believe his own words either. Ever since the King had tried to bring about a summit meeting with his nephew of Scots earlier that year and ever since King James V had simply not shown up, the English King had been determined to bring his nephew under his control. He wanted subjugation of him and of Scotland, for James to listen to him about reform upon his own Church and in truth to bring this neighbouring country under England's mastery. To this end, the King had unleashed a series of efforts to bring James into negotiation of a treaty of mutual friendship. The implication was that if Scotland did not enter a treaty of mutual friendship, England would enter a time of malicious revenge. So now James had once again refused to cross the border to talk, the King of England raided the territories of the King of Scots.

Not long after came the Battle of Solway Moss. Scots and English fought, and the English defeated the Scottish army. Two weeks later the Scottish King died, some said of grief. The only true heir to the throne of Scotland was an infant daughter, named Mary Queen of Scots, who had been born but six days before her father died. Scotland would now be ruled by a regent, the first being James Hamilton Earl of Arran, and the King of England thought there was an ideal situation here, for he had a son and Scotland had a daughter. Marry them, and Scotland would finally be brought under the control of England, for as the country belonging to the wife of this match, Scotland would be subjugated by England just as the infant Mary would be dominated by Prince Edward.

How foul are the minds of men.

It baffled the King that the Scots did not seem overly enthused about his marriage plans for Mary and Edward, but negotiations opened all the same.

More sad news arrived when I was told Ambassador Wyatt had died in October of a sudden illness. Some blamed the plague, and some said his wife, Elizabeth, to whom he had been forced to return, had poisoned him. The King was showing her favour, and it was said she had killed her husband to become Queen. I did not put much stock in such tales, they always arose when people died swift, but I mourned the poor man. He was but thirty-nine and fate had been often cruel to him. He left several sons, and his wife. I hoped the sons at least mourned him.

*

By December I had moved my household to Bletchingley, a grand house in my possession of which I was most fond. It was part of my annulment settlement from the King, mid-way between Kent and London, although closer to London. It was a modern place, having been built for the Duke of Buckingham – yet another once-companion of the King I had recently been told he had had executed – in 1521, so it was little more than twenty years old. It was a large building, boasting two courtyards and ornamental gardens arranged in appealing little terraces. Fishponds, or stew ponds as the English charmingly called them, always thinking with the belly, glittered in the grounds, and a stern northern gatehouse led from walled gardens surrounding the house into a great undulating deer park. There was thick woodland nearby for hunting, as well as much sweet meadowland. The house was warm and comfortable, with large windows, as only a duke could have afforded made, which let in the light. People of the nearby villages and towns were welcoming and sweet to me and my household, and since

I thought of my household as my family, this was a thing dear to me. Bletchingley was not as large as Hever, and although most of my household could fit within, some had to stay in the village, at the inn nearby, or with folk in the area surrounding. Had it been summer, I would have told them to camp in the park in tents, which was quite normal, but as frost came as a herald of ice and snow, it was not the season to be staying under canvas. Besides, my people always had a good welcome with my neighbours and so liked to spend their evenings amongst them.

We passed as merry a Christmas as we could there at Bletchingley. News of the war stalling as winter came allowed a little relief, and imperial troops pulled out of my mother's homeland, but still my heart dwelled in fear over what would come with the thaw. I worried for my mother, for Amalia, and although I worried for Wilhelm, I was more concerned about what he would do when the war opened up again in the New Year.

By January we were at Richmond again. I did not know whether to ask to be invited to court, fearing the King might still be considering marrying me, but when I finally did head there in March, by invitation, I quickly suspected there was no reason to fear. It seemed I had been called to court after the Lady Mary expressed a wish to see me. The King all but ignored me, made no effort to see me, and although I suspected some of this was because if he was allied to the Emperor it would not be politic to be seen making much of the sister of the Emperor's foe, I swiftly came to understand there was another reason.

"You have a new lady, Highness," I noted to Mary as we stood, drinking wine near the fire in the Great Hall of Hampton Court.

The reason I had noted this lady was because the King, who my nervous eye had been on, had little stopped staring at her since he arrived for the festivities. The woman who had caught his eye was tall, the little hair showing from her French hood a reddish-gold and she had arresting eyes, a dark grey which some might think hazel or green at a distance. Up close it was easy to see they were as water, a grey green, quite bewitching. She was clearly witty, given the constant cloud of laughter which surrounded her despite the widow's weeds she wore, and with her small, pointed face, delicate nose and dusky lips she had a captivating quality. Her figure, tall as it was, was also graceful and slim. I thought her perhaps thirty, but that was because of the clear intelligence of her conversation. To the passing eye she could have seemed younger, twenty-five or six perhaps.

Lady Mary nodded. "The widow, Lady Latimer. Her maiden name was Parr."

"And her first name?"

"Katherine, like my mother. She was named for her, in fact. My mother was her godmother. That is how Lady Latimer ended up in my service. My mother and hers were close friends, and when she was recently widowed, little more than two weeks ago, she asked for a permanent place in my house. Her dower lands are in the north, you see, but her husband, John Neville, died here in London, so she asked for a place so she could remain here in the south. The north holds some horrors for her."

"So she is a widow now? Poor woman." It was conventional, of course, to express sadness for the death of someone, condolences for those left behind, and yet frequently widows, if they remained single, had more freedom than other women.

Mary sipped her wine. "She is twice a widow, actually. The first was Sir Edward Burgh, then she was wed by her family to John Neville, the third Baron Latimer. Her last was an old man and the first young but sickly, she has in truth been more a nursemaid than a wife and had no children of her own." Mary paused. "Her last husband... my father did not like him. Latimer opposed the annulment of my father and mother's marriage and supported the Catholic Church, but it was more than that too. Lincolnshire rebels who rose in 1536 came to Latimer's very gates and threatened him with much if he would not aid them, then they took him captive. Some say he went willingly, but if he did so it was to protect his wife, Katherine, and his children who were inside the house when the rebels carted him off. She and her stepchildren were held as hostages during the Pilgrimage of Grace. Rebels threatened to kill them if Latimer did not join the rebellion."

"And did he?"

"He managed to persuade the mob away from his family, and he spent time with the rebels, but Latimer did always claim he was there under duress. He negotiated for the leaders of the Pilgrimage, represented them in the amnesty which followed, which my father loathed him for. I think, though, the Pilgrimage of Grace and how she was treated therein may have had an effect on Katherine. She speaks warm of the King's Church and reform and sets her mouth when the true faith is mentioned."

I coughed. "You should set your mouth too, my friend. The King's faith is the one we all follow, is it not?"

"I say such to you, Highness, and others I trust and that is all." Mary pursed her lips. "I invited Lady Latimer to my household because of her connection to my mother and because I thought she was one of the faithful. Her family were, and Latimer was, but I wonder about her. I think her experiences with rebels may have tarnished her beliefs. I do hear her first husband's family were reformers, Lutherans perhaps. Her first father-in-law served the Boleyn Queen and once ripped the badges from my mother's barge just to please his heretic mistress."

"I am surprised the King allowed her to court, if he suspected her husband was involved with rebels."

Mary shrugged. "There were conflicting reports as to whether Latimer was a prisoner of the rebels or a conspirator. Many men of influence spoke for Latimer, including Suffolk. Even Cromwell admitted he knew not which tale was true, and he was not a man easily fooled."

I glanced at my friend. Cromwell was not a man many spoke well of, even after death, and considering his religion and the changes he had made to the faith, not to mention the sacking of the monasteries, it should have been that Mary spoke not well of him, but it was not so. There was always a measure of affection, grief even, when she spoke of him. I had heard that he had been the means to save her when she was in danger after the fall of Anne Boleyn, and although he might have done so for selfish purposes, he still had aided her and perhaps this was why she always would speak well of him. When she had been standing against her father, refusing to recognise him as Head of the Church, her father and others had discussed her being arrested, perhaps even executed for treason. Cromwell as well as Chapuys had convinced her, so people said, to capitulate. In doing so, these men had saved her life.

"Latimer condemned the rebels, and Katherine's uncle and brother, both named William, spoke for him too."

"Why did her father not?"

"Her father died when she was a child. Her mother raised her, and her uncle, Sir William Parr of Horton, helped a great deal with Katherine and her brother and sister."

I had a thought, realising I had heard that maiden name before. "Her sister is Lady Anne Herbert? Who served me?"

"Indeed, her husband is Sir William Herbert, rather a mad gentleman, but a good soldier and many women say he is dashing. Anne served my mother too, and all the wives of my father."

I glanced at Lady Latimer. Anne was next to her, and it was clear they were sisters. I wondered how I had missed the resemblance before. There was the same delicate beauty upon each of them. I had always thought Anne a wit, and she was obviously highly educated. She had been the one to read letters in Latin to me, and she also was fluent in French, I remembered. "They both were well educated?" I asked.

Mary nodded. "Their mother spoke fluent French and was a great believer in the humanist method of teaching daughters well so they might be good use to their husbands and families. I believe the family were in some way related to Thomas More, and he was a great leader in the way of educating daughters. Another kinsman is Bishop Cuthbert of Tunstall, and he writes books on arithmetic, and encourages girls to be taught that art as well as boys. I understand their mother took it all to heart, and my mother was one to believe in the education of women, and she and Lady Parr were close, so..." Mary tailed off, waving a hand as if the rest did not need to be said, which it did not.

"What happened to her husband, then? After the rebellion?"

Mary kept her face steady, yet she sounded sad as she answered. "After the confusion about his part in the rebellion, Latimer never came back to court, but my father kept him busy. He sent him on almost constant missions up and down the country. Latimer's lands were in the north, of course, and Father sent him to arrest, try and execute rebels. Proof of his loyalty, you see? Katherine asked her husband to make a base for them in the south, since the north held bad memories for her. She will not talk of what happened when the rebels had her in their power and I suspect much ill might have been done to her. She started to come to court this past year. Her husband grew ill last winter and died early this year. He was fifty years, a good age for a man to reach, and I think she was fond of him. She is a rich widow, for Latimer left her as guardian of his daughter Margaret Neville and Katherine has a life interest in some of his property. She wanted to remain in London, and I agreed she would have a place with me. Her brother is William Parr, who I am sure you know for the gossip about his wife leaving him and running off with a penniless man."

I did remember the gossip. "The King seems captivated by her." The King, who was on his throne on the dais, was staring at Lady Latimer rather as a cat does a mouse. As she laughed with the younger Seymour brother, Thomas, the one I never had liked or trusted, Katherine looked aglow with life. I could see why the King wanted her. It was more than beauty, though she had that in abundance. She was pretty and witty, and other men wanted her, but there was also another quality in her, a spirit which made her shine. I knew it, for Catherine Howard had worn that same cloak. At the thought, I shivered a little. Katherine Parr was a remarkable woman, one who stood out from others at court for both obvious and subtle reasons. The King liked remarkable women. He liked to worship them, then bring them tumbling down as statues turned to dust, crashing on the floor.

I realised there had been silence a moment and glanced to my side, only to find Mary clearly unsure as to how to answer. I pressed her hand. "I have no wish to alter my state. Your father is of course a great man, but it was my brother who wanted us married again. I am happy as his sister."

Mary inclined her head. "So you have said to me, yet I always hear rumour that you are in tears for he does not offer you marriage again."

I chuckled. "If I listened to all that was said of me, I would think myself an entirely different person to who I am. Hear what comes of my mouth and believe that to be true."

Mary smiled. "Then I should tell you, yes, I think my father warms to her. He has sent many gifts, seeks her out to talk to since first she arrived at court. The lady herself... I know not if she is pleased. There were rumours that she and Thomas Seymour, even before the death of Latimer, had formed an attachment, and I believe she was hoping he might make her an offer." Mary glanced at her father. "But my father is the King, and Thomas Seymour is not."

The King had all but ignored me since I came to court, now I knew why. The widow Latimer was in his sights. He certainly did not want to be joined to me, and in time I learned it was not only because he found another woman more attractive than me.

Harst had come to me in February to tell me that through secret information exchanged between ambassadors he had found out that Henry of England and Charles of Spain had indeed made a pact, and in recent talks it had been said between them that my brother could be considered a common enemy of England and the Empire. The treaty had not been fully ratified, but it was likely to be so. If the King tried to marry me, it would be impolitic to say the least. My brother's ambassadors were still trying, despite this, to convince the King. Since the agreement had not been ratified, they thought there was hope, and they were desperate, Wilhelm pushing them for the sake of Cleves. There was reason for his desperation. By that February my brother's army, this newly assembled 30,000 men and 4,000 horse he had been so proud of, was in tatters. He had intended, against advice, to try to raid into the Low Countries, into Brabant to pay these thousands of men through the winter but had been prevented by deep snow. Unable to pay his men, or feed them, he found many were deserting him just as the season for war was approaching.

There had been tales Charles V was willing to negotiate but Wilhelm was not. My country might be undone by my brother's stubborn vanity.

"I hear the Emperor might offer again for your brother to keep Guelders during his lifetime and then it would go to Charles's kin, but your brother will not back down," Harst had informed me.

"Even though his army is all but gone? Can he not hold his men together? I hear they are deserting."

Harst looked uncomfortable. "What is it?" I asked.

"Your brother is not inspiring his troops, my lady, I fear. He has not appeared with them in battle as yet, relying instead on his generals."

"So, Wilhelm would send me to face death for our people, but he will not do the same?" I was incredulous.

His forces had won a battle of late, which was why the Emperor might have been more willing to negotiate. Maria, Regent of the Low Countries, had sent representatives to a city of hers located in Cleves. The town of Hinesburg was in want of food and had asked for aid, so she sent one of her commanders along with 10,000 foot soldiers and 2,500 horse. They resupplied the city but on the 24th of March, when camped before Sittard, they encountered my brother's forces, who offered battle. The battle resulted in the near devastation of the city and left 4,000 men and 900 horses dead. After the battle, imperial commanders gave permission for all soldiers who remained living to plunder the area, revenge if you will, which led to thousands of women being raped as well as theft, fire and devastation.

Despite all we had lost, this victory bolstered the confidence of my brother. Not long after we heard that Charles V and my former husband had ratified their treaty in secret, but Harst told me the Emperor was worried the King of England would not keep his promise about my brother being their common enemy and was pressing to have the King declare this as an oath in a letter, or to Ambassador Chapuys. In the meantime, there was to be another Imperial Diet at Nuremberg where a treaty was to be drawn up, intending to bring peace between my brother, the Emperor, the Regent Maria and Henry of England.

I doubted Wilhelm would make peace. He had not listened to reason thus far, why should he now that he had won one whole battle?

*

Whilst I was at court, I was given permission to often visit with Lady Mary, something I greatly enjoyed. It also meant I was able to have an eye on the woman the King was now interested in. From all I saw, she received his attentions with pleasure, but there was a measure of fear there too.

When Katherine Parr gazed upon Thomas Seymour, though, that was a different matter. I wondered at it a little. I had, admittedly from spare conversation, thought her an intelligent woman, and although Seymour the younger certainly was handsome, he repulsed me. There was something in his air I liked not, a leering lasciviousness I found repellent. It was not just my imagination, either, there were plenty of tales about him all over court. Once I would have gone to Kitty for such a story, but she gossiped little these days, thinking it not safe. My chamberers, however, were willing to share the odd tale with my ladies, who shared them with me, and my friend of Suffolk was always free with her information. Thomas Seymour had scant respect for a "no" from a woman, and there were plenty of stories about his wandering hands and callous ways. As far as I was concerned, he was a debauched old monster, his hands tarrying up skirts of young girls and his position forcing women into sex against their wills. That he was a young man with a handsome face did not alter what he was inside.

Yet Katherine Parr seemed entirely taken with him.

Perhaps it was that she had only had sickly or old husbands before, I mused. If he was nothing else, Seymour was young and handsome, fit and active, certainly not close to death. I supposed if one knew nothing of what he got up to with other maids at court, it could be easy to be charmed by him. But me, he left cold. It was all surface charm and trickery; I could see through him as easily as I could through a sheet of thin ice on a pond.

It was also true that Katherine's sister had married a man who was rather an adventurer. Seymour had had many exploits, and it could be said he was a dashing man of action, rather as William Herbert was. Yet although many would class the two men the same, I would not. Herbert was a "mad gentleman" as Mary had said, and others attested to. He could be wild and certainly had a hot temper. He had spent time in France after killing a man in a brawl and had served in the French army, then had been recommended to our King who heaped rewards on him for his military service. It could be supposed, looking at his record, that Herbert was the same kind of man as Seymour, yet I never felt that creeping unease in my spine when conversing with Herbert as I felt with Seymour. They were not the same kind of man. One, something in my skin and heart told me to fear, and the other caused no kind of concern.

I wondered if Katherine Parr would get her wish and wed Seymour. The King was keen on the widow Latimer, that much was clear, and it was also obvious to my eyes that part of the attraction might well be in the idea the King could wrest Katherine from Seymour. To gain a woman one of the most handsome and rakish men of court clearly wanted for his own? To snatch her from Seymour, thus proving the King was the greater man? When coupled with Katherine's own charms, how could a man of fragile pride like the King resist?

I shook my head to all of it, relieved it was not me and sorry for Katherine Parr either way her fate turned out. Neither match looked like a happy one to me. Instead, I turned to Mary, and since we were allowed to see each other often, made the most of it.

"Come to me in June, to Richmond," I said to Mary when the end of my stay at court had come. "Let me have you to myself for a while, away from court."

She pressed my hand. Hers felt thin. Yet another bout of illness had assailed her of late. Mary had many ailments although it seemed to me much of her nervous afflictions would have been cured had she led a simpler life, one less close to the throne of bones her father had constructed of his loved ones, and hers. "I would like that, and to see Richmond as well as you. My mother always favoured it, you know, the palace."

"She was a woman of wisdom. It is a beautiful place, so comforting in winter. I call it my warm box, you know."

Mary chuckled. "I shall tell that to Elizabeth, she would like such a phrasing."

"You visit her and Edward often? I should like to see them more. I am hoping at some stage your father will allow Elizabeth to visit me, perhaps in Kent."

Mary inclined her head, she knew I was referring to Hever, to showing Elizabeth the childhood home of her mother. "I will see if I can influence him a little," she promised. "It would have to be done with care, and the time is perhaps not now."

"Of course. With all that goes on in my homeland, I was amazed I was invited to court this time."

Her eyes became anxious for me. "You must be worried."

I swallowed. "I am, very much so, for my mother, brother, my sister, for my people most of all."

"I will pray for them, though they are the enemies of my cousin."

"I pray for peace, Highness. That would be surely what God would want, and it would be the best outcome for all if they never were enemies again."

Mary pressed my hand again. "You are right. I will pray for peace too."

When I returned home to Richmond, there was news unwelcome waiting for me. I was told on the 24th of June the Cleves army had abandoned Hinesburg without much resistance when the Prince of Orange and his forces advanced on them. Wilhelm still had not fought beside his men, and this was leading many to wonder why they should fight for their Duke. What was worse was Wilhelm's men had left behind all of their artillery, a double blow, and although the French army was seizing cities and small towns in the Low Countries and offered to send Wilhelm some 10,000 soldiers, things were looking bleak for my people.

The Emperor had published a manifesto on the war with Cleves, stating how my brother, a disloyal vassal, had betrayed his master and risen up against him. He said my brother could not speak a word of truth and had usurped Guelders. It was a justification for the war on my brother, and people would believe it, particularly if Wilhelm failed.

And it seemed he might, for as my brother moved troops into Brabant again, attacking Amersfoort, there was word the Emperor himself was on the march. Determined to finally subdue Wilhelm and Cleves, Charles V was only days away from Speyer, and he had an army with him.

It was 30,000 strong.

Chapter Five

Summer 1543

Richmond Palace

At the end of June, as I waited for news of my homeland, Mary came to me, as promised, and although we spent a merry time in company with one another, it was cut short. At first Mary did not want to tell me why and that alone gave me reason to suspect. "Your father is marrying, is he not?" I asked.

Mary was not a talented liar and her face, normally always a little pale due to ill health, flushed crimson. The colour continued to flood, a waterfall of blood, down her throat.

I tried not to laugh. "I keep trying to tell you, I am not offended by the King taking a new wife."

Mary shifted uncomfortably. "There are rumours at court that you have said the widow Latimer is old and less favoured than you in looks."

That was far less amusing. "Has the King or the new Queen-to-be heard this?"

"I believe Lady Latimer has."

I closed my eyes. Why was everyone in the world determined to make me an enemy to the Queen of England, whoever she might be? Was it just that I had once possessed her place? Did people also expect all masters to hate apprentices because once they had been in their shoes? "I hope you will convey to her, whenever the time comes that I am supposed to officially know of this marriage, that I harbour only wishes of friendship towards her."

"I will try."

Mary left a few days before the marriage, and on the 12th of July 1543, the most married King of England took yet another wife. Once Katherine Parr was married no one seemed to remember Latimer had been her name a long time. Perhaps it was the wish of the King, to try to think of his bride as a virgin rather than a woman who had already had two husbands.

I supposed, however, it was another way to protect himself, that he claimed this time a wife known *not* to be a virgin. Catherine Howard had portrayed herself as a maid when she was not, but I thought again of the other reason, beyond protection or passion. Thomas Seymour was apparently most put out by the match and left England not long after. The King had snatched Katherine from Seymour, claimed her as a prize. It was a signal fire on a hill, a sign of his dominance over a younger, more handsome, more active and adventurous man, that he could steal away what Seymour had thought was his. It was a sign to the court, too, of the supposed virility of the King.

To my mind it was a pathetic little display. Little as I liked Seymour, were it to come down to a fight between the men, the King would have been easily beaten, and had it come down to a true choice of Katherine's, she would not have chosen the King. She had married the King because he was the King and when he commanded something obedience was usually the only way to avoid arrest and possible death. If he was only powerful because of the position he held, then he was not powerful, not in truth. He had no strength in his body now, perhaps had not ever held greatness of spirit. The King was a weak man exerting a dominance over others based on fear of his position, nothing more. If he is to be truly impressive, a king must be impressive in *himself*, not some hollow man sitting under a ring of gold, hoping that metal will shine upon his face so brightly that none will see the true visage underneath, the visage of a coward.

"Lady Elizabeth and Lady Mary were at the ceremony," my friend of Suffolk told me. "And Lady Margaret Douglas."

I signalled for Kitty to bring wine. "She is at last forgiven for daring to love another Howard?"

"It would seem so, though the King keeps a close eye on her. I think Richard Rich is spying on her or has his men doing so on orders of the King. He wants no more clandestine matches for his wayward niece."

"Wayward... such a thing women are called for daring to love where they wish to."

Katherine took a goblet from Kitty with a smile. "You know what I mean. I do not disapprove of love matches, even between those not equal to one another. In fact, if the woman is higher, it can be a great advantage to marry a man below. I saw it with the Princess Mary and my Charles when they were wed. She was his wife, therefore by law subordinate to him yet she was a Princess of the blood royal and he the descendant of a flag bearer. That she outranked him allowed her much more freedom than most women have, and she relished that freedom. I always wondered if, as well as love, that did not factor into her decision to wed him. She did not like her brother having control over her and rebelled when she married Charles straight after old Louis, the bent and broken. Perhaps she did not want to take a husband, then, who would control her."

"An interesting thought." I sipped my wine. "I am glad to hear Lady Elizabeth was at the wedding. Is the King seeing her more?"

"The new Queen is determined to heal all rifts in the family, and has nurtured stepchildren before, Latimer's boy and girl, so she knows how to bring a family together. Indeed, her Neville stepson is rather a wild man by all reports. Queen Katherine is, they say, the only one who can temper his passions when roused. He listens to her and no one else, but I can see why."

There was a note of admiration in my friend's voice which caused a pang of envy in my heart. "You admire the new Queen?"

"I do, my friend. I know you little know her, but she is a gentle, wise soul. In fact, she reminds me a great deal of you. She has such a passion for education you know, speaks French as well as Latin and wants to learn Spanish."

"I know only English and my own language." My voice was stiff, jealousy pulling me taut.

"But you wished to educate yourself further, so did," Katherine washed on, seemingly unaware of the resentment rising in me. "The Queen is the same, and she is interested in the new learning. She wants to take the women who come to my salons and bring them to hers."

"Would you not mind that?"

"No, indeed, for the more the faith is discussed and spread the better. If the Queen of England approves of it, then Gardiner and Norfolk and all their little cronies cannot come after women of sense and rationality who want to understand their faith better."

"That sounds perilous to me, my friend," I said. "The King will not take to a Queen who holds great opinions on the faith."

"Katherine can manage him." My friend sounded so confident it chilled me. Women had thought that before and been proven very wrong.

"How will she manage him?"

A wicked smile appeared. "The King is enthralled with her charms, and she was a wife before, remember, to two men. She knows the bedchamber well, and what use it may grant a woman."

A look of disdain must have dawned over my face, for my friend tittered. "Though you do not know of these things, let me tell you; women have few ways to influence men, but through the bedchamber is one of them. Do not look down on the new Queen for this. She needs every weapon and shield in her possession in order to survive. This is one of them, and it is one that every past wife, save you and perhaps Jane Seymour, who never seemed to understand why anyone wanted to go to bed, used well."

Two weeks later the King came to me. He took care to dine with me, flood me with compliments and then tell me gently, as if I would be deeply sorrowed, of his new union.

"I have something to tell you, sister," he said as we walked hand in hand to the head table in the Great Hall.

Dear God in Heaven, I thought. *Once again, he thinks I do not know he has married.* Did the man think me deaf to all rumour flying about England, or blind as to how he pranced about the widow Latimer like a lusty plump peacock when I was at court? The King thought he was a man of delicate subtlety, when he was graceless and obvious as a boar in a henhouse.

"Anything you have to confide in me, Majesty, I am honoured to hear." Waiting for the applause of the people in the hall to soften, we took our seats, indicating for others to do so too. The King glanced appreciatively at his place where a salt cellar in the shape of a greyhound, his father's old emblem, as well as a rose were placed. He was more appreciative when the food began to arrive, for I had ordered every one of his favourite dishes from the kitchens, as I always did when he visited.

"The news I have, I know you will rejoice in." He tore bread in his fat fingers, dipping it in his pottage of carp and herbs and glanced at me. There was a challenge in his eyes and his voice; if I did not rejoice immediately, and make that obvious, he would be displeased. I could read this dangerous man well by that time. "I have taken a wife, for the comfort of my own self and for the procreation of another heir for England."

I turned to him, smiling broadly. "Majesty, my good brother, I indeed rejoice to hear this welcome news. You have been too long alone and deserve the comfort of a good woman. May I know the name of my new sister?"

"Lady Latimer, as was, Katherine Parr."

"A beautiful, gentle lady. I know her but little, but I was impressed with her regal demeanour when I saw her in the household of Lady Mary. Your Majesty obviously noted this grace within her and knew her potential to become Queen." I lifted my goblet. "May I drink to your health, and that of your fine lady, my good brother?"

He inclined his head, those beady eyes still glittering with not a little suspicion.

"I am pleased Your Majesty has taken a bride good in years and with experience of being a wife," I said. "Although she has not borne children with her two past husbands, I am sure this is because each man was not as hale as Your Majesty, and soon enough we will have a Duke of York to join blessed Prince Edward."

"You are not… upset?"

I smiled in a wry fashion. "Majesty, no doubt you hear rumour of me spread by malicious tongues who ever would want to cause discord between me and the rest of your honoured family. You have ever known my mind well, much better than these men who make up lies and guess the feelings of a woman. All I have ever wanted has been your happiness. I was not the woman to grant you that, and I sorrow for that, but I rejoice when I hear you have found love and happiness with another."

A rumble came from his throat, tears to his eyes. I was astonished, thinking I had done something wrong, but I had in fact managed to hit that thick vein of self-interest and sentimentality in his throat. "Sister..." he clutched my hand "... To have a kinswoman such as I have in you, one sent to me by God and not by womb, one who ever has my comfort in mind over her own... it is a blessing. *You* are a blessing."

I set my other hand on top of his. My lower hand was occupied, being crushed by his fingers. "As you are a blessing to me, Majesty. My own brother, I think, cares little for me, his concerns too many and his kinswomen too numerous. But you, Majesty, always you have provided for my needs and loved me as a good brother."

"I will ever be a good brother to you." There was a fierce blaze in his eyes I almost feared. "Be ever assured of our love. There have been in my life many accidents of fate, many times those I loved have turned on me. Such is the nature of kingship, but you are loyal, sister, this I always see for always you have supported me in all I do."

Not all you do, my mind snapped.

My mouth, however, knew what was acceptable to say if I wished to live. "I ever shall, brother. And whatever tales you hear of me, please believe them not until they come from mine own lips. There are many men here, even in our beloved England, who would speak against me or think to speak for me, but only I may do such, or you, brother, for you know my heart."

"Be ever assured of our love." Fiercely he kissed my hand as he repeated himself, leaving a small trail of drool which I then had to endure drying on my hand all night, though it made me nauseous. Wiping it away the moment it slicked upon my skin would have not been the most prudent thing to do.

The King stayed for two days, then rode back to his new wife. When he had gone, I sat in my own rooms awhile near the window to think on this new lady who now had to survive for as long as she could as his wife. I thought also of myself.

There was much in me that still loved England but there was now within me a great pull to be at home, in Cleves. The truth was that being within a country where I was still and always would be a foreigner was never an easy situation, but at a time when that country was to ally with enemies of my countrymen and my family, was to aid them, however indirectly, in the destruction of my own people was not a savoury thought.

If I was to cheer on the King of England – as I would have to or be called a traitor – in the obliteration of his enemies that meant I had to support him in the destruction of my people. Would I have to cheer if his soldiers joined with those of the Emperor, raced up the stairs of Swan Castle, took the head of my sister and raped my mother? Would I have to write letters of congratulations if my brother was in chains at the feet of the Emperor? And would I come under suspicion, an enemy inside the gates, to men about the King who never had been my friends and who liked not the position of wealth, power and liberty I was granted as the King's most entirely and beloved sister? Would jealousy cause them to create more dangerous fictions about me, ones which would send me to the Tower or to the block? Would ambassadors of other countries demand that I be arrested?

It was hard to say exactly what dangers I might face if I remained in England.

There was one more reason to return home. My mother. She had been ill. She was older now. I had no doubt Amalia was looking after her, but every good nurse needs a break from time to time and I had ever been my mother's favourite child, I knew that. It would bring her comfort to have me home. If she was truly ill, this might be my last chance to see her.

But to go home, even if the King would let me go, would be to surrender the freedom I had here, would place me back in the hands of my brother to dispose of as he wished or to keep me forever locked away in the Frauenzimmer. Did I want to return home to that? Could I even reach Cleves now, with the Emperor on the march towards my homeland? Staying in England was not without its risks, neither was returning home.

I knew eventually the question would become not which state was the more uncomfortable to live in, but which state would allow me to live.

*

Not long after the King's visit, I heard that Ambassador Chapuys was wandering about, telling people I would rather go home than stay in England and be further humiliated over the matter of the King's marriage. Chapuys said he had heard I had decried the Lady Latimer as inferior to me in beauty and fertility, since she had not borne any children. Whilst I had said something of this in passing, about fertility, to the King, I do not believe I ever noted to anyone I thought the lady devoid of beauty. Mary had told me gossip about that, which apparently had come from me, but never had I said it. I was also not sure how I could have decided Katherine Parr was inferior to me in fertility, since if she had borne no children, neither had I. I had not had a chance, of course, but all the same it sounded an illogical argument to my mind.

Yet here was the Ambassador, setting about that I had slandered the Queen and King. I had no doubt this was done to remove me and ambassadors of Cleves from England. The Emperor was poised to attack. He did not want his ally harbouring me, possibly he suspected I was making the King sympathetic to Wilhelm. I was a little tick in the side of the Emperor, a complication he did not need.

As for the wish to return home, even though I had expressed such a thought it had nothing to do with the King's marriage. I had wanted to return to be with my family as they were under assault, but such was impossible now.

"Chapuys says I want nothing more than to go home!" I cried to Kitty and my women. "What am I to do, march through the massing armies of the Emperor as he marches into my homeland? Does Ambassador Chapuys think me so foolish as to believe I would be offered safe conduct?"

The Emperor had 30,000 men, a force my brother and our small country never could repel, and soon enough the Emperor was demanding, much as I had thought he might, that Harst and other Cleveian ambassadors be expelled from England. Fortunately, the King refused. Such an action would have seen me isolated indeed, cut off from my family, and since I had accepted his new marriage with grace, despite the various rumours about all my weeping and bemoaning my state, perhaps he felt I was owed a few friends remaining in England. The King's council told the Emperor's men that they considered these ambassadors my servants, not those of the Duke of Cleves, and would not strip loyal men away from my household. In this matter I could breathe a little, for a while, but in others there was no good news.

"Your brother has appealed to his allies for aid, apparently the arrival of the Emperor caught the Duke off-guard," Harst told me.

"It should not have," I said. "The Emperor is determined to crush my brother, and our country. Cleves has wounded Charles V more, because Wilhelm was his vassal. France, he expects war from, but not a subject. This is personal." I paused. "Will François aid Cleves?"

"It does not look promising thus far, Highness." Harst played with his cap, anxious fingers rolling it in his hands. "There has been no word from France. They may be considering that abandoning this side of the campaign would be more sensible than continuing it."

"More sensible, but not more moral." I bit my lip. "They must have known Cleves would come under attack, or was that the point? Make Charles waste money and men on a smaller target so the French have more time to advance? Was Cleves always meant as a distraction?"

"It is possible. Your brother has sent men to negotiate with the Emperor. This is stalling the full invasion a little, but Julich is again under threat, Highness."

I set my hands on my hips and tried to breathe. "We should officially appeal to go home, Harst. The situation here will only get worse for us, and trickier for the King and his men. If Chapuys tries to darken my name any further, I could end up arrested."

He set his cap down on the table. "I know not how we would get home, Highness, even by ship there would be trouble, but I can certainly put it to the King's council, perhaps say you worry over the position that you remaining in England is putting the King in?"

"Yes, that is good," I agreed. "Make it clear it is for anxiety over what complications will fall upon my good brother that I wish to return, and for the wish to be with my family."

It was not allowed. The council thanked me for my concern, but I was a "good Englishwoman" now as the sister of His Majesty, and as such the King had no fear over complications about me remaining in England.

I doubted this was true. I might become quite useful to the King if he needed to bargain with the Emperor. A sister of the rebel Duke could come in useful one day, and the King liked to keep people who were useful to him close, for a while at least.

*

I paced my room, considering options, none of them good. A thought had come to me as to how to get the King to release me. Could I slander the Queen? Say things which people already were attributing to me, but worse? Be outspoken against her so the King would capitulate, finding me too embarrassing, and send me home? I might simply be arrested, but my country was about to be invaded, my mother was sick. If there was any way to get home, I needed to find it. Reasoning with the King, flattering him, had not worked, so would playing the jealous woman, a role most shameful for the King of England, work for me?

I was desperate. I knew not how I was to get home even if it was allowed, but my people needed me, my mother needed me. I had to be there, even if I was in danger. I had to stand with them. I had to find a way.

Just as I was considering whether I could adjust my morals and slander the Queen, I found I had an actual reason to dislike Katherine Parr, but it was not for jealousy over the King. It was for jealousy over a friend.

Katherine Willoughby would not stop talking about the new Queen. She came to visit me much more infrequently after Katherine Parr became Queen of England and every time she did come, she fair gushed about the Queen, Katherine's intelligence, her wit and her reformist beliefs. The Queen had formed her salon of learned and noble women who came together to discuss religious texts and new ideas. Quite frankly I thought it dangerous, for this gathering of women was more in plain sight than that of the Duchess of Suffolk's had ever been, and the Queen having any form of firm religious belief no matter if at present it agreed with the King's was not safe either. Yet meet they did, and discuss they did, and my friend the Duchess had found in her new Queen a similar soul, it seemed, someone to not only discuss religious matters with, but someone who apparently could guide her in them too. Katherine Parr had become a mentor to Katherine Willoughby, and I had come to loathe the shine of affection in my friend's eyes for another woman.

"I think it perilous, my friend, to be so bold in your faith," I told her after another visit, which came a long time after the last, where she praised the Queen no end.

I could feel, to my shame, my hackles rising each time Katherine of Suffolk talked of Katherine Parr. I did not want to dislike the woman, I barely knew her, but I was by no means a perfect soul, and to hear my friend, *my* friend, speak so well of the new Queen and clearly want to spend all her time with her, hurt me. I chastised myself, told myself I should be pleased Katherine had found a mentor, as it were, and the Queen was a little older than her so perhaps it was only to be expected, but I could not be pleased. I missed my friend and even when she was with me it felt as if she was not. Katherine was distant, often thinking on other things and if I would not engage in talk she wanted, such as of the faith which I made clear I thought unsafe, she often left sooner.

I started to feel as if my friend thought me dull company. The fire of reform was within her, and it was all she wanted to speak of. Sometimes we could connect with court gossip, but frequently, as is often the case when someone is immersed in a new obsession, Katherine would make it clear she found that uninteresting too.

My friend was drifting from me, my country was in peril, my mother ill, my brother clearly a fool who cared nothing for his people and my position in England was growing precarious.

Was there anything to stay for, yet was there any way I could leave?

Chapter Six

Summer 1543

Richmond Palace

In the summer of that year there was no good news for me. My friend remained distant and often was flitting around the new Queen as everyone else did, as if the Queen was a flower and all of court busy bees. My homeland was fast falling into peril. There was no sign of help from the French, the Emperor was coming for my people, and news was my mother was ailing.

For some reason, I had started to resent the new Queen for another reason. That she had replaced Catherine Howard, as if she had stolen the place and potential this young girl had had inherent within her. Catherine Howard had been determined to strike a middle way as Queen, favouring neither conservative nor evangelical, but the Parr Queen was clearly on the side of reform. Even though I knew it was foolish, even though I knew Katherine had no choice but to accept the King, still I felt she was an interloper.

Later I realised it was because I thought her an interloper in my friendship with Katherine Willoughby. Once someone becomes guilty of something in our minds, our minds find ways to link them to more crimes. In some cases, they are, of course, the King was guilty of much, but sometimes it is unjustified, based on unresolved annoyance about other matters.

Perhaps hating the Queen also just gave me something other to think on than the horror descending on my people.

In mid-July Wilhelm moved his troops to Brabant and I ceased to sleep, fearing to see dying, screaming people in my dreams. Maria of Hungary had withdrawn from the area to protect against the threat of the French in other regions, and as Wilhelm attacked small towns, he saw some success. There were stories aplenty – and how true they were I knew not since they came from imperial sources – that massacres took place under command of my brother. There were tales of entire towns and villages being put to the slaughter, of bodies in fields stacked as wheat, of children with their heads beaten in by boot heels, so soldiers could preserve weapons for battle.

Much ill is done in war, and I could not expect my brother to be transformed into an angel in a trade which made so many men monsters. Much as I hoped these tales were not true, I had reason to suspect they were. One of those reasons was that Wilhelm was not leading his men truly, his generals were still standing in his place, and if they were anything as lax as he was it was entirely possible they were not controlling their men when they encountered civilians. It is just as possible they allowed them free rein to act as they wished. Rewards stolen from townsfolk in war, women to rape, children to unleash their fear upon, these are boons generals sometimes offer their men, knowing it will keep them in the army. It was more than possible all the horrors I heard attributed to my brother, to my countrymen, were true.

"You need to eat, my lady," Kitty said gently one day as she took away another untouched plate.

I shook my head and said nothing. I had no appetite. Every day, thinking of my homeland, of what was going to happen, was consuming me, and as I was swallowed by a mouth made of darkness I had no stomach to eat.

In early August it was said my brother was convinced the French were turning against him and was demanding that his bride be delivered to him as a sign of their continued alliance. No help had come from the French for Cleves and the Emperor was not listening to any of the men Wilhelm sent to negotiate with him. The Emperor's patience had ended, it was said, and the Duke would now pay a heavy price for his betrayal.

"But why is my brother not appearing with his men? Does he not know it would inspire them to see their leader?" Even I, a woman never tested in battle, nor trained with any weapon knew this.

"His absence is blamed on his not having proper armour for battle." Harst watched me pace the room with anxious eyes. The scent of herbs was thick on the chamber air, caused by me mashing the rushes and herbs on the floor to dust with my nervous feet.

I let out a noise of exasperation, knowing this for the ludicrous excuse it was. My brother might not have been one of the richest rulers in the world, but he had money enough to buy himself a set of armour and to buy a horse who could carry him in that armour to the front with his men. "People will say my brother is a coward, and I will know not how to defend him."

"All I can tell you, my lady, is that morale is low amongst the troops and there is a sense of fear all over Cleves about the Emperor's impending arrival in our lands."

"And the leader of Cleves is nowhere to be seen," I said bleakly. "Once my father said that he wished Sybylla had been a boy, I understand why now. She would never have left our men without a leader."

On the 12th of August, Wilhelm finally appeared with his troops, but it was far too late. Morale had deserted Cleves, and the men knew it was only a matter of time before the Emperor crushed them. On the 20th of August the Prince of Orange assaulted Montjoie, a city of Julich, and a few days later the Emperor began a new attack on Duren. When the Prince of Orange joined his master, their combined forces numbered tens of thousands of men, and they possessed much artillery. Ambassadors from Saxony and other nearby states appealed for mercy, but the Emperor would not listen. Duren fell, one part of it entirely destroyed by fire.

"The Emperor marched then upon Niddegen," Harst told me.

"Ancestral home of my mother's kin," I whispered. "People always said it was too strong to fall."

But people had lied to me, to themselves perhaps. The castle of Niddegen, with its ancient high, thick walls, standing on a tall hill, fell to the Emperor's army, broken by mortars imperial troops fired upon it from a nearby hill. It was rumoured my sister was inside it as it fell, but this was only rumour. She was with my mother, drawn back to safety by our brother. That at least he had done. The castle surrendered, as did the City of Julich. Other cities in Julich and Berg surrendered without a fight, knowing they would be utterly destroyed if they did not. Charles marched towards Guelders and stopped at Venlo.

I sent an informal request through Harst to the King asking if there was any way I might be permitted to leave England and go to my home since it was in peril and my mother was in danger of her life, but my request was rebuffed again. The King said not only did the terms of our annulment mean that I had to remain in England for the entirety of my life but also that he would not risk his one and most beloved sister by sending her into a land torn by war. There was nothing I could do unless I chose to attempt to steal from England, something I knew would be entirely perilous for it was likely I would be recognised, for my accent if nothing else. I was trapped.

Then came the worst of news.

"How did she die?" I whispered.

"It is said she died of sorrow, my lady, for the fall of Julich."

I stared at the wall. My mother was a strong woman, strong in heart, mind and courage. I doubted she had died of sorrow, but I had not seen her for a long time. Perhaps she had changed, been reduced by the war. She was out of her wits with rage and sorrow in her last illness, Harst told me, reading from a letter from Olisleger, and died on the 29th of August. "Her body has been entombed on the island of Grav, at the Carthusian Monastery in Wesel."

It was said she was raving at the time of her death, her body consumed by fire of fever and her mind lost to her. To lose her was one pain but to know that she had died in such a way was an added agony. For a woman who had always prided herself on her measured calm, her stoic philosophy of life, for death to rob her of her sense, rationality, and her logical mind seemed a cruelty beyond measure.

Wicked death! I thought, my eyes aflame with tears. How dared he take a woman such as my mother and how dared he take her in such a way, having stripped away all that was important to her? Her homelands invaded, her people abused? The country she had been handed by her father as his only heir despoiled, ravaged by enemies to our people? How could Death take her at such a time when she was bereft of hope, when she must have desired more than anything to stay and to see her people made free again? And how could Death snatch from her what she had valued above all other gifts that God had given her; her mind? Death must have felt particularly vindictive on the day he stole my mother from this world.

It had been many years since I had seen my mother, yet any time I closed my eyes I could see her as if she stood straight in front of me. I could close my eyes and feel the softness of skin on the back of her hand as my fingers stroked it. I could feel the warmth of her fingertips as they pressed into my shoulder as she praised me about some piece of embroidery or some moment where I had made her proud. The old truth of life is that whilst we spend a great deal of our time as children and as growing adults wanting our parents to be proud of us, there comes a moment when we understand that we too are proud of them. If we are lucky of course. Some people never know the grace that comes with having parents one can admire. I was one of those lucky few.

She died but days before the total, crushing defeat of my brother. Perhaps it was not cruel that Death took her, then. Perhaps it was a blessing she never had to see that.

Wilhelm raged as our mother died, calling the French traitors and blaming them for not coming to his aid. Perhaps they could have sent men to help my country, but my brother was far from blameless.

"Word is, your brother will surrender," Harst told me.

"He has little other choice, does he?" My voice sounded not my own. It belonged to a hollow, lost person.

As my mother was taken from me, a sense of loneliness which had been coming upon me for a long time by that point fell on me then so heavy, so weighted that I could barely breathe.

The world was too bright, too hard, too harsh. The sound of people's voices coming from the river where ferryman took people back and forth, from gardens where kitchen girls gathered foods or herbs, from my maids as they chatted and laughed, it all became too loud. I loathed the sound of English voices where once I had welcomed them, thinking their accent charming. I despised the sight of English faces, where once I had thought them my friends.

I wanted to be home, but to be home in a time of the past when my mother was still alive so I could for the last time go into her arms and have them around me, encircling me, holding me tight against her chest so I could feel her heartbeat against mine, so I could lay my head at her throat and smell the perfume of her skin. I wanted to go home to a time when I was a child, so I could tell my mother all she meant to me, all that I had failed to tell her when she was in this world, and I had that chance.

I would never have that chance again. I should have gone home. I should have found a way. Guilt consumed me, like a mouth it opened wide and chewed me, yet into my chest and stomach too it crawled. I was guilt, I was pain, there was nothing of Anna of Cleves left.

My mother was dead, my father too and although I was an adult grown and a woman in charge of her own household and apparently her life, on the day I heard my mother was dead I felt like an orphan adrift in the world with no friends and no family.

There was a hole inside me, I could feel it gaping and echoing, calling to me in some indefinable language in the night. I knew not how to fill that hole. I wanted to fill it. Open as it was, it pained me. Every day as I woke and remembered my mother was not there it opened wider a little more, opened each time I thought of my sorrow or had some remembrance of her. I wanted to remember nothing of her and everything at the same time. If I remembered nothing then this pain would not be mine anymore, but I could not lose a single memory. So I tried to forget and at the same time to cling to every single one of my memories, to go through each one in my mind over and over so that she would not be gone from me, though she was gone from the world. I was torn by the two impulses, one for the peace of oblivion and one for the strangled cry of memory.

I hugged the ghost of my mother close to my heart, because I no more could hold my mother in this life. Her ghost was barbed, and it cut me, yet still I clung to her, my hands and arms and legs and chest bleeding as I wrapped my body about the phantom of hers and rejoiced as my mother's memory ripped out my heart, because at least then I could feel her hands on my flesh again.

I would have taken any pain, any of it, just to have her close one last time. The greatest pain was to know I never could. She was lost to me now, just as my homeland was to the Emperor.

Chapter Seven

Autumn 1543

Richmond Palace

Oh, that hideous year. It seemed never to end. There are times like that, endless wolf winters of the soul, when one is assailed on every side by horror and nothing good seems to happen.

The war was over, for Cleves at least.

On September the 7th the Treaty of Venlo was signed between my brother and the Emperor. Cleves was thrashed, all our men were in retreat, and to avoid the utter obliteration of his country my brother made peace with his enemy. My brother promised to surrender the Duchy of Guelders to the Emperor as well as the county of Zutphen, swore to renounce all leagues and loyalty with the French or any other princes, agreed that his country would observe the Catholic faith alone and swore to hold the United States of Cleves and Julich as a fief, subordinate to the Holy Roman Emperor.

The lands Wilhelm had fought for were lost, our mother was dead, other princes of the Germanic states thought him a blustering fool and he was now under the boot of the Emperor, kissing his filthy heel. Before, under my father and his father, our lands had enjoyed more anonymity. Now, Cleves was a prisoner to the Emperor as I was to the King.

Never had that been more apparent to me than when I had tried to leave, begging to return home so I could see my mother before she died. I never had liked or respected the King, and now I knew not how I was to look him in the eyes, for he was sure to see the loathing in me. It had become a living creature, with bright red eyes of wrath. How it longed for me to hurt him as he had hurt me, and so many others. How my hand twitched, stealing to my eating knife whenever I saw him after, wishing I had the strength to plunge it into the place where his empty, rotten heart had been.

But there were others to blame too.

"They say pride comes before a fall and never did I understand that so well as now," I said to Harst. "Wilhelm's pride led us to this. His foolishness too."

"The French could have aided us." His gaze roamed with concern over my thin frame, my eyes haunted by deep shadows of black and grey. I still was not sleeping. When I did, I saw my mother, and it made waking a torture.

I stuck out my chin. "Why should they?"

"Because they were our allies, Highness." His tone sounded as if he spoke to a child, explaining something she had forgot.

I laughed, a peal of bitterness. "What does that word even mean, my lord Ambassador? There is a fiction men tell one another of honour. It does not exist. Like justice and mercy, it means nothing."

Harst came to my side. "My lady, if you would hear an old man?"

"Speak as you will."

"It is easy, when we lose someone or something, to lose faith in all that is good in the world. You have lost much, more than many, and you slip into thinking there is no goodness, for you can see none. There is darkness of grief about you as a mist, obscuring your vision. But goodness is in this world, I know for I see it in you and others. It is a rare thing, it is true, but we should hold dear that which is rare and protect it. This is the one fight we never can surrender, Highness, to keep a light aflame in our hearts of goodness, and if we can find it nowhere else, then we must be the goodness in the world. You cannot let it die inside you. Your mother never would have wanted that. For her sake, you must not fall to darkness."

I took a sip of wine; it tasted of anger and grief, foul, like everything. "My mother is gone, Harst. What she wanted no longer matters to this world."

"But it matters still to you, Highness, no matter what you say now, I know that is true, just as I know that one day, as you begin to heal, you will honour her by remaining loyal to goodness."

Apparently just as Wilhelm surrendered, François was on his way to the United Duchies to deliver Jeanne and to ask for aid. It was so well timed I could barely believe the tale. On the way the French King learned that his ally had surrendered and was enraged, although by what right I knew not. Wilhelm dispatched a letter to François explaining his capitulation, but this was apparently not enough for François. My brother offered to send a delegation from Cleves to France to retrieve his bride but François and his sister Marguerite, Queen of Navarre, wasted no time in beginning the process of annulling this marriage.

It was said my brother, when he was free to marry again, would take a wife of the Emperor's choosing. Within days of the treaty being signed, of my brother dressed in mourning for our mother kneeling in ignominy before his enemy, the Emperor was off again to face the French. He took with him the remains of my brother's army. Another shameful sign of Wilhelm's complete surrender.

"And yet now, your position in England is less perilous," Katherine of Suffolk, who had managed to tear herself away from the new Queen, told me.

I supposed such was true. My brother was now the Emperor's lapdog, so England was his ally. I was no longer an enemy on the wrong side of the battlefield. "I may be part of the enemy camp no more, but I feel friendless here. During this time when my people were assaulted and my mother died, I was made to feel more a prisoner than ever I felt before."

"You are not friendless."

"I have few true friends here."

Katherine gazed at me. "I have been neglecting you, and I am sorry. My duties to the Queen are numerous, but I should have been here more, at your side, when this darkness fell upon you. Forgive me, my friend." She took my hands.

My heart felt so cold that when she reached out for my hands her flesh seemed to burn me. "I will ask the Queen that you come to court," she went on. "Now your country is friends with the Emperor there should be no trouble for the King if you were seen there. It would help him, in fact. And though you think I love the Queen more than you, it is not so, Anna. If you knew her better, you would see she grasps no love away from anyone. She is a creature full of love, as you are, and when you know one another more, you will call her friend and sister, as I do."

I was not so sure what I was full of anymore. Once I could have said in all honesty it was love and compassion, but now I knew not. There was a darkness in me now which, if I allowed it, could consume me. Sometimes I wondered how God had allowed all that had occurred, and my faith trembled within me. There were those who did not believe in God, the *nullifidians*, they said it was man alone who walked this Earth, no spirit guiding them. With all that had happened to my family, my country, my friends, I could believe what they said.

And yet, just as I had need of her, my friend had returned. Perhaps Harst was right, or perhaps the godless were. I knew not. But I knew I needed my friend.

"I would like to know the Queen better." I struggled to get the words to come clean from my mouth when all my jaw wanted was to mash them into a pulp. Jealousy may be a teacher, if we let it wash over us, showing us what we want to aspire to, I understood that well for my mother had told me so. But when it is not a fleeting feeling, a washing wave, but rather a deep sea that we fall into and whose tides try to drag us to the bottom, then it is harder to learn lessons from jealousy. Easier it is to fall within, become engulfed so blood runs no more in our veins but instead bitter salt water of the oceans of envy.

But I had mastered harder things than my dislike for the Parr Queen, and I knew it was petty, my anger and irritation at her. I wanted my friend back, so I would have to make friends with the woman who, to my mind, was trying to steal her away from me. Did I resent it? Indeed, but goodness is not always something which comes naturally. Many times, we must work at it.

I told myself there were harder things to do than try to like a woman who, after all, may have saved my life once by distracting the King as he was looking for a new bride.

*

On the 31st of December of that year my former husband formally joined the Emperor against François. At least it could be said that an offensive by England against France was now not an offensive against Cleves because of my brother's surrender to the Emperor.

"Your husband will be sent," I said to my friend of Suffolk.

"He will," she replied, "he has fought in France before, and the King trusts him as a commander. The plan is for the King and Charles to attack Paris, and men are being mustered as we to speak. It will probably begin in the summer, the winter not being a good time for campaigning."

"So it comes to pass..." I stared out of the window, wondering when I would feel hope again "... the country of my birth is now free of war even if its men still serve, and now the country of my adoption marches into that self-same war. Sometimes it feels the world is full of madness, and no one sees this but me."

Chapter Eight

Summer 1544

Richmond Palace

"The King does not think he will have children with Katherine," murmured my friend as we walked in my gardens that summer.

"I thought that was obvious in the spring of this year." My voice was just as low as hers.

I gazed out across the gardens. At the end of the last year and the beginning of this one I had thought it a thing impossible that I would ever appreciate beauty again. Lost had been my soul somewhere dark, unfathomable. Some mornings merely finding the energy to get out of bed had been a trial hard enough to consume my entire day with weakness. I had held but few entertainments, had no passion for games of cards or dancing or to hear laughter around me. Even music lost its pleasure. The gaping hole inside me, this wound my mother's death had torn and the shaming of my country had rubbed salt into, it was too large then for me to look about and appreciate any beauty in the world. But those who tell you that time will heal, they do not lie, even though at the time any of us are told such it sounds like a falsehood.

Lost in the darkness as I was, my hand had fumbled in that bleakness before me, and in the void something took my hand. It was not the enemy which reached out to me in that place where there was no light, it was not a demon or spirit of wickedness. I would never find out what it was that reached for me when I reached out, but I knew then that my own darkness was not a place of nothingness or evil, but a place of transformation and something was there to help me, to guide me as I stumbled through the blackness.

The darkness was not there to swallow me, but to aid me. It was a quiet place, where no harsh light shone to bruise my eyes, where I could simply *be* as grief washed over me, the initial cold shock becoming eventually warm waves as my body adjusted to the depths of my own sorrow. And when I emerged, I was the same and yet different, another Anna, another Lady of Cleves, my inner self having been dug deeper by the claws that sorrow bore, but my soul becoming stronger, too, for having endured. And emerge I had, blinking into this unfamiliar world, this world where my mother no longer lived, yet I knew she was somewhere, inside me if nowhere else. I knew not for certain, but I believed it had been her hand in the darkness, there to protect and guide me even when I could not see her.

I was not healed, not fully and perhaps I never would be, but my shoulders were stronger now and could bear the weight of my sorrow, and the wound which still hung within my chest, that hole so raw and bleeding, it was still there mistake me not, but I could feel the edges of it had been sealed by the fire of my grief.

There were times now I dreamed of my mother and woke with a remembrance of her love in my heart, as well as the sorrow of her passing. In the first days I woke only with sorrow. Now I had both, and both hurt, but they comforted too. It is a strange thing to learn that sorrow and grief are not enemies, they are the physical proof painted upon our bodies in our blood and in our tears of how deeply and truly we did love a person. They are teachers too, and their lessons are hard and harsh and yet they are worth learning, for they teach us, remind us that though we have lost someone we can show those who still are in our lives that we love them, while we have the chance to do so.

It seemed the King was at last thinking of a time he might not be there, and what would happen to the ones he at least claimed to love.

The Third Act of Succession of 1543 had been passed by Parliament in that spring of 1544. It confirmed a place in the succession for Lady Mary and Lady Elizabeth should the King have no children with Katherine Parr and should Prince Edward die without heirs. Whilst it was surely only an insurance policy the King was enacting, it also pointed to a potential loss of confidence in his ability to sire another heir. In a way it was remarkable for a man who lived so deep in fantasy as the King. I thought it might be one of the first moments he had considered reality for some years.

Catherine Howard and he had been married for eighteen months and there had been no child. Of course, he and I had been married for six months and there had been none either but that was because he had not touched me, not enough to make a child at least. That summer as my friend and I walked in the garden it had been a year since the King and Katherine Parr had been wed and there had been not even a suggestion that she had become pregnant.

Some might say this meant trouble for the new Queen, and certainly in the past it could have cost her a head, but I thought the King was finally simply seeing what the rest of us knew and was admitting he might be too old to father more children. Many people claimed men could sire children into their dotage, and it was of course possible, I had seen old men get children on young wives, but it was also true that it was not women alone who declined in the frequency of ease of creating life as they got older. It was a fact many men did not care to face, the illusion of their eternal fertility a lie many told, but in my herbals, there were frequent references to the weakness of the seed of men as they aged. I knew there must be many men who suffered so, because of the amount of remedies there were. It is a truth that there is no supply without demand, and these recipes had come into being, most likely, because generations upon generations of young women married to old goats knew their future prosperity relied on getting a son in their belly and into the line of succession for the house they had married into, so had sought aid from cunning women and abbesses with healing skill, in order to strengthen the seed of their husbands.

Many men would rather die than admit such, however, and in the past one of those men had been the King. Of course, he sent others to their deaths rather than die himself, but the truth of his need to blame all his other wives for lack of a prince or lack of children in general, stood.

Until now, until the sixth wife.

He had not shown distrust or dislike of Katherine because of her lack of a rounded belly; in fact he had honoured her greatly.

The King had set sail for France, the plan to invade Paris in his mind, and he had left Katherine Parr as Regent of England. True, she had a council of men about her which the King had picked, and some might have simply called her a figurehead, but they would have been wrong. It was clear to all of us even before the King left that Katherine would be the one making the final decisions. The inclusion of her uncle, Sir William Parr of Horton, as a member of the council just before the King's departure secured that in our minds. "She wants support," I noted to my friend of Suffolk, who had nodded.

"The Queen knows men will try to take her power, as does the King, but with her uncle at her side she will always have more of a voice. He was as a father to her and her siblings when their own died." My friend looked about and dropped her voice. "And I will tell you a secret, my friend. In many ways this time of regency is a test."

"A test?"

"Indeed. I have been told the King makes provision in his will that should he die before Katherine, she will rule as Regent for his son until Edward comes of age. This time, as she rules in England whilst the King is at war with France, it will be a trial, if you will, so the King can see who he can trust about his wife and who he cannot."

"But, it is for certain that he will make her Regent for Edward?" I was amazed. Although I had heard that Anne Boleyn had been named as Regent in the event of the King's death, and therefore it was likely Katherine of Spain had too, though no one had told me either way, I had thought the days of the King trusting wives so completely was long behind him, but Katherine Parr, as I had learned, was a woman of special talents.

She might well, as my friend of Suffolk had implied, use her wiles in the bedchamber to gain influence, but the truth was that was but one of her many talents. Grudgingly, I had come to respect the Parr Queen. The more I had learned of her, the more I had come to think of her.

We had little met. Perhaps the Queen had too much to be thinking of with the King away at war to take a great deal of time for me, or perhaps she still was unsure about me being kept long at court given my brother's only late obedience to the Emperor, but on the few occasions we had met, I had come to respect her. What I had learned of her from others only aided that.

Lady Mary had told me of Katherine Parr's gentle kindness to both her and Elizabeth, how she had asked for both to join her household and while the King was away, had indeed welcomed both into the palaces of England to stay with her. Katherine was kind to Edward too, and seemed to have won his heart, no mean feat for it was widely rumoured the boy had grown into a cold fish and had no heart to speak of. The King always seemed to be trying to make Edward into a mirror image of him – the way the two dressed was comically identical, especially since Edward was so small and looked dwarfed by the grand clothes his father insisted on – and perhaps people thought the King had succeeded in transferring not only his looks in dress to the boy, for Edward looked more like his mother than father in face and form, but also the coldness which had crept into the core of the King.

But if the King was coldness, his wife was a gentle thaw. Just as powerful as cold is the thaw, but how much more do people welcome it when it comes! It was widely said the inclusion of Mary and Elizabeth in the succession had come about at the Queen's urging, and perhaps this was true for the King had never made so momentous a decision to benefit his daughters before now.

There was more than this. Katherine was an outspoken woman when it came to faith, and like my friend she was of the reformed faith. She even argued with the King on the matter, debating and discussing with him openly, leading to much amazement at court that the King allowed it, and even joined in, apparently enjoying himself as an intelligent woman fenced with him with sword of words and shield of facts. She had penned books, published by the King's printer and endorsed by Cranmer, and the Archbishop was a great supporter of hers. Conservatives such as Gardiner and Norfolk liked the Queen not, thinking her a heretic, but Katherine had the full love and loyalty of the King. She surrounded herself with friends, ensured her ladies were not too beautiful – the King in fact called them a pack of crows, owing to the black velvet uniform they wore and also because they were not great beauties, aside from her sister, Anne – and she kept her people loyal. Better than any Queen had done for many years was Katherine Parr doing, and she maintained her position with a steady hand, a firm will and a heart of compassion.

And now the Queen had been named Regent. The King was in France, having travelled there to begin the siege of Boulogne. Paris had been the intended target, but it seemed that might have struck the King as too taxing a project, so a more acceptable one had been found. The English army had begun its attack on the 19th of July, and it appeared the siege was going to last a long time. The King himself had wished to be present for this and whilst he was there, Norfolk had been sent to march on other targets.

In all honesty, the English invasion was a muddle from the start.

Matters had begun with some semblance of order. Just before the King set sail for France, he had decided to secure relations with Scotland by marrying his niece Margaret Douglas to Matthew Stewart the Earl of Lennox. The King wanted friends in Scotland who were likely to support his bid to marry Mary Queen of Scots to Prince Edward. The Regent, Arran, was already largely on his side but more support was always a good idea. Most fortunately for Margaret Douglas, it turned out she liked this young man who had spent much of his youth in France and was handsome, tall and fresh-faced. It was widely rumoured that Lennox had a quick temper and possessed a mind never overtaxed by thought, so perhaps Margaret Douglas warmed to the match because thought she might have some control over him, but she also seemed to find him attractive. So, in June that year she had been married. Many called Lennox lusty and beardless – I learned neither was a compliment – but Margaret seemed happy enough and after all the misery she had experienced I wished her well of her marriage.

All had seemed to bode well for France as well, for the King had put together quite the largest force that England had organised since the days of Henry V. Some said 30,000 men were going to war, some said 40,000. The King himself had been in a fine mood, actually in love with his new Queen and fresh filled with fire of youth and lust for blood as he prepared to ride into France at the head of a conquering army. However, even before he left, apparently his ally was trying to dissuade him.

"The Emperor has been doing everything he can to persuade our King to stay in England," Katherine Willoughby informed me, "the Emperor tells him by all means to send his troops but cautions that he should stay at home."

"The King would never wish to do that; he would miss out on all the diversion of war." I was unable to keep scorn from my voice. I saw nothing good in war.

The King had, in fact become so buoyant I thought the prospect of invasion and spilling blood had become a greater elixir to him than marrying Catherine Howard. Having just had my own country invaded, this glee made me think even less of my former husband. He enjoyed the notion of all the pain he was about to cause, or perhaps did not even think on it. I would call it inhuman, but the truth is, it was a very human trait. We find no foxes banding together and riding out to make war on other groups of foxes. We discover no birds of the skies obliterating whole flocks of other birds simply for pleasure. It would be a pleasing thing to call war and mass murder animalistic traits of humans, yet no animals I have seen do such things.

The pleasure men take in trying to destroy their neighbours, other races of men entire, the lust men have to steal land from one another and shed blood, the honour they believe is in it, the respect they have for other men who kill hundreds or thousands of people... these are human traits alone. No animal is as cruel, as wicked as we have the capacity to be. No animals kill without reason, or in such numbers as we are capable of. War, murder, these are not animalistic traits, but are entirely human, human alone.

Something we should recognise, to our shame, is that animals of farm and field, bracken and bush and ocean, all of them, are more civilized than us. They kill for survival. We kill for land, for greed and for the pure, filthy enjoyment of it.

"I think the Emperor does not want to have to try to command the King of England in the field." Katherine lifted her eyebrows. "His men, the Emperor certainly wants, but the complication of another general on the battlefield the Emperor does not desire."

"The King is talking continually, so I hear, about marching his own troops into Paris," I said; this was before we knew the target had altered.

"That is his true desire now," agreed Katherine. "He wants France and most especially François to bow before him."

"All because he lost a wrestling match when they were young?"

Katherine chuckled. "The King, other men too, would scorn such a thought and say it is more complicated than that, but in truth I think you are right. The King has wanted vengeance since he lay on the ground staring up at François. What better way to take it than to have François bowed before him, his prisoner in war, and have his foe's entire country looking up to him? What better way to erase the shame?"

"And yet it would still hold that in single combat, François was the stronger man, and he beat the King."

"The more skilled, I would say. Wrestling is not all about brute strength, no matter how much it might appear so."

I affected mock horror. "That is even worse. The King was beaten by skill? No wonder he spent all his youth flying up and down tennis courts and jousting rings. He was trying to prove he was more than just the strength of his body." I sighed, humour falling from me. "And now, this old desire for revenge, to prove himself, it manifests to war, and he will wreak it on innocent people."

"How peaceful a world we would have, my friend, if not for the pride of men needing satisfaction."

"How peaceful a world we would have if people were not so petty," I scoffed.

The Regency Council left behind to consult with the Queen was made up of Archbishop Cranmer, Sir Thomas Wriothesley, Edward Seymour the Earl of Hertford, Thomas Thirlby Bishop of Westminster and Sir William Petre, clerk of council. The Queen's uncle Lord Parr of Horton had then been added of course, at her urging, and two days after the Queen's commission as Regent was signed another had been drawn up which granted the Queen and any two of her councillors the right to control money from the royal treasury.

"Archbishop Cranmer and Edward Seymour are sympathetic to the Queen, since she agrees with them about the faith, and are likely to vote for her whenever she requires it," my friend of Suffolk informed me, "so with their vote, as well as her uncle of Horton's, her power is secured, and the King knows it."

Katherine had proven a good Regent, keeping in touch with her husband whilst he was on the Continent, arranging supply lines for his troops, issuing proclamations, mainly to do with the war but on a wide variety of issues, some involving local squabbles. She had dealt with all issues with a straightforward approach which would brook no insolence, and my friend of Suffolk was fully assured that the Queen knew the King had made his will before heading to France and in it he had named his wife Regent of England for Edward if he should die. This granted her authority in many ways.

As the Queen had brought Elizabeth and Mary to court to be with her whilst their father was away, I was delighted to hear that young Elizabeth blossomed under the warm love of her new stepmother. The King had evidently approved this, for he sent his warm regards to his children as they stayed with Katherine.

Perhaps it was his confidence in her which gave Katherine Parr the conviction to act as a Queen should, so many in England were singing her praises, saying that never since Katherine of Aragon had they had such a good Queen.

Yet if the Queen was doing all she should, the King was not doing well with war.

"The campaign has largely been a disaster from the start." Harst's voice was lofty with cynicism. "Upon arriving at the sands of the beaches of France on the 14th of July, the King appears to have lost much of his enthusiasm for war."

"How so?" I asked, "and why?"

"Probably because he has found the reality of war is not as easy as he thought it would be when he was imagining it, Highness."

I almost giggled, and scowled at my friend for making me laugh at the King, something which had cost many a person their head.

Harst went on to explain that one of the reasons the King had lost much of his enthusiasm was because he realised that moving upon Paris would take him and his men far from their supply lines in the Pale, and he was having trouble also with the lack of support which was coming from his ally the

Emperor. This had led to the King deciding to change the city he would march upon. Paris was too far away and would require a great deal of effort, therefore he would make for Boulogne since it was closer, and the town was less well defended. An easy victory rather than a glorious one. What baffled me was how many Englishmen immediately acted as if this had been the plan all along. The power the King's fragile self-esteem had over his people was immense.

Whilst besieging Boulogne the King was apparently having a merry time, enjoying supervising his men and ordering them about, apparently in better spirits and health than he had been for ten years. Every other ruler of the world looked upon the English King gadding about, playing at war, and shook their heads in amazement.

On the 13th of September Boulogne surrendered, and the husband of Anne Parr, Sir William Herbert took to horse, heading for the coast and for England to relay the news to the Queen, who ordered all churches to hold Masses of thanksgiving and for all people to celebrate. The King rode into his conquered city in triumph. Once inside, he met the Duke of Suffolk and delivered to him the keys of the city then rode towards lodgings prepared for him on the south side of the town. The King ordered that the town's Lady Chapel be torn down, and the stone used to build a monument to his victory instead.

"How petty," I whispered.

Much to the disgust of the King however, on the very day of his great victory the Emperor signed a separate peace treaty with François.

The King only had Boulogne to call his own and the Duke of Norfolk, along with half the English army, was busy starving at an ongoing siege at Montreuil. Now the ally of the King had deserted him and made peace with his enemy. English ambitions to claim France were over.

"Little help was going to come from the Emperor," said my friend Katherine. "Charles, my husband, would not listen to me when I said I thought the Emperor would be short of resources after dashing this way and that, warring all over the Continent. The Schmalkaldic League are a continuing and growing concern for the Emperor and frankly, his war with France can wait." She turned to me. "Your family will give Charles V trouble now, and that is the trouble he will ride towards first, he fears them more than the French, and certainly more than offending the English."

"You said all this to your husband?"

"As much as I dared, and as carefully as I could, but he would not listen. He and the King, both were buoyed up with the notion they would claim all of France. They claimed one town, but they won't keep it long. All that blood, all those men and all that money and for what? Boulogne, for but a temporary time."

The final Treaty of Crepy was signed around the 18th of September, about a week after the surrender of Boulogne. Each King abandoned various claims to land and title. The Emperor relinquished his claim to the duchy of Burgundy, François did the same for the Kingdom of Naples and others. England was not mentioned, and now Charles V and François were at peace and the English King was the one on the wrong side of the field.

I could have laughed, were it not likely I might get caught. Finally, the odious man might get a taste of what he had done to me, to my country, to Boulogne, to so many people. Finally, he might be the one in danger, surrounded by enemies.

Charles V sent the King a letter telling him he had no wish to continue the campaign in France, and news was the King of England was incandescent with fury that his ally had made peace with their mutual enemy without saying a word to him. Once again, as when James of Scots had snubbed him, the King had been treated as if he did not matter, and there was no worse insult to a man as insecure as Henry of England.

This was no good news for me, however. If the Emperor was freed of dealing with his enemies of France and Cleves that meant he was now free to move upon the Schmalkaldic League, which included Sybylla's husband, her sons and of course, my sister herself.

"There is some good news however, Madame de Cleves," Diaceto told me. Madame de Cleves was a title I used from time to time, demonstrating I had been married. "There is word your brother is to take a Hapsburg bride; Maria of Austria, a kinswoman of the Emperor himself."

Whilst I wished my brother all felicity in marriage that was possible to bestow, I wondered if this was good news. If the Emperor was to move upon my sister and her family, it might well be that he would do so now with the aid of my brother, his new ally, and the men of our country. The men of Cleves pitted against those of Saxony? Was it not enough my mother had lost her life for grief, but now my brother's men would make war on our sister and her people?

All the same, no matter what might come in the future my brother was to be married in the present. I learned that the terms of the peace treaty with France ensured that Wilhelm's present wife, Jeanne, consented to an annulment of their match. And so it came to pass that my brother was free to marry the Emperor's niece. As a wedding present I sent two horses and two braces of greyhounds. However this would turn out for Sybylla and her people or indeed the people of Cleves, my brother was to be married and continue the line of our country. That was not the only present I dispatched that summer for I sent Lady Mary a gift of some Spanish silk.

There were some complications getting the King home, I learned. Gossip held that the French meant to capture him, but through the offices of Queen Katherine and his own "bravery" he escaped and made it home, his men following in bedraggled, starving lines behind him. I sometimes wondered afterwards if this was not all a feint, and there had been no danger at all, but to make him appear the courageous warrior coming home, rather than the abandoned, irrelevant ally, this gossip had been put about so all of England would rejoice to see him home.

If so, it worked. As he came riding back to London, his people cheered him like a conquering hero, yet all he had to show for all this effort was one town and yet another broken alliance.

*

Late that September, as I was in the mews visiting my birds before hunting season began, one of them a glorious osprey sent as a gift to me that New Year from Duke Albert of Prussia, I received the news that I was to lose someone else I had come to rely on.

"What do you mean you have been recalled?" I asked.

Harst stared at me in sadness. He did not want to go, did not want to leave me. I knew that. Regret was upon every fibre of his being as he stood before me. But he, like all men on this earth, was the servant of another and he, like all men, would obey his master. It was ever a wonder to me that men spoke so often and with such conviction about the natural, subordinate, position of women to men, when men, the vast majority at least, spent all their time bowing to other men. Women need reminding of this natural place under men so often by law and Church, that I think it is not natural to them, but other men, oh! How they love it! They bow and fawn with such ease. Peasants who rebel have more backbone than most of the men of this world who spy a higher authority and thirst to obey it.

Harst was the servant of my brother, and my brother had called him home. Why Wilhelm thought I could do without Harst I knew not. Did he think I required no information on the world, on home, on all that was happening, so had scant need of an ambassador? Perhaps he did not want me to know what was happening, shied from the notion that I would find out what his men were doing to our sister whilst under command of Charles V. Perhaps Wilhelm did not want another sister to hear of his lapdog-like lapping at the toes of the Emperor.

If so, it was too late. I did not think well of my brother already, even less so when he stripped Harst, one of the crucial links to the outside world I possessed, and one of my friends, from me.

"Chapuys is to be recalled too, next year," he told me. "A man named François Van der Delft will take over from Chapuys, and I am told will speak for your interests too, Highness."

I nodded. "My interests are the Emperor's. I see."

"Highness, Olisleger will return if he can. He has petitioned your brother, and advised him against his recall of me, but your brother is set on my return. Apparently, the Emperor advised it. Perhaps the Emperor does not want you to have as much influence here."

I laughed. "What influence do I have?"

"We may be able to persuade the King to release you now, Highness. You could come home with me, to see your sister, and your brother."

I shook my head. "The Cleves I knew, it is gone, Harst. My brother saw to that. Go home now and I will be as much in the pocket of the Emperor, a man I loathe for he killed my mother, as my brother is. And the King will not let me go. Send me off for the Emperor to command instead of him? I think not. The King has been treated as if he does not matter, again, and he will cling to anything which grants him any semblance of authority in this time of shame. I am one of those things. If the Emperor wants me, the King will cling to his 'good sister'. You know that, Harst, as I do."

I stroked the wing of my osprey, and a chirrup of pleasure came from her beak. She longed to fly free, as I did. Perhaps our wishes were the same, that we had in mind no nest, no country as our destination. We simply wanted to fly, wing into the heavens until we were so far from this world and all the men on it that they became as insignificant specks floating on a brown expanse of land.

"We will send information to you, Highness, through Diaceto we can manage." Harst fell to his knees before me, spoiling the fine fabric of his breeches and stockings on the dirty floor of the mews. But I did not stop him. I appreciated the gesture, dramatic though it was. He knelt before me as a man does when a king knights him, and I set my hands on his shoulders, gazing into his warm eyes. "We will not desert you, my lady," he said.

"I know you will not, my friend. When I lost faith, Harst, you offered it to me. I know such a gift is not temporary, and such a gift as faith, as hope, I will treasure all my life."

"As I am your brother's servant, I am yours, my lady."

"I know this, my friend." I touched his cheek. "I know."

Chapter Nine

1545

Richmond Palace

"So, my brother plans to marry both his sisters off," I mentioned to Diaceto.

Since Harst's departure the young man, growing older now as we all must, had become my new lifeline to the outside world. Harst had given his contacts to Diaceto, so I would not find myself blind in this world.

"Is there any news on exactly whom my brother expects me to marry this time?" Without waiting for an answer I continued, "I consider sometimes that the arrangement Princess Mary Tudor, late sister of my brother of England believed she had with her natural brother, should become as standard for all women; that once and once alone we are expected to marry where we are commanded by our families, then after we may choose whom we are to marry, and *if* we are to marry at all. Would that not be fair, rather than sending us hurtling from one husband to the next as fancies of politics alter as ever they are wont?"

"It saddens me, Highness, that the world is not fair."

"Whilst but one man of any country makes all the decisions and more than half of humankind is unable to make their own, Diaceto, it shall ever be unfair."

Diaceto, sympathetic though he was to me, assumed that expression I had often seen men adopt; a flicker of amused scorn, as if he were conversing with an infant, as if what I said was foolish, out of the bounds of human capability. He thought as many others did, that because this was the way of the world now, thus it always would be, so his mind belittled my comment as fanciful.

In part it was because it was common belief that it was ludicrous any woman could hold intelligent thought or be in any way capable of making choices for herself. Diaceto had been led in this way of thinking as all men had, therefore incredulity was bound to be his gut reaction.

Yet I was not alone in believing there could be a different world. People often surrender the notion of change as soon as it is suggested, and yet if they did not, if they considered it, much could be altered. I perhaps had more hope in humanity than those who would immediately condemn an idea of societal change as impossible. If Christine de Pizan had spoken more than a hundred years ago to argue that women were creatures of rationality, rectitude and justice, and should culture these virtues, that they were capable of contributing to their society and should be heard by that society, then certainly now, in our modern age, we should be considering women as more than mere cattle to be sold off to the most advantageous herder.

We should also be considering that it was perilous to place all our fates in the hands of but one man, one man with all the power and instability the King possessed.

Whilst I understood where it originated, it still baffled me at times that even a man of lower status and inferior education to me, like Diaceto, could believe he knew more than I did on this, or any other subject. There is an arrogance in man, where despite any evidence to the contrary, a person frequently will believe themselves to be right and all others wrong. I did not suppose such a thing, that I knew all, but yet I would have welcomed the chance to decide my own fate. Diaceto was not alone in thinking women incapable of commanding their own lives, however, for my brother, the coward of Cleves as men were calling him, had taken it upon himself to try to command destinies for his sisters once again. The man could not even turn up to fight with his troops, yet he thought we, his sisters, should obey him out of respect. I had no respect for him.

Negotiations to marry my sister Amalia off had begun, the intended groom either Karl or Bernhard of Baden, a Catholic house loyal to the Emperor, and there was word my brother was seeking a match for me too, perhaps into the same house with whichever son Amalia was not promised to.

I was ever in two minds about whether I wanted to return to the land of my birth. It would be suffused with memories of my mother and although part of me would have liked to walk in company with her ghost, another part of me believed it might be easier to stay in England, however hostile or friendly this country might become to me as tides of politics and alliances altered, rather than wander always with a phantom at my side, being reminded that I had let my mother down by not being with her in the last moments of her life.

I was not sure I wanted either to go home and to discover I had no influence on my brother, and find myself a more intimate part of a country which would not only not stand for Sybylla or the League but might well stand against them. Would I have to wait helplessly by, watching my brother aid the Emperor in crushing our sister? This match, too, would see me return, then be sent to another house again. What was the use? I might as well remain in England and be a prisoner, as go to another country and become captive to a man I knew not at all.

Marriage was in the air in other ways as well. It came with death.

My good friend Katherine of Suffolk suffered a loss that year as her husband Charles died in August. It was sudden and no one expected it. Brandon had asked for a quiet funeral, but the King would not allow it and had him buried in St George's Chapel at Windsor Castle in great pomp. The King was so distraught, men said, he could barely talk of his friend.

It was certainly more emotion than he had shown for the death of any wife, so perhaps he had loved Brandon.

Now the Dowager Duchess, her son Henry taking his father's title, my friend entered into mourning, yet there were immediate rumours the King might set aside Katherine Parr and marry Katherine Willoughby instead. He always had a fancy for her.

I knew where these rumours had come from; from the King himself, his eyes staring at my friend whenever she entered a room, that mouth bagging open so he could pant to relieve the pangs of lust which rose when on my friend he gazed.

It was no secret to the court that had Charles not been the King's good friend, Katherine would have become a royal mistress, and perhaps the King had asked this of his friend. Perhaps it had even been granted though I thought not, for surely my friend would have mentioned it. Although it was possible, I thought it untrue. The King was always more attentive to women he was chasing, not ones he had caught. Had he captured my friend of Suffolk in his bedsheets, he would have lost interest by now, but it was still possible he had asked his friend to share his wife. Although the King thought himself a paragon of virtue in matters marital, all others knew from the evidence presented that he had scant respect for the vows of matrimony. If he could have had his best friend's wife to warm his bed, I am sure he would have.

I doubted Brandon would have stood in the way of his master. Plenty of men had capitulated the moment their King had turned a leering gaze upon their women. Wives, sisters, daughters... what were ties of kinship and promises of protection to a man who wanted to further his interests by forcing a kinswoman to become a whore?

Brandon was not particularly strong in the first place, not in character, always he was a follower, therefore he probably would have succumbed and offered up his pretty wife so his master could rut between her legs, but I suspected that Katherine would not have agreed and the idea that she might refuse the King, using her marriage vows as a means to rebuff him, is probably what kept the King in check. He could not endure rejection, and I think he always knew that Katherine would refuse him if he offered her the place of mistress.

But what of wife? I wondered, if he offered, would she accept even knowing the dangers? The fact was Katherine Willoughby had become most fervent in her dedication to the new faith. If she thought there was a possibility she could influence the King to advance the cause of Protestantism in England, there was a possibility she might accept the risk of becoming his wife. But only would she have done so if she knew Katherine Parr would not have been disgraced and there are few ways a man may separate from a wife without defaming her, even I had not escaped unscathed. It was likely that, due to respect for the Queen, her good friend, Katherine Willoughby would turn down a crown for herself if offered. My friend had scruples and was loyal to those she loved. Those things, those qualities that make a soul great, would thwart any plans of the King to once again trade wives.

But there was word of another marriage.

Wilhelm's union to Jeanne was officially annulled on the 22nd of October by Pope Paul III and swiftly Maria of Austria, daughter of Ferdinand, King of the Romans, the Emperor's brother, was formally offered and approved by the Pope. She was around fourteen at the time, and the thought was that they would marry in the year to come, when she was fifteen.

This move of course tied my brother ever tighter to the apron strings of the Emperor, and this was not a good thing for our sister Sybylla. In the spring of that year, Charles V had promised at the Diet of Worms to discuss reform, or at least acceptance, however partial it was, of Protestantism. In reality everyone knew he was simply gathering support for his own causes at the Diet.

Talk of acceptance was just a distraction so his foes would look one way as he got up to much in another direction, where they were not looking. It is a common trick with rulers who maintain power through deception. A mirror dazzles the eyes of the onlooker with light reflected, as behind the back of the trickster something else entirely goes on. I had seen my former husband do it enough times to see it for what it was.

If the Emperor gathered enough support, it was believed he would be able to overthrow the Schmalkaldic League. He also had promises from the Pope that troops would be dispatched from Rome and from the Vatican to aid him.

I was worried for my sister, but in the meantime, I had a friend to console.

"I know you struggled in the last years of marriage," I said to Katherine as we rode our horses at a walk in the deer park at Richmond. My people were hawking, sharp October wind biting our cheeks, but Katherine had little taste for hawking that day.

"And in some ways that makes me feel worse." She stroked the chestnut neck of her fine horse. "I regret some moments between us. Charles was not a perfect husband, but what man is? I feel I could have been more patient, more kind to him, and now I cannot be, for he is gone."

"Regret is a good friend to grief, they often appear hand in hand," I told her. "I feel the same. Memories of my mother come to me, and often I have cause to regret I could not go home. My conscience assails me."

She straightened up, shifting her reins. "But you could not go home, the King would not let you. These things you feel, they are not based on the reality of the situation."

I smiled. "And thus, I turn your words back to you. You were a good wife to Charles. You gave him sons, which is all men seem to want, and you supported him, even when he did wrong. You were patient, understanding even when you were wronged. These things you feel, they are not based on the reality of the situation."

She smiled in return. "Perhaps, when the end comes and we lose people, we think of how much better we could have done everything. It is easier to know, with hindsight, what we should have done."

"You did well enough. The Duke was lucky to have you."

"Your mother was lucky you were her child, too. You could not have returned, Anna, for so many reasons, not the least of them war upon your country or the King not allowing it."

"And you could have done no more for your husband. Some of the responsibility for his life, his fate, must fall on him."

Katherine breathed in and let it out in a long sigh, staring at mist rising on the fields, spreading into the trees. "I suppose we must each try to listen to the other, to this good advice we give, and attempt to silence the voices inside us which tell us we were wrong."

"That, indeed, is the challenge," I smiled. "If we were, to ourselves, as good friends as we are to others, perhaps we would all be more at peace."

"It is harder to be a good friend to yourself, because you alone know all the darkness, the meanness, the bitter spirit inside you. Others, even the closest friends, they do not see this part of us."

I reached out to take her hand, stopping my horse and hers. "What others see is the result of the choices we make, Katherine. Remember that. No matter what darkness is within you, what evil thoughts that come, those are not the ones that you have acted upon, and friends see that. And whilst we all might carry wickedness within us, we do not all choose to act on it. Friends are friends because they like the choices we have chosen to make, the thoughts we acted upon. It is not what we are capable of which makes us what we are, it is not our impulses, it is what we choose to do."

"I sometimes think there is nothing of darkness in you."

I shook my head. "Plenty there is. It grows over the years, fed by disillusionment, but a man once told me the truest battle and one we must never lose is to continue to nurture goodness. At the time, I thought his words foolish, but the more I think on it the more it makes sense to me. If goodness were easy, all the world would be right by now. We must work at it, for the sake of all of us."

*

"The King weeps more for the loss of one ship than he did over any wife," I muttered to myself as news came of attempts to recover the King's precious ship the *Mary Rose*.

In the summer there had been word of French invasion, that 30,000 men were coming for England, and the King's navy, admittedly an impressive fleet under command of John Dudley, the Admiral, had set out to meet them. The English had sailed from Portsmouth and engaged the French, but at such long range the ships barely harmed one another, and no one was close enough to board. Battles at sea were much as they were on land; guns would fire, and men would fight once the ships were close enough. In truth, it was just a land battle on water. In the evening of the 19th of July, the *Mary Rose* had advanced, but she foundered. Though she was not far from port, about one and a half nautical miles, most of her crew died. Only thirty men or so escaped. Most sailors could not swim. Four hundred drowned within sight of English land, and with the King looking on, weeping. In all honesty I thought he wept for his ship, which had been with him thirty years or more, rather than his men.

The invasion was thwarted, however, battles fought on the Isle of Wight went the way of the English and the French retreated. The King was now hiring men to raise the ship, a company headed by a Venetian, hired by Admiral John Dudley.

"They will dive down, run ropes and cables under the hull and two ships will pull the ropes taut," Katherine explained. "This will bring the *Mary Rose* to the surface. She can then be taken to the shallows and pumped out, all the goods on her removed to make her lighter, and there she will be repaired."

"Is it not too deep to dive?"

"She is only perhaps forty feet below the surface. It is deep, but experienced divers can achieve the feat. The King is so pleased his ship will be returned to him; he wept."

"As he did when the ship went down." I wondered how many tears he had shed for the loss of his vessel, and how few he had shed over wives and friends sent to their death.

But the *Mary Rose* would not rise from the sea. Several attempts to lift her only managed to snap her masts. The King's beloved vessel did not want to return to him but would rather lie at the bottom of the sea, cradling the bodies of her dead. Perhaps, I thought, the ship did not want to leave her men until the sea had given them a burial complete. Or perhaps she simply had no wish to return to such as master as the King.

Chapter Ten

March 1546

Hampton Court

"I have for so long wanted to make your closer acquaintance, as a good sister," the Queen said to me, her tone gentle yet those grey eyes direct, "but I do wonder if it may be premature to call each other that. I would not... I am not the type of soul who may pretend affection where it is not felt, and I believe you to be of the same mind, Highness. They who know you well tell me often how measured, wise and diplomatic you are."

She had a way about her, Katherine Parr. Her voice was calm and dignified, gentle and sweet, yet she was straightforward, not one to avoid hard subjects. This I had learned with only a short acquaintance. It was a canny power. She fulfilled all that was expected of a woman with the tone of her voice, and yet the words that voice formed were more forthright than a woman was ever expected to be. Men were expected to talk thus, though plenty of them tripped their tongues about pretty, fawning phrases, dancing attendance and praise upon those higher than them. Some might have said Katherine took on the masculine and feminine roles in one, but I would not say so. It was men's privilege, not their nature, that they were permitted to be direct. Women, if allowed to be as they were meant to be, would be just as confident, just as frank, just as open as men. Were they *allowed* to. That was the clause. Most women were not permitted, but a Queen such as Katherine, confident in her husband's favour, she could let loose this side of her. She could be as she wished to be.

She had limits still, but the liberty upon her I could see. It was the same as that permitted to me, the licence to do as I would with my household, with my life, as long as the King approved.

Perhaps all freedom is only ever partial, and ours was dependent on the same man, but all the same we were more fortunate than many, and she more so than me.

Is it possible a woman has come who understands how to control this mad bear, the King of England? I thought. It was possible. I supposed that eventually, going through women as he did, he was bound to find one who could manage his capricious ways.

The Queen was at my side as we strolled the gardens. The sunlight was warm but not too hot, there was a light breeze blowing. It brought the scent of roses not far away to my nose, but also carried the scent of the river, further away but more pungent than any flower. I had been invited to court by the Queen and since I had arrived, she had been polite, welcoming, attempting to know me better. I had been a trifle more reserved, still something in my heart unwilling to warm to this woman who had done nothing except offer friendship to my friend, what a crime! That Katherine Willoughby had found another person more interesting than me to spend time with still pained me but was that the fault of the Queen for being that interesting person? It would make more sense if I was angry with my friend for abandoning me rather than being angry with the person she had abandoned me for.

Yet all those thoughts were things of sense, and the heart quite often is not a thing of sense. In some ways it is not always a bad thing to be led by one's emotions as long as emotions do not become one's master. If they are but part of the party travelling with us through life and not the one at the fore, leading us, emotions can be a good thing. But especially when it comes to poor emotions, ones we often are ashamed of, they frequently do not understand rationality and sense. Jealousy is possibly the worst of them and the one most likely to follow any track rather than one leading to logic.

The Queen wanted us to be friends, that much was clear to me. I had the impression one of the reasons she wanted to be friends was because of *my* friends. Despite differences in religion Katherine Parr and Lady Mary seemed to get on well and obviously my friend of Suffolk was ever in the Queen's company too. I had shied away from court more so over the past year, I had not been sent for, that was also true, and one could not simply turn up at the court of the King without an invitation, but it was also true I had sought no path to invitation.

Perhaps the Queen thought I was deliberately avoiding her due to jealousy over the King, there were enough rumours that she should suspect this. I had heard umpteen times how mournful I was, how sorrowed, how lost, how broken-hearted. I had in truth said little on the subject of the new Queen, wanting to wait and see what she did with her title. Catherine Howard, I had known as a sweet soul long before her marriage to my own husband. I therefore had faith in her from the beginning because I knew her. Katherine Parr, I did not know. Though I was willing to see the best in people most of the time, I had to see more of the Queen before I knew what to make of her, since my jealousy over losing my friend had tarnished her a little in my eyes.

I did have to admit, however, that an invitation to stay at court so that I might become friends with another woman was a gesture most generous and one Katherine Parr did not need to make. She had no cause to be my friend, and from the attitude of the King towards me over the past year I was getting the impression that I was a liability in England, one he could not get rid of, but also one he did not want. Perhaps it was embarrassing to have the sister of the Emperor's new ally here, when the Emperor had let the King down in France.

Mayhap it was also the fact I was an expensive liability, for my houses were many and my household, as a Princess of the realm, was large. I had a title to maintain, and the King, who had granted me that title, was the one who paid for it. I wondered how often the King himself now thought about sending me home, wondering whether his pride was more important than his purse. Perhaps enough time had passed that he would not worry about the shame I might cause by talking of our marriage, short though it had been.

It had been an odd year already. Martin Luther, he who had begun so much change in our world, had died in February. In Saxony and many other lands, he was mourned greatly, in others men rejoiced as if the Devil himself had been put down. Sybylla had written to me saying a great mind, and light, had gone from the world, whilst at court the King celebrated as if one of his greatest enemies had died. Of course, Luther had written many an uncomplimentary, witty phrase about the King of England, so perhaps one had.

I breathed in to answer the Queen. "Like many people, Your Majesty, I am perfectly capable of being civil on the surface, but you are right when you say it may be premature for us to consider each other sisters. Sister you are to me already by law since you are wife to my brother the King of England and I would like to know you better, so that title might become not just title to me, but truth. Those I think well of think well of you and since I bow to their judgement in many matters, I must respect their opinion on your worth as a woman and as a Queen."

"I have wondered if there was some reason why you might not wish to be closer." Katherine's grey eyes sought an answer in mine.

I sighed just a little. "No doubt you have heard rumour that I am jealous over your marriage with the King, but this is not the case, Majesty. There are many who would in such a fashion pit woman against woman, but I have never had cause to be sorrowful you married my brother of England."

"I am relieved to hear this." She smoothed her gown of purple velvet. I saw a trinket on her throat glimmer in the sunlight, one I knew had been Jane Seymour's, for it had once been mine after. I wondered if she felt haunted by those pieces of jewellery as I had, feeling them cold on my skin, as if the grave infested them.

Her eyes still searched mine, and I decided if she could be honest, I could follow. "Perhaps you will not be relieved when I admit that I am jealous of you for another cause, Majesty. Since you have become Queen, I have found close friends leaving my company and seeking yours. It is hard, I admit, for I often still feel like a stranger in these lands and of late I have lost much. My friends I hold dear to my heart, and they aid me when I feel low, so losing them not only because they wish to perform their duties to you with diligence but also because they perhaps find your company more engaging than mine, I admit, in that cause I am jealous. It may well be that that has caused friction between us which was not of your making and for which you are not accountable. I would set that to mending."

"And yet, when your friends are with me," Katherine said with a smile, "they so often talk of you. I have found myself wondering how I might live up to your reputation, Highness, and have felt pangs of jealousy all my own as people I love praise your wisdom and clemency."

I laughed a little. "Is it so? And to me they praise you, Majesty, for all you are and have done."

Katherine Parr's dusky mouth was twitching with amusement. "So, perhaps it is possible that we both have been jealous of each other and for small cause. Your friends who serve me, they are bound by duty and by position to be at court and perhaps I have clung to them in these first years I have been Queen. I have been finding my feet in this royal state to which I was not born, but perhaps it is also possible that if you are willing to come to court more and to stay here then these friends that we share might not have to decide between us, and you and I might also become friends. Then we could make of us all one large group of good companions, rather than a group of friends split down the middle, separated for no good reason?"

I smiled, feeling for the first time truly affectionate towards the Queen. I knew I was being flattered, but I also believed much she said. Katherine Parr was a clever woman, that much had been immediately obvious to me, hearing of her acts as Queen. What I had perhaps not quite appreciated before was the grace of character she possessed.

"I want you to know I welcome what you have told me about jealousy and friendship," she said, "it is not everybody who could admit such things to a woman they do not know well and do not know yet whether they can trust, but your honesty of expression has touched me and I think I can see a little of what your friends tell me so often is within you; a soul of honesty, loyalty and courage and such a woman as this, as you, Highness, I would be proud to call my sister and my friend, when you are also ready to do the same."

"I would like that too, Majesty." I meant it truly.

"Perhaps it would be good if you were at court in other ways as well," the Queen went on as we turned a corner in the gravelled path. "I am sure you are nervous, as I am, about the Emperor's plans against the Schmalkaldic League. I have ever urged friendship with Spain, but I admit I welcome their expression of the faith not, and that is how they decide enemies, over the religion a man keeps. Since Charles V disappointed my husband, your brother, in war the King has been speaking ill of him and, I admit under my urging, though I would not have many know of this, has been considering that it may be possible that England might consider uniting now with the League. England, after all, has more in common in terms of religion with them than with the Emperor, who is the lapdog of the Bishop of Rome." She stopped on the path, rocked back on her low-heeled boots, gazing at me. "I trust you with this knowledge, something which could get me into trouble with many at court for they think women, even queens should not encourage the King in terms of policy or faith, but you I will trust with this, Highness, because of your familial links to the League, and as a gesture to show I have struck faith with you."

I gazed nervously at the Queen. Was this what she wanted to be friends for, then? To use me in order to persuade the King to support her Protestant mission and have England switch sides of allegiance once again? Oh, England had been of her own faith ever since the King's split with Rome, but any fool could see the King had been retreating to Catholic practices for years. Yet he had seemed more interested in reform again since Katherine became Queen. I was sure she wanted to encourage that interest.

Did she hope for a link to the Schmalkaldic League through me, or hope that I might help her persuade the King to join them? It was as possible as it was unlikely. The Emperor was in a position of high power, in truce with France – though that would last as long as a snow shower in June – having bested my brother and won the war against him. A fool would take on the Emperor now, but the King had been abandoned by his ally, had been shamed by him and in such a state was likely to seek revenge. Joining with the League would certainly unsettle the Emperor, and that might be what Katherine was relying on.

Whilst it could not be denied that such a plan might help Sybylla, I thought it unlikely Johann Friedrich would allow the King to join, since my sister and he himself still harboured resentment over the King's treatment of me. Perhaps that was the plan? If I was firmly on the side of the King, I could convince my kin to accept him?

I also thought this a plan most dangerous. The King seemed to at least indulge Katherine's free-speaking mouth when it came to politics and the faith, and he had once listened to wives on such subjects, but those days of heady, strong influence had ended when Anne Boleyn went to the block. He had made it clear to Jane Seymour and to every wife after that they were not to meddle in politics unless it was something he commanded, yet to me it sounded as if Katherine was hoping to use her position to influence him, and was hoping that I would use mine to do the same. How far would the King's indulgence of his new wife go?

She caught my glance, evidently reading wariness in my eyes. "I understand," she said, "it can be a frightening thing to place oneself out in the open where all can see one's beliefs, for has it not been beliefs which have been used against men and women so often in these past years? The moment someone can see the direction in which you lean is the moment they can push you over, catching you off balance so you may well tumble."

"It is not so much a matter of belief or faith," I tried to explain. "To my mind, there is little difference between the faiths. We all worship the same God, Majesty, though we differ in how our God should be worshipped. That is my position, and I am happy to follow the King's directives on the faith, since he is a learned man and has led this country to many new freedoms, which I can only think please God since there is now a Prince in the royal household and two fine daughters elevated to the succession. God smiles on England, and there must be a cause. It is not therefore coming out into the light with my beliefs which makes me hesitate, but rather the notion that the King has his own mind and plans when it comes to the path his country should take. There have been times people have interfered with those plans and regretted it. I cannot deny that any help that could be raised for my sister and her family would be welcome, but I also can say to you that I have with care avoided putting myself in any situation political, for it has been made clear to me since I came to England that this would not be welcomed by the King."

"And yet he respects you," she pressed.

"I believe he respects me precisely because I stay out of politics, Majesty. I do not think the same would be true if I interfere and I am in a precarious situation here, being at once a daughter of England and of Cleves. I am in truth daughter of nowhere, for both countries have claimed me to be theirs, yet I stand not fully within either one. I am more than aware of how entirely reliant my present liberty is in the hands of the King, and I am also most aware, and have been made aware especially over the past few years, that all that I think of as mine, this freedom, this life, they are illusions and can be taken away from me as quickly as they were given, if the King so decides. If England, therefore, decided to unite with my sister and her family I would rejoice most assuredly, but I will not attempt to sway my brother to such a position. I think attempts to influence the King can have the opposite effect, in any case."

She seemed disappointed but it was also clear she understood me. I believe Katherine had decided at that time that she should be using her position more for causes she believed in and was considering that even if this put her in danger, it might well be a risk worth accepting. Her motto as Queen was "To be useful in all that I do" and Katherine Willoughby had told me in the end the Queen had accepted the King's hand not only because she had small choice, but because she believed God had placed her on the throne, that she might do some good. It was a worthy ambition, a lofty thought, though not an uncommon one. Most princes believed they had been placed above others in order to lead and organise them. For someone born lower, however, like Katherine, some might have considered it an arrogant thought.

I did not think this was the case. Katherine had made sacrifices as she was offered her throne, so perhaps she thought God was asking she surrender things for a purpose. Frequently in the Bible people were asked to surrender what they most valued, a test from God of their faith which would lead to reward. Katherine had surrendered love, and no matter how misguided that love was, it was to her a sacrifice.

When Katherine had become Queen, Thomas Seymour had left England and whilst she was Queen, he stayed away. All knew of their love and perhaps it was something to his credit that he stayed away, knowing that were he to remain in England she might be accused of loving him and he her, placing her in danger. Of course, there was an element of self-preservation to his actions, if motivated thus, but at least he was not endangering her. Katherine had been forced to surrender love, for all agreed that no matter how foolish it was to love a man like Seymour, she *had* loved him. Was it then unreasonable for her to strive to find a higher reason for her sacrifice? We all seek meaning to make life appear less pointless than it does seem at times. If God was asking her to become the wife of the King, was there a purpose to it? She seemed to think there was; to aid the faith, and lead people into the light.

She believed she worked for the good of others, and the ways she went about it were by education, conversation, writing. There are worse ways to attempt to convince people. As the years had gone on and the favour of the King had remained constant, she had done more for the faith, and as time had progressed, she had become only more confident that the King saw her not only as a wife, but as an equal.

She would shortly be disabused of this notion.

Up until that year, the King had indeed seemed indulgent towards his wife, but during the winter as he had grown sicker, there had come a change. He was less interested in her lectures on religion, less tolerant. Perhaps the reason Katherine was coming to me, bringing me to court and seeking more allies was because of this. She was surrounding herself with loyal friends, with men who owed their position to her, because she knew something was coming.

The King was growing tired of a wife who instructed him, and that tiredness, that irritation was just what Katherine's enemies had been waiting for. The Queen had inserted herself into every avenue of government, the royal family and the faith, and it was time, so thought men like Gardiner and Wriothesley, to get her out.

By April the Queen knew she was in trouble. The King was becoming more conservative just as she had reached the pinnacle of being outspoken about her clearly Lutheran or even possibly Calvinistic beliefs. In February there had been rumours of a new Queen to come, and sometime after that Katherine ordered new coffers, many said to hide books in her possession which should not be. In May there were rumours that heretics were hiding in the Queen's inner circle. My friend, the Dowager of Suffolk was named, as were Lady Tyrwhitt and the new Lady Lisle, Jane Guildford, wife of John Dudley, who had inherited his new title upon the death of poor Lord Lisle, my friend, who had died still a prisoner in the Tower. My dear Kitty had wept long and hard for her stepfather, most especially as it seemed there never was any evidence against him.

Lisle was not the only one who seemed to be being accused on scant evidence. On May 2nd Lord William Howard was summoned before the council and told he had been implicated in heresy but would be pardoned if he told them what was being said in the Queen's chambers. He said nothing, but it seemed he might have mentioned books on the faith, which the Queen should not possess, linked to an importer named Bale, known to the King's men as a trader in scandalous texts. The reason we thought this was that searches went on of many private apartments, and they were seeking banned books.

In the summer of that year a woman known as Anne Askew was arrested for preaching that the Sacraments were symbolic rather than literal. What she had said was revolutionary enough, but that a woman would dare to speak thus, to preach to men, was another heresy in the eyes of many. Askew had links to court, and it was rumoured Katherine and she knew one another.

The men who held Anne knew this, and they were looking for a link, for a reason, for something they might take to the King, to bring this powerful Queen down.

Chapter Eleven

Summer 1546

Richmond Palace

"*Does* the Queen know this Mistress Askew?" I whispered to my friend.

Katherine, widow of Suffolk, glanced about and kept her voice low. "The Queen never has said for certain, which is wise, but I think they knew each other, long before now, in Lincolnshire. The Queen certainly respects Mistress Askew and agrees with much she preaches. The Queen is not one to believe that women should be silent. In the faith, so says she, we all, men and women, have an equal path to God."

"The Queen is in danger, then. They will make this woman talk, and she might well say much against our Queen."

Our Queen, I thought, how swift my sentiments on Katherine Parr had altered. She had managed to gain my good opinion. She was not just the Queen, but *my* Queen.

"Are you in danger?" I asked.

Katherine nodded. "I think we all are. They have taken many of us in, Gardiner and his cronies, demanding this and that, promising much of safety if we will speak on the goings-on of the salons. I know none of the women of the Queen's salon have spoken. They are loyal to Katherine, and they know that one word will have the conservative faction after us all. But they are out for blood, Gardiner and the others. The King is sick and has grown impatient with his wife and they know this. If they could replace Katherine at this late stage, whilst the King is ill, it may be a Catholic Queen could be on the throne as the end of this rule comes. That would set them up for a Catholic Regency, no matter what Edward's faith might be."

"If the boy could choose, he would not want Catholic rule."

"But he would be a minor. The choice would be up to the Regent. Perhaps Norfolk and Gardiner, Wriothesley too, think they could dominate a regency council, or could use a new Queen Regent as a puppet, a figurehead. In that way they would have years to turn Edward to their way of thinking, years to install whatever changes they want to England. They could wash us all out of this country, by exile or by blood. They know the stakes here, my friend, and they do not want Katherine on the throne as Regent if the King…"

"I understand." I did not want her to mention the King's death, even in a whisper, and make more danger for herself.

Mistress Askew had been arraigned for heresy. It was widely known that although torture was illegal, she had been brutalised, but thus far at least she had refused to speak, not implicating the Queen or any of her ladies in heresy. We knew who they wanted her to name, the ladies Suffolk, Hertford, Sussex, Denny, Fitzwilliam and Lisle. Any of them would have done, for once one was named the others would be easy to implicate, then their husbands could be taken as well, for the husband was supposed to rule the wife so it was inconceivable to such men that the women could be acting on their own impetus.

But as events looked dark, it seemed the Queen would be saved. On the 16th of July that year, Anne Askew was carried out to her place of execution. She could not walk for they had tortured her so badly that her limbs did not work, and there she was burned at the stake, never having said a word to implicate the Queen.

It was an act of incredible courage. It was clear to spectators who saw Askew how badly she had been wounded, and it must have gone on for months, every day a new torture or constant repetitions of the same ones. Rumour was, Gardiner, Rich and Wriothesley had carried out her torture personally. They would have told her over and over the way to stop the pain was to name the Queen a heretic, and this good woman had refused to do so, had endured pain unimaginable, agony almost unending, never betraying the Queen, a woman she might have known and also who might well have been a stranger.

With Askew burned three men, one whose name I remembered well, John Lascelles. He had been the one to bring the accusations about Catherine Howard to light. Although I wished on no one the fate of death by burning,

I could not regret that he was no longer in this world when I thought of the young, good woman he had helped to destroy.

It seemed after the death of Anne Askew that Katherine Parr was safe but then in the last two weeks of July that year, Bishop Gardiner found another opportunity. Edward Seymour, one of the Queen's most outspoken supporters, was sent on a mission to France, and John Dudley, who supported Seymour and also therefore the Queen, was likewise sent away. As these men left, the council became largely conservative, and the King was ill and deep in misery as he always was when his body failed him. It must have finally occurred to the Bishop that in truth he did not need to construct a good case against the Queen.

All he really needed was for the King to turn on her.

One evening when the King was sick and ill, feeling low and sorry for himself, Katherine was debating with him, as ever she had done throughout the years of their marriage. As she left the chamber that evening the King happened to turn to Gardiner and grumbled it was a poor thing when a wife should think to instruct her husband. Seeing his opportunity, Gardiner sympathised with the King and in conversation that night and through another day managed to persuade his master that the Queen had secrets and should be questioned about her faith.

Initially it seems the King agreed, for a warrant was drawn up for Katherine's arrest, but perhaps the King even then had doubts, for he betrayed the entire plan to one of his physicians.

And then came one of those accidents of history which seem ridiculous yet alter the course of so many lives.

Wriothesley was on his way from one place to another, and as he walked the halls of court he managed to drop the arrest warrant drawn up for Queen Katherine. One of Katherine's ladies was not far behind him and seeing him drop the paper, she hastened to pick it up, and was about to call out to him when upon the page she noticed the name of the Queen. Quick eyes scanning the document, she understood what the paper was and what it meant for her mistress, and she ran to the Queen.

"What said Katherine when she saw the paper?" I asked my friend a few days later when she came carrying the tale.

"She said little but turned entirely pale, then immediately began stripping her clothes from her back. In all honesty, my friend, I thought the Queen had lost her wits, but she told us that she was sick and had to be put to bed, then we understood; the King's men, if they came for her, were unlikely to try and force her from her bed if she was ill."

"It was a ploy, to buy time," I said, "and I'll wager after that the King was told that his wife was ill? A way to gain sympathy for Katherine?"

"He was, and sent one of his physicians," agreed Katherine, "and it happened to be the physician that the King had told all to, so he advised the Queen in many ways, but she already knew what she had to do."

Of course she understood, do not all women? We have learned our lessons well, not just from men but from generations of women who survived before us. She had to pretend to be other than she was, so he would cease to see her as a threat.

When the King arrived that evening to see his wife, hearing that she was ill and having heard her crying through the walls, he found a woman who was terrified, therefore entirely willing to subjugate herself to him. Katherine described herself as a "silly, poor woman" and told the King that she was not truly ill but was instead afeared that his love had turned from her. She told him that she did not mean anything by her lectures or discussions with him over religion. The King did not entirely believe her for he said, "Nay, Kate, you have become a doctor and would instruct us." To this the Queen pleaded it was not so, and the only reasons she had to draw him into discussion were firstly, so she could alleviate his mind from the pain his body felt, and secondly, so she herself might learn from him, her husband who had a greater and stronger mind than hers and who understood such subjects of depth so much better than she ever could. If she took an opposing viewpoint, she said, it was only so she could hear him argue in full, thereby drawing from him all the knowledge he had within him and thus educating herself better.

"Is it so, Kate?" asked the King, "then we are perfect friends again."

"She flattered him into granting her favour again," I said. "She is a clever woman indeed."

"And a fortunate one too," my friend replied. "Had that warrant not been dropped…"

The next day when the royal couple were in the gardens, Wriothesley turned up to arrest the Queen. He no doubt had a copy of the paper the King had signed, and in lieu of the King's actual signature, had most likely attached the dry stamp to it, a stamp which held the imprint of the King's signature and could be filled in with ink. There was supposed to be a strict record of its use, but that could be swept aside when men of power chose to. As he turned up to arrest the Queen, Katherine turned pale to see him and the guards coming for her, announcing she was under arrest, but the King, at her side, rose from his chair and struck at Wriothesley with his ivory-topped walking stick, calling him a knave and telling him to be away. The man retreated and Katherine, pallid and shaking, knew that she was safe.

For now.

"She forgot," I said.

"Forgot what?" asked my friend of Suffolk.

"Through time and experience, Katherine came to believe she was safe in the love of the King," I said, "but she forgot he was not the only man she married. When first they married, she knew, did she not? I heard reports she was reluctant to wed him and thought it would be better to be his mistress. But then they married, and he was kind, indulged her, granted her power, so she failed to recall there was another man inside the King."

With steady eyes I gazed at my friend. "She forgot to watch that other creature, the one who hides behind the King's eyes. I pray she will not forget again."

Chapter Twelve

Summer 1546

Richmond Palace

The Queen was safe for now, but she had learnt a hard lesson, the one the monster inside the King had been intent on teaching her. He had done enough to exert his power over her, to make her afraid of him as once she had been when first they had married. In that first year, Katherine had been less sure of herself. She had ordered few dresses or jewels, had appeased both sides of court, had not spoken out a great deal. Then as time went on, she had grown more confident. It had almost led to her downfall.

The interesting thing was, I doubted the King had wanted her removed. It was true Katherine had been clever, she had seen the danger and played her part as the submissive wife, only concerned with the wellbeing of her husband so it could be said that she, unlike many of his other wives, had saved herself, but I believed the King had not wanted her gone.

He wanted her less vocal, less commanding, yes, but he valued her as a wife and as a woman who knew how to appease an old, sick man, how to tend to him. Did he want now to have to find and woo another wife? What effort that was! And to replace a woman who had many uses, and who he found desirable still, in what clearly was the end point of his life? What a fuss that would be. No, better to scare her enough to subdue her.

And now the King also had the perfect excuse to go after the conservative faction, who had been growing too bold. People said he turned on them because they had gone after his wife, and they had struck for Cranmer not a few times over the years too, and he the King loved perhaps more than any man, as far as he was capable of such an emotion. But it was not for either Katherine or Cranmer that the King went for the conservatives. He had never truly liked Gardiner or Norfolk, and now he had the excuse to put them down. Both found themselves out of favour with the King, he was short with them, shouted at them. Wriothesley too was in trouble. It was clear something ill was coming for the conservatives of court, and as Edward Seymour and his man John Dudley rose in favour, so Norfolk and Gardiner were falling fast.

Even if her enemies were being attacked now by the King, the Queen knew she had to be careful. She lectured him no more and was only and ever the dutiful, attentive wife. "She has even hidden the latest book she was working on," my friend told me.

The Lamentation of a Sinner was the title, and Katherine Willoughby, who had read it, said it was the Queen's greatest and most controversial work. In truth all the Queen's books had been obviously of the reformed point of view, but this one went further, and that was why she did not seek to have it published. It was not a book she wanted her husband to see, penned as it was in a time she thought herself safe. Now she knew she was not, and never would be whilst the King lived, Katherine stowed away her greatest work, knowing that to expose herself thus would mean death.

Katherine had no wish to die when she had not had a chance to live and though some might look down on her for changing and adapting in order to survive, I did not. She was a pragmatist, and they are survivors. I too had played the humble woman in order to keep my life. There were others amongst us, we wives of Henry VIII, who had not done so, and we knew what had happened to them. While they might well sit easily on the thrones of Saints in heaven, and perhaps we never would for we had not shown their type of courage, those women could no more influence the world, yet we who still lived had a chance to.

We would have more of a chance if we survived the King.

It seemed as if many of us would, as that summer my good brother became sicker and sicker. When I saw him at court, as I was now free to come and go as I wished, constantly welcomed by the Queen, I was amazed at the change in him, but I also knew hope where once I would have dreaded his passing.

I had always known when the King died, I might find myself in an untenable position. The King wanted me here in England, but men like Seymour or Norfolk were unlikely to. I had always before believed that one of them would become Regent, with a council to support them during Edward's minority, but as far as we all knew, the King's will, made when he had gone to France, still held. In that will he had named Katherine Parr Regent.

"I will look after you, sister," the Queen said quietly to me once when we walked in the grounds. I had expressed fears, without mentioning the King's death of course, that in the future men of England might not want me here, an expense to the country.

"It would be good to know I had a friend, Majesty."

Katherine pressed my hand. "A friend you have, fear not, and in the future, when matters are different, I would hope that you would feel freer to offer your opinion and influence than you do now." She gazed at me, and I saw a vision of the future in her eyes. "I understand now, much better than I did before, why you remained reserved in such matters with the King. Before now, I thought... well, I was wrong and I have been shown that you were right, but all things change, and when they do, I will have need of you as you will of me. I have the support of many men, but I would like that of women too."

There was a gleam in her eyes, not quite hidden by the dullness that fear had cast over her. I understood, Katherine played the subservient, obedient woman, but there was still that ambition in her. Deep now it was hidden, but it was there, and when she became Regent, when she was free of the King, she would rule as she saw fit.

She would need me because of my links to Sybylla and the Schmalkaldic League. In the future, when the King was gone and we were safe, there would be a Regent of England ready and willing to push forth reform and change. I might not agree with her on all matters, but Katherine Parr would support me if I supported her. I would be safe here, with her as Regent. I might even have influence and a voice in England.

The Queen who had existed before was not gone, she was not defeated. She had pulled her forces back a while, that was all. A tactical retreat. When the time came, she would be ready to take on the mantle and the power of the throne.

Chapter Thirteen

Summer – Winter 1546

Richmond Palace

Much that was ominous occurred that summer.

In June the Diet of Regensburg was held. Fraught were discussions on fidelity and rebellion. What it meant was trouble for the League.

At this time Wilhelm also negotiated his marriage to Maria, Archduchess of Austria but we all knew any peace of this union would become lost in the war approaching. On the 7th of June that year Charles V signed a treaty with the Pope and the Duke of Bavaria. The papacy provided promised supplies and troops for the cause of the Emperor against the Schmalkaldic League.

"The Emperor has also made treaty with Moritz of Saxony, Highness." Diaceto had news that morn. Olisleger and Harst had many ways now to send information to my man, bypassing the grasping hands of Carew, the letter thief, by using contacts in London and villages near my estates where good merchants of Cleves came and went, selling wares, and leaving information for my men to collect. "Moritz was so proud of capturing Henry of Brunswick in the late troubles that he wrote a book about it and brought it along to the Diet of Regensburg to show the Emperor, and others."

"What an odd man he is," I noted.

"The Emperor announced Moritz to be a loyal, trustworthy vassal," Diaceto went on. "And this will spell trouble for your sister, Highness, as well as her husband."

Moritz, or Maurice, of Saxony, I have spoken of before, but in case you have forgot, I will remind you. He was the Duke of Albertine Saxony, having taken the title from his father who had died some years ago. The man had been raised in the Protestant faith, and raised partly by Sybylla's husband, but Moritz loathed Johann Friedrich and since he came from the other branch of the house which once ruled all Saxony – both descended from Duke Fredrich II and named for his two sons, Albertine and Ernestine – Mortiz was a potential threat to the claims of Sybylla's sons. He was also apparently loyal to the Emperor, but there was one slim hope. Moritz was on friendly terms with Phillip of Hesse, another leader of the Schmalkaldic League and had married his daughter, Agnes. He therefore had more kin in the League than out of it. Perhaps because of this, we heard he had expressed that he would not take up arms against his kin, but would, as a loyal subject of the Emperor, provide his master with supplies of food and other things, which no doubt meant weapons.

"The truth is, Moritz will put in as little effort as he can, whilst reaping the greatest benefits possible," I said.

"I agree, Highness. The man has a hereditary claim to the Ernestine branch of Saxony's holdings and lands, and if the Emperor succeeds against Johann Friedrich, Moritz is the man most likely to be set in his place."

"Bringing all of Saxony together, all under the Emperor, through his little lapdog." My tone was bitter as lemon-laced vinegar.

Moritz of Saxony was later approached by the Schmalkaldic League, and he promised to be neutral, but that lasted as long as the promises of any ruler. I wondered what his wife would think of him when he broke his promise, but perhaps he did not care for her opinion. Perhaps she, like so many women, lived in silence, bearing children to men who slaughtered their kinsfolk and stole their homelands.

Then Charles V made the decision I had been dreading, and decided to put down Saxony and Hesse for all time. I had known it would come, of course, but to relive all that had been done to Cleves, this time through Saxony, my sister's country, to fear for her sons and her, her people too. I thought it would be enough to end the strength of my heart.

Charles was ready to use every bit of his great army to subdue Johann Friedrich and the League. Reports came, detailing how large the army was, and it was fearsomely vast. The Emperor, freed from other wars, was willing to turn all his resources on my kin of Saxony and their allies, and this was not just about defiance over land or rule, it was about religion. The Catholic Emperor wanted an end to the Protestant League, and for the sake of faith, something which was supposed to engender peace, he would make war.

"This is why I do not believe men when they say they are Christian," I noted to Katherine of Suffolk. "What is so different about our ways of worship, and why could we not entertain them all? One man says the Sacrament is literal, another says metaphorical, yet could they not both believe what they believe without forcing the other to their way of thinking? We have the same God, the same Christ, the same teachings of peace and love to our neighbours. Why do men not concentrate on that part of the lessons of the Bible, rather than trying to make all men agree with them over the way the faith should be expressed?"

"But under Catholic rule, the papacy rules the people," Katherine pointed out. "An ancient and unjust, not to mention corrupt, ruler."

"What other kind is there?" I asked. "And if men would accept the ways of others, the papacy would not rule us all. The truth is, religion is power to many people. It is not love, not a set of rules guiding the right way to live, it is power, it is judgement, it is being right where others are wrong and using that power to kill them. If God looks on our world, my friend, He does not sorrow when people differ in their ways of worshipping Him; He sorrows when we slaughter and torture each other. We are a strange, twisted creation. I sometimes think the Bible was wrong, and we were not the pinnacle of creation, but just another step along the way, a creation which God made and hoped would grow from a childhood of ignorance into an adulthood of wisdom, peace and acceptance. Men take our religion of peace and use it as an excuse to batter one another to death, to press women under blocks, to burn people to death, and for what? Not to save them, I do not believe such is true or either that that is what those who do such wicked things want. They torture and kill because they like it, because they take pleasure in it."

"Perhaps this is so," Katherine said.

"Never is the Devil more hard at work than in the heart of the man who judges others," I went on, so distressed by imaginings of what would happen to my sister that I spoke more honestly than I ever had about the faith. "And if these men were truly secure in their faith, they would not seek to rid the world of those who believe other things. They would accept them. They seek to exterminate those of other faiths because they are unsure of their own faith, and in that insecurity, they must have all other men agree with them, for then they will know they are right. Men who kill for faith, who say they kill for God, either they lie and kill only for themselves, or they kill to drown out the uncertainty, the insecurity in their own hearts, something they fear God will see and punish them for."

We heard that my brother-in-law and Philip of Hesse were meeting to see how to stand against such a force as the Emperor was assembling. There would be small time or space for negotiation. Charles wanted them gone, obliterated. They had to fight. The word was the League would attempt to strike first, and perhaps if they did enough damage Charles V would be willing to negotiate but the truth was, they had not the manpower the Emperor possessed.

It was at this time that the plan of Katherine Parr bore fruit, for whilst she had hoped I would be able to persuade the King to talk to my kin, at this time Johann Friedrich and Philip of Hesse reached out to try to convince my former husband to join the Schmalkaldic League. They needed allies. Past slights about his treatment of me faded to the background.

"Will he join?" I asked Katherine Willoughby, "he wanted to once before."

Her pretty eyes were sceptical. "That was when it was to his advantage to join. Now, it would be to the advantage of others, so it is less certain. The King retreats to conservative ways of thinking, even though he supports not conservative faction members at the moment. I am unsure which way he would turn, and he knows this would be a hard fight, not an easy victory, so it is less tempting there, too."

"He is still angry with the Emperor for what happened in France, would that be enough for him to take an interest in this?"

My friend did not know, and word at court was that the King was feigning interest, but then on the 30th of August he laid out his conditions for joining the League. Frankly, they were ridiculous. The King thought his potential allies desperate, so thought he could demand what he wanted of them. The King wanted to be made head of the League, not a mere member, and was to have a controlling vote. He also wanted it renamed, so it would be called the League Christian. The King wanted it to be that he would give aid to the League only when all other members did as well, as he supposed they would look for more aid from him than other members.

A week later and it seemed the King had been flattered out of the deal by Charles V, whose ambassadors had told the King that he, who was *so* fit to be an *arbitrator* between the great princes of Christendom should not be "seduced by these mean men of Germany."

Lutheran states in the League decided to take action against the Emperor without further alliance talks with England, and the Emperor was bent on war too, so by the summer of that year Charles V was moving men towards the Germanic states. 50,000 soldiers, he had, the imperial army assembling at the mouth of the Danube.

In Bavaria a group of Lutheran men seized Füssen and drove out imperial troops there. Their plan was to move towards the Tyrol to claim land between Italy and Austria. At the same time Johann Friedrich and all other leaders of the Schmalkaldic League were outlawed by an imperial ban put into force on the 20th of July. They were excommunicated by this ban which took away rights to property and permitted, if not encouraged, their own people to rise against them.

This allowed Johann Friedrich's cousin Mortiz, allied to the Emperor, to lay claim to Johann Friedrich's lands. He along with the Emperor's brother Ferdinand invaded, Ferdinand coming from Bohemia and Mortiz from his lands in Saxony.

"Fortunately, your brother of Saxony has been most successful in responding to their attacks," Diaceto informed me. "And as winter approaches, the time for them to make war fades."

"The Emperor thought he would crush them, and it is not so." Hope dared to rise in my heart like the arc of a swan's wing against the setting sun. "It is a shame my brother will not aid our sister."

"Cleves is bound now to the Emperor." Diaceto shook his head. "I fear, Highness, now he is married, this is the end of Cleves standing alone or with anyone but the Empire."

My brother had married his bride in the summer and returned home with her in July. Wilhelm was shifting many responsibilities to Olisleger, and I was pleased to hear it, knowing what use the man was. Olisleger was then Chancellor of Cleves-Mark but was taking on the offices of Chancellor

Ghogreff who was in charge of Julich-Berg. In the next year, Olisleger and his counterpart would argue that Protestantism should be allowed to take root where it was found, a clever move to try to support those of the reformed faith. They never argued for it to be officially upheld, but did push for it to not be exterminated where it had already come to be. Many times, small acts may help the world to change, small acts which pass unnoticed, yet come to mean so much.

"What do you know of my brother's new wife?" I had asked 'my' ambassador, Van der Delft, when he came to see me. The man was the Imperial Ambassador, but apparently, now my brother was allies with the Emperor, was also to act for me. I was not likely to trust him with much, but I thought he could be relied upon to know what his master's niece was like.

"I hear tell she is a beauty, Highness, and is almost intelligent."

I blinked. "What does *almost* intelligent mean, my lord? Does she know how to speak and breathe and move her feet at the same time? Or does that mean when compared to a man her education is such that would almost allow her to be their equal?"

"I have no answer for this, my lady," he said, "but I understand she has excellent manners, understands three languages and is attractive to any eye which beholds her."

"That sounds a little more than *almost* intelligent," I argued. "It sounds as if she is quite accomplished."

I also heard she was small of stature, long and narrow of body with a prominent lower jaw. "Of course," I said, all the Hapsburgs had jaws to rival those of horses. My new sister also came from a fertile family. Wilhelm was days away from his 30th birthday when they married, so he was twice her age.

"She is a granddaughter of Juanna the mad of Castile," I mentioned to Katherine Willoughby.

"And may have inherited some of that lunacy," replied my friend. "I hear she has mood swings most noticeable and violent."

"She is only fifteen." I shrugged. "We all of us have plenty of swings of mood at that time of life."

Perhaps it was more than mere swings however, as there was some fear reported amongst my countrymen, for it was said Maria possessed a certain instability of temper as noticeable as her chin. I thought it likely that she, a young girl sent away from her country to marry a former enemy of her people, who had found herself as a stranger in a strange and quite possibly hostile land, might well be feeling scared and alienated, leading to some fluctuation in her contentment. I doubted my brother was a wonderful husband, either. He had little paid attention to the welfare of his sisters, so was unlikely to care a great deal about a wife.

The trouble is, women hide what they truly think so well that when men discover one who does not conceal the storm of emotions which exists within the soul of woman, they find that one woman strange and unusual. But those few women who display their emotions to all are only letting slip the lie the rest of us tell.

Women are judged for all they are and all they are not, and even the best of us are found wanting, there is no way to win, so we learn to hide. We place masks on our faces to conceal what we truly look like. We slip silken slippers on our feet that we might dance away from any who try to see us up close. We cover the intelligence we own with the simple virtues men expect us to possess. We paint our faces so men will see only what we allow them to, and so we cannot be judged on all the rebel thoughts which live within our minds.

Men complain often that women are duplicitous, and we are, but not in the ways they think. We cannot live barefaced and open in this world because it was not made for us; it was made for men, and we are merely allowed to exist within it. My former husband was a true believer in this, I knew, for every woman who had not lived up to his ideal of them, in mind, in womb, in face, in expectation or in character, he had destroyed. If there is any dark lesson to the tale that he told, it is that if a woman disappoints a man, then that man may kill her and no other man will stand up for her as he batters her to the ground.

So, is it any wonder that we hide when if we are seen we will be killed? Is it any wonder we are duplicitous, when men do not want the truth from us? I think not. We are creatures set into the forest without fang or claw to defend ourselves. We are not allowed to arm ourselves; few are permitted education so we might plan an escape or a plot to survive. All we can do is run or hide. Those are the options open to women. We have learned to live within this world of men, this world of wolves where we are the deer. We disguise ourselves as part of the pack, and sometimes we manage to fool the wolves and sometimes we do not.

That was made clear to me in England too. Katherine Parr was not the only one who had been terrified into changing their ways, my friend of Suffolk suffered a change in heart much the same. After the execution of Anne Askew and the almost arrest of the Queen, I believe it became plain to my friend just how dangerous being so outspoken in her beliefs was. It did not change the intensity of her beliefs of course, but she put them more into hiding than she had before, knowing also now that Brandon was dead, she had even less protection. His friendship with the King had allowed her much freedom, but now she was alone, there was greater danger.

The Dowager of Suffolk came more often to Richmond. I think she was running away from not only the court where the wandering eyes of the King were ever on her but also in some ways from the Queen. However much my friend understood what Katherine Parr had done in stepping back from pushing the faith forwards, I think she also was disappointed. Perhaps something in her wanted Katherine Parr to be as Katherine of Aragon had, as Anne Boleyn had; a true martyr to their own cause. And although she herself also took the path of pragmatism rather than that of piety, I think my friend had been so fired up by the zeal of the Queen that when that zeal deflated and the Queen humbly stepped to the side and tried no more to push the King, Katherine Willoughby felt let down. She had thought the Queen was going to be a leading light in the process of reform, but it was plain now that the Queen could not be that light without setting herself afire.

But there might come a time soon when the Queen could shine.

One wolf was coming to the end of his tail. The King was ailing that year, no one was allowed to say it out loud, yet everyone knew it. He was growing old and was not a well man. At times I saw glances pass between Katherine Parr and Thomas Seymour, who had lately returned to England, and I thought of another Catherine and the man she had planned to marry when the King was dead. The dream of one Catherine might become the reality of another I thought, for if the Queen could survive long enough she might well outlive this dangerous man, might well be the only other woman besides me to escape his clutches.

There could be two wives who became survivors, perhaps.

*

"I can agree to this." My tone was grudging. "Bletchingley, once gone from my hands, becomes property of the Crown once more and it is up to the King what is done with it then."

Sir Thomas Cawarden, one of my own men, of my own household, wanted Bletchingley, my house. Behind my back he had gone to the council and put his suit to them. The King was ill but was not dead yet already vultures were after my property. I had known it would come when my former husband died, had expected it, but not now.

Cawarden had served on the Privy Council, and the King wanted to recognise his service, but as Cawarden asked that the house be granted to him, asked that we exchange houses so he could take the property, the King refused. The house Cawarden wanted to exchange was not, to my mind, a fair exchange and I would lose out in terms of what the estates could produce, besides I liked Bletchingley. It was a fair house, *my* house, in a good position to use when I travelled between Richmond and Hever.

The council had turned down his suit, however, on orders from the King who said that I had been promised Bletchingley for my lifetime and if I did not want to give it up, I would not be forced to. But the King had said that upon my death, the house could go to Cawarden. When I was dead, I would have no use for the house, so I agreed to this. I had small choice, but in truth I was wary about this move. The man now had a claim on one of my houses. I had a feeling that when the King was gone, Cawarden would make a move to take the house from me.

*

On the 4th of October that year the League made a move against the Emperor, attacking him and his forces at Noerdlingen near Ingolstadt. The hope was they could force him to make terms of a truce, but as time went on this seemed more and more unlikely.

"I hear imperial troops are being decimated by sickness spreading in their camps, Highness." Diaceto looked hopeful and worried at the same time. "Olisleger writes that although this gives some hope, in reality the League's chances to avoid defeat lie in forcing the Emperor into talks before he can call any more troops to his side."

"Winter will be hard on all of them." I tapped a finger on the table as I thought.

"And yet the League is short of money, my lady. It will be harder on them."

Men of Philip of Hesse began to desert early that month even though François of France had sent the Landgrave money to pay his troops. Perhaps they knew it was a desperate gambit they were involved in, and the word was they were not alone. My brother and his new wife were reportedly on a trip to see the Regent Maria of the Low Countries.

"He goes there so he might avoid Sybylla sending him requests for aid," I said bitterly. "My brother will run from the pleas of our sister."

As before, when Cleves was under threat, I felt entirely useless. I was aware I was not alone.

"I wish I could persuade the King to support the cause of your kin," Queen Katherine told me as I visited court, "but I fear, now, to speak on such matters. The health of the King is delicate, and whilst it is so his temper fluctuates."

"I understand." I did. Katherine could not put herself or her future position of Regent in danger now. She was too close to the end. Perhaps, if the King died in time, then England might be able to aid Sybylla and her family. It was a slim hope, but other members of the council such as Dudley and Seymour were secret Calvinists, this I knew. Seeing the Schmalkaldic League falling to the Emperor would not be in their interests and Seymour at least was fervent in his faith, though he took care to hide a great deal from the King. He and Katherine, though, along with Cranmer, had had a great deal of influence in choosing the tutors of Prince Edward and Lady Elizabeth. Both were being raised with the Protestant faith deep-rooted in their hearts. The reign that came after the King's would not be Catholic, and the men and women who would become powerful in Edward's minority would steer England on a different path to the haphazard one the King had broken.

I wondered sometimes, however, about the King's path, never fully rejecting Catholic practices and never wholly adopting Protestant ones. Perhaps, though it was not formed for any reason other than his own greed for power and wealth, there was something to this middle way. No one could be entirely outspoken, but both sides of the faith could exist.

That November, Duke Moritz completed his invasion of Saxony successfully. The land was almost unguarded, all the troops of my brother-in-law having gone to the front to attack the Emperor. By the time Johann Friedrich sent men to try to quash the invasion, it was too late. A large portion of Saxony was now in the hands of Moritz, to whom the Emperor had granted the electoral dignity. Recognised as Elector of Saxony, Moritz the betrayer, as I would name him, claimed victory over his hated kinsman.

"Have they lost all of Saxony?" I asked.

"Not all, my lady, but a vast portion is now in the hands of Moritz." Diaceto shook his head in sorrow.

"And my sister, and her sons?"

Sybylla's two youngest sons were with her, and they were safe, I was told, still within the territory held by her husband. Her eldest son was with his father.

That December Philip of Hesse and Johann Friedrich had run out of money to pay their troops and the force opposing the Emperor disintegrated. Moritz assailed Wittenberg that month, but Johann Friedrich pushed back and as Christmas approached he had secured his city once more. As strike and counter strike occurred, there were tales of Moritz's men committing atrocities in Anhalt by cutting off the breasts of women and the limbs of children.

As Saxon forces retreated to defend their own lands, and lack of pay caused men to desert, it seemed the Emperor had won the war of that autumn and winter with ease. The rest of the Schmalkaldic troops disbanded, and hopes of reinforcements faded as troops promised by Elector Friedrich of the Palatinate and the Duke of Wurttemberg failed to attack after their leaders promised, by treaty, to recognise the supremacy of the Emperor.

"The winter cold has set an end, in most parts, to the war," said Diaceto.

"It is only a matter of time." I pinched the bridge of my nose. "And my sister and her country need allies and money, not time."

Time had run out for another. By December, Norfolk was in the Tower along with his son, under a sentence of death.

Chapter Fourteen

December 1546 – January 1547

Richmond Palace

"It is said they committed treason by using royal insignia, the arms of Edward the Confessor – the three lions of England – on their houses and ornaments as part of their heraldry, but this is just an excuse," my friend informed me. "Surrey was within his rights to use the arms of the Confessor, but actually doing so was seen as a threat to the Crown. The truth is, the King has long loathed Norfolk and fears the wit of his son, the poet Surrey, so has sent them to the Tower and he will take their heads. He blames them for the actions taken against the Queen, the accusations of heresy."

I lifted my eyebrows. "He himself signed the papers for her arrest."

"The King is always blameless, so now, as he is convinced of the Queen's goodness, he must have someone to blame for leading him astray with regards to her treatment."

"But Gardiner was the man behind the plot."

"Where Gardiner is, Norfolk is not far away," said my wise friend. "You can bet there was a Howard bride ready and waiting in the wings for the Duke to throw at the King once Katherine was gone."

Surrey had actually been arrested for uttering slander, although about what exactly was unclear to me. Then there were rumours Surrey and Norfolk had intended to gain control over Prince Edward during the King's latest illness. This was likely to be true. I would suppose most men of power at court had considered it.

"There is rumour now they meant to restore the Pope." Katherine toyed with a ring on her finger. "But there is word too that Mary Howard spoke against Surrey when they raided Kenninghall."

Kenninghall, one of their properties, had indeed been raided by the King's men and when only Mary, daughter of Norfolk, Bess Holland his mistress and Frances, the pregnant wife of Surrey were found to be there I am sure the men sent by the King knew they could invent what they wanted. Who was to believe the word of women? One of the raiders was none other than Wymond Carew, the very man who had spent the last few years shifting through my letters. The others were John Gates, a gentleman of the Privy Chamber and follower of Dudley, and Richard Southwell, a royal commissioner who had taken part in the trial of Thomas More. They had no reason to find anything to exonerate the Duke or his son. I know not if they fabricated evidence, but many thought the charges false.

"Mary Howard went down on her knees and said she would conceal nothing," Katherine went on. "She told them her brother had pressured her to become the mistress of the King and influence him through her position."

"But she was married to the King's son, Fitzroy." My mouth was slack with shock.

"Indeed, which, although it was a match unconsummated, would make any relationship with the King incest."

None of this would stand for a charge of treason, however, yet the adoption of royal arms could. This was the charge they came away with to use against Norfolk and his son, accusing Surrey of asserting his family had a right to the throne by incorporating the royal arms of England into his.

"Of all the things he could have been arrested for, all the ill Norfolk has done, it comes down to some lions on a badge," I muttered to myself.

On Christmas Eve, the Duke, no doubt hoping to save himself, admitted he had concealed high treason "in keeping secret the false acts of my son, Henry Earl of Surrey, in using the arms of Saint Edward the Confessor, which pertain only to kings." Norfolk offered up lands to the King, hoping that, along with betraying his son, would be enough to save his wretched neck.

Katherine, sitting at my hearth, stretched her shoulders, sore from a chill wind which had gusted across her barge that evening. "The King believes Norfolk and his son mean to try to usurp the crown from Edward," she explained. "Seymour and Dudley have whispered it to his ear, and they might be right. The truth is, it is better for them if Norfolk is removed now. The Queen has agreed: she has no reason to trust the Catholic faction after they tried to have her arrested. Norfolk and his men would be a danger to the future of England when the King… when the future unfolds."

Norfolk finally learned what happens to men who turn on others. When the time comes, that favour is returned. All of Norfolk's family gave evidence against him, his wife, who by rumour he had battered all through their marriage, his mistress, and his daughter.

Surrey was convicted of treason and died on the 19th of January. Norfolk and his son had been attained by statute and Norfolk was rumoured to be about to be sent to his death.

But the slippery Duke slipped once more. He was saved from the block for the King could not sign his death warrant in time.

In the early morning of the 28th of January 1547, Henry VIII, King of England, died.

Chapter Fifteen

1547

Richmond Palace

In truth I did not know how to feel when men of the council came to tell me the King was dead. It was to remain a secret, for now, they told me. I was not even to inform my household.

"My good brother." I sat heavily on a stool in shock. In truth, though I had known he was ill all that year, and before, the notion that my former husband could be dead was unfathomable. No matter how ill, no matter how this reign might be better than the one that had come before with Katherine as Regent, it was unbelievable that the King was dead. For good or ill he had been a force of nature, something unstoppable. Everyone else had fallen, but not him. It seemed even Death would have to bow to him, and yet, he was dead.

"When will the Queen be announced as Regent?" I asked, feeling a little stupefied, and I looked into faces which scowled at me. It was then I understood. She was not to be. They were annoyed I had even been aware it was a possibility. I closed my mouth quickly on that subject. "God save King Edward, my dearest nephew," I said.

That pleased them more.

Later I learned the King's death had been a complete secret for three days as men ran about, doing deals with each other and organising how England was to be now. They had decided Katherine was not to be a part of this new England, not in the way she wanted and not in the way the King had envisioned.

"The King's will of some years ago held that the Dowager Queen might be made Regent," William Paulet told me, staying behind as the others filed out. "And yet as the end came, the King was convinced of another path for England and for his son; a Regency Council, headed by the Earl of Hertford,

Edward Seymour, which will as a body make decisions for the realm until King Edward comes of age."

Edward was nine years old when his father died. It would be another nine before he could assume full power. Until then, we were all at the mercy of this council, and, as I later learned, there was never supposed to be a head of it. Edward Seymour had arranged this.

"He has put himself into power," I whispered to my friend of Suffolk. "And what of the Queen? Where are her rights?"

"Stolen from her." Katherine's cheeks were hot with indignation, but her voice was kept as low as mine. "There are rumours, Anna, that even this regency council was not what the King wanted. The King's new will, this one which outlines this arrangement of governance, it was signed at start and end with the dry stamp, not by the King's own hand. Men are saying the King was too ill to write by the time it was drawn up, and approved the use of the stamp, which as you know is a carved impression of his signature that then can be filled in with ink, and such could be true, but it could also be true that this is not what happened."

"So, as the King was sick and ill, perhaps fading in and out of consciousness, Seymour and his men made a new will? And wrote the Queen out of it, out of power?"

"Indeed, and it is not unbelievable, is it? The King was shut away in his last illness, the Queen was not allowed to see him. He was surrounded by the men of one faction alone and his death was secret for days. Any will made could have been destroyed and a new one drawn up. Either they convinced the King to make these changes, or they simply wrote it themselves. Seymour was ready, he had his enemy Norfolk in the Tower thanks to Paget, who devised the plot against the Duke, and all the other men on the regency council on his side, either because they agree with him on the faith or, in the case of conservatives like Wriothesley, because they have been bought, and no doubt they have been promised much in return for their support. There is even a clause in the new will, so I am told, which allows members of the new council to reward themselves as they see fit. Titles are already being bandied about, as well as lands and money. Seymour has placed himself in control of the new King and the council, and the England we could have had under Queen Katherine, it is gone."

"Is there not something she can do?"

"She plans to protest, and I have no doubt she will, but, my friend, who will support her? Seymour and Dudley were her greatest supporters, and they will not back her now and take power out of their own hands. Cranmer wants reform and Seymour will bring that just as well as Katherine could, and perhaps with more confidence since he is a man, and it is seen as more acceptable for a man to bring about changes in religion where in a woman it is thought unseemly. Since Eve we have been seen as suspect and easily corruptible. The other council members, if they have been bought already by Seymour, Katherine can offer them nothing."

"It was a coup." I rocked back from leaning in to her, frowning.

"It was, and as the King ordered the Queen was to be kept away from him – he never liked her to see him when he was truly ill – they had the time they needed, as well as the three days after his death to alter anything they had not convinced him to change. They had the means to bring it about. Katherine was caught unawares, she thought they were her men, but she was deceived. She relied on the orders of the King being obeyed, but men, seeing their chance, took it."

Seymour and his men had possession of Edward and Elizabeth too. Edward was collected from Hertfordshire, where his household was, by Anthony Browne, who had attended the King in his last hours, and Edward Seymour, and they brought him to Enfield, where his sister was. This quick possession of the new King's person was done under the guise of the royal children needing to be told of their father's death, but it was also a way to take control of them. Lady Mary would have been harder to gain mastery of, but in truth with two of the heirs of England in their power, they had enough.

Edward and Elizabeth were told together of their father's end, and apparently the two, now fatherless and motherless, children fell into each other's arms and wept.

As they did so, I have no doubt Seymour was trying not to smile. Oh, it would not do to let the mask of caring uncle slip from his features, but the transfer of power was working just as he had wanted. On the 30th of January we heard the council had written to Seymour, asking his opinion on whether the traditional pardon for traitors should be issued, marking the start of a new reign as just and merciful.

"They are already deferring to him," I observed.

I knew not how to feel, not about the usurpation of the throne by Seymour, which, although he was to be called Head of the Council, was his position in truth, but about the death of the King.

In some ways we were all free, were we not? At one time or another every one of the people about the King had reason to fear him, besides our new King Edward. Mary and Katherine had been under danger of death from this man, I had been his politely held prisoner for years and at one time had feared he might arrest and kill me in order to be free and marry again. Elizabeth had been ignored and cast away. Even men of the council must at one point or another have suspected that their master might kill them. Only Edward, only the King's little legacy, this pallid boy who was not hale in body because the King much like his own father would not risk his only surviving son in sports or the joust, this little boy who was more scholar than sportsman, now was King and the King who had come before him had protected him from all the world could possibly throw at him. In truth I thought the boy arrogant and coddled, and he was clearly too young to govern alone.

Lord Chancellor Thomas Wriothesley told Parliament of the death of the King on the 31st of January, the same day I was told, and proclamations of the succession of King Edward were sent out. Wriothesley failed to mention the clause about rewards, as well as other specifics.

"Seymour does not want the people to know too much," said Katherine Willoughby.

"Can nothing be done?" I asked.

She spread her hands. "He has too much support, for the moment."

"For the moment?"

She expressed the slightest laugh. "He has been clever, mistake me not, but Seymour is not royal and yet sets himself into a position of authority. That never goes well with the people. They want to be ruled by the sovereign God has chosen, or at least by one, like Katherine, who was set there by marriage, therefore one could say by God. Seymour is humourless and charmless, clever he might be, but he has no way to win people to him other than rewards, and when they dry up? That is when he will find trouble waiting. There is nothing to be done now, speak out and he will pounce, but there will come a time when all this supposed unity between men following Seymour will crumble."

"You speak as if you know the future."

"I know men, and men of court most of all."

"Who is of the new council?" I asked my friend. "I feel I have lost track in all that has happened of late."

I was told there were sixteen executors who were to act as Edward's council until he reached the age of eighteen. Many names were familiar, Paget, Seymour, Dudley, Cranmer, Wriothesley, William Paulet Lord St John, Anthony Browne but also the Earl of Arundel and Thomas Seymour. There was further to these men, a supplement of twelve who were to assist the executors when called upon. Some believed that some names of the council had been forced upon the old King in his last illness, and some had certainly been kept away from him to prevent them being added. Bishop Gardiner, for example, had been refused access to the King during the last month of his life, and Norfolk had of course suddenly found himself accused of treason. The day before the King's death Norfolk's estates had been seized, making them ripe and available for redistribution, and although the old King had wanted the Duke dead, it seemed that King Edward was to keep Norfolk in the Tower. The thought was that starting the reign of the new king with blood might be a bad omen. Norfolk was nullified, in any case, which was all the new rulers of England wanted. The council was mainly a Protestant force, and they would steer the King, already convinced of the righteousness of reform, to continue the work imperfectly begun by his father.

There was a meeting not long after where executors agreed to honour the terms of the King's will but also, to avoid confusion, would set Seymour above them all to be "preferred in name and place before others" as head of their council. That was the first time any of us heard the term "Protector".

It was not calling him Regent, but it was what it meant.

The new King, by tradition, was taken to the Tower of London. Edward entered the gates of the city to great acclaim by his people, and with a magnificent shot of cannon in all places surrounding, as well as out of the Tower itself and out of ships on the Thames.

"I wonder they are not scared that some of this armoury might hit the King," I mentioned as we stood on my barge, watching explosions from boats upon the Thames assault the skies.

We heard the King had written to his sisters, telling them not to mourn their father's death since it was God's will. He said he would be to Mary and Elizabeth a loving and good brother. I could only hope the dour child meant what he said.

The next day, as preparations for the funeral of the old King went ahead, nobles of the realm, including myself, made our way to the Tower where we made obeisance to the new King and where Seymour was announced as Head of the Regency Council and Protector of the Realm.

The body of the old King lay in state for five days as a vigil was held. Access to the King's corpse was restricted, only nobles and council members were allowed to see him before he was embalmed. We shuffled past him in a line, and I curtseyed to this wreck of a man lying dead. He who had altered so much, not just for me but for so many others, he was gone, just like that. I half expected him to sit up and laugh, telling everyone it had been a fine jest intended to catch Seymour out, but he did not. The scent of corruption on his body wafted up my nose along with incense burning, trying to mask the odour. I had to fight not to gag.

They took him to be embalmed after. It was said when they came to let his blood there was not half a pint left in him. Perhaps his heart had used it all before then and then had run dry. They encased him in lead and put him in a coffin. For five days he lay in state, surrounded by the light of thousands of candles as his chaplains and Gentlemen of the Privy Chamber prayed for him. Masses were sung over him and all the walls were draped in black and covered with the King's arms.

On the 2nd of February, Candlemas, they moved my former husband to the chapel, and covered him in a rich cloth of tissue garnished with escutcheons of his arms. The coffin was carried by his gentlemen, and I heard even with all of them it was a hard task, the weight of the body, the coffin and the lead bearing down on them. The gentlemen kept watch over the King, until he had lain ten days in state.

"They will bury him at Windsor, with Jane Seymour." Katherine Willoughby stared into the flames of my fire, her eyes intent on much I could not see.

"And with Brandon," I added, and she nodded. "Perhaps the company of his friend was even more important to the King than the wife he will lay beside."

The procession taking the King to Windsor stretched for four miles. At the front 250 paupers led the others, carrying tapers to light the way for the King. Carts followed, bearing more torches, so any that went out could be replaced. The King's body was carried in a gilded chariot, an effigy of him on top of the coffin dressed in velvet and precious stones. I was told the likeness was uncanny, as if he was there, still alive.

"There was a ghoulish story from the one night they stopped at Syon." My friend of Suffolk looked quite excited by the tale.

The King's body had rested at Syon, at the very Abbey he had attacked and where he had sent Margaret Douglas and Catherine Howard as prisoners.

"It is said as the coffin was laid out for the night, people thought it had been shaken by the journey, for in the morning there was underneath found a huge puddle of blood, and when the men came to collect the King, they found a dog there, licking up the King's blood."

"It sounds rather like the prophesy spoken of Ahab," I mentioned thoughtfully. "That dogs would lick the tyrant's blood? Is it not therefore an invention?"

"Perhaps, or a stray hound had a royal meal."

Henry VIII was buried at Windsor on the 15th of February, in the same tomb as Jane Seymour, just as he had asked. Gardiner, who had by the King's choice apparently, been excluded from the regency council, preached the funeral sermon. Sixteen yeomen of the guard were required to lower the King's coffin in beside Jane's, using long linen towels, and officers of the King's household broke their white staffs of office and threw them into the tomb.

"Apparently, our new King was somewhat puzzled that later they all had their staffs again when they came to him at the Tower," my friend told me. "He did not seem to know they were not the same ones."

"Everyone speaks of how intelligent the King is," I whispered, shaking my head. "But do they tell the truth? I have had but small interaction with him these past years. In his letters he sounds a grave child, most serious and clever, but is he as adroit as men say?"

"I think that we will not know until later in his reign, and besides, my friend, there are many forms of intelligence, are there not? He might be a clever child in terms of book learning, but as for wisdom that is another matter."

Chapter Sixteen

February – March 1547

Westminster Abbey

Four short days after we buried one King, another was crowned at Westminster Abbey. It was Sunday the 20th of February and although the celebrations were long, as was the procession to the Abbey, the coronation was kept a short ceremony. It was thought the length of ritual inflicted upon adults might be harmful to a king of such tender age as Edward VI.

"It is also because the King is in favour of the reformed faith," Katherine Willoughby confided beforehand, "and many think the Catholic service of coronation has become inappropriate."

Short it was, but revolutionary it was also.

On the evening of the old King's funeral, lords of court rode back to London and gathered at the Tower, and there they were rewarded for their support of Seymour. "Titles are being handed out like sweetmeats." Katherine looked disgusted. "Seymour has made himself Duke of Somerset, Dudley has become Earl of Warwick, Wriothesley is Earl of Southampton, and the Queen's brother William Parr is now Marquess of Northampton."

"He supported Seymour over his sister?"

"It would seem so, but wait, my friend, that is not all. Peers have been made. Thomas Seymour wanted to be named Protector, although he called it governor, but none supported him, so his brother has bought his loyalty with a peerage instead, and he is not alone, Richard Rich, William Willoughby, and Edward Sheffield are all peers of the realm now. Dudley is Great Chamberlain and Thomas Seymour is made Lord Admiral. It is said Norfolk and Surrey's lands will be handed out, and there are many with their hands out now, my friend."

On the eve of his coronation, Edward processed on horseback to the Palace of Westminster from the Tower, through crowds cheering him and pageants performed, many of which I was told had been based on the last boy-king of England's procession, Henry VI.

Streets had been swept, fresh gravel thrown down. Tapestry and painted cloth hung from all the windows, making London a riot of colour. People thronged along the roads as Edward departed the Tower at one of the afternoon. He was dressed in glimmering white velvet embroidered with silver. Upon his jerkin were diamonds, rubies and pearls sewn into lovers' knots. His gown was of mesh of gold with a cape of sable, and the horse he rode on was covered in crimson satin smothered with pearls.

The King's messengers walked side by side in pairs in front of him followed by the King's gentlemen and trumpeters, as well as chaplains, esquires of the body and nobility of England on horseback. Ambassadors were paired to walk with members of the council.

"I admit, I was unimpressed by the spectacle, my lady," Ambassador Van der Delft spoke scornfully after the ceremony. "In the first place, I was kept waiting at the Tower, then when I was addressing the King in French, the Duke of Somerset interrupted and asked me to address the King in Latin which he told me the King understood better than French. In all honesty, I thought the King understood me not well in Latin either. Then in the procession I was paired alongside Archbishop Cranmer, who refused to speak to me because he opposes my religious beliefs. If this is the way the new regime begins, friendship with other countries is unlikely."

If the ambassador did not enjoy the procession, at least the King seemed to welcome some of the pageants; he chortled at a Spanish tightrope walker who tumbled for the crowds and played and danced outside of Saint Paul's Cathedral. I knew for we were there, far behind the King.

Sir Anthony Browne, the King's new Master of Horse, rode behind the King on a horse covered with gold cloth, and along the route gentlemen with staffs cleared the way in front. "They are all Somerset's retainers," Katherine told me as we paused at one entertainment in Cheapside where all the houses were hung with cloth of silver and gold. Tapestry had been hung from parapets erected for the occasion.

"The new Duke of Somerset seems to hold all the power now." I spoke with care, so none heard me but Katherine.

In truth I was not surprised Van der Delft was unimpressed; many of the pageants were not well done. Officials of the city had been given short time to rehearse, and speeches delivered by actors were either not done on time or the actors stumbled over their words. But there was one which touched me.

The King reached a stage where there was a scaffold erected and beneath its roof was a display of the heavens with the sun, stars and clouds painted on a backdrop. As the King watched, a phoenix descended from the heavens and took perch on a mound covered in red and white roses and bushes of hawthorn. It was a representation of Edward's mother, and although I had not known the woman, I hoped she was looking down this day, proud of her son.

As the phoenix sat upon her mound of roses a lion wearing a crown emerged, made signs of friendship to the bird by nodding, and as he did so a young cub walked from the bushes. Two angels descended from the heavens clutching a crown which they set upon the young cub's head. The lion and the phoenix then vanished from sight.

Although I understood the allegorical meaning, I felt it was sad, showing Edward, the young cub now crowned, also was so alone in the world. It was supposed to be a sign of divine favour and royal supremacy that angels had come to crown him, a sign of strength that he stood alone, but still, it saddened me.

There were many more pageants and songs all along the route, all of them representing the new King as favoured by God, beloved by his ancestors, and in possession of power unlike that any of his ancestors had wielded.

I felt we were being prepared for something, and I was right for the next day there followed the short, yet revolutionary, coronation service.

At nine of the morning on the 20th of February King Edward was taken by water to Whitehall and there in the chamber of the court of augmentations he put on his parliament robes. The procession made its way to Westminster Abbey. In the Abbey, the choir had been hung with cloth of arras, and two cushions had been placed on the throne to compensate for the small height of the King.

During the service of coronation, Archbishop Cranmer affirmed the royal supremacy and named Edward a second Josiah, but there was changing to the wording, so I was told by my friend of Suffolk, of the traditional ceremony.

The usual wording in the first part of the coronation address, which presented the King to the three estates, was to say, "Will ye sirs at this time and give your wills and assents to the same consecration, enunction and coronation?" but Cranmer had altered this to, "Will ye *serve* at this time?"

"So now the people serve the King, rather than the King serving his people," Katherine muttered, her eyes narrowing.

"What is enunction?" I asked. "I am unfamiliar with the word."

"It refers to the anointing of the King."

Cranmer had also altered the coronation oath. For hundreds of years kings had sworn to confirm liberties and laws granted to the English people by kings before them as well as those granted to the clergy, they had sworn a promise of peace to the clergy, the Church, and the people and had promised to be just and merciful and observe laws chosen by their people. Of course, I did not comprehend fully at the time, being unfamiliar with the coronation service in England, and the Archbishop gave a sermon where, to his mind, he explained all the alterations in the new oath, but it took my friend to explain the true significance.

"The references to laws and liberties have been removed," she said on the evening after the coronation. "It seems now that the King will decide what these laws and liberties should be. Peace and concord was promised only to the Church and the people, which excludes the clergy, and this means that the protection of their liberties is not something the King has sworn to. That means he may go ahead with reformation of the Church by royal prerogative. The King is now lawmaker, and in the final part of the oath, the meaning was reversed entirely. The people, not their King, now must consent to new laws, that means the King will make the law and exact the law, and the people must go along with it. Always before it was the King who would consent to uphold the laws of the people."

The clergy now had no right to hold kings to account, and the King once crowned could not be rejected. The coronation ceremony held no power over King Edward as it had over other kings. He could act as he saw fit. King Edward VI had come to the throne as no other before him. It had been said in a proclamation which had been issued on the 31st of January that he was fully invested and established in the crown imperial of this realm, and the men about him meant it. They had made Edward a King of supreme power, born as the defender of the faith, crowned with all the powers of the royal supremacy.

"They have handed him absolute rule," I said later that night. "When to his majority he comes."

"They have," agreed my friend.

"Should you not be rejoicing?"

"For the faith? Perhaps, my friend, I do not know. In truth the idea of a king, any king, being handed absolute power over his people is something I think dangerous. Edward is young now and he will be governed by others, but what about when he grows? Even his father had not this much power. This is a way to make a tyrant. If he turns out to be a good man, perhaps all will be well, but what if not?"

As the service went on the Archbishop had urged the new King to continue the Reformation of the Church of England, to banish the tyranny of the bishops of Rome from his subjects and to put an end to the worship of graven images. The new King agreed to all these things, and I believe he was probably in earnest.

He was a grave and serious child, and when he made a promise, I was sure it would be done, for good or for ill.

When Edward had been anointed and crowned, Somerset came forth to kneel before him, pledging himself to the new King. After him came Cranmer who swore the same, and then each member of the nobility was to step before the King, taking turns to kiss Edward on his left cheek. But eventually, because there was not time enough, the rest of us came forward in a group and knelt before the King as Edward Seymour declared we had sworn our loyalty to King Edward *en masse*.

"He now speaks for all of us," I said later to my friend.

"For now," was her reply.

That evening King Edward presided over a banquet in Westminster Hall, and he dined with the crown on his head as if now it was placed there, he would never have it taken off. Nobility took turns to serve the King at dinner and over the following two days there were many jousts, during which Thomas Seymour distinguished himself.

Everyone appeared to be enjoying the new reign begun, and there was, at the moment, a show of unity amongst the men surrounding the new King, but already cracks were showing, and I had concerns of my own.

What worried me was how lavish the handout of lands and honours to the new power group of court was, and how quickly it had begun. Katherine Willoughby had warned of it, this clause which allowed them to reward themselves, but all their new titles, and even Norfolk's holdings and money, great though they were, would not satisfy all of them, not given the rapidity with which the clause was used.

I had ever thought that when the King died, I would find my lands, houses and estates under threat and this surfeit of rewards gave me no cause to think otherwise. The old King had made promises to me, to maintain my household, but if men about the new King had not respected the wishes of Henry VIII about how his son's minority should be governed, why should they respect the promises made to me?

And the King's will, even in its new form, never had provided for the appointment of a Lord Protector but invested the government of the realm to the Regency Council that would rule collectively. The King had spoken of it to Queen Katherine and others, saying it was the only way he could be sure that no man would try to take power away from his son. Yet here we were, with a Lord Protector. What the old King wanted was no more important. I was not even sure the wants of my nephew, the new sovereign of England, would be taken into account either.

We had a new King, indeed, but his name was not Edward Tudor.

It was Edward Seymour.

Chapter Seventeen

1547

Richmond Palace

I hoped there might be outcry, that the English people would hear of Somerset usurping the throne in all but name, and protest, that they would remember Katherine had been a good Regent and press for the terms of the King's will, his true will, to be upheld. But of course, what had the people known of the King's plans? They had no information, so they held no power. Men of money had moved first and fast, and they had stolen the country from the one truly meant to govern.

And now Edward Tudor had been crowned an absolute monarch and Edward Seymour had been named ruler of that monarch, it was done.

We had to see what now would happen.

Katherine Parr tried to contest Somerset. She put up a brave fight, and brave it was for she had no one at her side. The Dowager Queen did not get far in attempting to assert her rights. They all abandoned her, these men who had sworn to support her.

Even her brother William Parr and the man who loved her, Thomas Seymour, had had their loyalties purchased. Somerset had pretended to be her supporter, perhaps he had been whilst Katherine had power, but the moment his chance had come, he had betrayed her and his former master. How long had he been thinking of that moment? Years ago, I had thought there would be a struggle for power when the King died, and I had supposed Somerset would be one of the combatants. I had even thought he would try to make himself Regent, but after that, hope had come when Katherine had become Queen, and the King had named her Regent. I had thought this would be respected, that men would uphold her. I had been wrong. They did not care she had been a good ruler, fair, honest and straightforward. They did not care she was of the reformed faith, like the King, and had been a good mother to him. She was a woman, they could take her power, and so they did.

Now a man with no royal blood, save a sliver that he claimed came from Edward III – and almost all nobility of England could claim the same – and a sister who had been Queen, had set himself up as the power behind the throne. In truth, Somerset *was* the throne, he was the chair upon which Edward Tudor sat, and he was going to use all his influence to keep himself there.

Men of the new council were still rewarding themselves with titles and lands so fast you might think one of them might have stopped, for shame, but they did not care. It was as children grabbing sweets off a platter, and just as such children become repulsive in their greed, so did the men of the new order of power in England.

It was a once-in-a-generation opportunity, I supposed, and they were determined to do what they could with it. And yet I believed if I was worried, I should not be the only one who was so.

Eventually, men consumed with greed would look to where greater rewards were, their present ones being not enough, for they never are. They would look to one place, to Somerset, and that man was no anointed king with a mandate to rule granted by God, he was no prince of the blood royal, his power was not even clearly defined, only agreed by other men.

My friend of Suffolk was right; Somerset was powerful, for now.

*

"Wriothesley has been arrested!" Diaceto's face flushed, he had hurried straight to me with the news.

I turned from my desk where I had been writing to my sister Amalia. "The Chancellor? But why?"

But I knew. For being of the conservative faction, for being a man Somerset thought he could not trust. That was why. It was only March, not quite a month into the rule of the new King, and Somerset was already clearing house. Wriothesley had supported Edward Seymour and had been rewarded, but could he be trusted? He had worked with Gardiner and Norfolk in the past, and Arundel, another conservative, was his ally. Would he continue to support Somerset? If he did not, he could be dangerous as Chancellor with the Great Seal of the realm – needed so it could be affixed to every patent and commission to grant authority – in his power. It was too much power. Wriothesley could veto the commands of the new Duke of Somerset. He had to go.

"The Chancellor told me personally, my lady, that he would resist any further alterations to the wishes of the past King," Van der Delft told me when he arrived later that day to deliver the same news as Diaceto. In truth I wondered if the Ambassador did not come to my house because he seemed to have warmed to me. He was an arrogant man who considered most things beneath him, but apparently, I was not one of those things. My brother having now married his master's niece, I was almost family. Of course, my sister and her husband were still at war with the Emperor or would be in short time when fighting resumed after the winter, but men are more prone to believe we women are led by male relatives rather than female, so my coward brother must be more influence upon me than my courageous sister.

I did not disabuse him of this fallacy. It was useful to hear what information he had.

"Is that why he has been arrested?" I asked.

"It has been told to me thus, my lady. Two days before the coronation the Chancellor commissioned for lawyers to hear cases in his absence. He thought he would be busy in council. Crucially they were to hear cases in his absence without the new King's warrant however, and a team of common lawyers declared that this was in opposition of common law. They demanded that the Chancellor be removed from his position, and this, Somerset has pounced upon. The regency council have expressed that they feel unable to pass judgement on the case, but it seems to me Somerset will not let Wriothesley escape now."

Indeed, he did not. The Chancellor was charged on the 5th of March, and it was said he had used unfitting words to the Protector which prejudiced the King's estate and hindered his affairs but had also menaced many learned men of the council. It was said peril might well ensue if the seal of England should continue to be held in the Chancellor's hands. The seal was taken from him, and he was placed under house arrest.

Now the only ones left on the conservative side were Gardiner and Arundel. I was told later that Thomas Seymour was calling for the former Chancellor and for Lady Mary to be thrown in the Tower, obviously it was thought that if a conservative coup followed the Protestant one, Lady Mary might be set on the throne.

But in the meantime, Somerset had other plans. On the 1st of March the many executors and assistants of the old King's will were amalgamated, making one Privy Council and on the 12th with only seven members of that council present, the council requested a new commission to grant the board full authority during King Edward's minority. At the same time Somerset's powers were widened. He was granted full power and full authority to decide private and public matters as well as foreign causes.

"He now can add or remove councillors as he wishes." Katherine looked troubled, as well she might. "He can convene the council when he wishes to, and can act without its approval."

"He truly has made himself King." I felt helpless, many did.

"And has begun to act like it, my friend. He has commanded that two gilt maces are to be carried before him by two pages at all times, and I hear that in a letter to François of France, Somerset called the French King his 'brother'. He has granted unto himself an annuity of 8,000 marks to uphold his state, a mighty fortune, and I hear he is soon to change his coat of arms so they will resemble the royal arms of his sister Jane. His wife has also become overbearing and proud and said she should be granted precedence above the Dowager Queen at court, since she is the wife of the Lord Protector."

My mouth fell open in shock. It was all so blatant. "How has the Dowager responded?"

"She is entirely indignant, as any of us would be to be usurped by the likes of Anne Stanhope," she said, "but I think this is not the time to respond openly. We must bide our time, for what do they say pride comes before?"

"A fall," I said, "but what a height the Lord Protector is setting himself to tumble from."

Chapter Eighteen

1547

Chelsea Manor and

Richmond Palace

"He is refusing to give you your jewels?"

The Dowager Queen had called me to her house to converse on matters, but I had not known they would be matters so base. Thievery of one kind was not enough for Somerset; he wanted to further his career.

"Indeed, even my wedding ring and gifts made personally by the King." Katherine Parr was twitching with anger, barely concealed under the surface of her clear skin. "You can imagine, much as the sting of being set aside as Regent, which I know was my husband's wish though men now lecture me, telling me the King never intended I should think so and female rule was ever abhorrent to him…"

That was a truth, though, I thought. It was not something to say to the former Queen, of course, but the path of the King's reign had crossed many possible ways for England and in none of them had he envisioned a woman on the throne. He would not have wanted Somerset on it either, that was true enough, but I wondered then if the will had not been forged. Perhaps the old King had been easy to persuade of the evils of female rule. After all, was not the reason we had a King now, no matter that he was a child, all because Henry VIII had thought it a horror to put either of his daughters, both older and one indeed now an adult proper, on that very throne?

"… but I know it was my husband's wish that I become Regent to guide poor, dear Edward in this task now given to him. But much as that stings, this barefaced, outrageous thievery of my property is another insult."

Somerset was refusing to hand the Dowager's jewels to her. Some, of course were indeed property of the Crown, but he was refusing to hand even her personal jewels to her, which as she said had been gifts from the King, including her wedding ring.

"And he even has jewels that my mother gave to me, which were mine long before I became Queen, and refuses to give them to me! Apparently, all is now the Crown's, or rather Somerset's, property."

"But why be so petty?" I asked.

She glanced about, though we were alone in the gardens, besides my maid Kitty far behind me. "The Crown is poor," she confessed quietly. "The treasury is depleted; Somerset needs reserves of bullion. He has also started to grant leases upon my dower lands without my consent. I know this, for orders I sent to one estate were not carried out and I was informed by the keeper of the park I was no more the master of those lands, but another chosen by Somerset was."

Stealing was not the only method being used to raise money. New plans to salvage goods from the *Mary Rose* went ahead. The ship itself was given up for lost, but there were cannon, anchors and guns as well as other goods on board which were worth a vast amount.

"It did not go well the last time," I noted to Katherine of Suffolk.

"The King means to employ specialists in the art of salvage," Katherine explained. "They will waste no time on the ship, but will dive to attach ropes to precious goods, that they might be hauled to the surface. There is one man in particular I have heard named, Jacques Francis, a man of African birth who is most skilled. The Italian salvage diver who heads the group, Corsi, recommended Francis most highly. He is to lead the team diving for cannons and other goods."

"He is coming all the way from Africa?" I asked.

"I hear tell he hails from Guinea, once lived in Portugal and now is a resident of Southampton, so a well-travelled man. The King is to pay Francis and Corsi handsomely."

I nodded. England had many Africans and Moors living permanently within its borders, many who had been here for generations and were known as English men and women, much as I, born of Cleves, was now named English. Unlike in some other countries, they were free people, often taking on specialist trades such as silk weaving and pin making, and as now I learned, diving. Plenty lived about ports, but London housed a large number too. There were many who were merchants, sailors, servants and traders, and I had several Moors who hailed from Spanish lands within in my household working as musicians. The King, and his father before him, had employed a man named John Blanke who had worked as a trumpeter for the royal household, a prestigious position. Although Blanke was not someone I had met, having died before I came to England, I knew his name for he was in a picture commissioned when the King and Katherine of Spain had had their first male heir, a boy who died after only living for a month.

I thought of these men, diving to the bottom of the sea. To find the cannon and anchor, would they swim through the ship itself? Along corridors where perhaps bodies still floated? I imagined most of the men who died with the ship would be bare bone by now, at least I hoped they would for the divers' sakes. What was it like down there, in the darkness of the water? Would they see where men had dropped knives or left their boots in the hurry to escape the sinking ship? Would they see the faces of the lost down there, or was there not enough light and they had to feel their way by hand? I hoped the King was paying them well, for to my mind it was not only hard work swimming and diving all that way, but hard for what horrors they might encounter. Men like Jacques Francis sounded unimaginably brave, to my mind.

But this gave me more to think on, for if the council were seeking to salvage goods from the sea floor, and were trying to steal from the Dowager Queen, this was ominous news for me too.

I was right to think so.

Sir Thomas Cawarden, freed from the restraints set upon his desires by the death of the old King, petitioned King Edward and his council for Bletchingley. He did not want to wait until I was dead to take possession of the house, he wanted it now. He had been made Master of the Revels, and was a supporter of Somerset, and as such his petition was listened to, and mine, countering his claim, was not supported.

"The King never intended houses such as this be taken from me in my lifetime," I protested to Sir John Guildford who had come to pretend to hear my side of the story when I objected most fervently to the King himself. "The old King made promises to me, good sir, is it too much to ask that my wise nephew the King uphold oaths sworn to maintain me as a Princess of this realm?"

In the end, Cawarden succeeded somewhat. The council ordered he was to take Bletchingley, but as my tenant, so in some ways the house was still mine. I had the right to visit and stay there, but the man acted as if I did not matter and immediately began making changes to the local church, which vexed me greatly as I knew the people there were traditional in nature and wanted no changes. He pulled down the rood-loft, whitewashed paintings on the walls and, as men of the village wrote to me in indignation, defaced the altar. There was nothing I could do. It was likely to cause only approval with Somerset and the King that Cawarden had done such, they wanted more reform, and word was it was to go ahead swifter than the last King had ever enacted it.

"Why is it men think that to destroy what is pretty and put in place what is plain will please God?" I asked the Dowager of Suffolk.

"A plainer church keeps one closer to God," she replied absently. "I do not say I approve of what was done to your property, or the church, but the costliness of churches are a waste. That money could be better spent elsewhere."

"And where will that money be spent, my friend? Not on the people, on the poor or needy, no, it will go into the hands and pockets of men like Somerset and Cawarden. And it cost money to whitewash those walls and pull down the rood-loft, did it not? So money was spent to make the church plain as it was spent years ago to make it pretty. If truly they wanted to help others with their money, why not leave the church as it was and put that money to aid the poor or to advance education?"

"I admit, you have a point, but you will have to hold your tongue. We will see more of this. The King is ardent about reform. Cranmer has convinced him he has a God-given mission to bring it about. Change is coming, my friend."

In exchange for my lost property, I was given Penshurst, which, seeing as it was not many a mile away from Hever, did not please me. What was the use of having two houses so close together? I still had to rely on Cawarden as a member of my household, too, which was not without its awkwardness.

When I stayed with Cawarden at Bletchingley – and we started to visit him at his property in Blackfriars too, for he was my tenant was he not? – my household, Diaceto leading them, wishing to use spite on Cawarden, left a trail of destruction in their wake. Rooms were used well, and nothing was tidied away. Some went out of their way to cause breakages. They did this out of annoyance at Cawarden because of the way I had been treated. I did not order it, but I admit I did nothing to stop it and did not berate them afterwards. Perhaps it was not my finest moment, but I too was annoyed at the man.

He objected to the council about this, which I understood perhaps, but also whinged about my habit of cooking. Cooking was a skill I had been taught in childhood, and it was considered an art worthy of a woman's time in Cleves, much as embroidery was in England. I had spent time in the kitchens of many of my houses, trying out new sauces and recipes, seeing if I could perfect English dishes. Cawarden seemed to think I was doing this at "his" house just to irritate him and complained about it to the King.

He also complained I sent a list of expensive items and foods which I required ahead of me each time I stayed with him. A list had been sent of course, but it was what usually was expected at any house at which I stayed. "The man is determined to find fault with me, and make it appear I am a profligate leech," I blazed to the Dowager of Suffolk, my usually calm voice gaining height and speed.

"The old King decreed you were to be maintained in a certain state." Katherine was examining the note of items Cawarden thought were luxuries. They included flour, candles, wood to burn, beer and meat, all to feed my household. True, there were spices which were costly, but my household was large, was maintained to a royal standard, and having been a part of my household, he knew what it took to feed them. "You were within your rights to ask for these things." She folded the paper and stared into my eyes. "That the man cannot afford the house he has stolen from you is not your fault."

"The council will back him, not me, however." I chewed my lip and tasted blood. "They want my properties to hand out to more of Somerset's people and they want to end the expense of me."

"Then they should let you go home," she said. "If they are to keep you here, they cannot keep you as a peasant. You were made a Princess of England, there is a standing to that, just as there is to the King's position, which must be maintained in order for the nation to be respected."

"Yet I am not of this nation, this they make clear here and now," I snapped. "Did you not tell me once that when Katherine of Spain lost her first husband she was kept in a low state, had to sell her plate and bargain for bread for her servants? She too was kept in a certain state whilst her husband lived, then another, much lower, when he died. She too was of another country. The old King protected my status whilst he lived, and now he is gone I may well be treated as Katherine of Spain was in those years after her first marriage and before her second."

"I do not think that will be the case, my friend."

I exhaled, my breath heavy and hot with fear and anger. "I do not know why you think it should be any different. At times I am accepted here and at times I am reminded that all I will ever be is a stranger, and if they are stealing lands and jewels from the Dowager Queen, they will too from the Lady of Cleves."

Chapter Nineteen

1547

Richmond Palace

I have often had reason to suppose when strands of destiny cross between two lives, they meet in many places rather than just one. As if we are threads in a tapestry, so our fates are woven together. It was this way for me with many wives of my former husband, so I felt, and became so with Katherine Parr, fate deciding to offer us almost the same path more than once.

Katherine saved me once from marriage, or rather remarriage, to the King by becoming the object of his affection, and in a way most similar she saved me again. Perhaps just as my own, personal ghost of another Anne was sent to aid me, so Katherine decided to as well, although unwittingly both times, I believe.

This time, she saved me from marriage to Thomas Seymour.

It was my nephew who suggested this man for me. King Edward thought I should not be living alone. Perhaps he already had been talked to by his men and saw me as an expense the Crown should not be supporting. The old reason for me to remain in England, my former husband's pride and worries over what I might say of his conduct, or perhaps rather his performance in the bedchamber, existed no more since he was dead, yet men about Edward were not willing either that I should be sent home.

Now the King had changed, and rumour had it right when it whispered that King Edward was more zealous in the Protestant faith than his father. Alliance with the Emperor, whom my brother was bonded to, might now not be as desired as before since he was Catholic, so from some perspectives it might be best to send me home and save England the expense of my houses and household as well as potential complications from my connection to the Holy Roman Empire. On the other hand, my sister was married to one of the leading lights of reformation, about to embark on war again against the Emperor, so there was a certain sense in keeping me in England, as a link which could always be exploited to open talks.

Either way, I was potentially an asset to England, but I was also an expense. The obvious solution was to marry me off to an Englishman, which would allow the Crown to claim back many of my properties outright, without me being able to object since they had been given to me as a settlement by the old King as our marriage ended. They were not dower lands, and even those were contested often enough, but had been left to me on condition I remain in England and did not remarry.

If I married again, most of my estates would revert to the Crown. Some might be retained by me by permission of the council, and those properties would of course go into the hands of my husband, making me a rich prize for marriage for one of Somerset's supporters. How much I would lose was not entirely clear, but I was sure papers could be found to support whatever outcome the council wanted. If they could fake the King's will, why not other documents? If I was allowed to retain anything, it would be only due to the kindness of the King, my nephew. At least some of the allowance I was granted would be lost too, for I would be taken care of by my new husband, so would not need a pension from the Crown. So, marrying me off seemed a fine idea.

The King thought the man for me was Thomas Seymour.

Seymour had gone to the King, his nephew, to ask whom, if any woman, he should marry. The King suggested me.

"Why me?" I asked Diaceto, horrified.

I had no wish to wed Seymour. Quite aside from the loathing I had for his brother, this upstart creature who was stealing from me and the Dowager, who lorded over England thinking himself King, the younger Seymour was no better.

On the surface Thomas Seymour should have seemed a fine prospect for any woman to marry. His dark looks were bold, his frame was tall and strong, and he had a reputation as an adventurer. By the time he was twenty-one, before his sister's marriage to the King, Seymour had been made a knight, an Alderman of London and had joined with the entourage of Sir Francis Bryan the ambassador to France. He had fought the Turks under command of the Emperor's brother Ferdinand and had an impressive record in military matters on land and at sea where he had fought the French as well as pirates who sailed the English Channel. Seymour wrote poetry and sometimes set it to music. He had a fine voice for singing, and often had not seemed a truly devoted man of any faith which had allowed him to skate through the muddy waters of the King's reformation with ease. So yes, if one looked only on the surface, he was a fair prospect.

But I did not like only to see the surface.

Seymour was vain, reckless and had scant respect for anyone but himself. He had no loyalty, had attempted to take his brother's position as Protector, and no matter that that position was a lie in the first place, it still did not speak well of his character to try to wrest it from his brother. He was eternally unsatisfied carnally, and all women of lower rank at court knew to avoid him. They had not the protection of rank that higher ladies at least sometimes enjoyed, so to men like Seymour were as game to be hunted.

They had been safe a while, the women of court, whilst he was in foreign lands, but he had returned in the August before the King died, and it was clear to everyone that the feelings between the Dowager and Seymour had not dimmed during the four years of her marriage. Yet now, apparently my nephew the King thought he should be *my* husband.

"I do not want to be sold off to Seymour," I objected.

"Word is, my lady, your wish is easy to grant, for it is said that Seymour was not asking in truth which bride he should take." Diaceto was grinning with a secret almost ready to reveal. "For he had one in mind already. What he wanted was to trick the King into suggesting the bride that some say Seymour has already taken."

"What bride?" I asked and then stopped. "She would not... she is not so foolish."

Diaceto was nodding. "People say they became lovers within weeks of the old King's death, Highness, and that Seymour persuaded the Dowager to wed him. I hear she was reluctant, knowing that it would not go well for her when the people of England found out, but she has loved him a long time, as all people know, and it is said his persuasion worked and they were secretly wed."

"But she is in mourning still, what if there was a child in her belly from the old King?" I stopped and stared. "God's eyebrows, what if there is a child from Seymour in there, if they have become lovers, and he tries to pass it off as the old King's child?"

Diaceto spread his hands and shrugged.

"Apparently, the King also suggested Lady Mary as a possible bride for already married Seymour. He said he thought his uncle could turn her away from the Catholic faith if married to him." My friend of Suffolk had come and when I whispered the rumours Diaceto had told me to her, she admitted it was the truth.

The Dowager loved him, Katherine said, and she had been scared of the dangers of accepting his hand, but more scared to lose him. "Consider, Anne, how long she has loved him, and how much she gave up when the King made her his wife. She has lived through heartache and terror; does she not deserve some happiness?"

"I am not sure Seymour could grant her that," I sighed. "It would seem to me the opposite. That man is reckless, he will bring her grief."

"Katherine could control the old King, and she will temper Seymour. Some of the best matches are made between people who own different characters, they complement each other." All the same, my friend did not sound sure of her own words.

"When will the King, and his men, know of this?"

Katherine lifted her eyebrows and widened her eyes. "The couple are hoping to catch the King, trap him, so he seems to give approval. In truth, that was what Seymour was after during the conversation in which the King suggested you, or Lady Mary, as his bride. He hoped the King would say Seymour should wed the Dowager, but apparently the thought did not occur to King Edward. He might well think it an insult that his stepmother should wed again. All the children of the late King seem to worship the memory of their father now, the way they talk."

"It is natural to think only the best of those we have lost, you did the same with Charles."

"That is true, perhaps it will wear off in time."

"I find it troubling the King wanted Mary to marry Seymour so he could turn her away from Catholicism." My brow furrowed in thought. "The King ever has seemed to love and accept Mary as she is, yet now he would marry her to a man not a prince, which seems to indicate he still thinks her a bastard, and he wants her converted."

"Van der Delft and the Emperor have driven home the point that Mary must be allowed to worship as she wishes," Katherine informed me. "And she is defiant about the new regime and its plans for the faith. She will not comply, that is why Edward wanted a husband for her, so she could be forced."

"Seymour was hardly the man to pick for a conversion. The man is as light of faith as a feather in the wind." I thought a moment. "Does Somerset know… about his brother and Katherine?"

"I do not think so, but he did support the idea of them marrying not long ago. It would be a good thing for him, as long as the King was not offended, of course. Katherine has wealth, and it would be kept in the Seymour family with such a match."

Katherine thought her secret safe from everyone, yet I was sure I was not the only one who knew. News leaked out slowly, then all at once. There were rumours Katherine Ashley, servant of Princess Elizabeth, had accosted Seymour in Saint James's park, questioning him about his plans for marriage. When Seymour told her he would "prove to have the Queen," Ashley responded that she had heard he was already married to her.

It was rumoured that their ceremony had taken place at Baynard's Castle, which formed part of the Dowager's jointure, and Katherine had given the castle to her sister Anne and Anne's husband William Herbert as a gift. As summer began to dawn the secret was out and everyone knew.

Everyone but the King and his sisters, apparently.

It was not a good time for this to emerge, for any support Katherine and Seymour might have had from his brother was vanishing. Not only was Somerset pilfering the Dowager's property, but the new Duchess of Somerset had taken it upon herself to wage private war on Katherine. Not content with taking precedence over her at court, Anne Stanhope had begun to slander the former Queen, saying before she had married the King, she had been no one of importance and certainly was not of the same dignity as her, the Duchess of Somerset. "I am she who will teach her," said Anne, and went on to name Katherine a "devilish woman".

"Many people think the new Duchess a woman of intolerable pride," mentioned Katherine Willoughby.

"She seems keen to prove this presumption correct," was my reply.

In this time of ill feeling between the former Queen and the man who had set himself up as King, now Katherine had to admit that she had married indecently fast – as some would consider it – after the death of her last husband. No one had thought it too fast when the former Lady Latimer had married King Henry only weeks after the death of her second husband. Then, it was acceptable. But to marry a lesser titled man so quickly apparently was not.

"It is strange, is it not," mused my friend of Suffolk, "that if we marry up in the world swiftly, then it is not a bad thing but if we marry down with the same swiftness, it is. Men will call women who marry up fortune hounds, but if we marry down, we are indecent in modesty."

"One could remain unmarried," I suggested with a smile, "and only occasionally in that state be called a whore."

Katherine laughed.

"What will the Dowager do?"

My friend told me that the clandestine couple hoped to secure from King Edward and Princess Mary goodwill for the match before knowledge of it became widespread. Apparently, the opinion of Elizabeth did not count. That summer as Seymour requested Princess Mary's blessing on a *potential* union with the Queen, Mary responded that she found the news strange. Mary seemed to think the very suggestion that Katherine might think to marry so soon after her father's death was intolerable, but she wrote that she was not to be a meddler in this matter.

With Edward they seemed to have more success.

"In truth he was deceived," Katherine of Suffolk revealed, her expression dour. "I would have told the couple what they did was not a fine plan, had they asked, but Seymour convinced Katherine."

"And the wise bowed to the fool," I said.

"The Dowager wrote as if in jest to the King, requiring help against the Lord Admiral and his suit to her, for he kept asking and asking her to wed him. This was presented to the King as if it was not a true marriage proposal but was a matter of mirth. Edward was convinced to join in this jape. Seymour managed to persuade the King, jokingly, into assuring Katherine that if she did think to marry again then he would support it. The King had no idea that he was offering support for a match already made. Katherine announced to others that since the King had approved her marriage to Seymour, she would go ahead with it."

The news of their marriage became public not long after Edward's letter written in jest was received by them, and much as I had thought, most people were surprised, revolted and angered by the match. Somerset, despite his former support, played true to character and immediately turned on the pair and condemned them. King Edward seemed insulted that his stepmother would marry again so soon after the death of King Henry, and many vile insults flew the way of the former Queen when the people of England learned of her union. Seymour was not mentioned in them, only Katherine. It was said that she had no moral compass due to the unseemly haste with which she had rushed into marriage. People called her a wanton and a fornicator; she was accused of sexual licence, and it was said that her barren womb had controlled her decisions.

"She will have no further influence with the Privy Council, I think." Katherine Willoughby sounded angry and sad. "There are people calling her chastity into question and as soon as that happens for a woman, she has no defence and no authority within the world."

"Had Seymour not talked her into marriage she might still have had some influence with the council and the King." Was love with a man like Seymour worth losing all that she had? I was furious at Katherine Parr. Where had her sense and mind gone?

"Only time will tell I suppose, if she might retain any," said Katherine. "The King knows that she deceived him about the true state of her relationship with Seymour, so has come to distrust her. If she had come out with the truth, this might not have happened. It seems as if her relationship with Princess Mary is also much damaged."

"I believe so." I had received a letter most unguarded from Mary in which she railed against Katherine and called me the only *"true"* wife of the King who still was within the world.

There was another repercussion. Just as people had said I was jealous the first time Katherine ended up with a husband people thought destined for me, so they declared I was the second time. Yet I say she saved me for I wanted not the men she was tied to by bonds of marriage. The rumours persisted, however. I had *loved* Seymour; the King had wanted our match to occur and had sanctioned it. *Licentious* Katherine Parr had *snatched* the Lord Admiral from the poor Lady of Cleves, who was a good woman and never would have clandestinely married behind the King's back. And was it not proved that I was a good woman, for I had not sought to remarry after my marriage to the King was ended? Katherine Parr had not tarried more than a few months!

"How much and easily people forget." I shook my head as I heard rumours of my jealousy. "At times I have been the evil siren, tempting the King from the bed of Catherine Howard and getting with child by him, now all that is forgotten. They have another woman to paint as the Devil, therefore I become their angel again."

I heard of much I had said, and bewailed, which never crossed my lips, and for good reason. It is to many minds, and particularly those of men, inconceivable that a woman should be happy by herself, as I was. Men, you see, are not happy by themselves, in truth they need women more than we need men for masters always need servants, but the greatest trick in the world is that those who rule us have managed to convince servants that they *require* masters, and love, in marriage or mastery, is a lie we are sold to keep us where they need us to be, serving them.

That was one reason I was upset about Katherine's marriage. True, she had lost much influence and her place as Regent, but she could have had some power had she not thrown it away on a man like Seymour. Had I been in her place, I would have done otherwise, but perhaps I was not a creature made to believe in love, as she was.

It upsets the order of the world, to find a woman who can live without a husband. One could argue I was not living without a man, exactly, for the King gave me my houses and filled my purse, but without a husband and happy, this is a thing the eyes of the world cannot endure. If more women could own their own property and fill their own purses, would men end up without wives? Perhaps this is what they fear.

And so, when the world finds a woman living by herself and without a husband it must be that she is sad, lonely and jealous of all other women for they have husbands, and she does not. That was why people thought I was jealous of Katherine. I was not.

In truth, I feared for her.

My friend of Suffolk claimed Katherine would temper Seymour, but to my mind it was a task she should not have to undertake. Was he not an adult, therefore capable of controlling himself? Katherine no doubt thought she had taken a man of action, a man of strength as her husband, and perhaps after three sickly husbands, two of them old, she had longed for such. But if Katherine had spent three marriages caring for men and thought this time would be different, I pitied her.

She was taking on the role of caregiver again, not in body this time perhaps but certainly in mind. Responsible for a man's reckless ways? There to temper his wildness? Such things as these are not as easy to cure as a rotten leg or a sickly stomach.

"God sends often times to good women evil husbands," Princess Mary stated some years later. People assumed she was talking of her mother. I wondered if instead she had meant her stepmother.

Chapter Twenty

Summer 1547

Richmond Palace

"But my sister, my sister is well? Her sons, are they safe?" I thought I might fly apart, fear dragging mind and flesh from bone.

Ambassador Van der Delft wore a grave expression. It had been his task to bring ill news to me, and although he was a servant of the Emperor and was supposed to think this tale was only one of victory, he had enough sense to comprehend my terror.

"Your sister is well and unharmed, my lady," he assured me.

The War of the Schmalkaldic League, in Saxony at least, seemed over. During the winter just passed the Emperor had not personally engaged in battle, and Johann Friedrich had succeeded in winning back some of his lands stolen by his kinsman Moritz. My sister had been appointed the Lady Keeper of Wittenberg by her husband, and Johann Friedrich left her in charge of the city as when the thaw came he headed out once more to fight, for it was said the Emperor himself was to enter the war. In late April my brother of Saxony and his army crossed the Elbe and destroyed bridges thereabouts. He only had 7,000 men to the Emperor's 27,000. Relying on poor intelligence, my brother-in-law set up camp just outside Mühlberg, not understanding how close he was to the Emperor's troops. But Charles V was well aware.

The Emperor attacked just as Johann Friedrich's army were getting ready to move out from camp. Some of the imperial army swam across the Elbe and the rest used a ford, catching their enemies unawares. Battle ensued and the small Saxon army fought with valour and ferocity, but they were vastly outnumbered. My brother-in-law became surrounded by horsemen of the Emperor and tried to fight them off, receiving a wound which ran down his left cheek, from the corner of his eye all the way to his mouth. He was captured and brought as a prisoner to the Emperor. My sister's eldest son was also captured during battle. Her other sons were with her in Wittenberg.

My sister then, as Lady Keeper of the city, had to prepare. She did not know whether her husband and eldest son were still alive, but she knew the Emperor was on the march, coming for her.

The imperial army burned the countryside and plundered small towns and villages, as Sybylla and her sons, John William and John Frederick the younger, made for the Castle of Wittenberg with the rest of her court. Wittenberg's walls were high and strong and there was a moat and swamp which surrounded the city as well, but the castle, although built to withstand a siege, was not constructed for counterattack. My sister ordered cannons which were mounted inside the two great towers of the castle to repel the imperial army, and she destroyed the bridge. She ordered earthworks to be built up as well, to provide more protection for the city.

But the Emperor was prepared.

Charles V had brought not only a huge army, but also long guns which would have no trouble reaching Wittenberg. He was also expecting reinforcements from Duke Moritz.

The Siege of Wittenberg began on the 4th of May and Charles's artillery pounded the walls. All said that my sister Sybylla, Lady Keeper of Wittenberg, Electress of Saxony and born Duchess of Cleves defended her city with courage and pride, coming out to spur on her troops and give orders herself.

I wondered if our brother heard, and shied away from the courage his sister had displayed against the Emperor, when he could not even ride out with his own troops.

As the siege went on, hoping to save himself from a sentence of death which had been passed upon him on the 10th of May, as well as save his family from destruction, Johann Friedrich surrendered control of Electoral Saxony to the Emperor.

On the 19th of May, Johann Friedrich entered into the Capitulation of Wittenberg and Sybylla was no doubt lost in wonder when the Emperor ceased to pound the walls of Wittenberg with his guns. Although he ceased to attack Wittenberg, his troops did not cease to assail the surrounding area. It was said that for months, if not years, afterwards rivers ran red with blood and fields were stained crimson.

A few days later, my sister opened the gates of Wittenberg and surrendered to Charles V. Dressed as a widow, for she knew not if her husband or son were alive, my sister, surrounded by her Frauenzimmer came from the gates of the castle, and knelt before the Emperor, asking for news of her husband. When she was told he was alive, she offered to exchange high-ranking imperial prisoners for his return, and that of her son.

"The Emperor was deeply moved by the courage of your sister," Van der Delft informed me.

No doubt he was greatly moved by her beauty as well, I thought.

Sybylla had always known she was a beauty, and her pale looks, that fair hair, would have been set off by the darkness of her gown and veil. My sister had shown courage in defending her city, and wisdom in the way she approached the Emperor, knowing that a woman, now in the hands of the enemy, must use any weapon she possessed.

"The Emperor lifted your sister to her feet and assured her that she and her two sons who had not fought against him would remain safe," the Ambassador went on.

"And what of her husband, and her son John Friedrich the middle?" I asked.

Van der Delft informed me that Johann Friedrich had been allowed to stay with Sybylla and their sons in Wittenberg during the end of May and into the beginning of June.

"And after that? What will happen to him now?"

"He has now been taken to Worms, where he will remain a prisoner of the Emperor, but his Imperial Majesty has graciously allowed your sister and her husband to write letters to each other during the period of the former Elector's imprisonment."

"How long will he be in prison?"

"That I do not know, my lady, but be assured the Emperor is now determined that peace will rain upon Saxony. He speaks highly of your sister, of her courage and grace, of her devotion to her husband. He will not seek further revenge upon her or Saxony."

I had news not long after that Sybylla had been 'permitted' by the Emperor to remain Lady Keeper of Wittenberg. Her husband was his prisoner, and Duke Moritz was to be the Elector of Saxony, but my sister had not lost everything. Her sons were allowed to stay with her, and some Ernestine lands were restored to them to govern.

They had lost much, but not all, and that was something.

I wrote to my sister, a long letter full of love and sorrow, mourning with her for the imprisonment of her husband, but full of gratitude she had not lost him to death – for the Emperor seemed to want him kept alive – and that she still had her sons.

As I mourned for my sister and her people, I found I had other problems all my own.

"I am in debt?" I asked. "But how can this be?"

Jasper Brockehouse, a man of my own country sent by the council to inform me of my predicament, and to attempt to solve it, was a kind man. He tried to explain.

What I did not realise until the old King died was that my former husband had, in essence, been protecting me in a way I never had known. The price of food and other essential items had been increasing as the population of England grew, and taxes had increased also. There had been an escalation in vagrancy, due to the King's dissolution of the monasteries and other matters, and when bad harvests struck, tenant farmers and others working the land had started to depart the country and come to the city. The old King had been debasing the coinage of England to pay for his lavish court and his wars, which meant he had ordered his men to mix base metals with precious ones in England's coins, damaging the economy. He had, in fact, become known in his latter years as "old coppernose" because as the slim silver layer on the coins wore away so copper underneath became visible. This debasement meant there was now a gold shortage, and England's coins were not trusted by men of other lands, causing trade problems.

All this led to one problem for me, many more for others; my income did not stretch as once it did. The King had, in fact, been supplementing my income so I never felt the repercussions of his policies on the economy, but now he was gone his son was not willing to do the same.

The old King had paid extra money to my servants to supplement their income too, had paid for doctors when I or my household required them. This I had thought was all part of our agreement, but the new council, and our new King Somerset, no longer wanted this expense.

My household was now hard to support, and my houses would not be looked after as they had before. I had always seen it as the King's duty to undertake repairs, since he was the owner of these houses, and I simply lived in them for the duration of my lifetime, but the council were not willing to maintain the houses in which I lived. I also had accepted into my house my cousin, Count von Waldeck, who was visiting England and had eight servants of his own. The Count did not respond well to Brockehouse being appointed as my cofferer, sent to try to straighten out the mess my finances were in.

"I do not understand, cousin," Waldeck told me when I said Brockehouse was there to see how to reduce expenses. "You are a born Duchess of Cleves, and Princess of England. Who should be maintained by the Crown of England if not you?"

It was a fair question, and since I had always been refused permission to return home, it seemed unfair to me too. I had been offered maintenance of my household by the former King and expected a certain standard of living as the former King's sister, yet now the new King, or rather Edward Seymour, seemed to want to strip this from me. It was not simply that I was accustomed to lavishness, and this was selfishness, which I believe was what those men thought, but that I was responsible for many hundreds of people in my service, in my household and on my estates. Their livelihoods relied on my position and without employment with me they would have to take lesser roles in lesser houses, if they could even get them.

Also, considering the vast rewards of lands and money and titles men of the council had piled upon themselves, accusing me now of intemperate, lavish living was rather hypocritical. The truth was, all they had was not enough. They wanted more, and the more they wanted was in my hands, and those of others, like the Dowager Queen.

Brockehouse became immediately unpopular with my servants as he tried to reduce expenses and my cousin thought him a swindler, sent by "idle men" as he put it, on the council. But Brockehouse also advised me as to how to gain the pension supposed to be paid to me. The council had been delaying and holding back payments.

I petitioned the King, and the council. Mindful of the promises of the former King and of my popularity in the country – since I was then being compared most favourably to poor Katherine Parr – they agreed that I was to have all grants and pensions I had been promised until King Edward reached the age of eighteen. This was a victory, of sorts, but I still had a shortfall in my income, as Brockehouse explained.

"The trouble is, my lady, even with all grants and pensions being paid, we still have not enough to cover the yearly costs of your household, and the transfer of the house of Bletchingley in favour of Penshurst was another blow to your income. The park of Penshurst is not as profitable as that of Bletchingley, and the old King's additional, regular gifts will no more be coming either, so we have more expenses mounting without funds to pay for them."

I came to rely on Brockehouse over the years and he worked hard, trying to save a penny here and a shilling there, trying to rescue me from debt. My pension from the council was often in arrears, and anything I was paid was paid slowly, grudgingly, often leaving me in trouble. Brockehouse was the reason I did not fall into despair over my finances.

"In truth, my friend, the debt matters little. Who is going to refuse you goods?" asked my friend Katherine. "The council will eventually have to capitulate, and you are popular with the people again, which goes in your favour."

I wondered about my position in England. In March my brother had begun again to send envoys to petition for my return to my homeland, I believe because he wished to marry me off as he was trying to do with Amalia. But the council were not willing to release me. They wanted me here, but they did not want to maintain me.

There was much talk of Richmond being stripped from me, my principal residence, but as I held my breath, nothing was done, not then.

I felt helpless, not only about my income and houses, but about my sister. Sybylla wrote to me, asking that since King Edward was my nephew – a wording which showed her desperation as ever she had referred to me before as the Queen of England, refusing to acknowledge the dissolution of my marriage – could I petition him to speak out and have her husband released? It was possible I might have persuaded my former husband to speak for my sister and her family, but he had died a spare four months before the Siege of Wittenberg. The English appeared to be making friends with the French again and although I knew that Edward's Protestant council were likely to support Johann Friedrich and his cause in general, I wondered if sympathy in faith would lead them to speak for him.

The English being friends with France posed another problem as well, since my brother was now allied with the Holy Roman Emperor. It was possible in that respect that my brother might be able to support Sybylla and her family, using his position with the Emperor to petition for release of our brother-in-law, but Wilhelm was not likely to speak up. He had not uttered a word of protest as my sister's country was sacked.

One of the reasons I thought the English would do nothing at that time was because they were busy. In the summer that year Protector Somerset invaded Scotland. Later people named it the "rough wooing". It had begun with Henry VIII, as he attempted to subdue Scotland in order that the little Queen Mary Stuart might be engaged to Edward.

Oddly, perhaps, it was events in France which led to this latest war. At the end of March François of France had died, rushing after his rival Henry VIII to the grave. The new King, his son Henri II, was determined to take Boulogne back from the English, and as he ascended to the throne the Guise family came to power anew. Marie de Guise was the widow of James V of Scotland and mother of Mary Queen of Scots, and as her family in France rose in prominence again, she succeeded in gaining ascendancy over her rivals in Scotland and sought to ally Scotland closer with France. Although the Scots had made a treaty with my former husband some years before, in truth it had promised little, but now the thought was Marie would refuse the marriage the English thought arranged between King Edward and her daughter.

Therefore, Somerset decided the way to convince the Scots was to invade Scotland, violence being ever the answer to dispute in many a marriage, even one not yet begun. The campaigns of King Henry had achieved little, and Somerset decided that nothing less than the total conquest of Scotland would do. At the same time, the English were wooing the French, trying to keep them away from Boulogne and from supporting Scotland.

"Somerset wants to set up garrisons in Scotland." Katherine Willoughby sounded unimpressed. "Which will be manned by English troops and mercenaries from abroad."

Somerset led the troops himself and reached Berwick on the 30th of August with 16,000 men. A naval force of 80 vessels and another 9,000 sailors sailed up the coast. There was an offer of peace made to the Scots which was conditional on the acceptance of the marriage of Edward and Mary but this being rejected by Mary de Guise, battle seemed imminent.

The place chosen was Pinkie near Edinburgh, and whilst it seemed the Scots clearly had the upper hand, for they had more men and the location they had picked was impregnable, they made a fatal error, deciding to attack rather than simply defend. English broadsides pounded the Scottish army, and it fell into disarray. The Scots broke and ran in three directions, one towards the beach at Leith, another towards the walls of Edinburgh and some into a marsh near Dalkeith, which was perhaps the wisest since it proved impossible to pursue them through the murky waters.

The English chased them for miles, for five hours, resulting in mass slaughter. Many Scots threw their weapons away as they ran hoping to gain speed and were hacked to death from behind. Some few put on a last stand, and many more feigned death. Some concealed themselves in rivers, just their noses sticking above the surface of the water. It was said some even died of exhaustion, having run for five hours from their enemies.

When the battle ended it was said the bodies lay thick and the rivers flowed red with blood. 13,000 Scots died that day.

"The King is overjoyed," my friend of Suffolk told me, "and has written to Somerset commending him for his victory and also lecturing him on the virtues of equity and justice. When the King was told that Catholic priests and monks had been within the front ranks of those killed, he seemed in ecstasy."

I felt ill to think a child thought of such a glut of death with glee.

There was a victory procession held in Saint Paul's Cathedral and a *Te Deum* was sung in English to give thanks. There were celebrations all through the night with bonfires lit and people dancing about them. Yet Somerset did not stay to press his advantage and there was a good reason for this.

"Whilst elder Seymour is away, it seems the younger will play." The Dowager of Suffolk's eyes sparkled dangerously. "Thomas Seymour is attempting to raise opposition to the authority of his brother and is voicing open condemnation on the administration of our Protector. Several members of the nobility have advised Seymour to keep his mouth closed and be content with his position, but the Lord Admiral will not listen. He is openly asking for support in case of rebellion, which many think he may well lead himself. There is gossip that he has entered into talks with pirates on the western coasts to try and secure their support for any uprising he might decide to undertake."

"You sound excited, Katherine," I observed.

"What is dangerous often makes one feel alive," she said, "probably because at such times we skirt close to death."

Thomas Seymour had influence over King Edward, for the young King thought him wild and bold and free and liked him. This, coupled with the news that Thomas Seymour had tried to form a faction against his own brother, led to Edward Seymour rushing home.

When Somerset returned, to the shock of many he did not dismiss or attempt to arrest his brother, but they merely had words. Somerset accosted Seymour for laziness in discharging his duties as Admiral. Straight after this Thomas Seymour ran straight to the King's apartment in Saint James's Palace and demanded an audience. King Edward did not appear since he was at his lessons, or perhaps he had been told not to by Somerset.

But it seemed Thomas Seymour was not to give up. Rumour was he began to visit his nephew frequently, whispering in his ear that the invasion of Scotland was a waste of men and money, and started to give presents of money to the King. You might think that a king would have little need for coin but in truth Edward had only a small allowance from the Privy Purse which was controlled by Somerset.

"My uncle of Somerset," the King mentioned to his men, "dealeth very hardly with me and keepeth me so straight that I cannot have any money at my will."

We soon heard Thomas Seymour was not the only issue Protector Somerset was facing.

"The rot has begun to set in." My friend could not quite keep a note of pleasure from her tone.

Chapter Twenty-One

Autumn – Winter 1547

Hever Castle

In September of that year the Princess Elizabeth became fourteen years of age, and I asked permission that she be allowed to stay with me for a time.

Elizabeth had quite recently been handed to the guardianship of her stepmother Katherine Parr, and her husband Thomas Seymour. It seemed the King, thinking well of his uncle now that Seymour was feeding him money, thought this the best place for his sister. Katherine Parr already was caring for Lady Jane Grey, step-granddaughter of my friend of Suffolk. Jane Grey was another claimant to the throne, though a more distant one, since she was descended from Mary Tudor, sister of the former King. Some viewed Jane as perhaps more legitimate than Elizabeth, despite provisions during the reign of the old King which had restored both Mary and Elizabeth to the line of succession. Jane's birth was not in dispute, however, unlike that of both daughters of the former King.

Jane Grey, however, had no pretensions to the throne. She was listed behind her cousins Edward, Mary and Elizabeth, and her mother Frances, and I think Jane would have been happy to remain ever in her chamber, reading, for she was a studious child. "And one much given to the true faith," boasted Katherine Willoughby with great approval. "Her mother has always been a little light of faith and her father Henry Grey is a cretin beyond measure of comparison, but Jane is a clever girl, one I am proud of. Her sisters Mary and Katherine are good women too, or will be in time, although Mary is sadly of a deformed body, but her mind is sharp."

Frances had experienced a difficult labour with her last child, and Mary's body had been cruelly twisted. It had been thought she would not live, but in one of those miracles of resilience, the girl had. She was short and it was said her spine was misshapen, but she had endured.

I sighed a little at mention of the true faith. I had expected some zeal to burst forth as the new King took his throne, but the speed at which matters had moved that year had shocked many besides me.

On Ash Wednesday Bishop Ridley had denounced images of saints as heretical, and many papers had been printed in London condemning the whole practice of Lent, leading to Gardiner and other conservatives on the council wailing in protest. Van der Delft had come to me to tell me he thought things in England were taking "a strange turn" which turned out to be a gross underestimation.

Fired up with the fervour of faith, and new freedom to express it, Protestants, Calvinists and all those interested in the evangelical way of thinking were splitting fast into segments and roaring into extreme and swift action. Even Somerset, adherent of the new faith as he was, appeared to think it was too much. Attacks on images in churches and statues being smashed became so common that in May a proclamation had to be issued stating that no great religious change was planned by the government, but people did not believe it. Widely people of the reformed faith were defaming the Sacrament, calling the bread of the Mass "Jack in the box" and furiously attacking the notion it could hold the real presence of Christ within it. The Sacrament was not literal, they argued, but symbolic and to think it was literal, as Catholics did, was to believe in magic and superstition. The very things that Anne Askew had been burned to death for not so very long ago were now being shouted as truths in the street. Some Catholics were already fleeing the country, in the fear that as images and statues were being attacked, so people would follow soon enough.

Then, in the summer, thirty commissioners had been appointed to visit the counties of England, carrying injunctions that sermons and services of the Church were to be delivered in English, Scripture was to be read by the laity, and image worship and pilgrimage were to be discouraged. Rosary beads were condemned, parish processions and the ringing of bells banned. Candles were not to be used except on the altar before the Sacrament and not in rood-lofts. Images were to be removed and even destroyed, which included not only statues, but stained glass. Cranmer and others were delighted by the changes, many of which reportedly came from King Edward himself, but for many people, especially the common people, this was a great deal of change, and it was too brutal, too fast. At the moment common people were stunned, paralysed by the changes, but in time I though they would find their feet and learn to move again, and then would come trouble.

Hearing my friend gush about the reformed faith, therefore, and knowing she was in full support of these changes was hard. I thought Katherine and many others were becoming caught up in something which would do great and lasting harm.

"I am glad she is interested in faith, my friend, but as for people being light of faith, I come to think that may be the best way."

Katherine frowned. "What do you mean?"

"Christ tells us to love our neighbour, to judge not, to offer our hearts to God. I will worship however the state of England commands and hold my own faith in my heart, but I fear all this swift change. It seems to me those light of faith may withstand the changes better than those who are deep mired in tradition, and for those who love the tradition of the Mass and the Catholic faith, all this change will be hard and will strike fear deep into them. The people do not yet understand all that happened in the last King's reign, for it happened so fast, and now change comes only faster. People are already fleeing England for fear, so what else will fear bring?"

"The churches are being rid of superstition, so people can become closer to God in a personal sense, this is a good thing."

I breathed in. "Perhaps, and there may be much to what you say, but to me it seems that one set of tradition, that of opulence and I might say beauty, is simply being replaced by another, that of starkness and personal faith. The new faith, though you and others might not wish to hear it, has as many traditions and customs as the last. I do not think God would want us to be so caught up in *how* to worship Him. I think He cares only that we do, but more than this, that we do not become distracted from the true teachings of His son by obsessing over the manner in which we approach our faith. All this concentration on detail, my friend, I fear it divides us and misses the larger points, to be kind, to be loving, to welcome our neighbour. We are lost, staring at the stitches on a tapestry, when we should be standing back, appreciating the glory of the finished work."

"But that is just what the removal of images and the services in English will do," as my friend argued, tiny spots of red appeared on her cheeks. I wondered, much as I loved my friend, if it was even safe to speak to her of my reservations. Katherine would not betray me, should it come to that, but another such as Carew might overhear and have me sent before the council as a heretic. I could little afford to be accused of such now, with men after my houses and the council seeking ways to stall on sending my pension. Still, though, I wanted my friend to understand my mind.

"As you say, and it might. I do not deny there is trouble with confusion in the Catholic Mass as people do not understand the words of Latin spoken, and I agree there should be more concentration on learning the teachings of Christ than on standing before a statue praying for a saint to intercede, but I think you miss my point. Both strands of the faith, they are arguing on *how* Our Lord should be worshipped, and not truly *following* the ways and paths of faith. Where is our acceptance of others in all this judgment? Where is our love for our neighbour when we condemn him? Christ did not ever state we should not love another man because he was of another faith than us, nor of another country. We are so busy, my friend, trying to be right that we forget to do what is right."

Katherine mused on my words a little, but she agreed with and supported the changes to the faith, so we were never going to fully concur on the subject.

"Jane Grey," she coughed a little, heading back to a safer topic, "is a good and studious girl."

"I am glad to hear it. Since the Lady Elizabeth is the same, I hope the Dowager's house will be a merry one, full of intelligent women of our generation and the next."

Elizabeth had gone to live with Jane Grey, whose wardship Seymour had managed to purchase at the start of the year, and with her stepmother Katherine. But it was said I might have the girl for a visit for a short time. I took her to the one place I had always promised I would, to Hever Castle, to the home of her mother. To a ghost I had made this promise, and I would always keep an oath sworn to the dead.

Before we left however, there was news of the further troubles of our poor Protector Somerset. Not only was his brother turning on him, stating that he had "read" – personally I doubted Thomas Seymour himself opened books a great deal – that in the past there had been the roles of Protector and Governor of the King in a minority – that of Henry VI – and therefore there should be one Protector of the realm and one Governor of the King, and of course Thomas Seymour should be the Governor, but now the Protector had other problems too.

Regarding the religious changes some were finding Somerset too mild. Cranmer and others thought he should be supporting the changes outright and pushing more forth, and he was not, and some thought him too extreme. Gardiner and the conservatives thought he should be speaking out, stopping the swiftness of change. The fact was, Somerset was acting in a more moderate fashion than any had expected him to, perhaps because he believed the faith should be altered by Edward, as Head of the Church, when he reached his majority.

Having said all that, however, Somerset was hardly stopping the alterations to the faith, and they appeared to have the support of the King, who was himself a tiny zealot, so why attempt to ride a middle path? Perhaps to keep his position, which was, for the first time, teetering a little.

It was true he still had complete control of the council and was also true he had started to disregard them in some areas, but faith in Somerset was waning and he had more than one critic. War with Scotland had cost much money and did not seem to have got England any closer to possessing the marriage rights of Mary of Scots, inflation was rising and commissioners sent out to ensure right practice of the faith appeared to be spiralling out of control. On the 5th of September images were destroyed in the Cathedral of St Paul's and all through England there was mass, somewhat hysterical obliteration of images and statues, stained glass and wall paintings. What Cawarden had done to my church in Bletchingley was done elsewhere as walls which had held beautiful paintings of images of the Bible were painted over with whitewash, and text from the Ten Commandments was set in their place.

"In Shropshire, the sacred relics, the very bones, of a saint were burned." Van der Delft was clearly scandalised. "And in Durham one of the commissioners got so carried away he broke a statue to bits with his own hands." He sighed. "Bishops Bonner and Gardiner attempted to protest and have been arrested and placed in gaol. Many are making a pretty penny from this. I hear that in Greyfriars Church near Saint Paul's men pulled up all the tombs as well as the great stones of the altar and walls of the choir, and they have sold the materials, saying God has no use for such trifles, but they need the money."

"It sounds as if England will descend into anarchy," I said.

"The council fears such, indeed, my lady, but Somerset is slow to act. He wants the support of the people, and the most vocal people at the moment are those screaming out for more change."

The council proclaimed any images "not abused" as in, not worshipped, could be kept, and stained-glass windows which held images of popes could be merely covered rather than destroyed, but it was too late. Assaults on churches continued. That November the rood-loft of Saint Paul's would be torn down along with images of Mary and Joseph, and two men were killed in the process. Open arguments erupted even during services between members of the congregation, and evangelicals attacked the Sacrament if they felt it was being venerated. More priests and men of the cloth went to gaol for speaking out against the widespread destruction, as evangelicals howled at such men that they were whoresons and heretics.

In this time of chaos, Elizabeth came with me to Hever for a few days.

"I have longed to show you this house." We rode towards Hever, stopping on a bank which undulated towards the pretty castle. "It was home to your ancestors."

She nodded but said nothing. Those dark eyes were careful. She knew not to speak of her mother. The reputation of Anne Boleyn was something which would haunt her for all her days, I knew that, but I wanted her to see her mother's home. To feel the spirit of her mother which I still felt there. I believed the lady had gone innocent to her death, and I believed Elizabeth thought the same. Only ever did she mention her mother when in extreme distress. Even at such a young age, she was cautious, not wanting people to link her with the disgrace in which her mother had died.

"Do you ever wish to return home, my lady?" she asked as we rode for the house.

"I have many times wished to, but I think now that by choice or not, the rest of my life belongs to England. My family sent me here to rule our people, at the side of the King, but that was not my fate, and if I returned now to my home, it would not be the one I remember. My mother, who was such a force in our country, she is gone, and my brother has lost much of its independence. I think I would rather remain apart, my memories of how Cleves was intact in my mind."

"Do you become lonesome, at times, Highness?"

I smiled. "We all do, whether we are with those we love or not. My household, these people are my friends, the family I made here in England. They are enough for me, along with friends of the nobility."

"Did you never think to wed again, after my father?"

I glanced at her. It was known by that time of course that Katherine and Thomas Seymour were wed, and Elizabeth could not be unaware that the Queen was being much vilified all over England for it. Ditties sung against her were rife in the streets. Elizabeth had said little on the subject, but I wondered if she felt as her sister Mary did and was aghast that her stepmother had so swift forgotten her 'love' for Henry VIII.

I shifted my reins to my left hand. "I did not. In truth, although I respected your great father, I married him out of duty rather than love, and I never have been offered a match which I thought would add to the life I was granted by your good father when we ended our marriage. I was left as a widow, in many ways, for I was set free of the shackles of marriage and was allowed to live free, alone, to manage my own time and household. I have never thought to exchange that state of freedom for the bonds of marriage."

"You speak as if marriage is a prison, my lady." We walked our horses down the path to the castle, birdsong surrounding us, trees in the park shifting gently in the breeze.

"It can be so, for women," I said. "You know this yourself, do you not? I heard that once you said to your brother's friend, little Robin Dudley, that you would never wish to marry. You are aware of the benefits of children and company that might come, so why make such a comment?"

She paused. "It seems to me that marriage can be death for a woman." Her voice was quiet, sorrowful.

Elizabeth had made that comment some years ago, when Catherine Howard died. The little girl must have been reminded, in the death of her Howard cousin, of the death of her mother.

There was silence a moment as we thought on each other's words. "You are happy, though, Highness?" she asked eventually, her words taking on a tone of true curiosity. "People say an unwed woman cannot be happy, but I have wondered, thinking of you and the tales of how you enjoy your life."

"I am happier alone than I ever was when married. Again, mistake me not, I respected your father, but we were not a good match, he and I. Others placed us together for reasons of alliance and duty, and we both attempted the marriage because of those things, but your father was right to separate from me. We were not for one another, and were far merrier as good friends, as brother and sister, than we ever were when wed. In truth, when we were separated from marriage was when we were able to know each other. I think, had we remained married, we might have been strangers to one another all our lives. The necessity placed upon us at that time was too much a strain, you see, but freed of it we could become ourselves, and close to each other. Friendship is a greater love at times than the love between married people."

"I think I will be married where I care not to be," she said. "People speak of it now."

"Where would you care to be married, if at all?"

"If at all..." She sounded wistful. "I envy you at times, my lady. You have the option of 'if at all' where I do not."

"If there is one thing I have learned of the future, it is that it is ever to be decided, nothing is set, nothing certain, and all is change. In such a condition of life, there is much that is possible, if a woman has a mind to will it so."

We clopped into the little courtyard, and I saw the girl looking up at the building about us, bright windows glinting the sunlight down on our faces. Servants came rushing out of the house. Some of them, the oldest, had served Hever during the time of her mother, and I saw them watching the girl with curious, affectionate eyes. Perhaps Elizabeth felt this welcome, this love already offered to her because of her blood-ties to this house of stone and brick, for she smiled at me with an unusual flush on her pale cheeks. "I think this a good house, my lady," she said.

"It is," I told her.

As we walked inside, I could almost hear a sigh from the ghost who wandered sometimes in my mind. A noise of contentment and relief, of love which death never could touch, and why should he wish to do so? Death wanders the world between the living and the dead just as love does, and both may touch either side. He would not want to take away a fellow wanderer whose hands stretched to link the otherworld and our world. In all probability, Death and Love were greater friends than any of us might imagine.

*

"Your brother will rebuild the palace, then, Highness?" Elizabeth asked as after dinner we sat in the hall by the fire. I had a letter from Wilhelm, which I had read to her.

She had not commented on the portrait of her mother I had left in her room, neither had Mistress Ashley, her woman. I had covered the section which had Anne Boleyn's name on it, thereby allowing any servants to deny they had seen the picture of Elizabeth's mother. It could be another woman of the Boleyn line, after all, but I knew Elizabeth would know her mother, just as I knew her servants were loyal and devoted, and many of them had been kin to Anne Boleyn, so would say nothing. I was not sure it was even a command anymore, that we were not to speak of her, and images of her were not to be hung on walls. Just to be sure, I had covered the name, but I wanted Elizabeth to look on the face of her mother. She would see those dark eyes in her own face had come from this woman in whose house we rested now, full after a fine dinner.

"He will, at some stage." I folded the paper. "It makes me sad, though. I am glad in some ways my mother is not here to know what happened to the City of Julich."

The letter was from my brother's wife. Maria of Austria was more communicative than my brother had ever been, though they had not been married long she had written to me often. This letter informed me that a great fire had destroyed what was left of the remaining old buildings in the City of Julich. There had been much destruction after the Emperor's invasion and my brother had already been rebuilding, but due to this fire now much of the city my mother had known was gone, like her. The thought of her death came to me fresh as the day she died. It stung a moment, then eased. I could think of her now without the barbs of her ghost tearing me apart. They still pained me, though. I thought they always would.

"But something new and glorious might be built in place of the old," suggested Elizabeth.

"It might."

"Perhaps to think of it as the new religious changes here in England would aid you, my lady." I looked up, disturbed by the sheen of zeal I saw in her eyes, a light I had seen all too many times of late. I knew Elizabeth had been raised as her brother, in the reformed faith, but all the same it was a shock to see that almost vacant expression of vehemence illuminate her eyes.

"To my mind," I said gently, folding the paper into my lap, "There is much schism caused by men wishing to stamp their way of thinking, and worship, on one another. Catholic or Protestant, how much harm do we do to one another as we try to impose what we think is right on one another?"

"Yet there is a right way to worship and a wrong way, my lady."

"So men will ever argue, yet when his men asked Him how to know the way to God, Jesus said 'I am the way, the verity and the life, No man cometh unto the Father but by me.' Christ was telling His men that the ways to God He had told them were the true ways."

"'If ye love me, keep my commandments,' said Christ," Elizabeth interjected. "Is not one of the commandments not to worship graven images?"

"And yet Christ did not say 'the' commandments, but 'my' commandments, and, although I am no scholar, my lady, it always seemed to me the two laws Jesus upheld in His teachings to His disciples were to love God and love thy neighbour. When men asked Christ who this neighbour was, He told the tale of the Samaritan who saved a man others left to die. Christ made it clear it was those who showed mercy to all, no matter their religion or race, who were to be upheld as the true inheritors of eternal life and the love of God. Mercy and justice were the two laws I believe Christ upheld, and it was those commandments of which He spoke."

"So, you think He was speaking of his own commandments?"

I held a hand to my heart. "I am not as clever as many who study the Bible, but I do not think Christ was being vague. Many of His teachings we follow rather than those of the Old Testament, do we not? Should it not be that we love our neighbour rather than seek an eye for an eye? It seems to me that at this time we have become obsessed with one commandment, about idols, and forgotten many others. Men may murder so that others will not worship idols, is that right?"

"Of course not, but the changes of my brother's government are done to bring the people closer to God." She put her long fingers against each other, hand pressing hand, in an expression almost of prayer, but it was a way to centre her thoughts.

"If that were all it was, it would be a fine goal, my lady, but I think it is not all it is. Men, insecure in their faith, seek to make others agree with them because they believe if more people agree with them, it makes them more right. But faith, true faith, needs this not, and when we start to force men to agree with us with fire and stake and murder, we forget we are failing to uphold another of the commandments. Christ told us to love, not to hate one another, and this change done now, I think it should be done gentler, not in such a rush. The people do not understand it, they fear it, and that could be dangerous for the King, no matter how much good he intends."

Elizabeth sat quietly for a moment. "My tutors tell me that the way of Catholics is the way of superstition."

"There is much that is ill in the Catholic faith. Eons of men seeking power in it, through the papacy, have corrupted much, but not all is ill in it, just as not all is good in the reformed faith. The trouble is that both are formed by men, these ways of worship, and not by the divine hand, and therefore much of man gets mixed up in the purity of faith. Reform should ever be a part of the faith, we should always seek to make our faith better, our worship pure and our hearts unhindered by the ways of man, but does it stand that the way one person chooses to come to God is so very wrong, if it is right for them?"

"What do you believe, my lady?"

I lifted my eyes to the ceiling, where Boleyn bulls were carved. "I worship in the way of England, and that is for the King and his men to decide. I will ever do so, for I was welcomed by this country and so it is not for me to go against the ruler of England in public. But in my heart, I have my own ways. I take parts of the faith I was raised in, and I mingle them with the reform I was taught. In Cleves, we were ever exposed to both sides, you see, therefore perhaps I have more knowledge of both sides than many others. I see their goodness and their flaws. I was raised in the gulf between them, and what I can tell you is that in seeing both sides, I would say they are more alike than they are different, when one gets down to essentials. Here and now, men are caught up with all that is different between them and are failing to see what is similar. That does not please me."

My eyes came to hers. "I think we, in this time and others, become obsessed with trifles, with slight differences in the way we worship and think about the faith." I stared into her eyes. "We all worship the same God," I said. "If men remembered that more often, there would be more peace, and God loves peace, that much is evident to me."

"So, you are of your own faith?" Her hands came to her lap, and she leant forwards.

"I think all people are. Does not the reformist movement encourage personal contact with the faith? The King is Head of the Church, therefore in loyalty to him I will worship as I am told, but my connection to God is my own, and ever will it be. I do not need anyone else to agree with me on religion in order for my own personal faith to be important to me."

She thought a while. "It is important, as you say, that all people worship in public as their ruler tells them. After all, if they do not then there will be schism and uprising." She smiled. "But I too think in ways personal about God." She paused. "I was a little sad, I admit, about the things done to churches, Saint Paul's most especially. I feel awe when I stand before stained glass and often when I see the beauty of a church, and to hear they are abused so, though my tutors said it was a good thing, does not sit right in my heart."

There was not that light of empty, mindless zeal in her eyes now, but a gleam of intelligence and consideration. That is the problem with the faith at times, and why, like any ideology, it is so seductive; it can lead people to lose their own thoughts, to abandon their minds to what they think is the light of God. I did not think that was the light of God, for God gave us minds and what are we to do with those but think? Blind devotion to one worldly practice of faith or the other was not, I was sure, what Christ had wanted. Devotion to the true lessons of the Bible, and setting them into action in our lives, the ability to think and consider good and evil for ourselves, that was what I believed Jesus wanted of us.

"It did not with me, either," I said. "Mistake me not, I do not think people should concentrate on saints or statues and not look to God, but I see no harm in the places we worship being pretty. Awe is one of the things which makes life worth living, is it not? Wonder, beauty… the appreciation of what God has granted, and God loves beauty, that much is obvious when one looks at this world of marvels He constructed. I do not think we should give so much to the Church that we cannot support the poor, or education for the young, but can there not be balance? Why does it always seem we must give all to one side and not balance out our giving to another? Why can we not have a way to all worship as one, united country, but not seek to obliterate those who wish to worship in a slightly different way? This argument over the Sacrament, it is slight in comparison to the other teachings of Christ, is it not? He never thought it important to say outright whether He meant the words of the Last Supper literally or metaphorically, so why should we spend so much time fighting over it? I think we would be better suited to read more of His good words on charity, mercy and peace, love, justice and kindness, and focus our passion there, rather than dispute endlessly about trifles of ceremony."

"I had never thought of it in such a way." Elizabeth sat back. "My tutors always tell me how important such things are, but you are right, Highness. Insignificant do these matters seem when one thinks about the rest of the teachings of Christ."

"Christ often condemned public displays of faith, especially if the people doing them were, in their own lives, not following His teachings on mercy and justice. What is important is what is in our hearts, in our actions, not how we flaunt our faith before the world."

Elizabeth nodded thoughtfully.

"Although I am glad you think as I do, it would be better not to argue thus with your tutors," I warned. "I would be in a great deal of trouble for trying to offer the idea of balance to you. No doubt both sides of the schism would name me a heretic."

"I shall say nothing, of that, you have my word. But I want to thank you, my lady. You have given me a great deal to think about. Perhaps my father was more right than he knew, to construct a middle way between the faiths. People have been telling me since my brother came to the throne that my father's way was confusing and did not go far enough, but perhaps he thought as you do, and saw there was a balance to be struck."

"Your father was a learned man, in many ways, not least of them the hearts of his people." In truth, I believed my former husband had adopted reform for the sake of power and retained Catholicism for the sake of fear, but I was not about to say that to Elizabeth. All she had left was the memory of her father, and I had no doubt it was a confusing enough love for her heart to contend with without me condemning him as a hypocrite. "Balance is something to be admired, just as peace is more profitable than war for a country and love more valuable than hate."

"And friendship above all." She beamed. "When it is true."

"Friendship is the greatest consolation of my life, I only hope you always have friends as I have been blessed with."

"My household are my friends too, my lady, just as yours are. I was in truth raised more by them than anyone else. My father was busy often, that I know, but I was left in the hands of good people."

"Keep those you love ever close," I counselled. "Trust where it is due, forgive often, and love much."

That night, her last with me in Kent, Elizabeth kissed my cheek and put her long-fingered hand upon mine. She said nothing more, but I could see her considering much anew and was glad of it.

A little more balance in this world of extremes, a little more pondering on peace rather than immediate adoption of war, even if carried by one only close to the throne and not upon it, could never be a bad thing.

Chapter Twenty-Two

1547

Richmond Palace

"But... it was promised to me. It is my primary residence, my home."

There was news; the council were determined to take Richmond from me. Stripping Bletchingley from me for Cawarden and replacing it with the smaller Penshurst was not enough. The King needed another London residence, and I had let Richmond get into a sorry state, so I heard, hardly was I caring for the property.

The council bleated, to whomsoever would listen to them whine, that I had not done anything to maintain the palace, which was true enough, but up until the death of the old King repairs had been taken on by his purse, since I was only ever leasing the house from him during my lifetime.

"But the old King was always the owner of Richmond and I his tenant," I protested to Brockehouse. "The King was happy to pay for repairs which needed doing. King Edward cannot think that I, his aunt and once his stepmother, should be turned out of my own house?"

I had returned to London, handing Elizabeth back to Katherine at her house in Chelsea, then had come home to this news. My primary residence! My Richmond! My warm box of London where I could stay close to the heart of court yet not within it, they wanted to strip it from me?

"The council are bleating that you are not maintaining the property as it should be, Highness, and as such they want it returned to the King." Brockehouse's eyes were sad.

"How can I maintain it now, when I have not money enough to sustain my own household in the state the King expects me to keep it in? And if they want me to make repairs, why not send the payments of my pension in goodly time, rather than always late?"

"Even if they were being sent on time, Highness, it would not be enough. In truth, I think the King's men do not want to pay to take care of a palace the King, and they, are not using."

I stuck my chin out in defiance. "I will not leave, Brockehouse. The old King promised me Richmond as my principal residence. It was his oath to me."

"I will let them know, my lady, but I fear it may only be a matter of time."

*

That November I petitioned the King, asking him to speak out for the release of Johann Friedrich from captivity. I knew not what good my voice might do, and I understood it might make my own situation with regards to Richmond worse if I irritated Edward and his council, but I wanted to do something for my sister. My brother could not be trusted, there was no evidence that he had spoken for leniency for Johann Friedrich, Sybylla or Saxony despite being closer to the Emperor than either of us.

My sister-in-law, Maria, however, had acted. One could say this was on behalf of her husband, and perhaps Wilhelm had asked her to do so, but I doubted it. He was too busy keeping his head down and rebuilding Julich in his new style – which Olisleger told me was a horror of a modern design my mother never would have approved of – to speak out for his sisters, one being slowly evicted from her principal residence and the other fighting to get her husband out of captivity.

Maria, on the other hand, was made of sterner stuff than the man she had married and appeared genuinely horrified about the treatment of her husband's kin by her own family. She appealed to the Emperor and wrote to King Edward herself, asking that he speak for Johann Friedrich. It was extraordinary, in a way, because she came from a fiercely Catholic family yet knowing Edward to be Protestant she appealed to him, hoping he would speak for one of his own faith. Maria was one who could find this balance I had spoken of to Elizabeth and set considerations of humanity above complications of human faith. Sybylla wrote in conjunction with her, and their petitions had reached King Edward before I came I to plead.

"Of course, we have great sympathy with the Schmalkaldic League and the imprisoned leader of Saxony," Somerset said smoothly. I looked to the King. I was on my knees before Edward, but Somerset was the one speaking. I was not sure, but I thought I could see a little glimmer of resentment in the eyes of King Edward. And *"we"*, said Somerset. *"We"*. Were he and the King the same person, then? Perhaps in his mind they had become so.

I stared straight at Edward. "The intercession of a King, great in mind and spirit, such as yourself, Your Majesty, would touch the Emperor, I am sure, and might lead him to think of mercy for my good brother of Saxony."

King Edward did not smile, but his pale eyes lit up at the praise. Not as much as you might think though. He liked to hear it, that was evident, but he was accustomed to it. Just a small spark did it ignite in his heart. Perhaps he was bored with so many men praising him and none of them hearing him, of being complimented and fawned upon as the new Josiah of England, this miracle brought to save us, yet being offered no power of his own. I wondered if Somerset was still holding back money from the King, and decided he must be.

"We are desirous of complying with the request of the Duchess of Cleves," King Edward announced, meaning my sister-in-law. His voice was high and reedy. "The release of Duke Johann is important to us, since he is of the true faith, and whilst the Duchess of Cleves would do well to look to her own method of worship, it cannot be denied that her request, like yours, my good aunt, is genuine and shall be taken up by us with all seriousness. I have already asked England's Ambassador to the Imperial Court to take a suit for clemency and release to the Emperor. If we can help to bring about liberation, we will."

The Emperor, however, sent a reply which did not please my Tudor nephew. Whilst he praised Edward, he also condemned him, supposing he had been easily persuaded by others, and since he was a "young prince" this was only to be expected.

"One should never remind the young they are young or the old they are old," I noted, hearing that the King was mightily indignant to be treated like a child. "The only people safe to call their own age are those in the middle of life, like me. We are happy to be named as old as we are, for there is no shame in it so far as the world thinks, but the moment one crosses the boundary of age either way, one is supposed incompetent by others, either a dribbling dotard, or a reckless, thoughtless youth."

Sadly, the King's sister, Mary, was doing much the same to the new King, treating him like a child. Every time he tried to lecture her about complying with the law and worshipping in the way he had set out for England, she resisted. Obviously, her faith was important to her, it had been in many ways the only thing she had to cling to that felt solid in a life of upheaval and loss, but the fact Mary kept reminding Edward he was too young to know his own mind was not helping their relationship. She felt he was being swayed in his youthful inexperience by men older than him, and he felt she was abusing her position of royal sister and challenging his authority. Both were, in truth, correct at least in part. I doubt Edward would have been quite so bent on the speed of reform if not for men like Cranmer, Latimer and Ridley being always about him, telling him it was the only way, but the siblings were also becoming increasingly afraid of one another, a schism driven between them by faith, the very thing which should bring men and women closer to one another.

Obviously the Emperor felt the same way about Edward as his cousin, and was not taking him seriously. The old King had not welcomed such treatment, and his son did not either.

"The Emperor will not release Duke Johann," the Dowager of Suffolk argued. "He knows that once the Duke is free, he would rise against him again. There is still too much disruption in the Germanic states for him to risk such. I wonder that the Duchess of Cleves attempted it, she must have known her uncle's will."

"It must have put her in a difficult position, his captivity." I examined a bracelet of pearls on my wrist, white globes of soft light, a touch of purity. Sometimes I thought they looked like tears. "She is Duchess of Cleves, and her own kinsman is making her the enemy of her own people. How is she to rule them in such a way? Saxony and Cleves have not always seen eye to eye, especially in religion, but my people remember that they sent a daughter of their house there, they remember how Sybylla was upheld and respected, and they certainly feel closer to the people of Saxony than to the Emperor and his men. Maria is in a hard position."

She was not alone. The council were sending letters continually about me giving up Richmond. They wanted me to surrender it voluntarily, you see, for then they would not be going against the wishes of the old King, and their scheme was to harass me out. Continual reminders of works that "had" to be done "immediately" and insinuations I was letting the palace fall down about my ears arrived weekly.

Soon enough, I would be forced out, I knew it, if I did not capitulate. Once more I was made to feel unwelcome, stuck in a country not my own, helpless to help those who needed me, and one of those people was myself.

Chapter Twenty-Three

1548

Richmond Palace and

Hever Castle

"There is nothing to be done, Your Highness."

I knew that was the case without Brockehouse telling me. The council had sent orders saying that Richmond was to be stripped from my hands. It was in such a "poor state" that I was ordered to voluntarily surrender it to the King so he might "put it to good order again". I had gone to London in May of that year to attempt to speak to Protector Somerset on this matter, but it did no good. In June that year I had to surrender the palace.

Losing Richmond left me without a good base in London, and my debts increased as my income dwindled, losing profitable estates to lesser ones. Whenever I complained about other problems, such as the continually late payments of my pension, the council would respond with an excuse, the King was on progress, or the administration of government took time. Often when I complained outright, they would pay me, but as often as they could manage it, payments were late and incomplete. It was hard to maintain my servants, some had to seek employment elsewhere.

One was Kitty, though it was not exactly employment she undertook. She had married in the year before, to Sir Henry Ashley, later a Member of Parliament and Vice-Admiral for Dorset, who, when she married him was a man who was not high and not low but seemed to love her dearly, and so I wished her well as she entered the state of matrimony and even more well when she told me she would retire from my service for at least a while that year, as she was expecting her first child.

"I wish you joy," I told her. "And a comfortable life."

"I wanted to thank you for all you ever have done for me, Highness." Kneeling, she took the bottom of my gown and kissed it. "Never did you abandon me."

In her place came Susan Boughton, a good woman who was as talented at her duties as Kitty, and rather more skilled at keeping her mouth closed before others. She was also excellent at gathering gossip both personal and political, a vital skill for the ladies who attend one higher than them.

But I was left with a problem — where to go as a permanent base now Richmond was taken? Hever was large enough, but it felt far from London, making it harder to see my friends, although the Dowager of Suffolk could come when she wanted since there were few roles at court for women now, and none in the King's main household. Until he had a wife, Edward's court would be a most masculine place, and there had only ever been a small amount of women allowed at court in the first place, mostly women serving the Queen or laundresses. Now, there were no roles for noblewomen to play. At feasts and dances they were brought in, the household of Mary, until recently, being quite welcome to offer relief of conversation and company to the men at certain times, but as the relationship between the King and his elder sister became only more strained over religion, Mary stayed away as much as possible, and until the King married there were few permanent places for noblewomen at court.

I had a house in Lewes, but I had never been there, and it was too small for my household. I could use Bletchingley, but as a visitor, and Cawarden made me feel most unwelcome whenever we went there. Bisham Abbey had a mansion house, and would suffice when I needed to visit London, but again it was not large enough to house us all a long time. So to Hever I went, using Penshurst nearby to travel to whenever Hever needed cleaning after my household had stayed there a while.

"They think if they can get me away from London, they can get away with not paying my income," I complained to Katherine of Suffolk.

"That may well be the case. And if it is so, appeal to your brother, make it obvious to the imperial ambassadors that you are not being paid on time, if at all."

As I departed, the King immediately ordered a thousand pounds' worth of "emergency" works on Richmond, as if to prove I had run the palace down on purpose. It was a small amount, truth be told, for such a vast palace and I thought it was done merely to make a point, demonstrating I had indeed done wrong and did not deserve the house promised to me. They tried to make me out to be a profligate waster of money, and yet still the council were rewarding each other with titles, lands and estates, never satisfied with the wealth they already had.

It was hypocrisy of the highest order, and I was amazed no one else could see it as plain as I could, but then, men are ever prone to believe women waste money and men do not. It is a convenient fiction, adding to the belief that we, poor simple-minded creatures that we are, need governing by men.

In truth, the old King had looked after me better than I had known. Was it out of guilt, I wondered, that he had supplemented my pension? Perhaps. He had always maintained himself in high state too, however, understanding that a king has a reputation to keep. Mayhap he had seen me, as his sister, as an extension of his own reputation, and had upheld my royal state for that reason.

I never thought I would have cause to bless his name, but in those days when his own son, my nephew, ran me out of my own house, I went to chapel and said a prayer for the soul of the old King, who had done much wrong and had caused me great fear, but had stuck by his promise to maintain me, at least.

I suppose we all may do one good thing, in a life of ills, keep one promise, in a jangled mass of lies.

Chapter Twenty-Four

1548

Hever Castle

"I am certain none of this can be true." My voice was firm as steel. "I know the Lady Elizabeth, and the Dowager, well. Elizabeth must simply have been sent away because the Dowager is soon to have her child, and the burdens of a large household are too much at this time."

"That certainly is the tale being put about." Katherine of Suffolk bunched her lips and lifted her brows, then continued. "But it is not the truth, and I am sorry to say, my friend, that the truth is indeed quite shocking."

Although the story being widely told about Elizabeth leaving her stepmother's household was indeed the one I had spoken of, a natural enough situation, the truth, as my friend had been told by Katherine Parr herself, was darker.

"Katherine does not blame Elizabeth, but I tell you, Anne, our friend has woken with a rude start to the kind of man she has married. She knows now Seymour has not respect or love for her."

Ever since Elizabeth had entered her stepmother's house, it seemed her stepfather had taken rather too much interest in her. Thomas Seymour had taken to visiting her room in the morning, when still only dressed in his bed shirt and without hose or stocking, so his legs and perhaps other parts were naked, to tickle the girl, who when this had started had been not yet fourteen. Later games had seen him chase her about her chamber, pouncing on her on the bed. Her servants had told him to desist and he would not listen. Elizabeth seemed to have responded with both fear and excitement, and people said they knew not if she was in love with the Admiral, or terrified of him. To me, it seemed both were possible at the same time. Talk in the household had begun and spread, and soon Katherine, then only newly with child, had heard of it but as proof that clever people may be blind, she had been persuaded it was all games, and "fatherly affection".

"Why did she believe so?" I felt ill.

"Because she loved him, and was pregnant with his child," said Katherine sadly. "Would you want to believe the worst of a man you loved?"

"I would wish to be clear of sight always, not blinded by such a thing as the deceit of love if this is what it brings upon us."

Katherine had started entering these 'larks' with Seymour, holding Elizabeth as he tickled her. Later 'games' had seen Seymour cornering Elizabeth in the gardens, and with Katherine's aid, cutting a dress Elizabeth was wearing to shreds with his knife, so the girl was forced to run into the house in almost nothing but her undergarments, with the eyes of the whole household looking on. "And Katherine held her, as Seymour cut her dress?" I was astonished, and appalled.

"She was again persuaded it was a game. Seymour said the dress was too old for Elizabeth and he did not like it."

Eventually it seemed things had come to a more serious head when Katherine had found Seymour and Elizabeth in some kind of embrace which could not be explained away as a game. "And she has sent Elizabeth away, in what, disgrace?" I asked.

"For her own protection. Katherine brought Elizabeth to her and told her she of all women had to take care, given how people would think of her in regard to the reputation of Anne Boleyn, but Katherine told me she said it only in warning to the girl. She has said little to Seymour on the matter and does not intend to, she must get along with him now. After all, she is so close to bearing his child and he has control over her life as her husband, but she blames him for what was going on. When she saw him trying to have his way with Lady Elizabeth, she understood what she had been blind to all this time; Seymour wanted Elizabeth, sexually and for lust, and he was using his position in the household to take her. Elizabeth was confused, so Kat Ashley said to Katherine, half petrified of Seymour and half in awe of him. In such a way has many a young girl without knowledge of the world or the ways of men been convinced they are in love and in a thrall made of awe and fear been seduced."

I paused, wondering on something. "What if it were revenge, also? Her father took Katherine from Seymour, married her. What if, in some way by claiming the daughter, he thought he would take revenge on the old King?"

"It is possible. Seymour is a strange man. There is also the fact Elizabeth is in line to the throne. Were she to become big with his child, the council and King might have had him set Katherine aside – and their match did not go ahead with royal approval as it should have, so annulment might have been possible – and had him marry Elizabeth to save a royal woman the shame of a bastard child being born. It would be a wild scheme, but had it paid off, he could have had a child in the line of succession, and found a place for himself as King, should Elizabeth ever become Queen."

I nodded. Wilder things had men done to gain power. "But, Katherine will continue to live with him?"

"I think we will see when her child is born. She needs him now, his houses and his good will. She is in a vulnerable position whilst with child, but I think when she has had her babe, she may petition the King for a separation, using this scandal to convince him. Some of her dower properties could be retained, perhaps her child could live with her too, if the King agrees, and then she can take her child and her broken heart and care for them both away from Seymour. Until then, she will play nicely with him, deceive him as he has her, and bide her time. If the King will not allow her to raise the child, she may have to stay with Seymour, for he, as the father, possesses all legal rights to the babe. She may have to play the loving wife forever, in order to remain with her own baby."

"And the Lady Elizabeth?"

"Will stay away with her own household, and for her own protection. Katherine said to me she was hurt by the girl too, she felt Elizabeth had betrayed her trust, but she admitted she also thought the Admiral more to blame. The Dowager will cover the truth of all this, hopefully no one else needs to find out, for the sake of Katherine's dignity, and for the reputation of Elizabeth."

"To think, she gave up the power to influence the council and the King to marry this man, and not a year later, this is how he treats her love." I shook my head in wonderment.

"Her life is not over, and she is about to become a mother, something she has always wanted," said Katherine. "Once she is free of Seymour, who knows what our good Dowager might do?"

We would never find out.

Days after bearing a girl, named Mary for the Lady Mary, Katherine Parr died. They said it was childbed fever which claimed her, in the country castle of Sudeley where Seymour had taken her for her confinement, playing the devoted husband who could not do enough now for his wife. She had come through birth fine, then sickened and eventually gave in to fever where she railed against Seymour, shouting that those she loved had betrayed her. Lady Tyrwhitt was with her at the end, and she said Katherine had claimed that the more good she willed to those she loved the less they willed her. When the Admiral had protested, saying he would not hurt her, Katherine snapped back that she thought he would. Her carefully stored-up rage and grief over his treatment of her, and perhaps Elizabeth too, came out in her delirium. She shouted she was not well handled, and people she loved laughed at her grief. It was a grim way to come to death.

Early in the morning on the 5th of September, Katherine Parr died. She had longed to be a mother, but a mother she was for only a few days.

"I wonder if she was able to hold her child more than once or twice," I said sadly.

Was marriage worth this? This destruction of woman after woman on the altar of childbearing, of their hearts on promise of love that never seemed to be real? Katherine Parr had been a leader, a writer, a thinker and a woman of genuine courage and compassion, and for a man like Thomas Seymour she had given all that up. To bear his child she had died, and died in the knowledge that he had betrayed her love and would have seduced her young stepdaughter under the same roof as his pregnant wife and might well have forced Elizabeth had he not succeeded in seduction. What a man to lose such a woman for.

I could not bear to hear his name after she died, could not bear to think on this fool who had wreaked so much devastation. Perhaps it was God's will that Katherine died, she was not young when she gave birth, but did she have to die knowing that all she had sacrificed in order to have love and a happy marriage was not worth it, and all she possessed was a lie? Death was cruel when he took Katherine, as cruel as he had been when every wife before her had fallen to death.

Was it some curse of the King's? That every wife of his would die a miserable death, knowing they had been abandoned by the one they thought was there to protect them? Was I to face this too?

"My lady, in the wake of the Dowager's death, we should examine something which may be of advantage to you," Brockehouse told me.

"What advantage is there for the world to lose a woman like Katherine, and to keep a man like Seymour?" I felt miserable as I stared out into the grounds of Hever. There was a low mist on the air, rising from marshes nearby. It was covering everything in a grey blanket, as if grief had become a ghost, and was overtaking the world.

"With the Dowager gone, God rest her, there is no one holding the title Dowager Queen of England, my lady, but if you were awarded that position, it might be an end to your troubles with income. In such a position, the council could not withhold your funds, they would be increased in fact, and the former dower properties of the Dowager might become yours, which would mean you would be financially secure again, my lady. You are the only woman left in England with any right to the title."

I did not turn from the window. "It seems crass to try to profit from the death of a woman I considered a friend."

"Men of the council will take her lands if you do not, and would she not have preferred you to have them?"

"She might, I know not." I sighed. It was true I needed money. "Make enquiries, see if you can get support for the idea. Do you know what will happen to her child?"

"Mary Seymour is in the care of her father, for now. It may be she would, in the English custom, go to another house when a little older."

There was another advantage to the notion of claiming Katherine's title. If I remained in England, this would indeed offer me an income I could easily live on, but if I was forced to go home – my brother was still attempting to arrange marriages for his sisters, though Amalia was being less than cooperative since she did not want to wed a Catholic – as Dowager Queen of England I would return with a title all men understood and my brother might be forced to respect, since technically I might outrank him.

Swiftly we heard that such an application would not be welcomed by the King and council. I would have to prove my marriage to the King should not have been annulled, and someone close to the King told Diaceto, when he enquired, that to do so would mean Katherine Parr and the old King were not truly married, which would pain King Edward, since always he had considered her his stepmother.

I thought this just an excuse, but told my men we might leave it a while, and when the pain of Katherine's passing was not so close, perhaps someone would be more willing to listen to me.

The death of Katherine Parr also seemed to remove all trace of restraint from her husband. Everybody was becoming more and more aware that Thomas Seymour was making a bid for power. There was a new King attempting to rise, determined to set down the old. Another Seymour wished to be Protector, though had he thought more about it, he should have started by protecting himself.

Chapter Twenty-Five

1549

Hever Castle

"Do you think the council will replace him?"

"They seem less interested in reading your letters now, Highness. There has been no word he will be replaced."

Wymond Carew had died. I could not say I would miss him, although as a member of my household I was obliged to pay for his funeral. Long had he spied on me and my servants, getting Kitty and Jane into trouble, others too. I felt little but relief to hear the viper curled at my bosom was gone.

But as one trouble departed, I had another.

By that year my financial situation had become so dire that I was forced to appeal to my brother, and Wilhelm sent representatives to attempt to obtain the payment in arrears of my pension. Continual petition to the council had done no good when it came from me, but Wilhelm asked Van der Delft for help on my behalf. This also led to my brother lecturing me on coming home. The reason I had not wanted to involve him was to avoid such a fate, but I had no choice. I had no wish to return home to try to live under the power of my craven brother.

I was not the only one with a fool and a coward for a relation. Thomas Seymour devised his own death that year.

It began, I believe, when Somerset attempted to gain complete power, as if what he had was not enough, over the King. Somerset had gone to Parliament the year before, attempting to set into law an idea. To secure his position formally, a bill would be passed which would confirm it, giving him precedence in the House of Lords, allowing him to sit alone in the middle of a bench next to the right hand of *"our siege royal"*. Such a position in law and the Lords would grant him almost royal status, and the wording of his patent of authority would change from Somerset being in possession of the title of Lord Protector until Edward was eighteen, to his powers to remain until the King wrote to him – securing a letter of release with the Great Seal and the King's own signature – that it was King Edward's pleasure to take on full power.

"Somerset could rule for his entire lifetime," I mentioned to my friend of Suffolk, kindly come down to Kent to fill me in on the latest in London.

"Indeed, and in response, Thomas Seymour objected most violently, saying he would 'make the blackest parliament that ever was in England' and would force through his own plans. He constructed a bill of his own, trying to make himself Protector, then went about court and beyond seeking support. He was trying to get the King to sign his name to the bill too."

"What said the King?"

"That if the council allowed it, he would sign, but not without their permission. The trouble is, Seymour was still offering gifts of money to the King and paying for gifts Edward wished to bestow upon others. The King had been signing recommendations for Seymour based on this and was being persuaded bit by bit to sign the bill. Eventually King Edward's men intervened and told him he was, to all intents, being manipulated, and he should not sign anything more the Admiral put before him. King Edward finally understood and agreed."

I popped a comfit of fennel into my mouth, offering one to my friend. "What did Seymour do then?"

"Scampered off to make friends. He told Henry Grey, my stepson, that he would get Jane Grey wed to King Edward, so Grey, never the quickest of thinkers, went in with Seymour in support."

"Edward to marry Jane Grey?" I was more than a little surprised. She was of royal blood, but surely men about Edward would want a foreign match, with many more benefits of alliance than a union with Jane could produce.

"Even I think it would not be a good match, when one considers international relations," said Katherine, "and I am her step-grandmother. Seymour managed to persuade the Marquess of Northampton, Katherine Parr's brother, to 'set up house' in the north. One can only imagine he meant to gather men."

"Seymour plotted rebellion?"

"It certainly looks that way. All the men he was speaking to were disaffected with the Protector and all could command shires to rise. Seymour reinforced Sudeley Castle, his own seat and began raising money. He also, as Lord Admiral, had ships to command."

"God's eyebrows," I breathed. "And I, away from London, could have been in the midst of civil war without knowing it."

"And Seymour had other ideas. Word is, the moment he was a widower, he started to look the way of Lady Elizabeth again. Some even now say he poisoned Katherine so he might take a bride with royal blood and once he had overthrown the Protector, he could set himself up as King."

"Elizabeth is involved in this scandal?" I was disturbed. The girl had been through enough as it was.

"She is, but I will get to her after. The last part of Seymour's story comes close, my friend."

"Then tell."

Katherine washed her mouth with a gulp of wine from a flask carried by Susan and continued. "Well, men were starting to hear of these approaches to Elizabeth, and sadly of what passed in Chelsea Manor too. Though Katherine Parr tried with all she had to cover it up, servants had seen things and talked. John Dudley, Earl of Warwick, and Lord Russell admonished Seymour for approaching the Princess, and he denied he had, but then he heard there was to be a bill passed in Parliament which would restrict the access of other men to the King – obviously Somerset was trying to keep his brother from Edward – and he was struck with fear. The Admiral declared he would stand against it in the Lords and men told him Somerset might imprison him if he tried. Seymour must have become desperate at that time, he said he would not go easy to prison and would escape, and then, perhaps fearing he would not have time to put plans of rebellion into action, he visited the King and told him he hoped King Edward would be managing his own affairs soon. I think he was hoping Edward might express a wish to break away from Somerset's power, but Edward did not. When

Seymour gained no answer from the King, he did a thing most stupid not long after."

"What?"

"He broke into the King's apartments at night. Through the Privy Gardens he came with two servants and a dagger in hand. The thought is he was trying to kidnap Edward. If he had the King in his possession, there was much his uprising might achieve, but Edward's favourite dog was in the chamber, and it attacked the Admiral as he snuck in. Edward cried out for help as Seymour killed the King's favourite hound, and Seymour was found in the King's chamber, wielding a knife and covered in blood."

"What did the Admiral say in his defence?"

"That he was checking the King was securely guarded," Katherine afforded herself a little roll of the eyes. "Of course no one believed him. The King was upset about his dog, too, which meant he little listened to his uncle's pleas. I think for more than a moment King Edward was sure Seymour would kill him."

"He would have gained nothing by the King's death," I said.

"Unless he meant to marry Lady Elizabeth."

"Mary is ahead of her sister in the succession, and I doubt Elizabeth would have agreed."

"Agreed or not, if he had her in his possession, and people are saying he had plans to, would she have had a choice?"

I shivered.

"They arrested him, and sadly all the tales about Elizabeth and Chelsea came out. Her servants, Mistress Ashley and Thomas Parry amongst them, were taken to the Tower and questioned and many of them spilled the tales of the Admiral coming to her room, the story of the dress… it all came out. Elizabeth maintains her innocence, and it seems the council may well believe her, but Ashley has been taken away from her, it is said she did not protect her ward well enough, and Elizabeth has been given to the care of the Tyrwhitts. Her reputation is in tatters."

Thomas Seymour walked to the block in March, on the 19th. Apparently, he had learned nothing after his arrest and had been caught writing letters to Elizabeth and Mary whilst in his prison, encouraging them to conspire against their brother. Elizabeth, still maintaining her innocence, was watched close when she was told the Admiral was dead, and all she had to say was, "This day died a man of much wit, and very little judgement."

I smiled when I heard. "She will recover from this," I said. "Elizabeth knows how to survive."

Chapter Twenty-Six

1549

Hever Castle

Since Seymour was dead and the little girl's mother was also lost to life, Mary Seymour needed a guardian. My friend of Suffolk was chosen.

"I understand why," Katherine confided, "yet I think another might have been more appropriate. I have little understanding what I am supposed to do for the child when the entirety of her father's fortune has been confiscated by the Crown. I am supposed to support the girl in the status to which she was born, the child of a Dowager Queen, but I am to be given no additional funding in order to do this. I have written to William Cecil, the man I trust most around Somerset, asking for additional funds, but I know not when I will have an answer."

Pity fell on me, like a cloak. "The poor child, her mother lost as she gave birth and her father sending himself to death through wild and impossible schemes."

"Were they so impossible? I wonder. Had Seymour not panicked and tried to capture Edward, I wonder how the rest of the scheme might have gone. The navy were with him, so I hear, ready to support him against his brother. It is just possible that with them, and the support of the other lords he contacted who even now are running around denying they ever knew what he was up to, this uprising might have succeeded. In truth, Somerset was too lenient with his brother in the past. Had he locked him away beforehand, the King would not have been in danger."

I twirled a diamond ring on my finger. "And yet the people call him a bloodsucking monster for sending his own brother to death."

"You have heard that down here in Kent? Personally, I think he paused too long. It shows something about Somerset I did not note before. I think at heart he is a merciful man, more given to redemption than revenge. That is a good thing in a man in general, but not in a man trying to be King. Others will have noted this and seen it as a weakness, mark my words. Dudley is the one to watch now."

"John Dudley, Earl of Warwick? The man who was my Master of Horse? But he is a great supporter of Somerset."

"Those who sit close to the seat of power covet that chair," she warned. "Dudley supported Somerset of course, the man had the higher title, the closer relationship to the King. Somerset was the one more likely to succeed in the first rush of this war for the power of the throne, but now Seymour is gone, the next battle is undecided. Watch news from court closely, my friend. Some even are saying that Seymour's wild scheme was put into his head by Dudley. There is no proof, but many of the arguments between the brothers, and many of the more reckless of Seymour's actions, especially his challenge over the Protectorship, they all seem to have a whisper of Dudley behind them. At the same time, he was at the side of Somerset, telling him what his brother was up to, how dangerous he was. I would not be risking a great deal if I put money on Dudley manipulating the relationship between the two brothers, pitting them against each other for his own gain."

"To what end? To gain the title of Lord Protector? But Somerset remains in post."

"I think there is a longer game being played here. Two contenders were too much to cope with, but perhaps now there is but one Seymour, he will be easier to remove. Besides, sometimes the Protector is popular with the people. If Dudley were to remove Somerset, he would have to disparage him in the eyes of those who support the Protector first."

"You think Dudley aims to be Protector, then?"

"I think all men on the council want to be, the real question is, who is most capable of taking the title?"

My friend was not the only one who saw trouble arising in the aftermath of the Admiral's death. It made Somerset most unpopular that he had sent his own brother to the block. People called him a ravenous wolf as well as a bloodsucker, and Hugh Latimer, that former Bishop and still influential preacher who seemed to breathe fire as he spoke, had to be carted out into

London to preach in order to clear the name of the Protector and smear that of Seymour.

"Not that Latimer needed a lot of help," I mentioned to Diaceto. "The former Admiral managed to adorn himself in the darkest threads of betrayal ever woven. Whom did he not betray? His own brother he was about to depose, his nephew he tried to kidnap, his wife's stepdaughter he was trying to force into marriage, pirates he was making deals with and the country he was seeking to overthrow. Really, if any man ever envisioned a scheme wilder or more selfish, I cannot imagine it."

Somerset, criticised now for one thing, was being condemned for others. His spending was one of them, the man lived a lavish lifestyle much akin to that of a king, and his wife flounced about court as if she was Queen. He expressed wishes of fairness to the common people, but then did not carry that through in his life, grasping all that he could for himself. "And his renovation of Somerset House causes great resentment." My friend of Suffolk nodded. "It is so sumptuous, so grand. People say he keeps the people and even the King in poverty and uses all the money himself."

The new palace, Somerset House, had begun to be built two years ago. The church of St Mary le Strand as well as a densely populated area of housing had been torn down to make way for Somerset's house. Religious buildings nearby, as well as the Cathedral of St Paul's, had been robbed of stone and brick for his house, but what had truly shocked people was that Somerset had ordered the charnel house of St Paul's, where graves of respected men and women of London had rested, to also be destroyed and the bones and graves had been scattered. This led to open dislike of the Protector, even his allies speaking against him. Despite his enormous income, he was accruing debts because of his grand house, which more people resented.

"The ongoing war with Scotland is draining the country of funds, and for no advantage," Diaceto said. "The promised bride of King Edward, Mary of Scots, has escaped England and gone to France for protection so the effort is futile in any case, and the recruits needed to man the garrisons cause resentment, since they are mercenaries and paid a great deal more than Englishmen in the army. The religious changes go too fast, and people are complaining that the clergy of King Edward do not even know how to read. Education has fallen aside, and support for universities has dwindled."

Unhappiness seemed everywhere. It had been decreed that the Host was no more to be elevated in the Mass, and the cycle of feast days that Henry VIII had begun to dismantle was continuing. People, even those who did not wholly understand the Catholic elevation, loved their ceremonies, and hardworking people required their holidays, so this was bound to cause discontent. Cranmer had even announced recently he did not believe in the transubstantiation and was working to ban mention of that as well. Plenty of people in England believed this as a fundamental truth. In the September of the year just passed, all licences to preach had been revoked, for some who favoured Catholicism were preaching one thing and reformers another, and some evangelicals wanted further change, thinking Cranmer and the King were not going far enough. It seemed no one was happy.

Poor Elizabeth was still suffering the aftermath of the Seymour scandal. All the careful protection Katherine Parr had offered her stepdaughter, Thomas Seymour had undone by being arrested and investigated so closely. There were rumours Elizabeth was in the Tower, which she was not, and that she was with child by the late Admiral which was also false. Elizabeth had written to the Protector demanding that these rumours be set down by the council by proclamation, but he seemed little inclined to help her. In response, when she was able, she rode out into the countryside to show herself to the people, demonstrating a wasp-like waist which carried no baby.

"France is on the verge of declaring war, too," confided Katherine. "Henri II wants Boulogne back, and they swear to aid the Scots too. The Emperor is the man to turn to, but King Edward does not want to ally England with the leader of the Catholics."

"This country is a mess," I said.

As were my finances, still.

"As long as my pension is paid, I am content to remain here," I told Van der Delft who, in addition to being sent by my brother to demand payment of the pension granted to me, had also been told by my brother to persuade me to go home. "What can my brother want from me now? I am thirty-five, Lord Ambassador, too old now for marriage and children. I am of no use to him."

In the end some money was paid to me, finally. The imperial ambassador managed to persuade Archbishop Cranmer to become involved, and although at this present time I did not support a great deal Cranmer was forging ahead with, my estimation of the Archbishop as a good man at heart had not changed. He spoke for me where many would have ignored me.

The ambassador had other news. In May of that year, we had been told the Turkish threat to the Holy Roman Empire remained an issue most dire, and rising taxes were helping not at all. "Your brother has however attempted to help your sister Sybylla by acting as an intermediary between the Emperor and Johann Friedrich," Van der Delft told me, "your brother, Highness, is trying to speak to the Emperor's son, Philip of Spain, as well, but I am told that his petitions are a little too delicate in their wording, and are not being taken with much seriousness."

I merely inclined my head, but in my mind, I scowled at my brother's feeble, lacklustre and late applications for aid for our sister.

Wilhelm gave up on his attempts not long after.

Chapter Twenty-Seven

1549

Hever Castle

"Enclosure," I muttered. "How can a word I had scarce heard of a year ago now mean so much?"

"I know not, my lady." Susan's brow was as troubled as mine.

There was unrest in the countryside, and it was coming for the towns and cities. In truth it was coming about because the government, and most particularly the Protector, were not issuing any firm position on the enclosing of land.

Enclosure was a process by which common land, often used by ordinary people for grazing their animals, or collecting foods and wood from, was seized by a landowner. They enclosed it, placing a fence or ditch or other boundary about it. Ancient rights people had to use such land was denied and since many depended on these customs, this was a high point of contention. It was no new phenomenon, but as with everything in the reign of King Edward much change happened fast, and many people were outraged about it. Many places now were being enclosed, some formally, some not, and some entirely illegally. Much of it was done for the purpose of setting sheep on such land, to profit from the English wool trade. Most of the people doing such were noble, of course. Common people responded fiercely, and the Lord Chancellor, that odious leech Richard Rich, was soon warning that rebellion was close because law and order were breaking down as common people were taking matters into their own hands.

That year a man named Hales tried to introduce three bills to Parliament to enforce legislation on landowners, but he got nowhere with them, mainly because plenty of the men taking advantage of enclosure sat in the Houses themselves. He did manage to introduce a tax on the amount of sheep a man owned, called Act for the Relief, which was supposed to somewhat rein in those enclosing land and driving out people to make way for sheep, but even though it went through it was deeply unpopular. Most of the nobility owned flocks of thousands of sheep.

The people seemed to think this would lead to revisions on enclosures done in the last few years, but instead the government issued a pardon for all landowners who had acted thus. Then a few weeks later Somerset sent out a proclamation that repeat offenders would be punished. It condemned landowners for greed, and seemed on the side of the common people, but in reality, it did little.

"Many think Somerset panders to the people in order to gain back lost popularity," said Diaceto.

Then there came news of riots.

"In Frome, Somerset of all places, men have taken to tearing down the fences erected over their common land and are claiming it is lawful for them to do so since Protector Somerset swore repeat offences would be punished." My friend of Suffolk exhaled noisily in frustration. "More men in more places have heard and are doing the same."

In Bristol there was an armed clash in a marsh over the destruction of more enclosures, which became so fraught the castle there was ordered to be armed with guns and manned with soldiers. Sir William Herbert's park in Wilton was destroyed and his enclosures were torn down, leading to the ever-heated Herbert sending 200 of his own men against the protestors and slaughtering them. There were some reports that common men meant to march on Herbert and kill him in retaliation.

Somerset sent out a proclamation against those who were rampaging, bringing down fences, and then sent another just a few days later promising to pardon them all as long as they repented.

"Many condemn Somerset, for he is all but allowing the confusion to continue," Susan told me.

In my own county there was trouble. A series of uprisings began, led by someone who called himself "A captain called Common-Wealth" and riled men up, telling them the Protector was with them, on their side.

"At present, I think there is little to fear, Highness." Diaceto, who I had sent to investigate, was still ruddy-cheeked from his ride about the surrounding area. "Although the damage is mighty on some estates, the tearing down of walls has been quite civilised. Men involved are even paying for their food and drink wherever they stop, and there has been no violence but to hedges and fences."

I was thinking it was a thing lucky I had given up Richmond, for whilst the flocks of sheep there had in truth been the King's, and the land his as well, I might have come under fire for such an offence since I was the tenant. At Hever I had some sheep fields, but they had long been given over to livestock, so it did not seem we were seen by the common people as causing offence.

By the summer, however, plenty of the nobility were finding that their parks were being attacked. Dudley had cause to whine to people that his park had been opened then ploughed by common men, and planted with oats.

Somerset appeared to be coming apart at the seams, from what I could tell. He was responding savagely to men about him as they questioned his continued support for the peasantry. He was popular with the people, despite the fact that he himself had claimed common land for his building of Somerset House and moved people out of their houses to build his own. The Duke was lashing out at everyone near him, so we heard. Then word came.

"Cornwall rises in rebellion." Diaceto came rushing with a letter from my friend of Suffolk, writing in warning.

The recent tax on an area like Cornwall, which was so heavy with sheep, had not been well received and the region, being so far from London, was often one that was somewhat a law unto itself. Cornwall was also still mainly Catholic, conservative of soul, so religious changes were not popular either.

When the new service of the Book of Common Prayer, Cranmer's great work, was first performed, there seemed little trouble, but by the next day men were rising. Priests were told to keep the old service by angry men who informed the frightened clergy that the will of Henry VIII had stated no religious change was to become law until Edward was eighteen and in control of the country. Priests duly put on their old robes and said the Latin Mass, but when a local gentleman tried to object, he was seized by the people and hacked to death. A Protestant lord, Sir Peter Carew, attempted to confront these men and in the process one of his servants set fire to a barn nearby, possibly as a distraction or perhaps a punishment. The people, enraged, began to rise, taking villages as their castles and fortifying them as Carew and local justices argued about the best plan to take. But as they argued, highways were being seized by men felling trees to set ambushes and imprisoning gentlemen they captured. The region was heading fast into lawlessness.

"It is said the Protector is calm, people think him deluded." Diaceto read to me from a missive from court. "The King is baffled as to why his people rise against him, so clearly he has not been informed about the situation, and Lord Russell has been sent to contain the growing rebellion and bring about order."

There was no military support for Russell, since it all was in Scotland, and the rebels had reached Exeter by that point. Russell struggled to gather soldiers from local shires and sent word he might have to retreat before he had begun. Two thousand rebels were now marching upon Exeter, along with Catholic priests, singing and preaching along the way, rousing more men.

"They carry the banner of the Pilgrimage of Grace," Katherine Willoughby wrote, *"The banner of the five wounds of Christ held aloft during that rebellion."*

It was, I was told by Susan, the image of a bleeding heart, that of Christ, surrounded by the five wounds he had received before death. The Pilgrimage of Grace had occurred in 1536, before my time in England, a little more than ten years ago, and clearly the people had never forgotten it. Soon they were making demands.

"They want the new prayer books to be burned, the Six Articles Act reintroduced, and the English Bible suppressed," Diaceto told me. "They want the Latin Mass back, and the Sacrament of the Host worshipped as was before."

There were other demands about communion and baptism, prayers for the dead to be resumed, and palms and ashes for Lent, and all services to be in Latin, not English. They were asking for the religious changes to be overturned and reversed.

"Cranmer has called them 'ignorant men'," said Diaceto.

"They do not understand all this change so fast." I drummed my fingers on the armrest of my chair. "It is not ignorance, but personal choice as to the way to worship. They cherished the old ways; the faith brought them hope in lives which were hard and brutal. They feel that hope has been taken from them along with the ritual of it."

They reached Exeter and encircled it. Outlying areas were seized and rebels set fire to the gates. Somerset wrote to the rebels, trying to bring them to order with promises that their costs would be reduced as he would regulate prices on food and livestock, then threatening them when that did not work.

"Then he sent out a proclamation they were traitors and would have property stripped from them." Diaceto frowned. "But the next day sent another, saying they would be pardoned."

"Threats against their property will mean little to these rebels. What is threat of such to men who think they have lost everything anyway?"

By July there were risings in other places, Buckinghamshire, Essex, Suffolk, Oxfordshire, Hertfordshire, and Sussex all were reporting outbreaks of rebellion. This had been largely brought about by another mistake. Nobles had met at Windsor to attempt to scramble an army together to meet the Cornish rebels, but as soon as they left their estates, men there, knowing they were away, rose up.

"These new rebels call themselves the Rebellion of the Commonwealth," I was told by Susan, who had news from the village. "The trouble is, perhaps knowing he cannot raise a force, Somerset is pandering to them, telling them their troubles are valid and offering pardons."

"I hear from court that Paget is all but screaming at Somerset that this will lead to further uprisings," Diaceto chimed in, "for the people will see the government is weak, but the Lord Protector will not listen."

Somerset issued yet another proclamation allowing men to not only investigate enclosure but to tear down enclosures if they found them to be illegal. Then came proclamation after proclamation, and each seemed to contradict the other. *"No one knows if the rebels are to be pardoned or punished, the people think Somerset is on their side and the nobility are up in arms about his wavering policies,"* wrote Katherine Willoughby.

Although the nobility were instructed to take no action, they clearly were done with Somerset's commands. Arundel managed to get men rioting on his lands to enter talks by inviting them to dinner with him, but Lord Grey of Wilton took another tactic and slaughtered 200 men rioting in Oxfordshire. The Earls of Shrewsbury and Huntingdon managed to take swift action and stopped trouble breaking out in the north, and Somerset was soon telling people no "great matter" would come of this unrest.

"Perhaps not, but not because of him," I said.

But just as it looked as though all might be well as the uprisings died down, it became not so.

That was the first time we heard the name of Kett, and Kett's Rebellion.

Chapter Twenty-Eight

1549

Hever Castle

If ever there was an unlikely man to start a rebellion, it was Robert Kett. He was not young and full of fire but aged fifty-seven years and a grandfather. He was an old man by the standards of our day, and by trade was a farmer and tanner, a reasonably prosperous background. He had done well enough for himself, was not reliant on the common land under contention, yet chose to lead a rebellion.

Perhaps he was simply one of those men who because they are respected in a community come to be a leader, in good times or bad, mayhap he spoke with eloquence as many leaders do, inspiring men. Perhaps he was just the right, or wrong man, for the time. Later, there were other theories.

"These risings seem different, more serious," Diaceto read fast as reports flew in from court, ambassadors trying to keep me informed and Katherine Willoughby too, not wanting me unarmed in terms of knowledge.

In Norfolk, Suffolk, and Cambridge were these latest risings, and this Kett, soon a name on all lips, was leading the Norwich uprising. Norwich was the second largest city after London, therefore a populated place, and the cloth trade was important there. There were also many poor, and a decline of the cloth trade had led many to be without employment, leading to further hardship. Desperate men do desperate things. Many marched out to join Kett. Soon it was rumoured he had 16,000 men.

"They call themselves the King's friends and deputies," Diaceto read from a letter from Van der Delft – which also requested an answer to assure him I was safe out in the country – which had arrived that morning. "This Kett keeps good order of his men, they say. He has named a tree the Tree of Reformation, where justice is to be dispensed, and has appointed governors to represent the people, arranged by their hundreds. Those who are plundering are being urged to aid the common people with what they take, and complaints are being heard."

"As if he is King." I stared at the tapestry. "Just how many kings will England have, do you think? How many can one country hold?"

Diaceto continued as if I had said nothing. "They are mainly holding gentlemen captured to account. The rebels escape most crimes lightly."

I turned my eyes on him. "That is to be expected, surely? This Kett does not want to turn his own men against him, so he pardons them."

"What is odd is that Kett's rebels do not seem to disagree with the Prayer Book, Highness, or the new services or changes to the faith. They are different in spirit to the Cornish rebels and seem quite behind the government and the King on the faith. What they want altered are enclosures. They are also fast making contact with other rebel groups nearby and winning them to their cause."

"How are the Protector and King responding?"

"The Ambassador says they are not. In truth, although he is fairly careful with his words, my lady, it sounds as if Van der Delft thinks they have lost their minds. Somerset has admitted affairs in Norwich are not quite as he would want, but the court is merry and apparently oblivious to the danger growing in the countryside."

They could not have been wholly unaware, however; 2,000 horse and 4,000 soldiers were swiftly drafted to become the King's bodyguard. My own guards, yeomen the old King had insisted I have for protection, were out patrolling my lands and house, and gentlemen who served me were on high alert even when inside the walls. I sent ale and food to them on watch, and thanks for keeping me safe.

A rumour grew not long after that King Edward had been deposed and murdered. The little King rode through the streets to show himself to his people, taking off his cap to make it clear it was him.

In the city, Cranmer preached against the rebels and the gates were fortified. The Night Watch was extended, and martial law came into force. No one was allowed to mention rebellion and if they did, as some dared, they were hanged. One bailiff went to his death protesting all he had said was there "were many men up in Essex but thanks to God it was quiet in London".

"Panic is upon us," I said.

Somerset was apparently still unaware anything was truly the matter, even though he sent William Parr to deal with the rebels. He wrote to Kett and the other rebel leaders, saying he knew them to be good men, but asked them to stand down.

"They ignored him, and now the City of Norwich is fallen." Diaceto was scanning another missive from court. "It says here the assault was led by 'naked and bare arssyde boys'."

"They bared their buttocks to the world as they attacked?" My eyebrows were high on my forehead.

"I remain unsure of the meaning, Highness, but what is for certain is Norwich is in rebel hands now. In Yorkshire it seems other men have risen and are demanding no King and no gentlemen rule them, and instead there should be four elected men who govern the realm. Lord Russell still has had no reinforcements. The Protector has not kept his promise to send more and Russell has such small funds that he orders his men not to loose too many arrows since the rebels will pick them up and use them against them. In Exeter the city is still under siege and food is running out." He folded the letter, gazing at me with a stable if troubled expression.

"Thank God we are safe for now." There had been no men marching on my lands, as yet.

At the end of July, the Protector suddenly seemed more resolved and sent orders to put the rebels to the sword. Russell engaged in a pitched battle with rebels, during which Lord Grey said he never had seen men, the rebels he meant, fight with more passion, but the rebels lost a thousand men and Russell only forty. Russell arrived to liberate Exeter, only to find the rebels had already left. Ringleaders were rounded up and some of the people, who had been starving, apparently managed to eat themselves to death on food gathered by Russell's soldiers, a sudden glut after long starvation sometimes causing more trouble than good. Grey and Herbert led attacks on rebels in the west and the protestors were overcome by superior numbers. Again, ringleaders were gathered up and hanged.

Brockehouse had news from a friend in the north. "In Norwich, there is trouble. Northampton was told not to offer battle, but he decided to disobey the Protector. He marched into the city and his troops were ambushed, the narrow streets and lanes became traps to his men. Lord Sheffield, a young noble, fell from his horse and was slain, beaten to death with a club. Northampton fled, causing panic. Men ran with him, leaving women and children behind."

"They were with the army?"

"I presume they were in the city, Highness. It says here some women who were with child were abandoned by their men and were left weeping in the streets as the two forces still clashed about them. Children too were abandoned in the chaos; many were slain, and buildings were set alight. Looting ran riot and Kett emerged the victor."

"Perhaps not." I tapped my lip with a finger, thinking.

"What do you mean, Highness?"

"He and his men declared they were acting for the King, that cannot be maintained now. The King's men will treat with him as an insurgent."

London was being fortified as news of Northampton's failure spread. Preachers known for spreading sedition were rounded up and men notorious for making trouble were imprisoned. Eventually it was said Somerset would ride out against the rebels with an army, and then only days later Henri II declared war on England, probably thinking it would be easy to take Boulogne now the English were otherwise occupied.

When the army marched out, however, it was not Somerset leading it.

"Warwick leads?" I questioned the messenger sent by the council.

"That is the way of it, Highness."

I wondered why Somerset did not. True, he had shown sympathy to the rebels, and perhaps that was why he did not want to go against them, but it seemed foolish. If Dudley lost things would be bad, but if he won, the popularity he might gain could be dangerous. Perhaps Somerset thought that with Henri II on the march towards English-held territory in France he was needed in London, or that someone should stay to defend the King. I know not what was in his mind. He had seemed so lost and confused through this whole time of trouble that perhaps he did not even know.

Dudley had been away from court as all this went on. First, he had been ill and then his estates had come under attack, although despite this he seemed, like Somerset, sympathetic to the rebels, not willing to send out an order to act against them. Eventually he had come to court and had been sent apparently to Wales with 500 men, although no one knew why. Then he was back and was sent to meet Kett's rebels with 5,000 men at his back, and his own sons in positions of command in the army.

He met with Northampton, marched north and when he reached Norwich gave the rebels the chance to open the gates. A pardon, excluding Kett, was offered, but when the herald came to announce the pardon to the rebels on Mousehold Heath, a young boy pulled down his trousers and did a "filthy act". No one told me what, but I could guess. Dudley's men shot the boy and there erupted much uproar, but Kett offered to meet Dudley and rode down the hill with the herald. His own men stopped him, however.

Dudley opened fire on the gates of Norwich and smashed them down. Fighting flooded the streets as Dudley rounded up forty-nine rebels and hanged them in the marketplace. The overcrowding on the busy gallows was so great they broke. Hearing this, other rebels and citizens came out and pleaded for mercy, but not all the rebels were done, and fighting and fire went on through the night. The next day a thousand Swiss mercenaries arrived, reinforcements from London. Kett ordered his men to withdraw to Dussindale, a wide plain, and there Dudley attacked. During the first volley the leaders, including Kett, fled as the remaining rebels fought on. Dudley exclaimed he was so moved by their courage that he offered them another pardon, and this one they took.

"Two thousand men were killed on the rebel side, and Dudley it is said lost around forty or fifty men," Diaceto said.

"Infantry, not well-armed, against men on horse, well-armed," I mused. "It was a massacre, in truth."

Executions began the next day, and Kett was hunted down and caught. He and his brother William were taken to London, and were sentenced to be hanged, drawn and quartered. In the end they were taken back north, William dying by hanging from the Abbey tower of Wymondham and Robert Kett hanged from the city wall of Norwich in chains. His body hung until the flesh fell from his bones and the bones fell to the ground.

"It seems odd to me a man with so little time of life left would risk all he had to become a rebel leader in the first place," I noted to Katherine of Suffolk. Come to me the very first moment she could, she had embraced me, glad to know I was well, and told me her own lands had come under some assault, but she and her sons, then at school, had been safe enough.

"Many think the same, and I shall tell you more odd things." The Dowager glanced about, her voice dropping but we were alone, only my man Otho Wyllik on the door and he would say nothing. "Kett, men tell me, was a tenant of Dudley. He bought land from the Earl of Warwick not long ago. Some say also that it is odd Kett would decide to negotiate with Dudley, though it was prevented, when he had refused to do so with other officials."

I frowned at her words, and implication. "What do these men think? That Kett was an agent of Dudley? The rebellion of Norwich was orchestrated by Dudley?"

"It is possible. No one really knows what Dudley was doing as the rebellions began. He said he was ill, then he had to hold his house, but what if he was not doing either of those things? And did he go to Wales? No one seems to have heard of a thing he was doing there, if that was where he was. There is another curious point. A man named Sir Richard Southwell, who is Dudley's friend and one of his stewards, has been accused by another gentleman of being an author of the rebellion. Southwell was treasurer for the King's forces and seems to have once employed William Kett as his deputy-bailiff. He visited Kett in the Tower, too. Dudley has spoken for him and men have dropped the matter swiftly, but there are links here which make for interesting thinking. Dudley is now popular in London, everyone heaping praise upon him, but what if he always *knew* he could beat the Norwich rebels? What if he was getting Southwell to fund them, to actually finance this section of the rebellion from the King's own purse, in order that he might take centre stage, and come to the attention of the King and the people?"

"It would be a mighty risk to take." I thought on Dudley. I had known him a little as Queen, he had been my Master of Horse, and we had talked here and there. He had, it was true, often ridden in the hunt with a degree of recklessness I had found amazing, but nothing else had struck me about his character. Yet, it was possible, was it not? Curious links to an odd man to be leading a rebellion, unexplained absence from court and the involvement of this Southwell. It was possible.

As Dudley became the darling of the people, given all acclaim for victory, Somerset was held accountable for the disasters of that year. All of them were taken as evidence of a failure of government. Other members of the council naturally laid all of the blame at the Protector's door and by October of that year Somerset was aware that he was under serious threat of losing his position.

And he was not the only one in trouble.

Lady Mary was.

Chapter Twenty-Nine

1549

Hever Castle

I had little seen Mary that year, but I had heard plenty of her and as the rebellion died down, there was more to hear, for men about the King were saying his sister might well have benefitted, had the rebels succeeded.

The reason of course was faith.

Mary had resisted all commanded changes to the service of Mass, or to her chapel. Her household had become a bastion of Catholicism, a refuge where those who wanted to worship in the old way had gathered, their Princess leading them in what amounted to open rebellion against the Crown. She had, most vocally, denounced the alterations in religion and made it vastly clear she considered Edward too young to approve any of them. Loudly Mary stated her brother was being led into evil by dishonest men who were manipulating the young King, who could not know his own mind or faith as yet, for he was still a child.

She might well have had a point, but no young man likes to be called a child, and no King, no matter what age, likes to be told he is a mere follower, in possession of no power of his own.

The court of Lady Mary had become this rallying point for Catholics still living within England, and where she led her cousin Margaret Douglas followed, her house also ignoring the new laws on faith. Two years before this time, Mary had started hearing at least four Masses a week, which became ones of great pomp whenever there was a new regulation introduced, and wherever she went she was welcomed by the people, many of them seeing her as a paragon of virtue standing for the true faith and others offering devotion, considering her a true, legitimate child of Henry VIII. Elizabeth's parentage sometimes was questioned by conservatives, but Mary was their beloved. The King had apparently told her that she might continue to practise her faith in private and the backing of the Emperor, who had stated he was determined his cousin should be allowed to hear the Catholic Mass, also lent weight to her cause, but despite any promises the King might have made, Mary's outward defiance of his laws was beginning to cause strain between them. She refused to use the new prayer book or to hear Mass in English and her priests were still elevating the Host, faithful to the old ways of the Catholic tradition.

As the rebellions died down, a link was found between some of Mary's servants and rebellions in the west. It seemed that one of her chaplains had been active amongst rebels in Devon and Cornwall and several other of her servants were linked to rebels in Suffolk.

Mary denied all such charges and said that the commotions in the country offended her just as they did everyone else. It was true in many ways for some of the rebels had destroyed enclosures of her park at Kenninghall, but declaring that the Lady Mary was "too poor for one of her rank" they had not taken any further action.

"Mary has cleared her name, most think," I said to Susan as we took some ale in the gardens. "But it is for certain a clash is coming."

"The King has always seemed most affectionate towards his elder sister, my lady."

"Affection wanes, sadly. The King is increasingly irritated that his sister is acting in open defiance of his laws, and if someone so close to the King is allowed to disobey him, why should anyone obey?"

*

That autumn, trouble was on the way for others. Like a sickness in the skies, it could be felt. Dudley and Somerset were clashing in council, and it was clear there would be a struggle for the position of Protector soon. It came sooner than I thought.

"Somerset was unaware for a long time Dudley was scheming." Katherine of Suffolk had rushed to Hever with the news. "But then it seemed all at once he was scared something was occurring against him and took action."

In early October there was word that Dudley and Arundel had turned on Somerset. The next day Somerset sent out a proclamation commanding men to come to Hampton Court, armed to defend the King – I wondered if he in truth meant Edward or himself – and declared there was a dangerous conspiracy afoot. The lords who had intended to confront him that very day heard of this and stalled, gathering forces to them instead. Herbert and Lord Russell, yet to return from the west, were told to offer armed support to Somerset.

Forces of Dudley and Arundel mustered in London and rode through the streets armed, preparing to take their stand, much to the amazement of the people who had not a clue what was going on. Was there another rebellion?

"Perhaps not rebellion, but we strayed close to civil war," my friend informed me as we wandered the gardens.

By the next day the city was full of armed horsemen and troops were massing at Ely Place, Dudley's house. Somerset took King Edward into his own lodging, something which caused much suspicion and Edward had to be produced by the Protector to prove he still lived. What the poor King thought of what was going on, no one can say, for the house was full of soldiers and people marching about, preparing for attack. Four thousand peasants assembled at the gates to defend their King, and Somerset addressed them, telling them Dudley and others had rebelled and meant to place Lady Mary on the throne as Regent. He warned that these traitors meant to harm Edward and told the tale of the princes in the Tower and Richard III to rile people up. Pamphlets about this flooded the streets, calling more men to arms.

"The other side sent out their own pamphlets, telling the people the Protector was an ill governor and was determined to keep King Edward his prisoner, not letting him rule," said Katherine.

"*Were* they planning to make Mary Regent?"

Katherine emitted a delicate little snort. "They deny it now, but it seems something might have been promised to her, for many who supported her seem to have gone to Dudley's side initially."

Aldermen of London were summoned to Dudley, and he and the other conspirators lectured them on the many ills of the Protector. Support for them grew. Seventeen of the twenty-five councillors took Dudley's side and some even went to Van der Delft, explaining the situation to him and other ambassadors. The men of London decided, after receiving letters from both sides, that they would defend Edward and the city, but would not offer an army of men to go against Somerset.

"It sounds as if they were unsure which side to support," I said.

Katherine shrugged. "Or they thought doing such could place the King in danger of his life."

Somerset was trying to organise his troops so that they could march on London, but many had to be disbanded because feeding the sheer amount of peasants who had turned up to defend their King was impossible. Sir Edward Wolf was ordered to take the Tower of London but found rebel lords had already secured it. As he came flying back, he met Somerset, King Edward and their troops who were on their way to the city. Hearing that the Tower of London had fallen, Somerset headed instead for Windsor Castle.

"What did the King think of all this?" I asked.

Katherine looked somewhat amused. "Apparently when on his way to Windsor he drew his sword and declared to his uncle that he and his vassals would help Somerset against those who wanted to kill him."

"So, he believed everything Somerset had said?"

"It would appear so."

At Windsor there was little food since the castle had not been expecting the King or his men, and Somerset's own party was breaking down. Confusion and division set in; Sir William Petre was sent to negotiate with the rebel lords but never returned. Letters flew back and forth between London and Windsor as the lords complained that Somerset never had listened to their advice and never heard reason or acknowledged himself as a subject of the Crown. Many people urged reconciliation but to all intents and purposes it seemed England was about to roar into civil war.

Men from surrounding counties, hearing this, started to march towards London for one side or the other, then Somerset heard that Russell and Herbert were urging him to step aside for the sake of peace.

"He knew then he had no chance." Katherine smoothed her gown. "The truth is, all the peasants in the world could not stand against the might of the royal troops now under command of Russell and Herbert. Somerset offered a submission to King Edward and his council at Windsor saying that he had never meant to cause any damage or hurt but just to defend if violence should had been attempted against the King. He asked the King to save him from his enemies, and Cranmer who had stood on the side of Somerset wrote to the rebel lords asking them to spare Somerset's life."

"Although rebel lords we may call them no more," I noted in a sardonic tone, "since they won."

Lords sent to carry letters promising clemency to Somerset also brought letters to King Edward, letters which described Somerset as ambitious and vainglorious and accused him of entering into rash wars and being negligent of the people. The Protector was denounced to the common people. Within hours all who had promised to stand by Somerset to the death stepped aside. They were given a signal to depart the castle, which came with a blast of a trumpet and as it rang out all the guards laid down their weapons and left through the open palace gates. Somerset was isolated and alone.

The lords arrived and Somerset found himself removed from his lodging which stood next to the King's bedchamber and placed in the Beauchamp Tower at Windsor, under arrest.

"When the lords came to Edward with their guards," said Katherine Willoughby, "the King believed he was to be assassinated, for Somerset had told him they meant him harm, but quickly they managed to assure him that they were there in fact to liberate him and Somerset had been the one keeping him prisoner. It was found the King was quite ill for he had caught some kind of cold on the night ride to Windsor."

Somerset was escorted to London surrounded by an armed guard of 300 horse, and despite his repeated protestations that he was not a traitor but a faithful servant of the King, his office of Protector was revoked. The next day he was placed in the Tower along with members of his household.

"He has been charged with twenty counts of treason," my friend told me, "there are all kinds of accusations, from discharging murderers to tampering with the coinage, allowing alchemy to be practised and neglecting Boulogne. The council also accused him of constantly ignoring their advice, and of supporting the rebels over the issue of enclosure."

"And where is the King now?"

"They took him first to Hampton Court then to Westminster."

"And has Dudley seized control?"

"Actually, at first Wriothesley was the man of the hour. Thomas Arundel was also promised by the King that he would be close to him, Southwell too. Wriothesley seems to have convinced himself that he was about to become head of a Catholic council, however since the Protector had fallen, executors of the old King's will were commanded to appoint a new Privy Council. Meanwhile, four chief gentlemen were chosen for the King, all of whom were Dudley's allies. What seems more surprising though is that the Duchess of Somerset was granted an audience with the King, and she pleaded for her husband's life, which seemed to surprise Edward for he asked where Somerset was, and when told he was a prisoner in the Tower and it was likely that the council would kill him, the King was much amazed for he had been told the Duke was ill."

"He did not know Somerset was a prisoner? How can that be?"

"I know not. He turned to Cranmer and asked him, 'Godfather, what hath become of my uncle the Duke?' Cranmer told the King that it was feared Somerset might kill him, but Edward said that his uncle could never have done him any harm and he had gone to the Tower of his own free will which showed his innocence."

I frowned, confused. "So, he did know Somerset was in the Tower?"

Katherine spread her hands, a ruby in gold winking on one finger. "But perhaps not the accusations against him? The King was quite insistent about wanting to see his uncle and stated that he certainly did not want him executed. I was told Dudley turned quite thoughtful at that."

"If the King is still fond of his uncle, then killing him might not be the best way to gain royal favour?" I suggested.

"Quite so, but it seems Dudley is swift ingratiating himself with the King, he is ever close to him, flatters him, makes it seems as if the King is in charge of all that happens. Edward has felt side-lined, I think, these past few years, so Dudley's charm is working well on him."

By November Arundel was asking Lady Mary if he could be taken into her service and Mary refused, evidently suspecting Arundel, saying she wanted nothing to do with any scheme to make herself Regent and also that she did not agree with any man who had acted against the Protector. I wrote to her, praising her loyalty to the King but also stating I was surprised she was so behind Somerset. Mary wrote back and also sent a personal message, one not written down.

"My good lady mistress said to tell you, Highness, that in truth she was troubled by the removal of Protector Somerset, for the man who lines up to take the position that once he held is by far the most reckless man of England."

I narrowed my eyes. "Did your mistress say why or how she knows this?"

"She did not say any more to me, my lady, but she never has liked Warwick. There was some incident between them some years ago, in the time of the Howard Queen I believe, when my mistress became convinced that Warwick was dangerous, and nothing has changed her mind since."

"Thank you," I said. "Please tell your mistress I miss her greatly, and I hope in these troubled times she will keep herself safe."

During the winter Wriothesley's health fell into decline and hope of a Catholic restoration began to crumble. Dudley too was ill that winter, but council meetings took place at his house due to his growing authority, which sprang from the support of King Edward. Paget as well as the Chancellor Richard Rich were clearly on Dudley's side, and Henry Grey, now Marquess of Dorset, and the new Bishop of Ely were too. Dudley's position grew stronger as he awarded new titles and rewards to his followers and on Christmas Day a letter was sent to all bishops ordering them to burn Catholic books and primers. The reformation of the faith would continue unhindered, it was said. Bonfires of Catholic books were burned in marketplaces and churchyards all over England. I was told Mary, hearing of this, lapsed into a melancholic sickness.

Wriothesley had been commanded to question Somerset in the Tower but found that Somerset gave no answer as to the articles drawn up against him, except to say that Dudley had been party to his every move. Deciding this was the best way to bring Dudley down, for if Somerset was found guilty then surely the Earl of Warwick would be too, Wriothesley conspired with Arundel and Lord St. John, William Paulet.

Paulet however marched straight to Dudley and revealed to him the conversation in the Tower, telling Dudley that should he seek to kill Somerset, it was likely his enemies would try to bring him down at the same time.

At another council meeting held at Dudley's house, where Dudley lay in bed pretending to be ill, Wriothesley spoke of the charges against Somerset and demanded his execution. At that point, realising he was about to be implicated with Somerset, Dudley jumped up out of bed, laid his hand on his sword and declared, "My Lord, you seek his blood and he that seeketh his blood would have mine also!"

Wriothesley had thought to arrest the Earl of Warwick but found himself captured instead. His supporters were rounded up too and ordered to remain in their houses. Arundel was deprived of his office and soon after Wriothesley fell into ill health – it was said he had consumption – and he died at the end of July at Lincoln House in London. Some claimed he had committed suicide.

"He left a gold cup to his 'friend' Dudley," said Katherine Willoughby.

"I think few will mourn him," I added.

"I certainly will not. I never can forget the role he played in trying to arrest Katherine Parr."

"And so now we have yet another King," I sighed.

In January of 1550, William Paulet became Earl of Wiltshire, Lord Russell was made Earl of Bedford, and Northampton became the Lord Great Chamberlain. There were many other honours, all of them given to supporters of Dudley. In February Dudley became Lord Great Master of the Chamber and Lord President of the Council. There was no precedent for someone so wholly unconnected to the royal family to inherit the position of Protector, but with these new offices the Earl had control of Edward's royal apartments and mastery of the council. Perhaps he was not Lord Protector, but I wondered if that even mattered.

"It is the power which is important," I said to Diaceto, "not the position."

Chapter Thirty

1550

Hever Castle,

Penshurst Place and

Bletchingley

We had thought Seymour would be immediately executed but he was not, he was held, and early that year he was released from the Tower, then even restored to the council. It was clear however that whilst it had obviously not been safe for Dudley to send him to death, Somerset's rule was done and John Dudley, Earl of Warwick, was the leader of England.

"Do you think him any better than Seymour?" I asked Katherine as we strolled about the gardens at Penshurst. I did not like this place as much as Hever, finding it rather old-fashioned with its huge Great Hall and draughty chambers, but sometimes Hever required a break from my household so it could be cleansed. The gardens of Penshurst were pretty, I admit.

"Worse, probably. He began as the Master of Horse to the Boleyn Queen, I think, then he was Jane Seymour's, yours, then Catherine Howard's and now he is an Earl and in command of the King. He has climbed well and strong, and when a man comes far, he only wants to go further. He does not come to a place and settle where he is comfortable. If he can manage it, he will try to rule the King himself."

"Sometimes I think to be the power behind the throne is better than the throne itself."

"And yet people always blame that person for any decisions of the King they like not. He might have great power, but more people will find him accountable than they will the King."

King Edward was reportedly delighted with Dudley and leaned on him. Dudley gave presents and flattered the King by pretending he found him intelligent. I had not seen Edward for a long time and whilst I had thought him a bright boy in his letters, I was ever chary about descriptions of him which seemed to err on the side of obsessive adoration. Kings are often made out to be more intelligent, more handsome and more talented than they are, mainly because people fawn on those with power, or those who will have power one day, and since this King was a boy and men were ruling for him no one knew what Edward might do when he came to his majority, therefore he might do anything. This led men to decide Edward would do all things good, and nothing bad. This is never the way for anyone, we all are fallible beings, subject to our own flaws and likely to err. But the trouble was this young King had been invested with power unlike any other king before him at his coronation. He would grow up hearing all that was expected of him, all these momentous achievements he would succeed at and either, I thought, Edward would become conceited and worthless, being so convinced of his own virtue he would see all his deeds as good and noteworthy, or he would be crushed by the weight of such expectation. Either fate was not to be desired.

There was the possibility that, invested with so much power, he might become a worse tyrant than his father. I hoped not, but it was possible, and Edward's reforms on religion gave me no reason to hope, nor did his increasingly aggressive treatment of his sister Mary.

Mary had not gone to the celebrations at court which marked the end of the most recent struggle for power. She had confided in Van der Delft as well as me that she was dismayed by Dudley's rise to power since she thought him "most unstable" and had therefore stayed away, but it was also the commands that had come about at Christmas over Catholic books and texts which had wounded her. I heard often she was ill, and no wonder, for from her perspective England was sinking into a pit of heresy and sin.

She was not alone in distrusting Dudley, but he had already rounded up his detractors and set them into prison. Ordinary people who spoke out were likewise silenced. It was clear who had the power now. It should perhaps be a surprise, then, that Somerset had not been sent to death. Perhaps Dudley was only too aware how fond the King was of his uncle, but I thought it quite likely the Earl of Warwick knew the people were behind Somerset too, for the most part. Nobles had not been happy about his treatment of the situation over enclosure, but many of the people thought the Duke was firmly on their side. Send Somerset to death, and Dudley might not only implicate himself if Somerset talked but he would also not be a popular man. Many praised Somerset's restoration to the council.

"He is the only adult Duke there is," said Katherine. "And so, in truth, he should be on the council to lead the peers. He shows himself as repentant and willing to serve, and King Edward seems utterly assured he meant no harm but simply became overzealous in his desire to defend him."

"I sometimes think Edward will believe anything he is told." I brushed a strand of hair back under my cap. "Like his father."

"Dudley has taken precautions, however, he does not trust Somerset yet. The King's guard is mighty, so many men, but there are other things. The King's tutors have changed, and Edward is now allowed to train with weapons, which Somerset never permitted. This has led to the King staring at Dudley as if he is a thing made of gold, for always he wanted to be able to enter warlike activities."

That March as flowers budded in the fields and fresh white lambs bleated to their mothers, a peace treaty was forged with France and six of Edward's companions were sent to France as 'hostages', as six young men of the French court came to England to be with the King. The new French playmates – for they hardly were hostages – took Edward more and more away from his studies and Dudley allowed whatever the King wished, indulging him to gain more favour. Peace, it seemed, had been restored and Dudley was the cause, but would it last?

*

Wilhelm's first child was born that year in Cleves. A girl, named Maria Eleanor. She was not the male heir all men want when their wives become great with child, but she was proof of the couple's fertility and could become an heir or rather could provide one by marrying a man to rule Cleves when she was grown, thus securing the future of our country. *A born duchess of the next generation*, I thought as I looked on the scrawl of my brother's secretary. Olisleger had sent the letter on to me, adding a note that Maria, Wilhelm's wife, had come through the birth in good health and although she had run a fever for a few days seemed now out of danger. The child was healthy, and all expected a male heir next.

Lady Mary wrote to me, sending congratulations and saying she was pleased beyond measure that we were now related through this little girl. We were in truth already related, several times over, through Edward I, but now one of her cousins had borne a child for my brother, I suppose it was true we were closer kin.

I wondered if people of Cleves thought of their own children as this one was born, so many of them dead in the late war, boys who had gone to fight, infants killed in their cities and houses, girls who had been abused, assaulted and murdered. We are ever told how common people rejoice in the births of new children of their reigning house, and perhaps for the sake of security for their nation they do, but how often do they think of how noble children are protected as their own are not?

And were we protected? I had been sheltered, it was true, had never known hunger or thirst as a peasant would, yet I too had been sacrificed for my country, for the changing whims of my brother. I was now trapped in another land, and although I did not want to go home to enter another trap, it was true I was beset here with dwindling funds, unsure of my place. My sufferings were few compared to people of lower status, I knew that, yet my life had not been without fear, without close brushes with death, without struggle to be allowed, to be permitted, to live as I wished.

The whole world seemed a cage at times, and I had not the key.

In that same letter I learned that Wilhelm's father-in-law was at odds with the Emperor. Ferdinand was King of the Romans, which made him Emperor Elect, the man most likely to become Holy Roman Emperor when his elder brother died, but it seemed Charles V wanted his son Philip to take the title of King of the Romans from Ferdinand and become his successor as Emperor.

"There is a great deal of unrest about it, particularly in the Germanic states," Van der Delft told me when I visited Bletchingley, so was closer to court. "But it is a natural wish for the Emperor to want his son to take his title."

"The title of Emperor is, I thought, my lord, one which the Electors *vote* upon," I said sweetly. I knew full well it more often was handed out to kin of the present Emperor. I just wanted to make it clear that in truth either man presuming the title should be his was not the way it should be.

Men of power think more power should be theirs, for no reason other than they desire it. That had been demonstrated enough for me to learn it as a lesson most important. And in England we had more than one man who wanted power. The Duke of Somerset had been set down, but there was word he meant to rise again.

*

In the summer of that year, I received an extraordinary message brought to me by Robert Rochester, one of the servants of Lady Mary.

"My mistress is determined to escape England," he told me, having asked for a private audience which I had granted. "She wishes to make for the Low Countries and her kinswoman Maria of Hungary is in support of the plan."

"Why do you tell me this?" I was somewhat aghast at the idea that I should be privy to such a plan which I thought reckless and foolish. Mary had come under increasing attack from Edward's government with regards to her religion, but she had withstood much harder storms and survived.

"My mistress wishes to ask you what your opinion is," he told me. "She values highly the strength of your mind, my lady, and although she has been driven almost desperate by the actions of her brother and is in many ways convinced that his council may find a way to arrest her, or even kill her, she still wavers on the plan, worrying that to depart England may be to surrender any claim she has to the throne."

"Then you may tell her that I wish to know no more of her plan, but my advice would be that she should stay. Her brother still has affection for her, as do the people of England, if she was to depart England and head to the Low Countries then any chance of her remaining the heir of King Edward would indeed be lost, and the dreams of her mother as well as her own ambitions would be over. My advice is that she should stay in the country to which she was born, she has a duty here and she still has many friends."

"I will indeed speak no more of the plan," he assured me, "and I will relay to her what you have said, my lady. I hope I do not have to say that this should not be mentioned to anyone."

"Not a soul will hear it from my lips. Her Highness is my friend, and I consider her close as any sister. Please counsel her well for I think whatever this plan is it will prove impossible. She would like as not be caught and that will place her in further danger, and if she should succeed, I believe it will be her ruination in another way. This is not Mary's destiny; I know that in my heart."

As the lady herself would later tell me, the plan was to escape by water. Mary moved to New Hall thence to Woodham Walter in Essex. Saying that New Hall needed cleansing, and she wished to take sea baths for her health, Mary's household, which was near the sea, was provisioned by boat often and it was thought that these deliveries of supplies would be ideal cover for a vessel organised by her men to come and take her to the Low Countries. Mary was to leave with only four ladies, as well as Rochester and two gentlemen whose names I never learned. She would take nothing with her except her rings and jewels.

But, at the last, the possibility of a boat being found in England for this mission failed. Van der Delft, who knew of the plot, was supposed to find another vessel for her, but he could not, and the Emperor did not seem in support of the scheme either.

In the end, almost at the last moment, Mary changed her mind. She would tell me much later that Robert Rochester intervened. She had of course already been told my message, but he told her much the same again and a ship which had been found, and was intending to take Mary away, was told it was not needed.

News of this however seemed to have leaked into court and Edward sent men to investigate. There were rumours that now the Princess was being watched most carefully and all attempts at escape in the future would surely be foiled. I was told by my brother's man that Maria of Hungary was quite impatient with her cousin and her failure to escape, but I thought Mary had chosen rightly.

Much later, in the future, I wondered if I should have told her to go, but at the time I was acting for a friend, one whom I believed in as a good and honest soul, a kind and compassionate heart. I did not think how time might change us.

Chapter Thirty-One

Spring – Winter 1551 – January 1552

Hever Castle

"I cannot thank you enough," I said to Doctor Herman Cruser, a man sent by my brother to appeal once again about late payments of my income. He had been the most successful out of all the men my brother and Van der Delft sent.

He bowed. "In truth, I would not have got far but for the support the Archbishop of Canterbury showed for your cause, my lady. He remembers you with great fondness, and I think the rest of the council, now hoping for peace with other nations, agreed with him."

"Then I will write to Archbishop Cranmer and tell him I am grateful again for his intercession."

In truth, although funds owing were paid that time, the next there was a slight delay and the next another. It seemed I had to constantly remind the council that I was alive in England, and my pension was something they had sworn to upkeep.

That was not the only promise they had forgotten. Lady Mary was no more to be offered clemency in her religious practice but was to conform. No matter the King had said she might worship in private the Catholic Mass, that was done.

In January of that year when the council wrote to Mary and told her that Mass was no longer to be heard in her household, she sent a reply saying that she was ill of health and could not answer them in detail but asserted that they had given promise to her cousin the Emperor about her personal religion. Neither the King nor his council were moved by her arguments. The King himself sent her a letter in which he rebuked her, telling Mary that she was his nearest sister, yet she wanted to break the King's laws, set them aside deliberately and of her own free will. Her resistance was fruitless and wayward, he told her, and the liberty she had been granted had been awarded only for a time in order that she might *"do out of love for us what the rest do out of duty."*

He meant to convert her faith, of course.

The King further raged that her constant comments about his age were no argument at all and that he thought his youth was an advantage for *"perhaps the evil that has endured in you so long is more strongly rooted than we suppose"* and if he gave her licence to break his laws it was an encouragement to others to do the same.

They had a tense encounter in person too, for Edward invited Mary to court. Thinking it might be a way to reconcile, she went that March, surrounded by an immense guard of supporters, but upon joining the court at Westminster found herself greeted at first by only one household officer, a sign of her unimportance. When she entered the palace, she was swiftly surrounded by twenty-five members of the council as well as her brother.

Edward spoke, reminding her of the letters that he and the council had sent to her, and the council then launched their own attack, announcing that Edward no longer intended that she should be able to practise the old religion. Mary fought back declaring that a promise had been sworn to the Emperor that she would be allowed to worship freely and Edward retorted he knew nothing of that for he had only taken a share in affairs during the last year.

"In that case," Mary announced, "that means the King himself has not drawn up the ordinances on the new religion."

She meant she did not have to obey laws which had not been made by the King.

"She has great bravery, if little sense," I mentioned to Katherine.

"Indeed. The council chose not to dignify that with a response and instead informed Mary that she, as sister to the King and heiress to the crown, must cease to observe the old religion because ordinances of the country have to apply without exception. So Mary once more called the Emperor to her defence, saying that she must await the Emperor's reply on this matter in order to know how to act. She professed loyalty and love of the King but then made a great mistake."

"What?"

"She turned to Edward directly and said, 'age and experience will teach Your Majesty much more yet'."

I whistled a little.

"'You also may have somewhat to learn, none are too old for that,' Edward snapped back. I am told he looked enraged. Mary told her brother that it would be hard to change her religion, in which her father the King bred her and left her at his death, because of her age, inclinations and devotion."

"What then happened?"

"There was some back and forth, they argued on what the old King would have done had he lived, the council told Mary she was subject to the Crown, and she said their authority only went as far as her marriage not her faith. She also accused them of negligence, in a way, that her father had ordered two Masses to be said for him every day, as well as other ceremonies which the council was refusing to observe. Then she said her father had never done anything prejudicial to Edward because of the paternal love he bore him, so it was reasonable to suppose that he alone cared more for the good of his Kingdom than all the members of his council put together."

Dudley lost his temper then, shouting, "How now, my lady! It seems Your Grace is trying to show us in a hateful light to the King, our master, without any cause whatever."

Mary denied this and turned once more to the issue of the Mass, saying that even if there had been no promise made to her or to the Emperor, she would hope since she was his sister, Edward would show her enough respect to allow her to continue in the observance of the old religion and to prevent her from being troubled in any way.

My friend smiled at my worried face as the story unfolded. "Lady Mary came to the end of her argument in the strongest way possible as she asked her brother directly, 'Might it please you to take away my life, rather than the old religion in which I desire to live and die?'"

I expelled a great gulp of breath. "God's blood, she has some daring."

"Indeed. Edward was much astonished by the remark and replied that he wished for no such sacrifice. Mary begged her brother not to hear those who would speak ill of her about religion or anything else and assured him that she remained his obedient sister. Edward said he had never doubted that, and their meeting ended."

"She fought well," I noted later, relaying the tale to Susan.

"But they will press her continually, Highness." Susan looked troubled. She herself was of the old faith.

All that year, the government and council used all their influence to try to make Mary submit. Members of her household were attacked. Robert Rochester was questioned about the Mass being held in her house and in August he, along with two others, was summoned before the council, only to be to be accused of being the instruments which kept the Princess in the old religion. They rejected the accusations saying they were but servants of the Princess and were subject to her will, which showed how in control of her household Mary was. They were incarcerated in the Tower. Rochester stayed all that winter in his prison, only to be released the next year on grounds of ill health. Her other servants were allowed out, one under house arrest at first, but eventually all of them returned to her. Mary was feared by her servants but also much loved, like her father in some ways.

The council attempted to replace Rochester, but Mary protested that if that happened then she would leave, by means of death. She protested that she was sickly and would not die willingly but, "if I shall chance to die, I will protest openly that you of the council be the causes of my death. You give me fair words, but your deeds will always be ill towards me."

Soon all the country knew of her words, for Mary shouted them from an upstairs window in her house at the King's officers in front of crowds who had turned out to stand by her. She told them at the same time she wanted Rochester back, for in his absence she had been forced to become her own controller.

Jean Scheyfve, Lord of Sint-Agatha-Rode, who had replaced poor Ambassador Van der Delft who had gone home due to illness only to die almost as soon as he reached his native land, appeared at that time to fight for the Princess, and the might of the Emperor was used to threaten the council. It was said the Emperor was threatening war if his cousin was not permitted to worship in the old ways.

"How seriously they will take it, I know not," I said to Susan as we sat at our embroidery one day. "Many times, the Emperor has promised to come out fighting for his kinswomen and never has he appeared. It was said he would invade for Katherine of Spain, his aunt, then for Mary when she was mistreated by her father and neither time did anything come of it."

Suddenly the pressure upon her eased as Dudley, now made Duke of Northumberland, decided Mary was not so great a threat as was thought.

"Northumberland believes that Edward will deal with her when he comes to his majority, which is not now so very many years away, and it would be better that she was dealt with by her brother and not by the council," Katherine told me.

"When Edward comes to his majority, do you think he will rule in truth?" I played with a flower fallen from the hearth, winding its stem through my fingers. The stem snapped as I played.

"I think he will, with Northumberland at his side. In truth, Northampton will not need to manipulate him a great deal in time, he has become Edward's tutor in the means and method of power and the boy responds to him. Dudley has many sons, he knows how to raise boys."

"He is not alone," I smiled. "How are your sons?"

"Well, doing good work at school in Cambridge. They are in St John's College now and their tutors are impressed with them. I hope this means they are indeed learning. Henry is almost sixteen. I fear he will be running after the girls and the ale soon, so it would be good for him to grow his mind as much as possible before he starts losing his wits to wanton pleasure. Charles copies everything Henry does, so there is no hope there either." She chortled, with affection.

"Your sons are good boys, and they will be good men, I am sure."

I was wrong. They never had the chance.

That summer the sweat fell upon England, hard and hot and full of fury it came. It had not been seen in England for so long, not since 1528 had it appeared, so few expected it to come again. Hever was immediately shut off from the countryside, not even messengers allowed into the house, as older servants told me how they had almost lost the Boleyns to the sweat. "Master George, Sir Thomas Boleyn and ... Anne, they all were ill of it and almost died," said one of the older women, Mother Lovell. The old servants were getting used to the notion they could say the name of Anne Boleyn. The old King was many years dead and no one was going to assault them now if they mentioned her, but it had become habit not to say her name, and so she came back slowly, carefully.

"I will take all precautions," I assured them, and I did. Many others did too but some were lucky, and some were not.

My friend Katherine was not.

As this plague raged through England, we heard tales from those delivering goods at the end of the path to the castle. They would stand away from my gentlemen, leave bread or meat and step away, money was left in dishes of vinegar to keep coins clean, but news was always exchanged, sometimes messengers left notes and missives too. People were well in the morning and dead by supper, we were told. It was dangerous to sleep during the first hours of sickness, for that seemed to carry more people away than it healed. A whey posset of ale and milk, as well as feeding the patient sorrel and sage and mustard, would bring on a sweat that might save a man. One man even wrote a treatise blaming the sweat on a lack of fish in the diet of the English, which seemed remarkable since many kept to the old ways and ate fish on half the days of the year.

And then there was news. My friend of Suffolk, closed away in her house at Kingston, heard that both her sons had the sweat. They had moved from Cambridge when the sweat struck there, to Buckden, the home of Margaret Neville, stepdaughter of Katherine Parr, but as they came to Buckden, both fell ill of the dreaded sweat.

Katherine was ill herself when she heard, but from her sickbed she rose and with the aid of her Master of Horse, Richard Bertie, she rode hard for her sons. As she arrived, she was told her eldest, Henry, was already dead.

As Katherine went to her son Charles, servants tried to hold her back, but Katherine and Bertie pushed through them. At the last door was a doctor. "My lady, you cannot enter this chamber. If you go in there, you surely will die."

Katherine drew herself up, all the power and majesty that grief may bestow upon a soul flowing through her. "Fool," she breathed with scorn. "My son and heir is dead, his brother to follow him to the grave. Do you think I care if I die?"

"Stand aside," Bertie shouted at the man, his hand on his dagger, and the doctor stumbled to one side as Katherine swept into the chamber, pulling her little boy into her arms. She had been too late to comfort Henry as into darkness he fell, but she was there as her son Charles died, so he knew he was not alone. His mother was with him as the end came.

Katherine retired to her estates after her loss, not wanting to see anyone. I sent letters, and gifts, knowing nothing could replace her children, but wanting her to know I was thinking of her. I heard from her but little for some time. Locked away with her sorrow, she had entered a dark time.

My friend was not the only one who lost children. An orphan girl died of the sweat that year too. Mary Seymour, daughter of Katherine Parr, passed from life at Grimethorpe.

*

"Only a year was he free," I said in October of that year, "and now it seems he is to fall."

Edward Seymour who had been humbly serving, a little too humbly some thought, as a member of the council may not have been as meek in truth as he was pretending. "It is likely that he was plotting to return to the position of Lord Protector," said Brockehouse, "and Northumberland was not about to let that happen."

Of course he was not. It would have meant his death. One of them had to succeed and the other fail. They could not share, that was not the way of men.

That summer had seen many smaller uprisings gather once more due to changes of religion or land enclosure but the response of the government this time was swift and brutal. Somerset was commissioned to maintain order in Sussex, Oxfordshire, Hampshire and Wiltshire, and relations between Northumberland and Somerset had seemed quite friendly. Somerset was being treated with respect at court and men said he would be fully reinstated soon. There was even a marriage arranged between Northumberland's son, Lord Lisle and Somerset's daughter, Anne. The King himself attended the ceremony.

What was odd was that Northumberland, rather than attending his son's wedding had gone to his house at Hatfield three days before the marriage and there were rumours abroad that trouble was brewing between the two men.

Gardiner, still imprisoned in the Tower, had been visited by Somerset amid rumours that the council was to seek a reconciliation with the Bishop on condition that he accept the new prayer book. Gardiner agreed, though grudgingly. His acceptance was enough for Somerset but not for Northumberland who wanted Gardiner to apologise for his contempt and to sign a confession of his guilt. Gardiner would neither apologise nor sign the confession, and Northumberland spent time railing against Somerset for his "lack of good consideration". The peace so dearly bought between these two men appeared at an end.

It seemed Somerset had been starting to plot against Northumberland, meeting with Arundel to discuss how to bring about the downfall of the new Duke. There was noise from abroad too, from Maria of Hungary who was talking about organising an invasion to set Edward at liberty from the hands of his malignant governors.

John Dudley moved first.

In October of that year Edward Seymour was sent to the Tower on a charge of treason.

Lords who supported Northumberland had already been bought with rich rewards, as Henry Grey became Duke of Suffolk, William Paulet took the title Marquess of Winchester and William Herbert became Earl of Pembroke. They knew which master to follow; the one with the open purse.

Somerset was not alone in the Tower. Paget joined him there near the end of October and Arundel and Lord Grey of Wilton followed. Somerset's apparent plotting was revealed, and it was said he had intended to seize the Tower of London and destroy the city before sailing to the Isle of Wight. Not many people believed the accusations and thought instead these were lies made up by Northumberland. The prisoners were interrogated and Northumberland believed he had enough evidence to continue.

Somerset was taken to Westminster by boat at five of the morning on the 31st of November and there it was announced that Somerset had intended to deprive the King of his royal dignity, seize the King's person and exercise royal authority. Somerset remained defiant, defended himself well and as crowds gathered outside Westminster Hall, they cried "God save the Duke!" so loud that it could be heard inside the hall, which left lords who were trying Somerset ill at ease.

Perhaps this had a bearing on what happened, for Somerset was found not guilty of treason. Outside the crowds erupted into celebration, and when King Edward was told Somerset had been acquitted, he replied that he never had believed Somerset could be a traitor.

The sentencing however was not done.

Somerset was found not guilty of treason, but he was found guilty of committing felony under legislation which had been passed to stop the gathering of unlawful assemblies. He was sentenced to death by hanging for this crime.

The Duke fell to his knees and requested pardon from Northumberland, Northampton and Pembroke and asked that his wife, family and debts be taken care of.

At eight in the morning on the 22nd of January 1552, Edward Seymour, Duke of Somerset walked out of the Tower surrounded by armed guards and was taken to Tower Hill. Northumberland had attempted to stop a crowd from gathering by shifting the time of execution three hours ahead, but a huge crowd had gathered. There was much talking amid the masses that a pardon would be sent at the last minute for it was for certain the King loved Somerset and would not see him die for a mere felony.

But the pardon did not come.

The King had graciously allowed Somerset to die by the axe rather than by hanging for it was a kinder death. Somerset made a speech but as he talked a clap of thunder rang in the skies, leading people to believe that God Himself was protesting the execution. His speech interrupted once, Somerset continued, asking the people to keep themselves quiet and still, so they would not disturb him as he died.

He knelt before the block, put his head down and his end was swift.

"God knows what will happen next," I wrote to my brother and his wife, and I think I spoke for most of the country in that letter. What would come of this?

In public it was said King Edward showed little emotion at the news his uncle was dead but, in the future, anytime Somerset's name was mentioned, Edward would sigh, and tears would slip from his eyes as he said that his uncle had done nothing in truth worth dying for and he regretted not giving the clemency of a Prince.

The clemency of a Prince, I thought. *Does such a thing exist?*

Chapter Thirty-Two

1552

Hever Castle

"And now the true, unopposed reign of Northumberland may begin, grown from the blood of Somerset," I said to Katherine Willoughby. "What will Dudley do, I wonder?"

"I think him more a schemer than Somerset." My friend was pale, still in mourning for her sons. For much of the end of the year, even after the sweat had fallen away and travel was safe, she had stayed alone, wrapped in her grief. She had wanted to visit me and talk though by that time, not wanting, as she said, to be left alone with her thoughts anymore. For a protracted stay she had come, saying Hever offered her comfort somehow. "This place has known much loss, as I have," she had said when first we walked together. "Somehow it reaches out to me."

I understood, for I felt the same. There are places which seem to call to us as we walk within them, ghosts which reach out in friendship, echoes of the past which resonate within us.

That day, she continued with her thoughts, "Somerset was at least truly dedicated to the faith, no matter his other issues. Dudley is subject to one god alone and it is not the one we all worship, however differently we come to Him in custom."

"What God is his?"

"The one which lives in his purse." She adopted a wry expression. "Dudley is a man of gold before God, dividends before deity."

Perhaps I should have worshipped at this altar. I had two years been in debt and was still sinking. It accrued slower when I was paid on time and faster when I was not. I had petitioned again of late for the payment of my pension, and for additional funds to clear debts which had mounted in all the times I had been waiting for my pension. The council would barely see my men at that time, making it hard for me to fight my case. At my lowest moments, it made me feel unwelcome, as if I should fight instead to leave England. In Cleves my brother and his wife had had another daughter, this one named Anne, after me and after a Hapsburg aunt of the same name. Amalia had taken on her care and that of her sister and wrote to me often of the charms of our nieces. It made me consider that there were things I was missing in Cleves, things it might be worth returning for.

But there were things to stay for, and one of them was my friend. One day as we walked in the gardens, looking out over the park, Katherine stopped on a soft slope and said out of nowhere, "I took them for granted, Anna."

"What do you mean?"

"My sons, I took them for granted. I always loved them, always was proud of them but, and this is odd for I know not why, I never thought I could lose them. I know not why I was so blind, Death stalks us every day. Perhaps because they were Charles's sons, I thought them sturdy, like him. I never thought I could lose them, and certainly not both, one hour after another, like this."

She smiled, her eyes filling with tears. "I remember the days when I would appear suddenly, back from court. I always told my servants not to tell them, so it was a surprise. They would come flying down the stairs from their rooms when they saw my party approaching, would run to me to tell me all the small doings of their days, and I would tell them of court. They longed to go, and when they were allowed in Edward's household, how happy they were! It was as if I had promised them a fairy tale, and it had come true." Her mouth twisted. "Had I known I had so little time with them, I would have come home more often, had them at court with me, I would have spent every day I could with them. I took it for granted they would always be there."

"You did not take them for granted. You loved them and they loved you."

"But I did, Anna, because I thought I had all the time in the world with them. I was a fool to believe I was special. I never thought that... but this? This small, short time I had in the end, a few years?" Her voice cracked, shattered by sorrow. "I thought I would hold their children, Anna. I thought I would be infested with grandchildren. They never knew what it was to be men, to grow up, to fall in love."

She wept a while as I held her, and then against my breast she said, "Sometimes I question my faith. Does God hate me? Why would He punish me so?"

"God does not hate you." I hugged her closer. "Although I am not sure of many things, I am of that. My mother always said when hard times came that there was a plan to all things, and we had to trust God. Sometimes I wonder if this is so, but, my friend, not knowing what else to do, I follow the advice of my mother. She was right about many things."

"Trust in God, though He may be cruel?"

"I do not think God thinks of death as we do," I said quietly. "Perhaps to Him, it is not so different to life, so He does not see it as punishment."

We were silent a while. "There is no one left in the world who is mine," she said finally.

"I am yours," I told her. "And always will I be, until the end of my days."

Katherine looked at me and took my hands in hers, squeezing tight. "I am yours."

"You are not alone, my friend," I said as she leant her head upon my shoulder.

We sat on a hillock, watching nothing but the sky together that afternoon, hands clasped tight about one another so that even if the wide world sometimes felt as if it was crashing in about us, there was a firm point left in that world, and that point was where our hands met, in friendship.

Chapter Thirty-Three

Autumn 1550

Hever Castle

"Well, it is one thing they have done right."

That autumn the council had had the decency to write and inform me that *"through the offices of King Edward"* my brother-in-law Johann Friedrich had been set free from his captivity. I knew it was not via the offices of the King he had been freed, but I was glad they thought it important to tell me. I already knew, since Amalia had written to me, but at least it showed the council had some notion of civility.

Part of the reason Johann Friedrich had been set free, I believed, was because the Emperor could no more trust Duke Moritz. The usurper Duke, sent out on more missions for the Emperor than he wanted to undertake, had conspired instead to ally with France and had that January signed a treaty with Henri II to become General Colonel of a set of allies against Charles V. I could have laughed when I heard. Talks came about later between Moritz and the Emperor, and my brother sent representatives too, to bring them back into peace together. Part of the terms ended up being that Philip of Hesse, who had been a prisoner of the Emperor too, was set free along with Johann Friedrich. This was set out as a boon to Moritz, but I doubted he had campaigned for his old foe and rival to be set free. I believed there was another reason.

"The Emperor thinks he might have more success with Duke Johann ruling what is left of his lands in Saxony, and that with my brother-in-law free, he has something to hold over the treacherous Moritz," I said to Katherine, still with me at Hever. "Charles V was a fool to trust Moritz in the first place. Once a man betrays one master, he will turn on a second only faster."

"These things of evil become habit, then when practised enough, they become character."

"How true," I said.

I glanced at her man, Richard Bertie. He was not far away, seeing to our horses with my man Otho, but no matter where he was, he always had an eye on Katherine. She was his mistress, so it was natural for him to be attentive, but I thought it more than that. At her side he had been through this hard year, had stood strong for her when she needed it when trying to get to her sons. I was fairly sure the man was in love with my friend. It was not a match that was likely, of course, he being so below her in status, but even without hope I knew he felt much for her.

Katherine had always been an attractive woman, in soul, mind and body, but the last year had done much to her. It had not robbed her of any beauty, mistake me not, but it had plunged some of her lightness of spirit into a place of darkness. She thought a great deal more before she spoke now, she prayed a great deal, either trying not to lose her shaken faith or to regain it; possibly both. There was a sense to her that was both strong and fragile at the same time, a depth of spirit and resilience that only those who have battled through sorrow that should destroy the soul may contain. She was the same, and she was changed, and still she was fighting to remain standing, to remain upright and not become crushed by the weight that grief had placed upon her. I knew she thought herself weak, but she was one of the strongest people I had ever known.

If only we could see ourselves through the eyes of our friends. If only we could feel all that the hearts of others feel for us. What wonders would be revealed to us then.

I was having a few issues of my own, although of a much lesser kind, with my cousin, Count Von Waldeck, who seemed to view the highly valuable Jasper Brockehouse as some kind of demon sent to humiliate me. My cousin thought the man ought to be spending his time extracting more money from the council, rather than ordering my household to spend less, and they came to blows frequently. I had recently told the Count I could support him no longer and he had agreed to return to Cleves, although I worried what he might tell my brother. "I will say how rudely you are treated here," he assured me, as if that should be something I would want.

"That would not be in my interests," I informed him.

"Your brother should hear how the English defame a born Duchess of the land of Cleves!"

When I begged him not to, he began to scowl as if he suspected I was saying such so I would not bring the further ire of the council or King upon me. Waldeck seemed to believe there was a giant conspiracy surrounding my being held in England and the lack of money offered to me. He suspected my servants of holding me here with some kind of magical influence, but there was no conspiracy. It was easy enough to see for nothing had altered. The council wanted me kept in England as a potential political asset, especially with my sister's husband now free, and they did not want to give me more money because they wanted it all for themselves. It was plain as porridge to me.

But I was right to worry. When my cousin returned to Cleves, he went straight to my brother to tell him all the ways I was being mistreated, one of those being that my servants were against me. Brockehouse, Waldeck said, was untrustworthy as were others, such as Gertrude the wife of Jasper, and Diaceto and Otho Wyllik. They were instruments of the council who were trying to impoverish me, Waldeck raged.

This was not true, although it was true the council were attempting to push me further into financial trouble. They wanted me to exchange another property. Bisham Abbey was the estate they desired this time, and they intended to exchange for one which was highly inferior. They wanted it for Sir Philip Hoby, a diplomat who had done well of late for them in France, managing to negotiate an engagement between King Edward and Elisabeth of France the year before. Since that had been agreed, hopefully bringing about lasting peace with France, Hoby was to be rewarded, and they wanted my estate, a rich one, to grant to him.

Bisham was worth a great deal. Once it had belonged to Margaret Pole. The mansion house was situated on the River Thames. A monastery had once stood there, but much of its stone and brick had been taken away to enhance the mansion house, which the King had owned before me. In places, the arms of Margaret Pole and her husband were still set in glass and stone about the house. It was a pretty place with rich land, and in an excellent position for accessing the river. I did not want to surrender it.

Knowing, however, they would force me if I did not agree, just as they had done with Richmond, I suggested instead that a fairer exchange take place, that I should give up Bisham, but be granted Westhorpe instead. This was actually a property of the Lady Mary, but I had already approached her on the matter, trusting the friendship between us and hoping she understood how ill I was being treated in financial matters by her brother's government. Since she was being treated badly over religion, I believe she understood only too well how unreasonable the council could be.

I could have simply given in without a fight, but I refused to and wrote to Mary stating that *"for the amity which hath always passed between us"* I did not want to offend her, but I wanted a fair exchange, so I was not left even more in financial strain.

Mary sent word she would not go against this exchange, she had plenty of properties and money left to her due to the generosity of her father's will and the council did not dare try to take them from her, and so once more I traded houses, although this time with small loss to my pocket.

There had been repeated efforts all that year to try to get me to surrender lands in Kent for others of lesser value. I wondered at times about Katherine of Spain, and how desperate she had felt when she could not pay her servants or maintain the house she lived in. I could not even sell off anything I owned, for in truth it all belonged to the Crown.

When the council came after me, trying to pluck more of my lands from my hands, I felt alone in England, yet it was but a feeling, and not the truth. I was not alone for I had my friend, just as she had me.

Chapter Thirty-Four

1553

Hever Castle and

Penshurst Place

I set the letter on the table. "It is something,"

"But yet not enough to plug the hole, Highness." Brockehouse had ink stains on his fingers, deep and old and formed in my service. Like scars they were. Seeing them brought a small thrill of affection fluttering to my soul.

"At least it goes some way, we may pay some of the men demanding money."

"That is true."

The council had at last sent funds that April, but Brockehouse was correct in saying that they were not enough. Three years I had been in debt.

But the council had other things to worry on. In February of that year the King had become ill and despite many people saying that he was well enough and was improving, it did not seem to me that this was so. Edward was little seen outside his rooms for many months and only a limited amount of people were allowed in to see him.

"The chambers are strictly controlled," my friend of Suffolk whispered, "as are all the men who are allowed in to see him. When he had measles the year before, he was not this close guarded. Something ill is going on, my friend. The amount of security, the secrecy surrounding the King's health, these signs tell us the King is in danger of his life."

She looked lost for a moment. I knew she was thinking of her sons. Edward had mourned them deeply, I had been told, for both had been his close companions. Sometimes it seemed that Death was hungry for the young.

"And then what will Northumberland do?" I asked in a low tone, "for if the King should not survive this, then Mary will come to the throne, and she will restore Catholicism and set Dudley down. She never has liked him."

Katherine looked not a little worried herself. During the reign of Edward, she had made her views on religion plain to all who would listen, had enthusiastically attended reformed services of the Church, and had funded the education of evangelicals, so it was clear to all on which side she stood. Should Mary ascend to the throne, should Catholicism be restored in truth, my friend might find herself under attack and her dower properties under danger of confiscation. She had lost much already, as her stepdaughter became Duchess of Suffolk after the death of Katherine's sons, and Henry Grey, Frances' husband, became the new Duke of Suffolk in respect of his wife. Much that Katherine had had access to as the Dowager and mother of the Duke of Suffolk had gone. She still had the properties of her father, the dower lands left to her by Charles, but her living and estates had become reduced.

Although rumours grew at times that the King was dead, they were quashed each time by Northumberland and the council. But it showed how little Edward was seen that year, that these rumours were so easy to believe.

That May there were further rumours when a sudden spate of marriages took place, Northumberland forming alliances. One was the sixteen-year-old Lady Jane Grey who was married off to Lord Guildford Dudley, a younger son of the Duke of Northumberland.

Although the descendants of Margaret Tudor who had been Queen of Scotland had been excluded from the succession by the will of Henry VIII, either for being born out of this country or for being thought illegitimate, the descendants of Mary Tudor, his younger sister, never had been. Lady Jane Grey was a direct descendant of that Princess of England and although surely her mother would be considered above her in the succession, it still seemed to many that her marriage to Guildford Dudley, a man many said was a brute and an idiot, was done in order to give Northumberland a foothold in his climb for the throne. Frances Grey had no sons, but if his son could get one on Jane Grey, there would be a male heir entering the line of succession where at the moment there were only women. No Queen

Regnant had ever ruled England, and perhaps Northumberland thought that if his son could get a son on Jane Grey, if anything happened to King Edward, that son might well have more support for the throne than Lady Mary would.

Some men might even prefer it. They had done well out of the minority of Edward, after all. With a baby left as heir to the throne, ordinary men of no royal blood would have longer to remain in charge of England, and longer to line their pockets.

"Do you think this means something? About Edward?" I asked Katherine of Suffolk, "that your step-granddaughter would be being sold off to a child of the Dudley line?"

"I know not," she confessed, "and I cannot get a straight answer out of anyone in the family. In truth I think Frances has always resented me and now the fact that she will not answer my letters on this does make me wonder what it is that Northumberland is cooking up for this country, with ingredients the Greys are providing. Once Northumberland promised he would marry Jane to Edward, if you remember? Henry Grey was interested in that match, for it would certainly have made his daughter Queen and her offspring direct heirs to the throne. This match, now, it puts Dudley's heirs and Greys surely closer to the throne."

That year the King would vanish for weeks and sometimes months, his health delicate. Then there would be news he had recovered again and there was rejoicing. Then he would vanish again, only his men and doctors seeing him. It was said he coughed up black bile, sometimes green, and was weak and ill, his lungs soft and his breathing hard. In time it was said he was coughing up blood.

"Consumption," said a doctor who came to see me when I was ill of a fever that summer. "Many of us think it is so for the King, my lady. I would not want to say it means we could lose him, but consumption has haunted the Tudor line. Prince Arthur, they say died of it, although there was talk he had a canker too, but the Duke of Richmond, King Edward's own half-brother, certainly died from it. We must pray the Lord God will deliver our King from harm."

Not long after I had word from Edward's council asking that my man, Diaceto, be sent to Denmark. There was a message that required delivery, and it was thought this man of my homeland who had long been in the service of England, through me, would be able to deliver it, travelling through the countries between us with ease due to familiarity and a talent he possessed for languages. Not wanting to lose my man but wishing to comply with the ever-fractious government, I agreed and Diaceto left. It would be some time before he returned, and when he did, much had altered.

The Imperial Ambassador Jean Scheyfve visited court often and sent word to me that Edward had recovered a little upon moving to Greenwich where the air was good and clean, but he had fallen ill again and *"it is held for certain that he cannot escape."*

The last time anyone saw the King was in the summer of that year, on the 1st of July. He appeared at a window in his palace of Greenwich, and onlookers were horrified. He was thin, pale, wasted in appearance and although he waved and they cheered, it was plain as day the King was a very sick young man. Rumours that Dudley was poisoning him soon emerged, although I did not believe them. I could believe much of the Duke of Northumberland, but it would have been to his advantage for Edward to live. Northumberland was established as the power behind the throne, the King apparently now looked his way every time he went to make an answer to a petition or a lord, Northumberland's power over the King was complete. He could have ruled England through Edward, perhaps for the entirety of the King's reign, as long as he played his dice with a skilled hand. Killing Edward, even with his son married to the eldest Grey, was not to his advantage.

Jane Grey was, as it turned out, more to be thought of as a back-up plan, and not one dreamed up by Northumberland alone.

Something was coming, another change on its way, and after the last few tumultuous years of conspiracy and back-stabbing, all the country held its breath to see who, this time, would emerge victorious.

I am not sure any of us expected what happened.

*

We did not know until much later for it was kept a secret most guarded, and I perhaps knew less than most, being relegated to the countryside, but poor young King Edward coughed out the last of his life and died on the 6th of July 1553. He was just fifteen years old. It was only three months until he would turn sixteen and might have taken on more powers, for he was already working closer with the council than ever he had before, and it was only a few spare days since last he had been seen at that window in Greenwich, but his condition worsened, and as he neared death something King Edward had been working on came to the fore.

Apparently, the King had thought on the problem of the succession before his last illness and eventual demise. His tutors often had him construct essays on various topics, such as war, faith, love, and the King had taken the succession as one of these subjects. Deciding in this theoretical exercise that both his sisters should be excluded despite his father's will, Mary on the basis that her mother and father had not been truly married and because of the nature of her faith, and Elizabeth on the notion that she too was a bastard, Edward struck his sisters from the line of succession and settled instead on the Grey line.

Frances Grey, daughter of Mary Tudor and Charles Brandon, was the eldest of this line which contained only daughters. Her sons would be the ones to succeed, but Edward's *Devise for the Succession* held a caveat that these male heirs would have to be born before Edward's death. Frances was thirty-six and it had been some years since last she produced a child. She was not with child as the King was dying, so therefore the crown would pass to the next in line, Frances's eldest daughter, Lady Jane Grey.

Jane Grey, or rather, her *"heirs male"* were the ones chosen. Jane was not in truth Edward's choice for the throne, a boy who came from her was. It seemed Edward was much as his father, and did not believe in female rule, but as, in June, the fact that he was dying became clear to the King, he changed his *Devise*, adding a word or two. The throne would be left to "Jane Grey *and* her heirs male". With the alteration of a sentence, so Edward tried to do as his father had, and control the succession. His *Devise* was made into letters patent that June, and it seemed that Frances, who must at some point have been told, willingly stepped aside without challenging the King's wishes, to allow her daughter to be Edward's heir.

Although there were letters patent made of the *Devise*, strictly it was not legal, since changes to the succession had to be approved by Parliament. Jane was an heir, had been named as successor to Edward by the King himself, but that alone did not give her the right to rule.

Nevertheless, Northumberland was charged to see Jane made Queen. Since his own son was wed to Jane Grey, and therefore would become King, or at least King Consort, even though such a thing had never existed in England before, I doubt he had too many qualms about the outrageous betrayal the King was about to enact upon his two sisters, both of whom he had claimed to deeply love, but neither, it seemed that he respected.

The King's death was kept a secret while Northumberland made his plans. On the 10th of July Lady Jane Grey was taken to the Tower and on the same day was proclaimed Queen of England and Ireland in the streets of London. All about those proclaiming this girl Queen there was muttering of discontent. Some little knew who she was, but all of them knew Mary and Elizabeth.

At the same time Northumberland sent guards to attempt to take Lady Mary into custody but Mary, kept apprised of Edward's delicate health after being allowed to see him in the February of that year and finding him most ill, had already left her estate of Hunston House near London and fled to Kenninghall in Norfolk. She had many loyal supporters, and they had informed her she was in danger. When she reached her estate, she was told the King was dead.

Northumberland immediately sent ships to the coast of Norfolk trying to prevent Mary escaping to the Continent, or what he probably feared more, the arrival of reinforcements to aid her cause sent by the Emperor.

On the same day as Jane Grey was proclaimed Queen in the streets of London, the Privy Council received from Mary a message which asserted her right to the throne and commanded them to proclaim her Queen, as she had already proclaimed herself. When the council sent word that Jane was Queen by Edward's command, they added that Mary was illegitimate and would be supported only by a few "lewd, base people".

But if it was only a few people, why were they so worried? Because they were well aware that support for Mary was growing. In London people were crying out she was the true Queen, and men began to flock to her.

Supporters immediately rallied around Mary, not only Catholics hoping for the restoration of their faith and return of the country to Rome, but also those who saw her as the lawful claimant to the throne. No matter that she might be a different religion to them, her blood and honest claim outweighed considerations of religion. As Mary gathered troops and supporters, Northumberland was forced to surrender control of the council in London in order to launch into a pursuit of Mary into East Anglia where innumerable masses of common people were gathering to aid her, as well as nobles. On the 14th of July Northumberland marched out of the gates of London with 3,000 men and reached Cambridge the next day. Mary gathered her forces at Framlingham Castle in Suffolk, and as I rested at my house in Hever, eager for any news, I heard that her army now numbered 20,000.

"I should go to her," I said.

"I believe that would be impossible, my lady," said Brockehouse. "Northumberland is on the march, and the quickest route to Mary would take us on roads close to London. There is much unrest in the countryside, and it would be dangerous. Besides, you can offer her no men, and it is soldiers she needs now."

"She needs support," I insisted. "I shall at least send to her a message."

"I believe that would be premature, and should it be known that you sent support to Mary, if she loses then we will be penalised only more by the government of Lady Jane Grey."

I did not think Mary would lose. The country was behind her, not Jane. I sent my message, offering whatever support I could, though I knew it was little, and sending her a bag of coin she knew I could ill afford. Mary was once my daughter, and she was my friend. I wanted no harm done to Jane Grey, being beloved of my friend Katherine, but Jane Grey was not the Queen England should have. Mary was.

"This time is what you have been saved for," I wrote to my friend. *"This time is why you did not leave England."*

I never had a reply, for Mary was busy.

Things were shifting in her favour. On the 19th of July the council, no longer under the control of Northumberland, realised they had made a deadly mistake. Led by the Earls of Arundel and Pembroke, the council turned heel and publicly proclaimed Mary as Queen. Lady Jane Grey had been Queen for nine days when her father came to tell her she was no more. Apparently, she abdicated more than willingly. She would have taken on the throne had it been God's will, she said, and done much for the faith, but if it was not God's will, it would not be.

There was wild joy and singing throughout London and when Northumberland heard, alone in Cambridge and drastically outnumbered, he himself proclaimed Mary Queen there, as he had been commanded to by a letter from the council.

William Paget and the Earl of Arundel rode to Framlingham to beg Mary's pardon, and Arundel occupied himself in arresting Northumberland on the 24th of July. A month later on the 22nd of August, after renouncing Protestantism in an effort to save himself, Northumberland was beheaded.

It seemed however our new Queen, Mary I, first Queen Regnant of England, was of a mind to show mercy to her cousin Jane. It made me peaceful of heart to hear it, for Mary must have realised Jane had been used as a pawn in the plots of Northumberland, and the *Devise* of Edward. Jane was not pardoned but she was not executed. She was held in the Tower of London as the triumphant Queen rode into London and prepared to be crowned.

And as she did so, Mary sent word to me at Hever, inviting me as her *"beloved kinswoman and loyal supporter"* to London, so I might ride in the carriage directly behind hers at her coronation.

Chapter Thirty-Five

1553

London

Immediately was I invited to court, and when shown into the presence of the new Queen, I fell into a deep, respectful curtsy and remained upon my knees until found myself raised up by the hands of Mary herself.

I gazed into the face of my friend. Mary was much changed since last I saw her. She was older now, and the trials she had faced of religion and fear in the reign of her brother showed on her face. Pale and thin she was, yet glowing with the love of her people and the recognition of her title. She smiled and kissed me on each cheek as a roar of approval went up about the Presence Chamber.

"I am so pleased, Your Majesty, to see you take the seat to which you were born," I breathed as she released me.

"I too am grateful to be here, by the grace of God and because of the support of my many loyal men and loyal people of England," Mary replied in her deep voice.

"I wish I could have ridden out to join you, Majesty, but my men feared for my safety, and I had no soldiers to offer you." I had, of course, my yeomen guard, there for my personal defence, but they were few in number for what Mary had required and sending them would have left me almost defenceless.

"I would not have had you in harm's way, God knows the face of war was scarce the place for a woman, and I *had* to be there!" Mary laughed. "But there was small resistance in the end. My people knew the claims and machinations of Northumberland were false, and my claim was true. They flocked to me, and all was well. The schemes which tried to deny me and my sister our rights are done, and the will of our father is restored."

Elizabeth was within the throng. Standing to one side, she smiled at me a little. Dressed in green and white, her Tudor colours, she shone like a being of silver and forest. I thought of my sister's tales of the hidden folk as I saw her dark eyes and a peek of red hair under her French hood. She was an arresting looking young woman now, not beautiful exactly, but captivating in her own way.

Mary had brought Elizabeth to her so they could enter London together. During the time of Jane Grey's spell on the throne, Elizabeth had claimed to be ill. I thought it more likely the clever young woman had been watching to see which side would prevail. I had no doubt however she was glad Mary had. Had Jane continued as Queen, Elizabeth's claim to the throne would have been swept aside, perhaps forgotten. However much she had loved her brother, which I did believe she had, and however much she admired her sister, which by the gloss in her eyes I could see was also true, Elizabeth was more than aware that now she was but one step from the throne, and Mary was old to think of having children, being thirty-seven years.

The Queen took me to one side.

"You must not think I blame my unfortunate brother for what happened, for I believe that in his weakened state before death his poor young soul was corrupted by Northumberland." She sighed a little and took my hand. "I also know that during the long years of my brother's reign you suffered as many of us did, for I know that in your heart not only are you a true Catholic, so the terrible, heretical changes of the Church must have been dismaying to you as you found yourself forced to worship in the way the council and Cranmer… " her face took on an expression of loathing for a moment, which harrowed my soul "… prescribed, but that you, like myself, suffered as others tried to reduce your position and your standing as well as your income. I will have you know, Highness, that I intend to uphold all the promises my father made to you in terms of your household, income and position in England. I may not be able to restore all your estates and houses, but you shall no more have to struggle as my mother once did with the burden of attempting to maintain a royal household yet not being paid adequate money in order to uphold that august position. You will struggle for funds no longer, my friend, my royal aunt, my good sister and kinswoman. Your days of being destitute are done." She kissed my cheek.

Tears came to my eyes. I had not been destitute but ask any person who has struggled with their finances what it means to find oneself suddenly free of worrying about money, and you might understand how I felt. The relief was as a weight tumbling from me. "Thank you, Majesty." I fell to my knees and kissed the edge of her gown. Mary raised me up again.

"You are restored to true position and respect, as the only wife of my father still living, and as his beloved sister," she said. "No more will men try to treat you with disdain."

I could see various members of the council in the room looking nervous. Mary had announced her Privy Council was to be huge – unwieldy was the word many used – comprising trusted members of her own household who in truth had no experience for the roles they were being granted, but were there because Mary knew they were loyal, as well as existing members of Edward's council, who had all the experience but none of her trust. Since plenty of them had acted not only against me, but Mary herself, in Edward's reign, I knew why this conversation made them deeply wary.

Mary was true to her word. Determined as she was to uphold the benefits that her father had promised me just as she was determined to uphold his view of the succession, my accounts were investigated by officers of the Crown, debts were paid, and my pension came regularly. Certain houses were still not restored to me, but I thought if I waited then in time Mary would see to that as well. As it was for the present moment, I was more than happy. At last, I had a friend who was Queen, and Mary's council, under orders from their sovereign, were disposed to be kindly and generous towards me. I could forget and forgive. I even had hopes of more and reissued my request to be known as the Dowager Queen of England. Where Edward's government had refused to consider it, Mary said she would certainly put it to her council.

But if I was happy, many of my friends and those who had supported me in hard times became more than worried after Mary became Queen.

Katherine was troubled, as was Cranmer, supposing the changing of the faith was likely to occur with swift speed. They were correct. The singing of the Mass in Latin was restored in England by that August and a proclamation was issued which strictly forbade Protestant preaching. Mary declared she would be lenient and would give people time to return to the old faith, but swift changes, this time in the other direction, seemed to confirm all the worst fears of the Protestants around me and raised concerns for many others, even ones who were Catholic.

Mary was uncomfortable with the title of Head of the Church and meant to restore England to the power of Rome. Plenty of people might want the old customs back, but they did not want to see the Pope at the Head of the English Church again. Mary's father had demonstrated how a king might become Emperor and Pope within his own kingdom, and many of the English now welcomed this unique idea of their faith. Many more did not want to pay taxes or tithes to Rome, and others did not want their land, taken from the Church in the days of Henry VIII, stripped from them.

It seemed even I would not escape, for in that month I had a note from Mary's council to say that I had not been observed in church yet, which pained the Queen since "she knew" I had been desirous of the faith returning.

In actual fact, the only reason I had not been to public Mass was partly for my health, which seemed to have decided, now all was well, that I should take a break from being healthy and fall to sickness. It ever is the way of things, as soon as we have a break in some form of stress in our lives, as we relax more troubled spirits of sickness are sent to assail us. But I had another reason. Unsure as to what the method of religion would be in England now, I did not want to go against the old decrees of Edward, or his father and did not want either to turn up to church to find a service being said in English which might offend the new Queen. Some preachers were still saying Mass in English as some had reverted immediately to Latin. Was I to command them to say the Mass in Latin? I had thought it safer to pray in my own private way until everything was decided, but apparently, I was being watched by the Queen, and she was not happy with what she saw.

Lady Elizabeth had also not been seen at Mass, and this made Mary suspicious of her. That I had not been seen at the same time was apparently making the Queen, or those about her, suspect that Elizabeth and I were in cahoots and that we, along with other Protestants in England, might be plotting to resist her religious changes. I thought Elizabeth was either thinking the same as me, and waiting until the rules were clear, or that she was attempting to signal to other Protestants, for we all knew she was that way inclined, that she was on their side.

If so, it worked, for even in the first months of Mary's reign, people of a Protestant bent were saying Elizabeth was clearly on their side. This did not please the Queen, and in response Elizabeth was "invited" permanently to court, where the Queen could keep an eye on her.

"And yet the Queen promised tolerance on religion," I said to Katherine.

I received an arched eyebrow in return. "Queen Mary may promise such a thing as she ascends to her throne, all rulers do, but whether she will keep true to that promise is quite another thing. There are rumours already that she means to marry into Spain, perhaps to the Emperor himself, to whom she was promised as a child, and all knew that match was her mother's wish, well… when Katherine of Spain was not promising her to Reginald Pole."

"He is a Cardinal, is he not? She cannot wed him."

"He is not ordained a priest, but I do not think she would want to. Edward Courtenay has been mentioned too, but Mary would see such matches as beneath her. She will want a lord of her station, a prince or archduke, King or Emperor, and her mother would have liked her to marry a man of her homeland."

I frowned. "The Emperor is rather old now, and not a well man."

"If not the Emperor, the Emperor has a son and if Mary marries into Spain, then the Protestant religion will not be respected in this country, it will in fact be persecuted. Monarchs make many a promise when in the first flush of their ascension but as the bloom fades, so do promises sworn. Mary will not offer tolerance. There will be some who will manage to hide their faith and go underground but those of us who made ourselves obvious in the reign of King Edward, we will not find hiding so easy. Cranmer knows he is deep in danger. Mary wants him removed as Archbishop, and I think she wants to prosecute him for heresy. She blames him for the religious changes of Edward's reign, well, him and Northumberland, but it was Cranmer who wrote the Prayer Book and pushed forth with the changes. It will become dangerous here for those of us who wish to follow the reformed faith."

"You cannot be thinking of leaving England." I turned to her, horrified. "It is your home; it is everything you know and what would I do without you?"

Katherine smiled. "You, my friend, I do not worry about. You are the only wife who managed to survive into this reign, all others fell long ago. I have no doubt that you will do what is required in order to continue on. You are a pragmatist, Anna, where I never was. I see now as perhaps I did not before the wisdom you have always adopted in speaking little even on subjects which mean a great deal to you and keeping your opinions to yourself. Had I done such in the last reign I would have been safer now, but we all thought Edward would live, did we not? We all thought the way he had established was the path we were to follow, and now abruptly the path changes and I find myself not on firm footing. I fear, my friend, there will be no space for me, or for my husband, as Mary comes to her throne."

Katherine slipped that little shot of information in and then was astonished when all I did was smile. "So, you married Bertie," I said calmly. Her mouth fell open.

"You knew? But how? I told no one until now."

"I saw the way he looked at you, and you at him. When did you decide to go ahead?"

"Last week," she confessed grudgingly. "I will be a great scandal soon, but I thought, if we slipped this in as Mary came to the throne, I would not be the subject of so much gossip and talk. They will be busy talking of the new Queen, all the gossips of London and beyond, so will have less time to be scandalised by the crazed, old Dowager Duchess marrying her Master of Horse."

"I wish you all the happiness of the world, and you are not old."

Katherine assumed a pained expression. "Sometimes, my friend, I think all that wisdom we credit you with, all your insight, is nothing of the kind. You have simply trained yourself to react calmly to every situation, so it appears you know all, that you understand much before we ever know it ourselves. It is not really insight; it is simply being able to master your expression."

I sniggered. "Ah, well, you will never know, will you? Since I have such a good mask."

Katherine grinned. "I am happy, he loves me, and he is a good man. He stood by me as grief tried to consume me, and he helped me to walk when I thought I had fallen too hard to get up again. You did the same, but sadly, I cannot marry you."

I chuckled. "A sadness to me too, my friend, but I am glad you are happy."

"And I have a husband who cannot try to control me."

"You think he would try?"

Katherine's eyes took on an edge of darkness. "He would consider it. It comes to all men, no matter how good they are. They think that to dominate a woman is the natural order, and eventually that impulse will rise, even over love it will spread. Some may recognize it and control it, and I hope Bertie will be one of them, but many fail and I know this. That is why men beat their wives; they have to prove they are stronger than them. It is why once loving men run off with other women, and it is why men turn cold and cruel, treating wives as if they do not matter. Dominance, control, it ruins their lives as well as those of their women, for it isolates them, destroys love, turns men into monsters."

"And knowing this, you marry?"

"I outrank him. Free as a widow I was, but as a woman married who outranks her husband, I am still at liberty. Try as he might, if that path he chooses, I will always be higher than him and because of obedience to hierarchy he must bow to me at times. It makes us equal, in a way, you see, a balance of power. Each must defer to the other, so if there comes a time that love dries up as a leaf in the desert, and the urge to dominate me grows strong, he will never be able to fully command me. I choose a husband with my heart and my mind this time, my friend."

"And he is of the same faith as you," I said.

"Which makes us even less safe here," she sighed.

"So you think to leave England?"

"To leave England for a time, if it comes to that, though I know not where we would go or where we would be safe. The Schmalkaldic League has been put down by the Emperor, its leaders are humbled, many countries where the great reformation was begun are now in trouble. France and Spain are Catholic, and the Emperor is determined to hunt down and root out the people he calls heretics. If England becomes not safe for us, we will have to go and we will have to find ways to survive, but we all know other truths. Queen Mary is old for the getting of children even if she marries right away, and there is waiting behind her a most Protestant Princess and a wise one. Many of us now look to Elizabeth. She is our future."

"But not yet would you go?"

"I am willing to see if Mary will be tolerant, as she swears."

Chapter Thirty-Six

Autumn 1553

London

Mary's coronation was held in September, and I was invited to be amongst the ladies in attendance upon her. Mary spent the traditional night at the Tower of London and from there was to process to Westminster Abbey. On the night before we all left, she called me to her.

"Mine will be the first coronation of a queen since the woman who displaced my mother was crowned," Mary said quietly when I joined her at the window overlooking the courtyards below. I thought of people who had died in that space, now so still and quiet. Light rain pattered on cobbles. Light of torches glimmered on the wetness. It was a scene of peace, yet there so much violence had taken place, lives had been stolen, futures obliterated. Mary, it seemed, could see past the peace of the night and perhaps like me could hear the whispers of those lost. To her, however, they meant something different than to me.

"I feel as if the people will remember this, and they will compare me to her, to the woman who destroyed my mother's life, and my own. Although I am eager to take my place on the throne, to be accepted by God as Queen of England, I feel this most keenly upon me and I fear it, my friend, I fear people looking at me and thinking of Anne Boleyn." She turned to me, her eyes haunted.

I touched her hand and she almost flinched. Perhaps she was not accustomed now to being touched, her position removing her from all others, but she did not pull away. "This is indeed the first coronation of a queen since that time, but it is not the first coronation of a *prince*, Majesty. You are to become England's first Queen Regnant, but you are also a princess of the realm. I believe the coronation that people may compare yours to, if any does, would be that of your brother. That would be the most recent memory any have of a coronation, for some it will have been the only coronation they will have seen. Disturb yourself not with dark imaginings, thinking that you might be compared to a woman you hold responsible for the end of your parents' marriage, for I think your people will compare you to your brother, and you should keep in mind, Majesty, that whilst you say this woman destroyed your mother's life and yours, that is not entirely true; you still are here and at this moment you are to rise to the position of greatest glory, a position you were granted by your father and by God, so your life has not been destroyed and it is not at an end. In truth, it is only just beginning."

I thought of the tale of the Swan Maiden Sybylla had told so long ago. Those had been her words, had they not? The part all thought the end of the tale was only the end for one. For the Swan Maiden, that end had been her beginning. How strange it is that something said so long ago could come back to me now, my sister's wisdom emerging from my mouth to bring comfort to another soul. My heart ached to touch my sister then, and, knowing I was not able to, I hoped she could hear the sound of my heart singing to her.

Mary clasped my hands, sudden tears in her eyes. "You are right, she tried to destroy us, but she did not for I am alive. I am here and to be Queen and though my mother fell during the war we all fought, a part of her lives on in me."

"Though I never knew your mother, I think she would have been proud of you this day," I said. "I was told once that your mother envisioned you as the first queen of this country, when she was still married to your father. I think perhaps she saw this fate for England."

*

"And how are you this fine morning?" I said to Elizabeth as we came to our carriage which was to trundle behind Mary's own in the coronation procession. All about us was a flurry of activity, people in fine clothes getting into position, pages and servants running hither and thither, fetching or carrying messages. There was a hum of conversation on the light wind, muted by respect. People were smiling and their lips, as well as all the jewels which had turned out that day to be appreciated, glittered in dun sunlight.

"Highness, I find myself well and bright, content of soul." Elizabeth looked fresh and pretty, her dark eyes shining. "My sister takes her rightful place as Queen which many tried to deny her, and she claims it with courage and fortitude. I am proud on this day of my sister and of my Queen."

A diplomatic answer, and she was dressed in a diplomatic fashion as well, for whilst during Edward's reign and particularly after her brush with scandal with Seymour, Elizabeth had dressed in plain Protestant colours of black and white, as her most Catholic sister ascended to the throne Elizabeth had set aside such robes and chose instead regal hues. Her style of dress for the day had of course been commanded, as mine had, but still, the swiftness with which the Princess had altered her appearance was a telling sign of intelligence. About court too now she was a riot of colour.

Elizabeth and I were both in the same colours, in almost twin gowns, made of crimson velvet with cloth of silver, our robes done in the French fashion. Elizabeth's gown, however, carrying more silver than my dress, was more elaborate and certainly more so than those of the women of Mary's household following us. It marked her as higher of status than them and me, which as the albeit unnamed heir of England she was, but lower in status than her older sister, who was dressed in a mantle of cloth of silver with a gold circlet set with precious stones and pearls upon her head, along with a jewelled veil made of tinsel fabric. Mary's kirtle was also made of cloth of gold, trimmed with miniver.

"I am told you have not appeared willingly at the Mass as yet," I mentioned quietly as we took our seats. Susan helped me to arrange my skirts then fell back, to take her place in the procession far behind.

"I have been sadly much ill, Highness, afflicted with stomach troubles." As Elizabeth looked about, she saw me lifting my eyebrows at her and smiled. "It is *very* true," she said.

"Never protest that something is most certainly true when you are lying, it belies the falsehood," I advised. "I would consider that whilst sometimes it is good to show those who look to us for leadership or guidance that we are on their side, that when there is one with great power over you, a little compromise must be made. The Queen has yet to name you her heir, if she suspects your religion, she may not. There will be a time for you, later, but this now is the time of Mary."

"May my sister live long and rule over us," said Elizabeth, arranging her skirts.

I touched her arm, and she turned those black eyes on me. "People I love, and respect are already talking of fleeing the country," I whispered. "That will not be a path open to you if you wish to remain thought of as Mary's heir. Much as I wish the Queen will be clement and kind, we must always consider the opposite may be true. If you cannot run at such a time, hide you must. There are people counting on you."

"I am sure my sister means to deal with her people only with love." I knew that was not what Elizabeth thought at all, but I nodded.

"With all my heart, and for the sake of our new Queen herself, I hope that will be the case," I said. "I love your sister, we have been as friends a long time, but power changes people, that much I have learned. You are clever, Elizabeth. Remain that way and act always with pragmatism in mind."

"I think I may promise that. *Semper Eadem*, it is how I am and how I mean to remain."

"That was your mother's motto, one of them," I noted.

"And now mine." There was a note of pain in her voice, but she turned her head to smile at French Ambassadors who were wandering past.

I glanced to one side and saw Thomas Cawarden in the throng, getting ready to depart. I had to control my face. I had hoped he might fall from favour, even though I was still reliant on using "his" house, but Mary had granted him a warrant to perform a play at Saint James's Palace of late, and he had a knack for such things. It seemed he was to haunt court, perhaps gaining more favours. It was odd, really, for the man was an avowed Protestant. Perhaps it was a sign Mary did mean to be neutral? One could only hope.

As we set out, Mary's golden carriage at the head and our silver one just behind, four ladies in waiting rode on horseback beside the litter of the Queen. These ladies were the Duchess of Norfolk, the Marchioness of Exeter, Marchioness of Winchester and the Countess of Arundel, their appearance marking and honouring not only the high titles of the land, but a return to favour for Catholics.

After them came women of the royal household, some in carriages and some on horseback. These ladies were all dressed in crimson velvet. Many were to serve the Queen in her private chambers. Behind them came noblewomen and gentlemen also dressed in crimson satin, followed on horseback by maids of honour, one of whom I was most pleased to see was Anne Bassett, who, having served many of the queens of Henry VIII was now serving his daughter. Behind them came chamberers all in crimson damask. There were probably seventy women in total riding behind the Queen and following us came servants and their masters of the court dressed in green and white, the Tudor colours.

As a snake formed of crimson, white, gold and green, we emerged from the Tower gates and into the streets. The noise was thunderous. People screamed the Queen's name and blessings upon her, and when they spied Elizabeth and me, they called out for us too. Elizabeth lifted her hand and waved to all, and they screamed her name only louder.

"They adore you, Highness," I said to her.

"As I do them." She beamed. "Look how they turn out for my sister, my lady, bringing presents they can ill afford to give to her. Generous are the hearts that love."

Mary's entourage were swamped by these little gifts, it was true. Bread rolls baked as roses and light ale freshly made, possets of herbs, bunches of flowers. Many were flung into our carriage too, and as Elizabeth deftly caught one that almost came flying for my head, people laughed and applauded her.

All along the route from the Tower to Westminster there were pageants with music and speeches and plays performed. In many places there were banners in Latin proclaiming the Queen as the saviour of her people, and of God.

Hans merchants put on a show at Gracechurch corner in which there was a fountain running with wine and an actor flew down a rope just as the Queen passed by, which caused much applause and not a little laughter as he landed awkwardly. At the other end of the street Florentine merchants had built an arch with three entryways and six actors above them hailed Mary as she approached. On the very top a statue of an angel dressed in green played a trumpet to bid her welcome as well.

I was not so sure about the Florentine pageant, truth be told, as it compared Queen Mary to Judith of the Bible, who had defeated and decapitated her enemies. When I looked puzzled, Elizabeth smiled a little and said it was to celebrate Mary's triumph over Northumberland.

I thought of Jane Grey, still in the Tower. Mary had said she wanted to release Jane, but it had not occurred. This pageant, therefore, left me a little uneasy.

But it was a fine day in truth, the streets were full of supporters who threw their caps in the air and must have known they never would find them again as hundreds fell to the floor like dandelion seeds blown to the wind. Screaming people almost beside themselves danced, shouting support for Mary. I hoped it made her happy.

To the Palace of Westminster that night we came, weary from all we had seen. My head was ringing from all the screaming and from the sound of church bells pealing all over London.

On the 1st of October Mary arrived by barge at the stairs of the old Palace of Westminster and walked from Westminster Hall to the Abbey in the morning with three naked swords carried before her by the Earls of Westmoreland and Cumberland. They represented spiritual and temporal justice. The third sword, the Curtana, the sword of mercy, was carried by the Earl of Derby.

Once again Elizabeth and I attended Mary as she processed into the Abbey and in a train behind her countesses and noblewomen walked in pairs.

The Queen's train was carried by the Lord Chamberlain, John Gauge, as well as the Duchess of Norfolk, and as we entered, we saw the quire of the Abbey was hung with rich, bright tapestry, and the floor strewn with rushes and sweet herbs. As Mary entered, the Bishop declared the Queen's pardons for prisoners, excluding some held in the Tower of London and some in the Marshalsea. Sadly, Lady Jane Grey and her supporters were amongst those who were excluded from pardon. I tried not to sigh aloud, for I had hoped now would be the time my friend's granddaughter was set free.

I understood Jane could still be dangerous to Mary, not because Jane herself was, but as a figurehead. All the same, Jane was Mary's cousin and Mary herself had admitted she thought Jane innocent.

Mary walked to King Edward's chair with two nobles beside her and after a moment she was joined by Stephen Gardiner, Bishop of Winchester who was now, much to my disgust, Lord Chancellor, and stood with her on the raised scaffold in sight of all the people. Mary was never going to allow Cranmer to crown her, after all. Grudgingly she had allowed him to officiate at Edward's funeral, and after much persuasion had allowed her brother a Protestant service. She had wanted to bury him with Catholic rites, deciding even in death she knew what was best for her little brother, but men had persuaded her in the end. As the funeral had gone on, Mary had held a Mass, hoping perhaps to cleanse the stain of the last truly Protestant service she would allow from England.

Cranmer himself could not conduct the service of coronation for another reason. He was in the Tower. So were Hugh Latimer and Nicholas Ridley. Cranmer had refused to bring back the old Mass in Canterbury Cathedral and had stated loudly that the doctrine set forth by King Edward was purer and more according to God's will than any that had been used in England for 3,000 years, so he would not betray it. Mary and her men took this as sedition and commanded him before the Star Chamber. That day, he had been sent to the Tower.

He was not alone. Much was changing. Reformed bishops, priests and other clergy had already been pulled from their offices and replaced with Catholic ones. Others had been arrested. Bishop Bonner had been restored, Gardiner had been promoted and released. It was said Cranmer, and the others, would be put on trial for high treason, and I had no doubt it was so. Mary loathed him.

In truth, the speed at which Mary had moved on religion had frightened many, me included. I had thought it a mistake that her brother attempted so much reform so fast, and now, I thought this swiftness of restoration a mistake also. She did not see she was doing the same as Edward had, and it would cause the same problems.

"My sister comes to the four corners," Elizabeth whispered, standing at my side. Perhaps she had seen my mind wandering and called me back to the present.

The chair of King Edward was placed on a higher platform with ten steps and Mary showed herself at the four corners of the scaffold as Gardiner introduced her as Queen, a part of the ceremony Elizabeth told me was known as the *recognition.* Of course, I had seen a coronation before, but Edward's had been shorter and in all honesty we had been so caught up with concentrating on all the changes Cranmer had made at that time, I am not sure the significance of the rituals performed had sunk into my mind.

As Gardiner asked for the people to recognise their Queen, we all cried out in one voice, "God save Queen Mary!"

I should have been nothing but pleased to see my friend take her rightful place, but whilst I always would believe she had a right to her throne, I was coming to fear what she would do with it, what people I loved she would harm. Cranmer had spoken for me in the past, he had worked, I believed, to save Catherine Howard, he had spoken for Somerset when few had. I did not agree with all he had done, nor the speed, but we all knew what happened when a man was accused of treason in England. I did not want him to die.

Neither did I want to see my friend Katherine arrested or driven out of her country.

And these were only my closest friends. What of all the others, all these frightened people watching Mary take her throne? So many would fear this day as others welcomed it, and as the service went on I could feel them in my heart, their dread, their worry.

I watched as Mary was taken to a richly draped chair at the high altar where she made her offerings. The Bishop of Chichester gave a sermon on the theme of obedience, and it was clear he was talking mostly of the faith. Mary made her promises and the choir sung *Veni Creator Spiritus*. Our new Queen was then anointed, although first she went into a space curtained off under a canopy, so she could be undressed by her ladies and re-dressed in a different costume in order that the oil might touch her skin.

"The oil must be allowed to touch every part of her skin, from where it is applied to where it decides to drain," Elizabeth murmured, "for this is God choosing His Prince for England."

Her eyes were shining with a brilliant light as she gazed upon her sister, and I could see much that was in her mind. It had been said before that no woman could rule England, yet her sister was about to, and men had supported it. If one goes before you, it is easier for you to follow, a path once broken becoming easier to walk. Elizabeth was looking on the coronation of Mary, but she was seeing a path now open to her, made more possible by the ascension of her sister to the throne as a ruling queen.

Mary was anointed by holy oil obtained by the imperial ambassador from the Bishop of Arras, as the stock of oil left over from the reign of her brother was considered no more to be sacred.

The Duke of Norfolk, yet another past prisoner now released, brought the three diadems Mary was to be crowned with; Saint Edward's, the Imperial, and one newly made for Mary. Using each in turn, Gardiner crowned Mary. The crown of Saint Edward was only allowed to rest upon her head for a brief moment for it was so heavy, weighted down with jewels, that it was quite possible it could have snapped her neck. Upon her finger Gardiner placed a ring, marrying her to her country. The master of the jewel house brought a pair of bracelets which were set with precious stones and pearls for her to wear also. Now that Mary had been crowned all nobleman put on their caps and coronets which they had carried into the church, and Gardiner and the earls about him made homage to Mary. With the Queen kneeling, Mass was celebrated. In her hand she held the royal sceptre which was topped with a dove. Once more she entered the curtained section then reappeared in her coronation robes carrying the sceptre and orb and all people in the Abbey burst into furious cheering and weeping. Our Queen was crowned. For that they were pleased.

It was what she might do with the power invested in her which some feared, but from the gloating expression on Gardiner and Bonner's faces, they were not amongst those who felt any trepidation.

Chapter Thirty-Seven

1553

London

After her coronation was done, and all of us had feasted with her in Westminster Hall, with the elderly Duke of Norfolk riding up and down the hall on a horse challenging any who would contest his Queen's right to rule – a ridiculous pageant which I was told was traditional – and with Elizabeth and me sitting in places of honour on the end of the high table, our new Queen made it plain to those about her that she wanted to marry as soon as possible and was considering candidates. She wanted to know who her people wanted her to marry.

Whilst many believed this idea of offering candidates was merely an exercise in appeasing her people and the nobles about her, for most thought her heart was already set on Spain, it was a chance for more moderate candidates to be suggested, perhaps those who whilst being Catholic might encourage the Queen towards toleration of the faiths rather than obliteration of the Protestant religion, and those who followed it.

"English candidates are popular," Katherine Willoughby told me, playing with a gold bracelet on her wrist. "Edward Courtenay most of all."

"Is he not a little… simple?" I had met the man a few times now at court. True, he had been imprisoned for most of his life, ever since he was a child, but he seemed to have remained a child, as if never having been free meant he never had grown up.

Handsome he was, and perhaps ten years younger than Mary, so probably fertile. He came of royal stock, since he was a second cousin of Mary and Elizabeth through the line of Edward IV, his paternal grandmother being Catherine of York, sister to the Queen of Henry VII. His house could also claim descent from Edward I. Mary was fond of him as his family had supported her mother, and she remained great friends with Courtenay's mother Gertrude. His family had been imprisoned by Henry VIII in what was known as the Exeter Conspiracy where it was said his father and other family members had conspired to convince Reginald Pole to lead a Catholic invasion of England, which would end with Courtenay's father, Henry, Marquess of Exeter, being placed on the throne. As the King's cousin, he had held a claim.

I frequently found this conspiracy a little confusing, for it was said the Poles and Courtenays had worked together to bring this plot about, yet the Poles had an equal, if not better, claim to the throne since Margaret Pole had been the daughter of George Plantagenet Duke of Clarence, the brother of Edward IV. Clarence had died a traitor, but still, the Poles' claim stemmed from a male ancestor where the Courtenays' came of a female, and the male was usually favoured. One had to wonder why the Poles would then support the claim of the Courtenays over their own? This, amongst other questions led people to believe the conspiracy was probably fabricated.

Courtenay's father, Exeter, had lost his head for the plot, as had many others, but his mother was eventually released, and Gertrude and Mary were close. Edward Courtenay had never been released, however, both Henry VIII and his son Edward seeing him as too much a threat to the Crown.

But Mary had set him free, and now plenty of people wanted her to marry him, a romantic idea.

Yet I thought she would not. Not only was he below her in status, he was very much a boy still, bounding about court open-souled, careless with his words. He would make an awful King, although Mary might consider him since he would hardly interfere in her affairs. He knew nothing of the world, so how could he?

They were in truth plenty of candidates. Mary could marry within the nobility of England, or she could wed a prince of Europe. Her father had married subjects to the Crown as had Edward IV when he married Elizabeth Woodville, however it was known that when prince married pauper, people often resented it, and it caused problems within the country. The only English men with royal blood were Edward Courtenay, who I thought too much a simpleton, Reginald Pole who was a great-nephew of Edward IV and was a Cardinal, Henry and George Hastings who were three-times great-nephews of Edward IV, and Henry Stuart Lord Darnley, son of Margaret Douglas, and a grandson of Margaret Tudor, Queen of Scots.

Lord Darnley and George Hastings, many stated, were both rather young to be considered, since they were both around thirteen years of age – people seemed to forget girls were married off at this age in droves – and Henry Hastings was married, so unless he set aside the daughter of the dead Duke of Northumberland, he was unsuitable as well.

That left Courtenay and Reginald Pole.

Gardiner favoured a match with Courtney. Both men had been in the Tower during King Edward's reign and had grown close. Gertrude Blount was also pushing her son on the new Queen.

"But it is widely rumoured," my friend of Suffolk whispered, "that Mary is not keen at all, and considers him most unsuitable. He is much younger than her and a subject with no lands or power of his own."

"I do find him rather lacking in judgement, too."

"Yes, he is almost childlike, I suspect from being placed inside a prison as a child and never having any knowledge of the outside world. The Queen snapped at Gardiner when he suggested Courtenay again to her recently and said that his friendship for the man was not a good enough reason for her to marry a subject."

Irritation passed over Katherine's face as she mentioned Gardiner. She had hoped, as had many of us, that his arrest and incarceration during Edward's reign might have been the end of him but now he was out and in a position of greater power than before.

And Gardiner did not like her.

"What about Pole? I understand he was suggested as a match for Mary many years ago, perhaps by those who led the Pilgrimage of Grace?"

"It is not a match her father would have looked well upon," said Katherine, "there would also be problems. He does not know England well since he has been in exile since the early 1530's and although he has not been ordained a priest, he is a Cardinal and very much a scholarly person rather than a leader of men. He also remains a subject of the Queen and thus far she has made it clear that she would prefer to marry an equal, not one who was set below her by God. I think she has another plan for Pole in any case, for I am sure she wants to reward his family after they supported her, and she respects all that he ever said on her mother's marriage to her father; he was ever in support of Queen Katherine of Spain. I think she wants him to lead the Church, to take Cranmer's place."

We both paused as we thought on our friend, and what his fate might be. There was nothing we could do – speak out and Mary would suspect us, setting us in danger. I had no power to free the Archbishop. All I could hope was Mary would play true to the goodness I knew was in her and set him at liberty. Jane Grey still was held, so there was hope for Cranmer. *Mary is good at heart,* I told myself.

"So, if a native match is unsuitable," I said, "then she must choose a prince."

"Some put forth Eric the Prince of Sweden, who she said was too young but in truth it is because he is a Lutheran. Another candidate is Dom Luis of Portugal, he was suggested as a husband for her many times in the past, is her first cousin and ten years older than her. She may approve of that for she seems not to like the idea of a younger husband. He is not a king in his own land therefore would be able to spend much time in England and he is Catholic, and old enough to possibly have maturity and judgement although many men are lacking that."

I smiled. "And then there is the Emperor Charles himself, or his son Philip, both of them are widowers."

"I think she would prefer the father over the son. She believes, however erroneously, that he has protected her for her entire life, when in actual fact Charles has done little for her other than bluster from a distance. It is more likely that Philip will be the suitor put forward, even though he is at present negotiating for a marriage with another cousin, an Infanta of Portugal like his first wife. I also hear he has a long-term mistress who he loves more than life itself."

I went to the Queen with a candidate of my own; the Archduke Ferdinand.

There were actually two men of the same name who might be possible; Ferdinand of Austria who was a cousin of Mary and had been widowed for some years, and Ferdinand's son who owned the same name and was unmarried and of a suitable age for Mary. The elder Ferdinand had thirteen children and seemed constantly occupied in war with the Sultan of Turkey and helping his brother the Emperor with maintaining Hapsburg dominance over his lands, so it was possible he had little incentive to marry again and was likely to be an inattentive husband if he did, but his second son who was twenty-four years of age was a possibility.

This Ferdinand of Austria was the brother of my brother's wife, Maria.

"He is not a king within his own country so will be able to spend time with you and devote himself to your country, Majesty," I said when I presented the idea to Mary. "He is twenty-four, a grown man and one who has lived in the world. I hear tell he is well educated and loves music, much like yourself and he is a Catholic and kinsman to the Emperor, your cousin. His father has been in devoted service to the Habsburg Empire all his life and if you wish to marry into your mother's family, I believe this would be a good option for you."

I thought this man, although Catholic, might be more moderate than his kinsman of Spain.

The people of England were not in favour of the idea of a Spanish match, thinking the Inquisition would come to England as well as burnings for the faith. A man of Austria, although of the same family, might prove a compromise for Mary and for the English people, he might be Catholic enough and Hapsburg enough for her yet not hail from the country many seemed to fear. Maria, my sister-in-law, also had sense enough to plead for people not of her faith, and although I could not guarantee her brother would do the same, it was possible.

"Such a match would make us closer in kinship, too, Your Majesty," I said, smiling, "so I do admit there is another motive for me to support this match."

Mary looked interested and she said she would consider all I said but as I looked into her face I knew she would not, for in those deep blue eyes I seemed to see the rising sun of Spain.

Chapter Thirty-Eight

1553

London and Hever

"I am *quite* the scandal of London." Katherine sounded at once a little amused and worried.

She was indeed the talk of town. News of her marriage was out, seeing as Katherine herself had informed the Queen who greatly disapproved of the match, but now it was done, Mary said, she could not set they who were joined by God apart. Frances Grey and her husband looked down on the match, but they were bound to. Frances was the only reason, most of us thought, that Henry Grey had escaped losing his head along with Northumberland, since Frances had managed to remind Mary, despite her support for her daughter Jane as Queen, that they had been close friends before that. Where Mary led now Frances was sure to follow.

"But you are happy," I said. "And you have weathered worse storms than this."

"That is true. And Bertie… you know I must get used to calling him Richard, yet I never can after all these years. He says he likes it, but I sound like a mistress still, calling him to order." We both laughed a little. "Bertie, he is not a man as Charles was, thinking of me as only a pretty ornament to put up on his sleeve and wear so other men become jealous. Bertie has respect for me and values my mind as well as what I look like."

"And he cannot order you about."

Katherine smiled at me bringing up the subject anew. "You find it fascinating, do you not? This reason for selecting a husband? In truth, I wonder if I did not think of the marriage between Charles and Mary Tudor, and in considering they were at least mostly content but that he could never command her because he was of lower station than her, I came to think that marrying down in rank could be an advantage for me just as much as other people think it a disadvantage."

"You sound most pragmatic, are you sure you love the man?"

"I do love him," she said, "I love him a great deal, but I am also aware from past experience how a man may change over the years as he becomes accustomed to his wife, and how things perhaps buried deep within him might come to the fore and become more noticeable. Charles was the same. We started out with romance, but it seemed to become more like fellowship or business by the end. The part of me that still fulsomely wants to believe in love is overjoyed and giddy, make no mistake, but there is another part of me, a part with a wiser and more ancient voice, which speaks to me at the same time. That old voice tells me that a part of me must always be protected, even or perhaps especially, from the man I choose to love, and so in choosing someone who is lesser than me I do protect myself, I protect my mind and my spirit, my ability to speak and my will to be heard. He cannot dampen me as Charles tried to on occasion and he cannot set me down, for I am the one who raised him higher. He is a dedicated Protestant as I am but should our views on the faith ever stray from one another, he will not be able to restrain where my feet take me. Should it come to pass that he changes and what he once cherished he then tries to control, he will not be able to. That is my protection, my friend."

I nodded carefully, thinking how sad it was that women had to think thus, think always of ways to protect ourselves, even from the men we loved. That we had to think of a time beyond the first giddy strains of love, think to a time when the man we loved might alter into someone we knew not. That even in matters which should be purely of the heart, where we should be lost and carefree with love, we could not be. Women had to use their minds and protect themselves. It made our worlds smaller than they should have been, less free.

I could not deny, however, that my friend had made a sensible choice. Others thought not of course. The idea a woman would marry below her station? And for love? Ridiculous!

"It is a funny thing, my friend, that women are often accused of being materialistic and yet whenever we dare to marry for love, people look down on us," my friend told me. "It is almost as if whichever path one chooses it is never the right one, almost as if whatever women do, we will be condemned. I may as well therefore do what makes me happy, at least at the present time. We will see what the future brings. That is all we ever can do."

*

"They will die?" I had hoped Mary would show mercy. The core of me shook. Hope, something I had felt for my friend, *in* my friend, quivered.

On the 13th of November, Cranmer, and four others, Latimer and Ridley amongst them, as well as Lady Jane Grey, her husband Guildford Dudley and Henry Grey, Duke of Suffolk had faced trial for high treason. They were found guilty, attained by legislation passed by our Parliament. Grey, as I mentioned, had been saved from sentence of execution due to his wife pleading with the Queen, her cousin, but he was set under house arrest. Many people thought Jane and her husband might be spared too, pardoned by the Queen.

Cranmer, Ridley and Latimer, however, seemed another matter. They were condemned to death for heresy. Cranmer had spoken heresy, had written heretical works and had encouraged heresy, so said his accusers. It was not known when they would die, but everyone said it would be by fire.

"That is the punishment for heretics, Highness." Gertrude Brockehouse's face was sorrowful.

"I thought I knew my friend, that she was a woman of mercy," I said, "but this Queen I do not know."

"It may be the sentence of death is there to scare them, so they might convert."

"You think this is what the Queen wants?" I thought of it. It would be a victory for Mary, that was true, and she sincerely believed in her faith and that others who did not believe as she did would go to Hell. Perhaps she indeed meant to scare them so they would be saved. Perhaps just as people said Jane Grey and Guildford would be eventually pardoned, so Ridley, Cranmer and Latimer might be too.

How easy it is to delude ourselves when we do not want to believe what is happening straight before our eyes.

*

"But that is nonsense, they have not been married long, and they have demonstrated they are fertile enough," I huffed with scorn.

"I know, Highness, yet still rumours come flying out of inn door and alleyway." Brockehouse spread his hands.

Gossip had started at the beginning of that year, swearing Wilhelm would never have sons. Some claimed he was cursed for making a pact with the Emperor, some said it was for failing to aid Sybylla. In any case, as another daughter was born that November, Magdalena, people were all agreed he never would have a son.

Whilst this nonsense went on in Cleves, another charade was coming to an end in England. All those suggesting candidates for Mary's husband were clearly wasting their time. It was becoming more and more obvious that Mary had decided she would marry into Spain and that was that. Following on my suggestion of Archduke Ferdinand, however, the King of the Romans had sent ambassadors in November of that year to discuss the match with Mary. The Queen put on a good show, pretending interest and asking questions about him, but speak to any of her ladies, as I did for I was often at court that autumn, and it was entirely clear that she was not enthused.

"Her Majesty would like a husband the same age, or older than her," Jane Dormer, one of Mary's women, told me.

Elizabeth had made a few pointed jests about the women in Mary's chambers. It was true many were older than the Queen, and rather conservative of dress, dour of expression, but wicked little Elizabeth had a wily tongue and soon everyone was calling them "the murder about the Queen" after Elizabeth had compared them to crows. Jane was one of the younger, pretty ones and once had been good friends in childhood with King Edward. She had escaped the slander. Personally, I had not been impressed with Elizabeth's spiteful observations. As a woman in possession of a mind, the Princess should have understood women are too often judged on what we look like when there are numerous other qualities we may possess to recommend us to people. But Elizabeth was still young, and we all make mistakes when we are growing up.

I thought on Jane's observation about Mary. Were I feeling cynical I might say what our new Queen wanted was a father figure, one who rather than rejecting her as her own father had done would instead choose her. We all at times act out a pageant in our own lives where we replay events of the past but attempt a different outcome, as if by doing so we might heal wounds the past has inflicted. This was what I believed Mary was doing, and why she rejected any man younger than her. A younger man might well have had more advantages, especially because what she wanted the most was a child, therefore picking a man who was young and virile would have been sensible. Mary however was not a sensible woman. Frequently she acted on emotion rather than thought, little considering what might happen. Men would say this was because she was a woman, but it was not. She was in truth much like her father.

Mary never had been a pragmatist, and many times had set herself in grave danger by refusing to back down on viewpoints or her faith. I had never really considered how different we were, until that time.

Her wishes for a Spanish match were, however, deeply unpopular, but she did not want another choice, even mine.

It was not only Mary who did not want the Archduke Ferdinand to become England's King, or King consort – it did not seem anyone had quite decided what the status of Mary's husband would be – there were others opposed to the match, several within England and one very powerful one outside. The Emperor did not want his kinsman to wed Mary, he wanted his son to take that position. The Emperor did not welcome the idea of his brother getting too powerful, since he was already contesting him over the notion Philip take on the title of Emperor Elect, but Charles V had also long wanted control of England and through this marriage he could not only take control of it in the present, but in the future if Mary and Philip had children. Charles V would be able to guide the destiny of this once heretic, rebellious country, keep it always an ally to Spain. I heard through my ambassadors that Philip of Spain was not keen on the idea of marrying Mary at all and thought her an old woman, long past her prime, yet he was willing to do his duty and marry her to bring England under the mastery of Spain.

It seemed the English feared this too, as on the 16th of November that year a parliamentary delegation marched to the Queen to formally request that she select an English husband.

They wanted Edward Courtenay, recently created Earl of Devon, but the Queen appeared convinced that the safety of England lay in forming bonds with princes overseas.

On the 7th of December that year a marriage treaty was presented to the Privy Council favouring Philip. It had clearly been carefully put together, for the terms favoured England and included many safeguards to be put upon the power of the new King. England would not have to go to war if Spain did, and the King would have authority in England only during Mary's lifetime, and not beyond. But many thought this false, thought England would be drawn into war on the side of Charles V and might well become just a province of the Hapsburg Empire. The idea of the Inquisition arriving frightened many, and a king must have power over a queen, people supposed, therefore Philip would surely rule Mary, and Spain would dominate England.

"Many nobles are up in arms about it," Katherine confided, "they believe that because of this the Queen will want them to pay greater subsidies and taxes, because if England enters into foreign wars, those wars will need money. Many others, much like me, are worried that the Inquisition will come here, and we all know the stories of the tortures they inflict upon people they see as heretics."

"I hear France also fears this alliance," I murmured, "Antoine de Noailles, French ambassador to England, has apparently begun many intrigues with any malcontents at court he can discover and has also threatened that war may come with France."

The people of England did not like it either and before Christmas arrived that year ballads were being sung in the street defaming Spain and its Prince, as broadsheets condemning the match were handed out in the streets of London.

I decided to return home to Hever after the Christmas celebrations, which I had to attend at court. Elizabeth too was forced to remain for a time, but managed to persuade her sister to release her, so she could keep Christmas quietly on her own estates. Mary was growing impatient in any case with her sister continuing to resist the Catholic faith Mary kept trying to impose upon her, so seemed to release her with relief.

Perhaps both of us leaving around the same time was something which linked us in the mind of the Queen, a link that to both of us became most dangerous as January fell upon England.

For with the coming of the New Year, so came rebellion.

Chapter Thirty-Nine

January 1554

Hever Castle

"This is a foolish time to start a rebellion." I gazed out into a frozen landscape. Frost in shapes of fern fronds covered my windows, spirals of ice and silver. The shutters were up in most rooms to keep in the warmth, but I had demanded some light that morning.

"It is still a danger," Diaceto said. My gentleman had recently returned from Denmark. "Wyatt is here, in our very county."

"I think us far enough away, but have the guards close up the house and we will not venture out."

"Maidstone is not far away, Highness, but twenty miles or so. A marching army could be here in two or three days."

"We are the wrong way from London." My voice was calm, controlled. "Kent is not the focus, it is but a rallying point, a place to gather men. I am sure of it."

"All the same, your yeomen are on guard and gentlemen of your household will be fully armed from now on, Highness. The grooms will watch your stables in case of theft, and patrols will go out about Hever and Penshurst too if we can cover both."

"Very well."

I was right, however, for the focus of rebellion this time was London and Mary rather than fences or the faith. "There have been so many uprisings over the past years, since the death of the old King, my brother. It seems now that anyone who is disaffected in any way thinks to rise up and march on London first before considering any other course of action."

"There is a pattern now to follow."

"Do you think men fear the children of Henry VIII less than they feared his father? I know there were rebellions in his age, but not as many as we have seen since his death." I stared thoughtfully at the flames.

The hall was warm. I had been making additions to Hever since it came into my possession, and more since Mary came to the throne and my finances improved. I had had work done on the Long Gallery, first envisioned by Thomas Boleyn, to widen it and bring in more windows for light, and had added another gallery on the first floor, linking the two wings of the house to the entrance hall. The castle, pretty before, was more modern and useable now and since it continued to be my main residence it needed work to adapt it for my household. The work was done in sympathy with older parts of the building, for I had no wish to make the house look disjointed, as if it stood in two ages, but it was more serviceable now.

I thought of the man who had granted me this house, of the wife he had taken who lived here before me. I always felt her imprint on this place, every day as I wandered the gardens or the corridors I could feel Anne. My former husband I had never heard whisper of after his death, but perhaps I had never appreciated just how strong the sense of fear he held over his country had been. It had been horrifying, indeed, there was no denying that, but it could not be denied it had held the people in check. Was Machiavelli right, and the way to control a populace was through fear? I thought love would be better, if the people truly loved their ruler, would that not lead to greater peace?

I did not know if the people loved Mary. They had been willing to at first, just as I had, warming to the notion my friend was a good soul, but almost as soon as she had her throne there were problems. Mainly it was the Spanish match. Had she wished to please her people she should have wed Courtenay and been done with it, but Mary wanted to please herself.

It was not an unreasonable thought, to want happiness of her own, and had she been a king there would have been small opposition to a foreign marriage. It was because she was a queen, a woman, that there was trouble. With a foreign bride coming in to wed a king no one would suspect her country meant to try to dominate England, or not unless they were exceedingly paranoid, but as a wife was subject to her husband so the

Queen would be to her King. Men could not see it any other way. Spain was on its way to mount England, and England was bending over willingly.

And they would not have it.

Much as I wished Mary happiness, I was realistic enough to appreciate there are times even rulers must follow the wishes of the people, do what is best for the country, rather than what is best for themselves. I had not wanted to marry, but for my people I had walked into a union with surely one of the most dangerous men a woman could be wed to. Had she done what was pragmatic, Mary could have wed Courtenay and been rising in popularity at this moment. Instead, there were men rising against her.

The trouble this time was, it was not peasants, badly armed, fed, and trained that had begun a rebellion, it was men with land, minor nobility, and not so minor.

"Henry Grey," I was somewhat in shock when informed, "you mean, the present Duke of Suffolk whose daughter still is a prisoner in the Tower at the mercy of the Queen, is one of the men who has risen up?"

When Susan assured me it was he who was mentioned, I shook my head. What was the man doing? It seemed the purpose of this rebellion was not to place Jane on the throne, rumours were the rebels wanted Elizabeth and wanted her wed to Edward Courtenay. If Mary would not do as they wished, her sister would be forced to.

I am sure Elizabeth wanted the throne, but I knew she would not support Mary being deposed, or herself being forced to wed a man of the people's choice. Elizabeth had ambition, I knew that for I had seen it in her eyes at the coronation, and because she had made repeated attempts to resist the Catholic Mass, knowing that Protestants in the realm would look to her to restore and protect their faith when to the throne she came. But Elizabeth was clever enough to know if she came to the throne in such a way, through rebellion, she would always be in danger of losing it in the same way. She had respected her sister and brother's right to the throne, believed each had been chosen by God to rule, just as her father had. She was a pawn, a figurehead the rebels were using, I was sure.

And here was Henry Grey, sacrificing the safety of his daughter and the friendship his wife had forged with Mary, which had saved their family, in order to support Elizabeth for the throne. In truth, he simply wanted a woman there he thought he could control. Grey was also potentially placing my friend of Suffolk in danger, since she was related to him by marriage. Grey was a known Protestant, but I thought his involvement was less about faith and more about power. He had been left out since Mary came to the throne. His wife had some influence as friend of the Queen, but he little since he had supported Jane. In truth, he was fortunate still to have a head. The Queen had been lenient, I doubted she would be again.

Sir Thomas Wyatt was the man leading the rebellion. It was not Ambassador Wyatt, since he had died in the same year as Catherine Howard. This was his son.

He had men following him, of course. Sir James Crofts was mentioned, who I thought an odd fellow to have joined as he had never seemed to hold strong religious beliefs and did not appear to have ever objected about Mary marrying into Spain. "He served once in the military," I said. "I remember his name being mentioned."

"Perhaps money is his motivation?" Diaceto shrugged.

"Perhaps, or he thinks he might become more prominent under Elizabeth. He has not found favour under Mary."

Sir Peter Carew was another conspirator, was a man many called a pirate, and he was a passionate Protestant. I remembered a Spanish ambassador had called him the greatest heretic and rebel in England, and Carew had supported the match with Courtney. He seemed affronted that the Queen had chosen a husband herself.

Edward Courtenay himself had also apparently joined this rebellion, but I thought it quite possible he had no idea what was going on. The man was so innocent that he might be told it was a game of war often played in England, and he would go along, grinning like a fool.

It seemed the idea for it had begun in the November the year before and by Christmas it had been decided that these four leaders of the rebellion would raise forces in their counties and march upon London. Once the capital was taken, they would replace Mary with Elizabeth who would marry Courtney, and a fleet of ships would be set loose to prevent Philip of Spain from reaching England. In this way would England be saved, restored to the Protestant faith, and Spain would be vanquished.

That is the trouble with rebellions. They sound simple, straightforward. This lie deludes men until they think that bravery or ideals alone can win wars. They forget how many men a sovereign might command. They forget that any war is not won through the spirit of those fighting. Usually that is what the victors praise about the enemies they defeat, how bravely those men fought as they fell in desperate battle, as if those men had any other choice. It is strategy which wins war, more important than numbers is this, and most rebellions have no strategy other than an end goal. That is why they fail.

The other reason they fail is because frequently those involved are bold, incompetent and foolish.

I later heard that as early as the 29th of December Spain's ambassador to England had informed Mary of a suspected plot in which certain persons were trying to coordinate to seize the Tower of London and set another claimant on the throne. However uninformed this rumour was, much of the rebellion's plotting was discovered when Carew began to attract attention. In Devon, Carew appeared to be making little effort to hide his raising of support for rebellion, and when he managed to overtake Exeter Castle, he naturally attracted the attention of the Privy Council. On the 7th of January they sent a letter calling on him to appear before them to explain himself, and since he did not appear the council sent a letter instead to the Sheriff of Devon, commanding him to bring Carew before the council. The sheriff decided to tell Carew about the letter and Carew went running away to France. The French welcomed him and there was much talk that he would be supplied with arms, vessels and coin. Carew and his French allies plundered Flemish and Spanish ships, swearing they would not allow Philip to set foot on English soil.

Just before Carew fled poor, silly Courtenay was arrested after having been rather outspoken to the wrong people about the plans of the rebellion. He confessed all to his friend Gardiner when people started talking, and Gardiner told the Queen. Mary had Courtenay immediately arrested. When questioned, the man admitted that he had been approached by individuals concerning several matters touching religion and the marriage with Spain. Evidently, he gave them names, as after he had spoken two or three more men were arrested.

As his allies fell, it was clear to Wyatt that the rebellion could not wait until the 18th of March – a much more clement month for a rebellion to begin – which was the date they had agreed so the next day Wyatt called his supporters to him, and they decided to move ahead with the rebellion. This meant they were even less prepared, and they had lost the element of surprise. Mary knew something was coming.

We heard that Henry Grey had been ordered to come to court, but he gave the messenger a reward and a drink, then promptly slipped out of his back door, gathering as much money and men as he could. He rode to Lutterworth where others in the rebellion met with him on the 29th of January. The Duke of Suffolk read Wyatt's proclamation about the rebellion, its causes and aims, to the public in Leicester, and the next day led his troops towards Coventry, believing that his allies were there, and they would open the gates for him. Unbeknownst to Grey, the rebellion had been discovered, and many of his allies had already been arrested or were on the run. The gates were closed to him, and he also found the walls well defended.

Henry Grey went to his brother, Lord John Grey, and they hid in the cottage of one of Lord Grey's gamekeepers. Intending to find a way to escape England, the Duke of Suffolk at one point decided the cottage was not safe so he hid instead in the hollow of an old decaying tree where he stayed for two days and a night in the midst of winter with no food or drink. The gamekeeper betrayed his hiding place and the Queen's men found Henry Grey out in the open, holding out his hands to a small fire which he had built because he could not stand the cold any longer. His brother was also found, and the two were arrested and taken to the Tower of London.

Crofts managed to raise forces in Wales, but the council had also caught wind of this and sent orders to the Lord President of the Council of the Marches to stop rebellion there. Finding his forces surrounded by council troops, Crofts' men tried to fight their way out, but most were massacred.

Crofts surrendered and found himself, too, marched to the Tower to join his friends.

That left only Wyatt, and he had decided to take men of Kent, the very county my house was in, against the Queen.

He had started the Kent uprising on the 25th of January by raising his standard at Maidstone and reading a proclamation stating that Mary's marriage to Philip would bring upon this land most miserable servitude and would establish popish religion. Even *Catholics*, Wyatt shouted, would join him for they had no wish to be subject to Spain. Claiming the Spanish were already at Dover and had come with a force of men to subdue the English, Wyatt gained many supporters.

His headquarters then moved up, towards London, to Rochester.

"They head for London, not Hever." Although I had predicted this, I admit I breathed a sigh of relief. The rebels had gathered very close to us, and I was a relative, albeit by marriage, of the Queen. It was possible they could have come for me and whilst I had more guards than before, due to the Queen's attentions to my income, I doubt they could have stood long against a rebel army. It was said Wyatt had 2,000 men and more were marching to join him every day.

"I thought you not worried about Wyatt's rebellion." Diaceto eyed me with some amazement. "You seemed so calm, Highness."

"It does not aid anyone to panic," I said, smoothing my skirts. "Clear thinking does not come from wild imaginings, and clear thinking is what we needed then, and now."

In addition to his 2,000, another 500 meant to join Wyatt but they were met by a force of 600 of Mary's supporters and were routed. Sixty men were taken prisoner.

"The Duke of Norfolk has taken 500 men, they are calling them the white coats as they wear white with a red cross on the front, and they have been sent to deal with Wyatt at Rochester," Diaceto told me.

Sadly, this did not go as planned. As the white coats and their now ancient Duke came down the hill, the white coats called out, "We are all

Englishmen!" and promptly joined the rebels. Norfolk and his personal guard were forced to flee.

Wyatt's troops, a portion of them, had also managed to march out and gain control of some of Mary's ships which were waiting to escort Philip, as well as some cannon, and his forces had grown to about three thousand men. The white coats urged him to move upon London and within three days the rebels were on the short road to the city.

"They were halted by delegates sent by the Queen who had instructions to discuss and negotiate Wyatt's grievances." Diaceto, now that Hever seemed safe, although in truth they were still not far from us, seemed rather exhilarated by the adventure of the uprising. "Queen Mary declared she wanted to understand the cause of the rebellion."

"She is playing for time." I fully understood Mary. She did not want to understand the causes of the rebellion, she did not have any sympathy with men rising against the Crown but if Wyatt refused to negotiate with her men, Mary would be able to name him a traitor, knowing that he intended to overthrow her.

Wyatt told the delegates that he was no traitor, and the purpose of the rebellion was to defend against England being overrun by strangers and foreigners. He refused to meet Mary, however, and added the requirement that he be given control of the Tower of London, with Mary in it, and sole discretion for replacing members of the council at his will.

"He must have known she was not going to agree to that," I said, "although some men do have spare limits to their fantasies of arrogance."

Mary knew her city was under threat. Men were on the edge of London and soon they would march within. She had put trust in the men of Norfolk, and they had betrayed her. What if the rest of her people did the same? She would be overthrown.

Mary rode to the Guildhall which was full that day and delivered a speech full of fire and love, telling her people of her desire to end the rebellion by mercy instead of justice of sword, and she shared Wyatt's insolent and proud demands. She addressed her marriage to Philip, saying that she was already married to the people of England and "nothing is more acceptable to my heart nor more answerable to my will than their welfare and wealth."

"All Tudors have one thing in common, no matter how different they are," I said to Susan.

"What is that, my lady?"

"They all wield the power of words."

By the next day there were 25,000 men of London ready to protect Mary and the city from Wyatt. The rebels had 15,000. Wyatt was declared a traitor and there was a reward of one hundred pounds offered for his capture, dead or alive.

On the 2nd of February Wyatt's army arrived at Southwark where they meant to cross the Thames and gain entry to London by way of London Bridge, but they found the gates were closed and the drawbridge had been flung down into the water by the people of Southwark. Guns of the Tower of London were aimed at Southwark, and the people there begged Wyatt to leave, to save their houses from cannon fire.

On the 6th of February he went to Kingston, marching by night and meaning to surprise Mary at break of day. The bridge there was broken but Wyatt's men repaired it, costing time, and crossed over, continuing into London but the rebellion had lost the element of surprise and many of his men deserted.

By the next day, however, his forces had reached Hyde Park, and fright took hold of court as it was said Wyatt and his men were coming for Whitehall, where Mary herself was. Men started to flee court, but the Queen herself emerged from her council chamber and called for calm, telling those who were panicking to consume their minds with prayer, and God, whom she trusted above all, would not deceive her. "Better news will come," she told them.

Mary was right. Royal troops sent out into the streets were heading for Wyatt and his men.

As what was left of the rebel army continued on, they encountered artillery fire and attacks from brigades of horses in the streets. When they arrived at Ludgate, they found it too well defended, so the rebel army turned back and headed towards Westminster where they were met by more forces loyal to Mary. There was a brief battle and afterwards Wyatt surrendered. He and his supporters were marched to the Tower of London.

The Queen emerged victorious, yet as the fire of rebellion died down, flames of suspicion rose. Mary looked about for more whom she considered to be guilty of traitorous acts towards the Crown.

Her eyes came to rest on her own family.

On her sister, Lady Elizabeth, and on me.

Chapter Forty

1554

Hever Castle

"She trusts no one, it is part of becoming Queen." Diaceto stopped, correcting himself, "Well, she seems to trust the Emperor and his son, but no man of her own country, or woman."

"I have done nothing."

"We know that Highness, it is the Queen who does not seem to. People place rumour in her ear."

A messenger had come from Katherine Willoughby. From William Cecil my friend had heard that I was much suspected in the Wyatt rebellion. Imperial Ambassadors close to Mary were telling her that Elizabeth must have known of the rebellion, must have supported it, and they were telling the Queen I had too. Cecil was close enough to the heart of court to know much. He had initially supported Northumberland but later turned on him, as all had at that time, and had laid a full account of the attempted usurpation of the throne before Mary, which was why she had spared him. Cecil had since bowed his head and gone to Mass, obeyed all the Queen wanted, and was therefore still active at court and was a member of parliament. There was some word he would be chosen as Secretary of State, a post he had held before.

But he was also involved in the administration of Elizabeth's lands and was the cousin of one of her most trusted women, Blanche Parry, who had rocked Elizabeth's cradle when she was a baby and remained with her ever since.

Cecil was a clever fish. He kept his head down and did all he could to survive, and was doing well, but in certain circles, those my friend of Suffolk was close to, he was known to be a supporter of Elizabeth and was in communication often with her man Thomas Parry. Cecil knew of the threat against Elizabeth and Courtenay and knew too that my name had been mentioned. Elizabeth had been warned, as had I.

"Read it again," I said.

Brockehouse frowned, his eyes scanning the page. Diaceto was biting his lip, standing near the fire. "It has been reported to the Emperor and thence to Mary that your brother, Duke Wilhelm, was promised by the French King Henri II that the French would attack England as the rebels rose up. There is another strain of talk which says your brother has promised the French he will attack Mary.

"It is said in both these rumours that this would be done to prevent the marriage with Spain and that the French King promised Duke Wilhelm revenge would be taken for the old King repudiating his sister, the Lady of Cleves, and that you, my friend, had requested this vengeance. This French invasion would then give the Emperor's Germanic subjects the chance to rise against him in their territories. It is being said that all this was the plan of Lady Elizabeth, Edward Courtenay, and you." Brockehouse looked up from Katherine's missive. "No doubt the location of the rebellion in Kent has led to some men of the council linking you to the rebels, my lady," he said, looking bleak.

"Did my brother promise any such thing?" I was pacing the room in agitation. I certainly had not asked for any of this. When my cousin Count von Waldeck had gone home, just what had he told Wilhelm? That I was shamed beyond measure for the old King ending our marriage? Or was all of this an invention? Just how many enemies did I have at court?

Diaceto crossed his arms. "We know not, Highness, but it seems that the Queen does indeed suspect her sister was involved in the rebellion. The Lady Elizabeth has been called in for questioning, but thus far she has not appeared."

"How has she resisted this?"

"She protests she is ill and has taken to her bed. The Queen has sent doctors to check her story. It is likely the Queen will arrest her sister if she does not appear willingly before the council."

"Will she have me arrested too? Should I take to my bed?" I turned at the wall and came walking back towards them.

"We know not, but it is being said in London that since you spoke for Archduke Ferdinand as a suitor, you may still be loyal to your brother and that might make you suspect in loyalty to the Queen. If she thinks you loyal to your brother and it is found he did indeed talk with the French about invasion, you may be in grave danger, Highness."

That was not all. Soon there was another link besides my location at the time of the rebellion and gossip about my brother.

Cawarden, my old retainer, had come under suspicion and his house, my old one of Bletchingley, had been searched. Many arms, many more than one man required, were found within. "He must have been planning to join the rebels." I could have cursed the man! "Or it was a storage place for another uprising which was never put into action?"

"Many lines of the plot did fail," Diaceto said. "It is suspected he was part of the rebellion or was planning to rouse a private force of his own."

"He is a dedicated Protestant." I remembered all he had done to my church there. "That would have been enough for him to join against Mary. He never wanted the Spanish match."

The trouble was, I had visited Bletchingley not long ago, on my way from London to Hever. We had only stayed a night, and I had thought Cawarden seemed a little less welcoming than usual, although he never did want me staying there. He must have worried I would see something, although I had blithely gone about, noting nothing. This made me once again suspect, and Cawarden knew Elizabeth and had conversed with her many times, as well as sending her letters. This painted me in darker shades of betrayal.

I became worried about a letter I had sent to Elizabeth as rebellion seemed on the rise, even though it had contained little more than to tell her to remain on her estates whilst this trouble went on in London. I had written it out of concern for her safety, but I worried now that my words might be twisted and used against both of us, as if I knew something of the rebellion and what their plans were, or that both of us were involved and had been conspiring together behind Mary's back.

There was an additional problem as well for citizens of Guelders had been calling for Wilhelm to become their Duke once again, and no matter how she felt about me the Queen could not publicly show any honour, affection or respect to me whilst there was this possible problem looming for the Emperor within my brother's old duchy. Mary was about to wed Philip of Spain which would ally her only more firmly with the Holy Roman Emperor, therefore any trouble being brought about by my family for Philip's kin she would have to oppose. This could also be used against me as a possible reason my brother might well be conspiring with the King of France.

The last problem was Diaceto. Since the man had returned from the Continent unfortunately just before the rebellion took place, some were saying he was suspect. His bag, containing all his documents from that time as well as a gold chain the King of Denmark had given him as a reward for good service, were seized and Diaceto was ordered from my service.

I thought they might arrest him, but records of the mission he had been sent on still survived from the chaos of the end of Edward's reign, and several members of the council remembered the message he had been dispatched to deliver. All the same, given the suspicion I was under, he still was thought dubious and was commanded to return home to Cleves.

"I will object," I said.

"I think, Highness, that would be most perilous at this time," my good man said. He had been in my service for fifteen years, and now I was to lose him. Diaceto was one of my most precious links to home.

"So, I am to just stand aside?" My lips bunched as I held back tears of frustration, fear and anger. I felt so helpless; I could barely stand it.

"I see no other course. The truth is, Highness, you are under suspicion. Act in a way to draw more attention and you could be in grave danger." He kissed my hand. "You will not be forgotten here. We will find ways to send word to you, and aid if you need it."

As I said a tearful goodbye to a man who had only served me loyally, I waited nervously at Hever to see if a delegation would arrive to take me prisoner, but they did not. Cawarden was interrogated but released, then arrested again the next day. Seventeen cartloads of weapons were taken away from his house. In the end, however, they could find no evidence he had been involved, and he claimed those weapons were to be used in defence of the Queen. He remained suspect for the rest of Mary's reign, however, and not without reason considering the arms he had possessed.

In the meantime, hundreds of rebels were surrendered to the Queen's officers, so many indeed that all Her Majesty's prisons could not hold them. Churches had to be employed. A general execution of common prisoners began on the 12th of February that year, gallows were erected all over London. For weeks prisoners were tried daily and were hung. Some were beheaded or quartered or both and then their parts were displayed on gates and walls around London. I heard tales of thousands dying, but actually only 150 were in the end, still too large a number to my mind. Many of the rest, the more fortunate, only received a few days in prison.

Others were not so lucky.

"Imperial ambassadors have convinced her that England will not be safe for Philip to come to if Jane Grey is alive," I told Susan, staring at the words written by Katherine Willoughby.

Jane Grey and her husband Guildford Dudley, who had been free to wander the Tower gardens in December of the year before, were to be executed. Mary was keener than ever to marry Philip, despite all the blood which had already been spilled for this marriage, but to go ahead, the Emperor and his men were demanding England be made safe. "She would not do it," I whispered. "I thought she would not kill this girl, her cousin."

But Mary obeyed the Emperor. Jane was to die on the 9th of February but was given three days to convert to the Catholic faith. She refused. On the 12th Guildford was beheaded as Jane watched from her window. Then she was taken out. Jane made a speech and asked the headsman to dispatch her quickly. Then there came a horrible moment when the seventeen-year-old girl was blindfolded, to reduce her terror, and fumbling, could not find the block where she was to lay her head. Until that moment, Jane had been calm, but as her hands drifted through the air she cried out, "What shall I do? Where is it?"

"She feared he would take her head before she had found her own way to death," I said sadly.

I thought of Catherine Howard, practising her death all night before her execution, the block having been brought to her rooms. There had been to her mind a solidity in the thing she would lose her life upon, a sense of something holding her at the end. It was the same for Jane, I thought. Little had I known the girl, but I along with everyone else knew she had wanted nothing of the plot to make her Queen, and she had done nothing at all in this recent rebellion. I had known of many unjust deaths in my time, and this was one of the worst.

And my friend was responsible, all to marry the man she wanted.

Disillusionment is a hard, uncomfortable place to come to. There is a mirror there which shows us much truth of the world behind us, and of the person staring into it. It is not an easy place to stand, but stand I did, staring. Mary had done this, was capable of this. The person I knew, the Queen I believed she would be, was not who she was. Duped I had been by my affection for her. I had been a fool.

They helped Jane to find the block and she laid her head on it, praying to God to take her soul. Her end was swift, mercifully.

Henry Grey went to his death eleven days after his daughter, whom many believed he had condemned to death. No one but Frances Grey cared for her husband, but plenty cared about Jane. Her death was widely condemned by Protestant countries, who decried it as a horror that Mary had taken the life of an innocent, learned girl.

I agreed.

*

"Highness, are you quite well?"

"Perfectly."

They were staring at me. I knew it for I could feel their eyes, though I was staring at the tapestry.

"And you understand what we have just told you?"

"Perfectly, also." I looked at the messengers come from court. "Please leave me now."

As the messengers as well as Susan and the Brockehouses filed out, I walked to the tapestry. A hunting scene near a lake was laid out in thread. Men held armfuls of dead birds and hare; deer were upside down on spits not far away. By the edge of the water there was a swan. She swam, not worried by all the death about her. Her beak was open a little, and I wondered if she sang, marking the death of all those about her, as she continued on.

"Sybylla," I murmured, touching white feathers on the cloth.

My sister was dead, her husband too.

Sybylla had been ill for more than a year, at one stage she had even been given the Last Rites there was such a fear for her, but then she had recovered, grown stronger. I had hoped she would be well now for a long time, but it was not so.

Johann Friedrich would not leave her as she entered her last illness that February. By her bedside he sat, their children present too. My sister's lungs had become weak, her heart and legs had also become frail. She had grown thin.

She died at Weimar on the 21st of February 1554 at nine of the morning. She was with her husband and sons when she slipped away. Her people mourned her greatly, remembering their kind, brave Duchess. They called her the mother of the Church, for despite all her trials never had she lost her faith.

Her husband lived only ten days without her. He died on the third day of March. Not long had he been free, but at least at the last he and Sybylla had each other.

I felt numb, truth be told, as if my mind had heard this news but my body refused to believe it. I went about that day in a daze, hardly saying a word. My servants, Gertrude and Jasper, Susan too, they all followed me, not asking if I was well, for they knew I was not, but simply there to ensure I did not fall in my deadened and confused state. I put my fingers to the scar on my eyebrow often that day, as if it could link me to my sister, help me find her.

But she found me.

That night I dreamed of a lake of swans, and amongst them was a voice. One of the swans was singing, a portent of her own death. As I looked to my side I saw my sister.

"It sounds as if she is happy," I said, pointing to the swan. "Though she is dying, is she not? They sing only when death comes."

"She sings a song of joy." My sister turned to me, placing her hand on my cheek. "Do not fear, Anna, we will wait for you. You are not alone."

I woke, wondering if this meant I was soon to die, the Queen to take my head, and yet in ways strange I took comfort from the dream. I wept long for my sister when my numbness melted, which eventually it did. As when my mother had died, I curled up about my own torture and allowed the claws of grief to cut into me deep and hard. For a long time, I could not wake without losing Sybylla again, for I would awake and not know why I felt sad and heavy and then I would remember that with the leaving of my sister's soul there had come a weight upon me to balance out this world.

Perhaps that is the true function of sorrow, that we are handed this weight of soul which once belonged to those we loved, to allow their spirits to rise, to the next life, and that in time, as we bear this grief long and learn to carry it, they come to attain their place in the world beyond in part because of us, because of our love, our willingness to carry this burden.

I know not if any has thought this before and I steal the thoughts of another, but the notion I carried my heavy grief for a purpose, to aid my sister and her beloved husband, helped in ways I cannot describe.

They were waiting for me, my sister had said so. I was not alone.

Chapter Forty-One

1554

Hever Castle

Wyatt's trial went ahead on the 15th of March. No doubt to Elizabeth's intense horror he named Sir William St Loe, one of her servants, as one of the men who had initiated the rebellion. Wyatt pleaded guilty to treason but claimed he never intended any harm to Mary and only wanted to prevent the coming of Spaniards to England. He also apparently claimed that Courtenay was an originator of the rebellion and accused Elizabeth of having been involved in the conspiracy. Wyatt was sentenced to death by hanging, with his body to be drawn and quartered. He went to death on the 11th of April, but before he was hanged Wyatt told the crowds that neither Elizabeth nor Courtney were involved in the rebellion. He admitted he had testified falsely at his trial. Many thought he had been promised his life in return for false testimony and when this was retracted, he came out and told the truth.

But Mary still suspected her sister.

Mary had been summoning Elizabeth to come to London and Elizabeth had continued to claim illness. Queen Mary sent her own physicians as well as council members to her sister and although the physicians found the illness was genuine, they still put Elizabeth into a litter and had her carried to London. She had arrived on the 23rd of February and left the curtains of her litter open so that the people of England could see that she was pale and ill.

"I read here she was dressed in white and wearing a haughty expression," Susan said.

"White, for it would make her look paler, and more ill," I said, nodding. "So the people would believe her about her illness."

"Do you think she was ill, then, Highness?"

A slight smile lifted my weary face. "Not for a moment. I think she remembered her stepmother, Katherine Parr's trick when the King was to arrest her. Katherine pretended illness, which bought her time and sympathy. Elizabeth does the same. She knows the danger she is in here and now, and she knows now, as we all do, that Mary is capable of murdering young women who have done nothing wrong. If Elizabeth is found even a little involved in this, I think her sister will kill her. If Elizabeth has the people on her side, however, there may be hope."

Mary refused to see her sister despite Elizabeth asking many times and put her in a secluded part of the palace surrounded by guards.

Elizabeth was examined time and time again and although she had friends on the council who spoke for her, there were plenty who wanted to see her executed, Gardiner and the imperial ambassadors not least amongst them. Told eventually she was to be moved to the Tower, and fearing that meant she would die, Elizabeth made an appeal to Mary in writing. She wrote of her innocence and her loyalty to Mary, but her sister did not answer. On the 18th of March Elizabeth was taken to the river and then to the Tower by water where she was examined again. But the captive Elizabeth continued to protest that she was innocent and by that April letters were being distributed throughout London in favour of her. It seemed there might be another uprising, or people might even rush the guards about her, were she sent to the block. Unrest was grumbling everywhere, so loud it was as a creature growling.

"The people don't want to see another girl on the scaffold," I said. "Jane was bad enough, but Elizabeth is Mary's own sister, blood of Henry VIII, and the people love her."

Susan played with a clasp on her bracelet, one I had given her. "That is what the Queen fears, I think, Highness"

"And fear sometimes holds us in check. I only hope there is enough sense and decency left in Mary to hold her back, to have her not listen to the men trying to kill Elizabeth."

I still wondered about my own fate. No letter had come demanding I was to present myself in London. No men of the council had turned up with questions to ask. Perhaps the Queen had enough to deal with, with her sister.

Then, there was news.

A death warrant had been sent to the Tower for Elizabeth, to be carried out the next day, but when it arrived the Lord Lieutenant of the Tower had been suspicious of the seal and signature. Rather than executing the warrant, he sent word direct to the Queen, asking if she had issued it. Mary had not, and was shocked someone – I suspected Gardiner, personally – had issued it without her knowledge.

Perhaps it was this that moved Mary. Realising men about her would do anything to have her murder her own sister, even circumvent her own sacred authority as Queen, she came to suspect them. This made her more sympathetic towards Elizabeth and others. Not long after a messenger came to Hever.

"Her Majesty would have you know, Highness, that certain late suspicions were raised against you in the matter of the Wyatt rebellion," William Cecil said, as if we both did not know this already. "But despite the persuasions of men about her, she never could bring herself to believe that you were involved."

"I am glad to hear that," I replied, studying the earnest man. He was about thirty-four then but seemed younger. I knew him for a friend of Katherine's, so trusted him as she did. "I never had any involvement with the rebellion, and I am certain Her Highness the Lady Elizabeth did not either."

There was a flicker of interest in his eyes at that, but he continued. "Her Majesty wishes to bring you to court so she may demonstrate to such men that she considers you not a threat, but she will not be able to meet with you in person. The current conflict arising in Guelders between your brother and the Emperor makes that impossible. She would have you know, however, and said I was to tell you this particularly, Highness, that her good faith in you is assured in her heart because of two times in the past when you offered her advice which she believes saved her life and allowed her to take her throne. For those times and your aid, she thanks you, and wishes you to know they have not, and never will be, forgotten by her."

I nodded. "So, I am to come to court, and be ignored?"

"That seems the way of it, Highness."

I came to court and was ignored indeed. When she did see me in passing, the Queen was cold and distant, although never rude. On those few occasions, I could see a great grief inside Mary, one she could barely contain. The throne was separating her from people who had long supported her, and from her own blood. It was a power, yes, but it came with isolation.

Perhaps as another sign she had come to distrust the word of men about her, on the 19th of May that year, the anniversary of her mother's death which had taken place in that very spot, Elizabeth was taken from the Tower. She was not set free, but she was not executed either. She was to be taken instead into house arrest at Woodstock, by then a dilapidated, isolated palace.

"The Queen thinks to remove her from the eyes of England," I said.

"But at least she is alive, Highness." Susan dabbed her eyes. A Catholic she was, but she, like many of us, had lost faith in the Queen. The fate of Elizabeth haunted her, as it did many in England.

Many thought Mary would have her killed there, some quiet way, hidden away from the eyes of the world, but Elizabeth had friends and support, and both were growing in number. Thomas Parry and her other servants followed the Princess there, and word from my friend of Suffolk was that Cecil was the man covertly chosen by Elizabeth's supporters to supply important, secret information from court for the imprisoned Elizabeth. There was an underground movement forming in favour of the daughter of Anne Boleyn, and it was growing stronger by the hour.

The Queen, however, had pushed her sister out of the light of day, for other things were on her mind.

On the 20th of July that year Philip of Spain finally arrived in England to wed Mary.

Chapter Forty-Two

Summer 1554

Hever Castle

I ordered celebrations to go ahead for Mary's union, little as I liked what had been done to bring it about and wrote to Mary to congratulate her upon on the occasion of her marriage, but I was not invited to court, and the Queen remained distant. Although this worried me of course, it also saddened me; Mary and I had once been close and now we were not. I felt as if my earnest, courageous friend had died and there was someone else in her skin.

Cranmer, Latimer and Ridley were still in prison, Mary still hoped to convert them it was said, but all over the country there were people being attained for not going to church, and I knew that whilst my friend of Suffolk was busily pretending she lived only a quiet life in the country now, at her estates with Bertie, she would be examined and in danger soon enough.

I soon heard rumour that whilst the new King of England was a charming man, most attentive to his wife in public, in private he did not seem impressed with his bride. "He thinks her old and sour," Gertrude Brockehouse told me. "It is said he went through the wedding night with a sense of duty but does not want to remain long in England. The Queen, however, is fulsomely in love with him. She talks of nothing but *her* Philip and gives gifts and fawns on him every day. People say she thinks herself already with child."

I wondered at this, it was not impossible, but Mary was thirty-eight, almost the same age as me. I had long ago said to an ambassador it would do no good for my brother to bring me home to marry off for I was past my years of childbearing. Could it be that Mary could even get with child? She had never been hale since I had known her. Her women had told me her courses were irregular and often stopped altogether when she fasted. Her mother had become pregnant many times but miscarried often too, yet within weeks of marriage, Mary was convinced she was carrying a babe.

By September, the Queen was sure. It was reported she had stopped her courses, had gained weight and was ill every morning. A child was in the belly of the Queen.

It was then men came to see me, sent by my friend of Suffolk.

"You are aware what you ask here is dangerous to me and the Lady Elizabeth?" I stared into serious eyes.

"We are, my lady."

"And yet you ask."

Cecil nodded. "And yet I ask. I am aware of the risks you would take, but our mutual friend of Suffolk believes you have great love for your kinswoman and would wish to aid her."

I nodded. "I have always considered Elizabeth as a daughter, though the title of mother was taken from me."

They wanted a way to send intelligence to Elizabeth. Quite what, they did not say. A man named John Gaier had been selected by Cecil as a court messenger who had no prior links to the Princess or her cause, but sympathised with her plight, still imprisoned in Woodstock. Cecil was seeking ways to get messages to Elizabeth herself, but also to her man Thomas Parry who had ensconced himself in the village near Woodstock and was passing news of the doings of the world on to the Princess, along with messages of support.

"The Queen seeks to remove her sister, the rightful heir to England, from the world, Highness," Cecil told me. "We cannot allow this to happen, nor can it be that Elizabeth, if she were to be brought back to court should come unawares of matters occurring in the world. She would be defenceless. We must become her eyes and her ears, my lady, and for that we need your help."

"I am not in favour with the Queen. You see me here, sent away from London as the royal marriage was held and as the Queen announces she is with child? When recently I was told of the death of my sister and her husband..." I paused to take a breath so I did not lose my composure "... an imperial ambassador even had the temerity to say to the Queen that this ill, sorrowful news was but a front so my brother could discuss rebellious activities with me. I am not the best person to choose."

They wanted me to write to Elizabeth, and using that, would send secret messages to her and to Parry.

"The Queen may not bring you to court, my lady," Cecil pressed, "and yet in private, to her women, she speaks of you as someone she trusts. She has said many times that in the reign of her father you offered her advice which saved her life, that you and Chapuys were then the only people she could rely on to tell her the truth. She followed by saying that once, when asked on the matter, you told her not to flee England when she was under threat by her brother, and that advice allowed her to take her throne. If you ask to write to Elizabeth, I think it will be allowed."

I thought a moment. "I could ask to send on some letters I still have, ones written betwixt King Henry and me. If I said I hoped they might bring comfort, and instruction, perhaps the Queen would allow it."

"And the letters, yours to Elizabeth and these of the old King, they would be taken to the Queen, and she would read them and see there was nothing in them to be concerned about." Cecil's eyes were shining. "Our true message would be sent by mouth, not on paper."

"I do not want to know what information you are sending her," I warned. "I could end up in captivity or on the block for this."

"We will keep you in perfect ignorance, Highness, if that is what you wish... but, you will do it?"

I inclined my head. "I will, for love of my stepdaughter. I know what it is to dwell in ignorance and captivity, not knowing why men wish you ill. I would have her know she is not alone." It was not this alone which moved me. Elizabeth, I loved, but England I did too. Mary was not the Queen I had hoped she would be, but another could be, another who might cause England to become a better place.

I paused. "Is Queen Mary really with child?"

"Many have asked the same, and none know, though the signs look as if she is."

"But others doubt?"

"Others *hope*, my lady. And in Elizabeth we place our hope. She has all the passion of her father and a greater mind than her brother, and she is determined, my lady, to bring balance to a land which sore needs it. She says sometimes and only to those she trusts that all this dispute over religion is foolish bickering over trifles, and we all of us worship the same God. Where her brother and sister have forced their people into one strain of faith or another, Lady Elizabeth is bent on following her father's way, the middle path. With her, my lady, England has a chance to be united as one people."

I was silent a while, feeling tears smart my eyes as I heard my own words echoed back to me. *"We all worship the same God,"* I had said that to Elizabeth, so long ago. It seemed the girl had listened and the woman she was becoming might bring about this balance I had so long hoped for.

I agreed to be part of their scheme. I wrote the letter to Elizabeth, and another to Mary, explaining why I had wanted to write and sending on the letters from their father I had dug out of an old chest. My letter to Elizabeth counselled nothing but obedience and faith, telling her to set herself to prayer and her heart to loyalty to the Queen. The letters I found from their father were straightforward enough. My former husband had many times taken to the feat of both praising me and lecturing me on certain points, so it was easy enough to find letters which struck the right tone of obedience and good behaviour in women.

I dispatched my petition to Mary and the Queen agreed to send on the letters. They went with Cecil's messenger. I never found out what was in the message he sent to Elizabeth or her man Parry. I did not need to know; I only hope it helped.

At the same time as I received the Queen's reply, telling me the letters would be sent on and thanking me for trying to aid her sister in proper behaviour, suited to a lady of England, I had another message. It told me that my request to be titled Dowager Queen of England had been refused. In truth I had almost forgotten about it, and was not surprised that it had been refused, given all I was suspected of.

The irony was that I had been refused this position because of suspected treachery, yet I finally had turned traitor to the Queen, and for that treachery she had thanked me, and praised my name.

Chapter Forty-Three

Summer 1554 – February 1555

Hever Castle

Once more I found myself at odds with the council, who suspected me still. My one *whole* year of being paid on time for my pension was at an end, and I once more had to petition and request for funds on which to live. I doubted it was Mary ordering delays and underpayments. She was so busy gloating over her belly she barely had time for anything else. Men of the council, Gardiner in particular, were the ones trying to punish me.

"We have lived through worse," I told Brockehouse.

"You could appeal directly to the Queen, Highness."

"I may, in time." In truth, I did not want to bring myself too much to Mary's attention, considering my involvement in the messages to Elizabeth.

But soon there was another who needed aid.

"I need your help, my friend, the time has come. We are under suspicion, and it is only a matter of time now before the Queen's guards come for us, I am sure of it."

Katherine of Suffolk stood before me, Bertie hovering at the edge of the room. I had been expecting this, but all the same, I had never wanted it to happen. They were in trouble.

Mary had rejected her father's split with Rome and had appealed to the Pope when she first ascended to the throne to return England to the jurisdiction of Rome. Of late, Philip had managed to get Mary's Parliament to reject the religious laws of her father, and Mary had already abolished Edward's laws. Talks with the papacy had been ongoing however, as Mary knew that to demand land and estates back from her nobles would be suicide for her reign. There was word the Pope was on the verge of agreeing that confiscated land would not be restored to the Church but could be retained by those who owned it now. The Heresy Acts of former centuries were due to be revived as soon as this agreement was confirmed. They were ancient, one passed by Richard II, one by Henry IV and one by Henry V. These acts having been repealed by Henry VIII and his son, Mary meant to reinstate them. It would mean Protestants could be arrested and executed by law for their beliefs. It was a death sentence for any not willing to hide their beliefs or convert.

There had been recent investigations into the finances of my friends, for Gardiner was saying Charles Brandon had owed money to the Crown upon his death, which Katherine was liable to pay. It was an excuse, we knew, to interrogate the couple. Katherine had recently sent money to Latimer too, still in prison, to allow him to pay for a few comforts and ease his suffering. He had been her chaplain once, and she still had affection for him. But if this was found out, it was likely they would be pulled in for questioning.

Bertie had a way out. He had managed to persuade Gardiner that he would seek to recover money owed to the Brandon estate from debtors on the Continent. One of them was the Emperor. A royal licence had been issued, and he was to leave in a few days, that June. Since he would be travelling in lands of the Empire and his wife and their new child, Suzan, were still in England, it was supposed he would not try to escape.

That left Katherine.

"I understand," I said, "there are things in place already. Ways and means for you to use in your escape."

I had spoken already to my men in Cleves, to Diaceto, to Harst and Olisleger, finding names, contacts who could aid them with places to stay, with travel, with the language. Katherine spoke French, Spanish and a little Latin, but they would need more than this where they meant to travel. All I had gathered would help the Dowager Duchess, her husband and their baby escape England and make their way into the United Duchies governed by my brother. My cousin Count Von Waldeck had promised to send men to help them when they arrived, and Amalia had sworn to do what she could. My sister was by that time in charge of the ducal nursery and was intending all children of Wilhelm be brought up to be good Protestants, whether my brother wanted such or not. She had been left there, unmarried, she told me in a private message sent vocally from Cleves, as a mission from God, that she now understood. As I had been sent to England to become an aunt to children who needed me, so she had in Cleves.

I had not contacted my brother on this matter. He could not be trusted.

It would perhaps not be safe for Katherine and Bertie to stay in Cleves for good, but with my brother and the Emperor at odds again, and many people willing to aid me, Cleves would be at least a starting point which, if they could reach it, would allow them to rest a while before escaping into a Protestant land where they could worship in peace, until it was safe to return.

"Bertie is to take to ship now, and come back for me as the year turns," Katherine told me. "We have much worked out already, a ship to take us to the Low Countries, but we need somewhere safe beyond."

"Cleves," I said without hesitation.

"I dared hope you might say such," she breathed.

"Of course, as you are my sister, so my country will be yours, at least for a time."

I told her all I had been up to; gave her the lists of names and contacts she was to use. "When you reach my brother's lands, these people will aid you to arrange places to stay, and transportation further on if required, perhaps to Sweden, or another Protestant country where you will be safe. I have no further contacts in such lands, but I am sure you will do well."

"You thought of all this?" She blinked at me. "When?"

"When first you told me it might be necessary. I would always want to keep you here, my friend, but not at the risk of your life. If I know you are safe and well, that is enough for me."

"Will you not come with us?" My friend gazed into my eyes, and I could see the love she bore for me. It was enough to break my heart. "England is not safe for you at the moment either, this year has proved that."

"I cannot go with you. I would endanger you. I would be missed too fast and too easily and Mary would immediately know where we all had gone. My brother's trouble with the Emperor would only increase and I might even bring war on my people." I shook my head. "Besides," I went on with a smile. "What if your friend Cecil needed to send another message to Elizabeth, and I was not here?"

Katherine clasped my hands. "I thought to come here only to tell you that we might go any time. To ask that perhaps we might use your name if to the lands of your brother we went, and here you are, having plotted so much for us." Her eyes filled with tears. "What will I do without you?"

"I am still here, my friend. Though we might soon be far apart, we will only be so in terms of miles. I am yours, Katherine, as I promised, and you are mine. Friendship cannot be broken by such things as land and distance. You are never alone, for I am with you."

"I am yours." Tears fell on her soft cheeks. "In this life and the next, my friend. My love for you will never die."

My friend escaped on New Year's Day of 1555, with a small party of servants, her infant girl in her arms. It was indeed a while before they were missed, but they were not alone. Some eight hundred people fled England in Mary's reign, and they were the ones with names people remembered. I suspect many thousands more left, their names never recorded.

Katherine moved to the Barbican where her London townhouse stood and at around four of the morning, Katherine and her small party snuck into the darkness. My friend was dressed as a simple merchant's wife and was accompanied by seven servants who had been told of her plans at the last moment so they could not possibly betray her. The slight noise as they left their house early in the morning roused a man named Atkinson, an untrustworthy keeper of Katherine's house. In haste to leave before he found them, Katherine had to leave behind a bag which contained clothes for her daughter and a pot of milk. Her men were ordered to go ahead to Lion Quay between London Bridge and Billingsgate which was where they meant to sail from, as she and her women hid in the shadows of the Charterhouse. Atkinson saw nothing and Katherine and her party scuttled out into the night.

Through Finsbury Field they raced, all meeting together at Moorgate, where they passed to Lion Quay. The barge was waiting there, and they reached Leigh, below Tilbury, later that same day. At Leigh Katherine was housed with a London merchant, and he told people she was his daughter. There, Bertie found his wife and child and they spent their last night in England at an inn, where they were almost betrayed by someone recognising Katherine, but managed to escape.

They had to wait some time before passage was arranged from Gravesend, and three times they set sail but each time winds forced them back to England. On one of the occasions the Queen's officers came to shore suspecting that Katherine was on the ship, for by that time she had been missed, but all they found was a simple merchant's wife, so they abandoned their search for the Dowager Duchess of Suffolk.

I wondered sometimes if Mary had let Katherine escape. It was clear that she knew something had been planned, otherwise why would people have been keeping watch for Katherine? But perhaps she did not send her best men, keeping in mind all that Katherine's mother Maria de Salinas had done for her own mother.

My friend landed at Brabant, dressed like a woman of the Low Countries, and from there they went to Cleves. She and her companions made it to Xanten, which was not safe, as it had already been rumoured Katherine had fled there, so to Wesel they went. Using the contacts I had given them they headed farther to the east. Mary's officers and those of the Emperor tried to track them down. The last I heard from my men was that they were heading for Mannheim and Katherine was pregnant again. I wish her all the joy in the world.

I knew not where they ended up – though there were many rumours of Frankfurt and Poland – for it was hardly safe for a letter to be sent, but I knew my friend was safe, was alive. She was a mother again now, twice over with God's blessing, and I hoped one day her daughter and her other child would be able to come home with Katherine and see this England their mother loved.

I missed my friend greatly, so greatly that it pained me every day almost as much as the death of Sybylla did, yet it seemed to me there was some connection between these events, that in the same year I should lose my sister I should also lose my friend, but lose her in a way which kept her and her family alive in this world. Perhaps when Sybylla had said to me I was not alone, there was a reason she echoed my words to Katherine when her children died. Perhaps my sister of blood had wanted me to aid my sister of friendship.

It was possible. I had ever thought that Katherine and Sybylla would have liked one another. They were kin of soul. It was what had drawn me to the Duchess when first we met.

I missed her every single day, but at least I knew Katherine Willoughby was alive and I had helped her to be so. I had often felt helpless in the face of the great changes enacted upon England, in the face of the fearsome power others wielded, and yet when it had come to it, I had been able to do something. My acts were small compared to some, but they meant a great deal to people I loved. Katherine and Elizabeth I had aided, I had risked peril for, and I would again if they asked it of me, if they needed me.

Little acts of courage may alter the path of fate just as well as large ones.

Though she would suffer on her journeys, though Mary's officers were always hunting her and her family, though there would be trial and tribulation as she was away from her homeland, as long as my friend was alive there was always a chance that she could come home.

If Elizabeth came to the throne, there was a chance.

There were many then speaking of the Lady Elizabeth in quiet tones of respect. She was the one in whom they placed their hope, these people who had to flee the country in fear of death, and those who hid their faith for terror of arrest and execution. Elizabeth was their hope for the future. I understood that only more as the year went on.

Chapter Forty-Four

1555 – 1556

Hever Castle

"I know nothing of the escape of the Dowager, and I am sorry for it," I told a messenger sent to me that February, right around the time Katherine and Bertie were trying to sail to the Low Countries. "I am stunned such a thing would even occur to the Dowager, given that the mother of the Duchess, Maria de Salinas, loved this land so much that she stayed here with her mistress, the Queen's excellent mother, and raised her children here."

I hoped he might pass this on to Mary, remind her that Katherine had once been her playmate, her friend, and their mothers had been close too. Perhaps Mary might remember the comfort Maria de Salinas had given to her own mother as she was dying and allow my friend to escape because of that. Any aid I could offer my friend I would. But for the most part, that year became about hiding away at Hever.

It was not safe in England, that much was certain. We heard of more and more people fleeing the country before the heresy laws were brought in. Mary continued to fuss over her belly, telling all who would listen that her child was the saviour of England, the one brought to her by God. It was clear, was it not? To Mary it seemed so, to the rest of us perhaps not.

But not all was ill. That is an important thing to remember when crisis falls on us. Even when all seems dark, there is always a little light to see by.

Lady Elizabeth emerged from captivity in April and many of us let loose the breath we had long been holding.

Elizabeth was commanded to court so she could witness the birth of Mary's child. The Queen had swelled, and all said it was for certain she carried a babe. I had suspended my disbelief since my friend of Suffolk, as last I heard, was carrying her second child at the age of thirty-six. But as the Queen's due date arrived, there was no child.

Another child did arrive. A male heir to Cleves was born at four in the morning in Swan Castle on the 28th of April. At least the birth of my nephew Karl Friedrich put paid to rumours that no male heir would ever be born to my brother. "There is no end to the foolishness people will believe," I mentioned to Brockehouse. "At least now Cleves is saved from falling into Saxon hands, or Imperial. I could not rest if Duke Moritz claimed our lands as well as biting plenty from my poor sister's children."

Sybylla's eldest son had inherited what was left of his father's lands, but not all that was truly theirs.

But for the Queen there was no child. April passed, then May. As June came, then July and there was no baby, the Queen quietly left her lying in chambers and emerged into the world again, humiliated and defeated. She had not been with child. The swelling had gone down, her monthly courses had returned. People spoke at length of how a woman who desired a child could be tricked by her own body, and it seemed this had happened to the Queen. Others claimed the Queen was ill or had been possessed of a "great wind" which slowly had released. I had never heard of such a wind being held in the body that long and thought it more likely the first explanation was true, and Mary, who had ever loved children and desired a family of her own, something stable in this changing world, had tricked herself through hope into believing she was with child, and her body had followed suit.

Her misery was only more increased when Philip, who had delayed business on the Continent for a long time, left England to command troops against France in Flanders.

But it seemed something might have shifted between the sisters, for Elizabeth was not sent back into captivity but remained at court. Some said Mary and her sister were friends now, and the younger had offered the elder great comfort in her time of trial. Some whispered Mary merely wanted Elizabeth close, so the wily princess could not get up to anything.

"There is a suggestion Elizabeth should wed the Duke of Savoy, Emmanuel Philibert," I was told by Gertrude. "But rumour holds the Princess herself is not keen at all on the match, and darker rumours come, saying that Philip perhaps means to wed Elizabeth himself, so he may remain King."

"I sincerely hope the Queen never hears that rumour, both for the sake of Elizabeth and because it would destroy her," I said.

"Nevertheless, before Philip left it was said he was mightily fond of the Princess, my lady, and it was he who insisted Elizabeth come to court and talk with Mary."

"I am glad there was any reconciliation, but still I hope Mary does not come to think her husband desires her sister. There is enough Mary believes Elizabeth is trying to steal from her, without adding jealousy of love to the pot."

*

In January of 1556 the Emperor abdicated his throne, and Philip was declared King of Spain and was busy making peace with France. Sadly, this all fell apart in February when Ambassador Noailles was named in a plot against England.

"Henry Dudley, a cousin of Northumberland, was, it seems, attempting to organise a force to invade England from France," Brockehouse informed me. "The men of England involved have been captured, but it appears the French Ambassador's name is all over this plan. The Ambassador has left England and Dudley remains in France."

"Do you think it is real, or that all this was contrived by Spain as a way to bring England into war with France?" Mary's marriage treaty had held that England was not to be drawn into conflicts of Spain or the Hapsburg Empire, but if a threat came to England itself, from France, England could enter indeed, and Spanish relations with the French were fragile. Many expected war would break out again imminently.

"Philip has, people say, often tried to get Mary to involve herself in the war, before the recent treaty, so it is possible."

There was another kind of war breaking out in England for the time being, however. One of faith. I attended Mass strictly, observing all the laws of England, and made all my household do so too, no matter their leanings, telling them God would forgive anything done to survive this time. In those years, you see, the burning times came.

In September of 1555 Cranmer had stood trial for heresy. He had already been found guilty of it, and considering Mary's reinstated heresy laws, we all knew it would not go well for him. The truth was, Mary wanted two things; to make a spectacle of him, as well as Latimer and Ridley, to show people what would happen if they failed to convert, and to take revenge. She never would have admitted the revenge part, even to herself, but it was clear to me now. It had been Cranmer's ideas and his theories which had driven the annulment of her mother's marriage to her father, which had led to her illegitimacy. Unable to ever blame her father for his part in this, Mary had always blamed Anne Boleyn for enticing the King away from her mother, and Cranmer for making their separation and the split from Rome possible. The two, I believed, were intrinsically linked in her mind. Cranmer had been the spark which had led to the implosion of her world, everything she held dear.

And he would pay for it.

The burnings had already begun in Smithfield. It was an old practice, to save the soul of a heretic they were first threatened with fire, an earthly inferno being not as bad as that they would taste in Hell, and the hope was they would convert. If they failed to, they were burned, a punishment for heresy and one meant to deter others from following the same path.

Mary's father had burned men and women for heresy. Cardinal Wolsey had overseen some, but he had been more lenient than Thomas More, when he came to be Chancellor. During Edward's reign only two people had been executed for heresy, the most famous being Joan Bocher who had died for her Anabaptist views. Perhaps because of this, when Mary seemed resolved to bring back the punishment of burning for heresy, the people of England were shocked. Perhaps they thought the practice was to die out, or only be used in extreme cases, but as the burning times began it was clear this was false hope. Mary's laws made heresy a religious and civil offence, and it was treason for a person to believe in a religion other than that held by the Queen.

John Rogers was the first to burn, losing his life at Smithfield in 1555, but the deaths which stuck most in the minds of people were those of the bishops of the past reigns.

Cranmer had refused to be moved for a long time. Mary had hoped, as all knew, to force him to convert and in doing so she would have won a mighty victory which might well have swayed others, but Cranmer continued to insist that the Protestant religion was true, the Pope was the Antichrist, the transubstantiation was false, and that Mary herself was failing in her duties as Queen by offering Rome dominance over England. He said her coronation oath meant she was bound to uphold the liberties of the English people, to protect their customs and laws, and by putting Rome's laws ahead of English, she betrayed her people.

Fearing he was never going to convert, Mary sent Latimer and Ridley to burn at the stake in October of 1555. They too had been outspoken, but in truth it was another way to persuade Cranmer to convert. At Oxford it occurred, and Cranmer was taken to the tower of the gatehouse where he was imprisoned so he could watch his fellow men of the faith burn. Latimer was almost seventy years old, Ridley perhaps fifty-one or two. They should have died in their beds, not in flames and agony.

"It is said that when Latimer and Ridley were brought out, and Ridley shook to see the pyres, Latimer turned to him and said, 'Be of good courage, Master Ridley, and play the man. We shall this day light such a candle by God's grace in England as I trust shall never be put out'," Brockehouse told me.

"Brave words." My voice was quiet. I had hoped Mary would never do this, yet she had. "I hope they did not suffer long?"

Suffering on the stake was guaranteed. Sometimes family members would pay for good timber to be near the person dying, so they would perish faster. Sometimes I had even heard a small bag of gunpowder might be snuck in, tied to the throat, so death was even swifter, but if greenwood was used the fire would burn slow and the death would be agonising, endless.

"Latimer, I am told died quickly." Brockehouse's face told me to ask no more, but I did.

"And Ridley?"

He shook his head. "He was not so fortunate, my lady. His fire was green and ill made. The pyre was too high, so it burned heavy, but could not reach the man's body. His end was long."

Cranmer, faint with the horror of what he had seen, was taken back to his prison and there Reginald Pole, who had come to England as papal legate and had been instrumental in the revival of the heresy laws, was to reason with him. Pole was soon to be named Archbishop of Canterbury, Cranmer's post, but first the old Archbishop needed taking care of.

Pole did not meet Cranmer, who he despised as a heretic, so he wrote to him. Under fear of the burnings of his friends he had seen, and under persuasion that he might be spared, Cranmer suffered a crisis of mind and spirit in January of 1556. He recanted his beliefs, hoping it might save his life. For a while it seemed it might, but then in March there came news that he was to burn.

"When a man asks forgiveness, why should it not be granted?" I could not eat that day, sick to the stomach.

I was not alone. The people were horrified that a man might recant but still be condemned to death at the stake. Many had expected mercy for Ridley and Latimer, then for Cranmer, and it had not come.

This is a trouble we have, we humans. Sometimes we believe too well in the best in people. We think because we uphold certain values, others will too. We think people we believe in will live up to the potential we see in them. I had convinced myself for a long time, despite all I could see of what Mary was becoming, despite all I knew she might do, that she would act according to the goodness in her. Based on my assessment of her as good at heart, I fooled myself into thinking she would not act according to the worst of which she was capable. This is how we allow evil to rise, unbidden and uncontested; we put hope in the best in people.

The people of England were disabused of their belief in Mary at this time. Most of them at least. Some cheered Mary on.

In truth, I think condemning Cranmer after he had repented was one of Mary's greatest mistakes, and she made many. To decide to go ahead with Cranmer's execution made it clear that even if people recanted it was no sure promise they would escape the flames, so why not go to God in the faith they believed in? What the burnings also made evident was that there were plenty of people willing to die for their beliefs, and the burnings created martyrs to the cause of the Protestant faith, which only strengthened the resolve of many.

On the 21st of March, the day after Pole had been ordained a priest and a day before he would rise to the position of Bishop and Archbishop of Canterbury, Cranmer was brought out. It was a wet day, mizzle in the grey skies, but Cranmer appeared calm. He was, people thought, to die a Catholic, one being punished for his former beliefs, but Cranmer, brought to speak before death in the church of the university, had other plans.

"He renounced his recantation of his former beliefs," Jasper Brockehouse said. "Cranmer said that in fear of death he had rejected the true faith, but now that fear had gone, and he rejected all bills and papers he had written since his repudiation of his faith. The victory the Queen and her men hoped for vanished. The church was afire with talk and Cranmer kept on shouting, saying that the Pope brought only false doctrine to the people, and he was about to reject the transubstantiation when they hauled him off the pulpit. They ran him through the streets to the stake, and there, Cranmer thrust his right hand, the one which had signed his recantation into the flames first, saying it deserved to burn before the rest of him, since it had betrayed the faith."

"How long did he suffer?" The man was sixty-six when to this grisly death he walked.

"His end came swift, I am told. His last words were to ask Lord Jesus to accept his spirit."

"This will make people turn on the Queen."

"Indeed, it has hardened the resolve of many."

In the next years, hundreds of people would burn for their faith. In truth, I think Mary's father burned more, but it was the amount of people marched to the stake in a shorter period of time which most struck those who witnessed it. Views that had been legal and upheld only a few years before now could send a person to death. People informed on neighbours, those who they owed money to, even former friends at times. Fear wandered England as a beast in those years, clawing at the hearts of people. Some learned to hide their faith, as the Princess Elizabeth did, and many died like Cranmer, Latimer and Ridley, choking on smoke as the flames consumed their flesh until from bone it fell.

And this was done, ordered, by a woman I had considered my daughter, and friend.

*

"Does my brother mean to isolate me from all people completely?" I asked that September, feeling almost more weary than angry. Almost. All I had left here in England was my household. They were my friends and my confidants, the ones I set my trust in, and my brother was trying to strip them from me.

Wilhelm had been told, yet again, apparently this time by ambassadors and Count Von Waldeck had supported them, that numerous members of my household were untrustworthy. My brother was demanding that Mary order these people be removed from my household. In a time when my sister had so recently died and I had lost my greatest friend too, in a time when I was carefully keeping away from court so any involvement in Katherine escaping or the letters to Elizabeth might not be uncovered, the threatened removal of more people whom I loved and trusted from my house, just because my brother thought they were not good influences or because other people had lied to him about them, threatened to strip away everything that was dear to me about this world.

In truth they were being taken from me because they were being blamed for my resistance to my properties being taken away from me, again. The council had been pressuring me to exchange property, just as they had in Edward's time. Mary was protecting me no more.

My brother wanted Jasper Brockehouse and his wife, who apparently had driven me "mad", removed, along with Otho Wyllik and two others. My brother also approached Philip of Spain, thinking, quite rightly, that where he led Mary followed.

In September these people were ordered before the council and although I protested, they were commanded again to appear. Brockehouse and his wife were commanded to leave my service, and return to Cleves or at least leave England, only to return at their peril. Otho was likewise commanded to depart my household, and no one would listen to me as I protested they were loyal servants and my good friends.

"It is clear to us that these people have not served you well and have much deceived you in the manner of friendship," the council wrote. Apparently, my brother and Philip of Spain knew more than I did about my own friends.

As they left, I wondered what I had left in England. Many friends were gone, Katherine fled. Mary was much a stranger to me, even though she had invited me to the Christmas celebrations that year. I thought of Elizabeth, and I was brought some comfort, but rare was the time I was allowed to write to her. I knew I had friends, but scattered they were about the world now.

I had Susan, my gentlemen and guards, and a young woman named Dorothy Curzon came into my service soon after. Dorothy was young and sweet, and was constantly amazed by any tale of Princess Elizabeth, so I knew she looked up to her.

I lived quietly, spent time with my maids, played cards with my men. I read letters from those who loved me who I could not be with, and I prayed for a time when all this might change, and I might be reunited with those I loved, who still lived in this world.

*

That Christmas I was invited to court, and, wishing to appear a subject obedient to Her Majesty, this woman now a stranger to me, I went. Mary was oddly friendly, perhaps believing now I had been separated from all these people her husband believed were a bad influence, I would have come entirely back to the fold.

"You have been long away from us, my good aunt," she said when we met before others in her Presence Chamber.

I had to try hard to control my face. The truth was, I had not been invited to court since the Wyatt rebellion. "I live a simple life in the country, Your Majesty," I told her. "Walk, prayer, chapel and thought, these are my friends now."

There was a little flash in Mary's eyes at the mention of friends. She must have known I was passing comment on those she had stripped from me. Sometimes I wondered if my household had been reduced as punishment for Katherine escaping. It was possible Mary had found out something in the years her men had been hunting my friend in the east of the Christian world, and certainly the fact the couple had made for Cleves first must have given her pause. But she said nothing of it. "We are pleased to have you here, as family, for this Christmastide," she said.

"As I am pleased, always, to be invited to your court, Majesty."

Where did you go, Mary? my mind asked. Where was the young woman I had known? In truth, even though Mary was pale and thin where her father had been obese and ruddy when I had known him, she reminded me of him more and more as the years went on. The stubborn unwillingness to follow any path but hers, the killing of those who would not comply, the growing paranoia and suspicion of those about her... mistake me not, most rulers do the same, but this was not the Mary I had known when we were younger. It was odd to me that one who could have idolised her mother so greatly, appeared to have turned so completely into her father.

I gave the Queen presents for New Year, a purse of half-sovereigns, worth twenty pounds, and she gave to me a covered bowl, a gilt cup and a gilt cross. They were not special presents, and I remembered once hearing of a gift her father had sent her, of a gold cup with a lid, and people saying she had been sad to see it, for it was no sign of favour but a gift he gave to everyone. Many other nobles had the same as me.

But I did manage to see Elizabeth, however briefly.

"King Philip is hounding me about the match with the Duke of Savoy," she whispered as we walked in the gardens. "I have heard that if I do not agree, I may well be kidnapped and carried out of England, forced to marry the man."

I kept my face steady. "Have you told your men to keep watch on you?"

"I have, but still I fear."

"I did hear tell the King had set his sights on you as a bride for himself, in the future," I whispered.

Her face blanched. "I have no wish for the husband of my sister to look at me so," she told me. "Such an idea is repulsive. But, I admit, the same thought occurred to me."

She already knew what I was thinking, of course she did. Of all the clever women I had met, Elizabeth had the potential to be the most intelligent, but there was much else in her I loved too. A ready humour, willing to laugh at this life which so often had harmed her, and a wily sense to her nature. Elizabeth was a survivor, a more adept one than her sister ever had been, and Mary had faced more than most. Elizabeth was a good Catholic now, to the eyes of the world, but people suspected she never had lost her Protestant beliefs. Where my friend had fled, Elizabeth was hiding herself, hoping her time would come.

"If the King believes you would take his hand, he would surrender attempts to marry you elsewhere."

"I have implied as much to him. I know not if it has worked. I have thought..." she glanced about with care but only her women and mine were nearby and they were not close to us "... I have considered, leaving England."

"Do not." I smiled, nodding at a passing lady and her gentleman out for a walk with the first flush of love on their cheeks. My voice was no more than a murmur as I continued, "The same I told your sister once. Leave, and you abandon the throne. Stay, survive, and endure, and you will find your destiny. I believe it is here, in England." I gazed into her eyes. "And many others, some people I love dearly, are relying on you too."

She nodded. "My sister threatens to make the law name me a bastard again and leave the throne to Mary of Scots if I do not take Philibert as my husband."

"The people will never accept the Queen of Scots, she is promised to the prince of France. Were she to take the throne, France would too, and the people would rise up. If Philip accepts your implied offer, all of this pressure to wed will go away, so you must convince him. That way you remain free, unwed and can choose your husband when the time comes."

"I look at my sister's marriage and think once more I do not want any husband," she muttered.

"That too is a choice."

Chapter Forty-Five

1557

Chelsea Manor

"Another forced exchange of property," I said, almost to myself as I read the letter, "and my household being stripped from me I have fewer allies to defend myself with."

Brockehouse might have spoken for me in this matter, but he was gone.

A man named Sir Thomas Cornwaleys wanted me to exchange my property of Westhorpe in Sussex, one which had already been an exchange, for another. Once more the property he wanted to swap with mine was lesser in value. I had told him I would accept not the house he suggested, but the house and park at Guildford, and that was the only way I would exchange. I had come to Chelsea Manor, once the house of Katherine Parr and a property granted to me by Mary, in order that I might be closer to court, so I could appeal to Mary if possible.

The good thing was Cecil was largely handling this and although men were telling the Queen I was stubborn, and my household were encouraging me to be so, a Master Freston in particular who had become my cofferer, as well as my maids who were a constant bad influence, Cecil was helping me fight my corner. In all honesty, it seemed sometimes that as I got older – and I was not in truth that old, being forty-one – people seemed to believe I was turning to a rambling dotard, devoid of thought.

I wondered if Mary knew I had talked to Elizabeth, and this attack on my remaining property had come about because of that. I doubted she knew what we had said, but she knew we had talked a little in the brief five days Elizabeth was at court, and that might be enough. The marriage between her and Savoy had been dropped of late, so it might be that Elizabeth's plan to promise her hand to Philip had worked. The other reason was that in January the French had broken the truce made with Spain and had started war with the Hapsburgs again, so talks of marriage had dwindled as everyone spoke of war.

Two months later and Philip had appeared in England, playing the devoted husband as he tried to get Mary to go to war. Much she had pleaded with him to return before, but as soon as he needed something, he was there by her side.

He had brought with him two members of his house, the Duchesses of Parma and Lorraine. I was much amused by the appearance of Lorraine, for she was Christina, once widow of Milan, who had married the man I was intended for, Francis of Lorraine, and she once had rejected my former husband, leading to him making an offer to me.

Although it had been widely rumoured these ladies had come to take part in a plot to kidnap Elizabeth, just as she had feared, soon it vanished, and Philip was his "good sister's good friend." I thought therefore Elizabeth's scheme had indeed worked and he would not see her married off to a kinsman because now he thought there was a chance to take her himself.

And now he was occupied in persuading his wife to go to war, so had little time for aught else.

"It is said Mary is in favour," Susan told me. "But the council are not."

We all knew it was only a matter of time. When Philip clicked his fingers, so his wife ran to his side, obedient as a lapdog who knows where the treats are kept. People had, as it transpired, been right to fear that Mary as a wife would obey Philip as her husband, and war was declared in June of that year, not long before my birthday, after a nephew of Cardinal Pole himself, with aid from France, invaded England and seized Scarborough Castle. His possession did not last long, but it was enough to tip England into war.

"There is trouble between the papacy and England now," Dorothy told me, bringing some ale to me in bed, "since the Pope is allied to the French King."

I found I little cared. An illness was upon me that month. It came suddenly and stripped me of strength. I had been tired a long time, perhaps when my servants were taken from me it had come first, and now a fever had me which came and went and came and went. I thought of the days I had pretended sickness to avoid the old King making a fresh offer of marriage to me, and I smiled.

"You are pleased about the war, Highness?" asked my maid and I shook my head.

"No, child," I said. "I was thinking of the past."

*

That July I drafted my will. Weak I had grown, sleeping so much I was losing sense of the days and nights. Sudden had my sickness fallen, but I knew I might well not recover. Part of me was sad, thinking I had much still left undone. Part of me told me I had done enough.

My will said I could be buried where it pleased God, asked the Queen to pay my debts and provide for my people, and I left gifts of money to my women. To Susan and Dorothy, I left money for their marriages and smaller gifts to my laundress and to Mother Lovell, who had attended on me at Hever when I was ill. To each of the gentlemen in my house I left ten pounds, and did not forget my yeomen and grooms, or their children. I had not much, but I gave all I could. My brother was to be sent a ring of diamonds and his wife one of rubies. I sent another diamond ring to Amalia, and left one for Katherine, my friend of Suffolk, smiling at the thought that, when I was gone, Mary could no more come after me for being friends with a heretic.

To my cousin Count von Waldeck I gave another ring, and left one for the Countess of Arundel, who had been kind to me on more than one occasion. I left funds for the poor, to be given out from my estates at Hever, but also from Bletchingley, Richmond and Dartford, places where I had met and loved the people, and lastly, to my stepdaughters I made bequests. For Mary *"for a remembrance"* I left my best jewel and to Elizabeth my second best. I asked that Elizabeth take my woman Dorothy into her household, at the request of the maid herself.

"I have surrendered what is left of me in this world," I said to Susan. "It is done now, and I am prepared."

Her voice, full of tears, came as I closed my eyes in weariness. "Prepared, Highness?"

I smiled. "For what comes next."

*

And now they sit near me, all these people of my household. Some weep; some pray. They want me to recover but I will not. In some ways, I do not mind. I have fought a long time to live in England and now I will die here. Many I love are already gone.

I wish I could have seen what would happen to Elizabeth, perhaps she is my regret, and I do wish that I could have looked on the face of my friend of Suffolk once more, met the son she is rumoured to have now. But if these things are not to be, they are not to be. I know I am to join other loved ones. I do not fear, perhaps that is strange, perhaps not.

Catherine Howard asked one thing of the King before death, that she should die a private death, not under the eyes of the world. I have been granted what she never had. The eyes of the world turned from me long ago, they have other places, other people, to rest upon and that is well. Never did I wish to live in the glaring light. Always the shadows I preferred. And now I have the death she asked for, to slip away as England roars into war, without the eyes of the world staring at me, but only the eyes of the people I love in my household watching over me.

"I can hear the swans," I whisper to Dorothy, and she smiles. She thinks I cannot hear such from here, but I can.

I hear the swans on the river, calling to one another. I think, if close I listen, I will find there is a song in their voices, a single voice amongst the many singing to me and the voice which sings to me is that of my sister, calling me to her, calling me home.

I belong to those who love me, those here, weeping for me and those far away who will hear I am gone and remember me. And they belong to me. I am surrounded by those I love, even those who are not here are with me, and my heart sings, roaring with all the love they hold for me, with all the love I contain. I am made of love, suffused by it, awed to feel now all the hearts joined to mine in this world, to know in the core of my soul how deeply I am cherished.

"I am not alone," I whisper, and the song of the swan comes, stronger than before, filling my ears as my eyes are taken with the sight of feathers, wings of light which fold about me, bringing on the dark.

And in the darkness, there is a hand, reaching out, clasping mine.

The End.

Author's Notes

This book is a work of fiction, although based on research of the events and people of the time period in question. I read a great deal of sources for this book and the others in the series, which I include as a bibliography at the end.

Anna of Cleves is a much-maligned figure, the Queen of Henry VIII who was cast off after he decided he didn't like her looks, but I've always wondered about her, because of all the wives of Henry Tudor, she did the best. In the rhyme about his wives, Katherine Parr is noted as the one wife who survived, but that's not true, because Anna of Cleves survived too, and not only Henry, but Katherine Parr as well.

I think we would do better to remember her as a survivor, and a clever one at that, rather than as a cast-off wife.

Her looks will always be up for discussion, as portraits of the time might be accurate, and they might not be, but I think Anna had a great deal to recommend her which had nothing to do with looks.

For the most part in this book I have tried to stick to the historical events as they happened, but a few things I have invented.

Katherine Basset, sister of Anne Basset, was one of Anna of Cleves's serving women and was taken in for questioning due to a conversation held between her and Jane Rattsey. I invented Anna's pet name for her (of Kitty) mainly because there are so very many Katherines in this series, so to avoid some confusion I made this Katherine a Kitty. It was a common pet name for Katherines in the Tudor era. Jane Rattsey, I made one of Anna's ladies, but I have found her listed as a "lady" and as a "common woman" depending on the source, so in all honesty I remain unsure of her social status. Some sources listed her as one of Anna's women, some did not. I included her as one of the household.

Plenty of biographies of Anna of Cleves state that she was keen to marry Henry VIII again, but as I read the source material it seemed to me much of this apparent enthusiasm was coming from ambassadors, mainly of Cleves, who had been told to re-open and push the marriage negotiations after the execution of Catherine Howard. There are also various mentions of Anna slandering Katherine Parr, but considering the fact that at the time of this alleged slander there was a conflict building between Duke Wilhelm and the Emperor, as well as a concerted effort by imperial ambassadors to remove Anna and the ambassadors serving her from the English court, and country, I have chosen to approach these rumours from another angle in the book and put them down to a plot to darken her name in order to remove her and other people of Cleves from England, due to a fear they might influence the King, then the Emperor's ally, to be lenient towards Cleves. It is possible she slandered Katherine Parr but considering their later friendship it seemed unlikely to me.

I have two reasons for believing Anna had no wish to marry Henry VIII again, (aside from the dangers of being married to him, which any logical person must, by this point, have been aware of, and Katherine Parr certainly was since she commented she would rather be his mistress than his wife). The first is Anna's illness which arises suddenly and occurs just at the time when her brother was sending his men to urge Henry to marry her again. There are not many reports of Anna being ill, in fact aside from her last illness she seems to have been a woman with a strong constitution, and yet just at the time Wilhelm is urging her to wed the King again, suddenly Anna is so sick she cannot go to court. It could well have been a genuine illness, but the timing seemed interesting to me. There are repeated examples at this time of women faking illness, or the severity of an illness, in order to avoid dangerous situations or protect themselves, Katherine Parr and Elizabeth both used this tactic. Therefore, I think Anna may have too and was avoiding court and the King for the simple reason that she had no wish to be married to him again and only agreed to the idea due to pressure from her brother and duty to her country. If she did want to marry him again, I can only think it would have been because her country was in grave danger from war with the Emperor, and she was trying to protect her people.

The second reason was a comment Anna made when she learned Katherine Parr had married Henry VIII. I have read it in several forms, but the most common runs along the lines of, "A fine burden Madame Katherine has taken upon herself." Some have said this was simple, petty jealousy, but if that was the case why not say the King was taking on the burden rather than Katherine? This comment sounds to me as if her sympathy is with the Queen, not the King. The later friendship which appeared to spring up between Anna and Katherine, too, is I think quite telling. Numerous sources say Anna did not like Katherine, but once Cleves was united with the Empire due to her brother's surrender, Anna became a constant visitor to court, apparently invited by the Queen, and Anna was there much more frequently than she was when Catherine Howard was Queen. Most people accept that she and the Howard Queen got on well. If Anna did not resent the woman who immediately replaced her, why resent the one who came after her? This is all speculation, and as an author of fiction I may put my own spin on events, but I think the timing of the slander apparently done by Anna towards Katherine Parr, the timing of Anna's illness, and this comment, raise questions about traditionally accepted ideas about Anna's wish to marry the King again, and about her feelings towards his sixth wife.

With regards to Katherine Parr's brush with arrest and death at the hands of her husband, there are various tales about how she found out he was planning to have her arrested and questioned and I simply picked my favourite; the one of the dropped document found by one of her ladies. I had used it in my series on Elizabeth as well, so used it here for the sake of continuity. Another story has Katherine genuinely falling ill and the King's physician telling her what was about to happen to her. This is of course possible.

Then we get to various historical mysteries. Was the will of Henry VIII fabricated in order to facilitate the rise to power of Edward Seymour? We may never know, but certainly I think either Henry VIII was encouraged to makes changes, or changes were made whilst he was not in a state to correct them. Seymour certainly claimed more power than Henry ever intended him to. Which leads us to another question. Did Henry intend Katherine Parr to rule as Regent? Another mystery. It is true that at one stage he named her Regent, when he went to France, and may have thought she could rule for Edward, but I do wonder if, at the end, his continual and constant belief that a woman could not rule England and hold the country together might have prevailed. Henry might well have considered the idea of a female regent for a short span of time, his grandmother had acted as regent for him for a matter of months until he attained his majority, after all. The trouble was, perhaps, that knowing he was dying when his son was so young, Henry might well have thought that nine years or so was too long for a female regent to rule and may well have fallen back on the idea of a regency council instead.

Another mystery is Kett's Rebellion and the question as to whether John Dudley had anything to do with it. There are certainly questions as to what he was up to at the start of the rebellion, where he seems to be curiously absent from court at a pivotal and dangerous time. There are the links between Kett and Dudley, and the involvement of Southwell, but again, most of this is speculation. One of the reasons all this slight evidence looks suspicious, I would add, is because with hindsight we're all quite aware what a schemer John Dudley was, and the lengths he was prepared to go to in order to achieve his ambition. With such a courtier, much is possible.

No one really knows what happened to Mary Seymour, daughter of Katherine Parr. Records of her cease when she was around two years old, and it is thought therefore that she died in infancy. I had her die in the outbreak of the sweat which claimed the sons of Katherine Willoughby, but the true cause of her death is unknown. Some claim she lived to become an adult, but there is spare evidence for this. Sadly, like many children of the time, she probably did not live into adulthood.

I would like to add a slight note that Anna's comments about Penshurst Place do not reflect my opinions of the historic house! I have her being rather denigrating about the building, but mainly this is because in her day it was a smaller house than it is now, and it would have been considered a little old fashioned. It was expanded in the Elizabethan period but retains many original features. Anna's opinion of the building emerges, in truth, from it being forced upon her in one of the many exchanges of her properties. Penshurst Place is a stunning building, boasting an amazing medieval great hall, glorious rooms and truly beautiful gardens. I have been many times, and I adore it, so if you're ever thinking of visiting, please do and don't let the Anna of this book put you off!

Another alteration to fact is that it is highly unlikely Lady Mary sent word to Anna of Cleves to say she was thinking of escaping England. They were friends and Mary honoured Anna, but it is likely that this escape plan was kept a secret, for obvious reasons. What I wanted to do, however, was to create a bond which I thought might explain why, during the Wyatt rebellion, Mary did not bring Anna in for questioning. There was almost the same amount of evidence against Anna as there was against Elizabeth. It was mostly rumour and little could be substantiated, but Anna was linked to the rebellion in many ways. Personally, I do not think she was involved and that much of this "evidence" against both Anna and Elizabeth was coincidence and hearsay (although I do believe the rebels probably contacted Elizabeth directly, and I believe she gave them no firm answer of support, which was the way canny Elizabeth would play many intrigues when she rose to the throne), but Elizabeth was taken in for questioning and Anna was not. I wondered why and came to believe there was a bond of trust which Mary had with Anna which she did not have with Elizabeth. In thinking where this was forged, and knowing the two had been friends, especially after Anna's marriage to Henry VIII ended, I came to think of pivotal times Anna might have supported Mary, leading to this trust. This time of Mary's potential escape from England came to mind, and I decided to use it.

In the case of information being sent to Elizabeth whilst the Princess was in captivity at Woodstock with Anna's letters being used as a cover, this did happen. Whether Anna knew her letters were used as a cover is unknown, and what intelligence was sent I do not know, but I think this is an interesting scenario. Anna certainly regarded Elizabeth as her daughter at one point, may well have feared greatly for her during the reign of Mary and I suspect would have wanted to help her. I have framed it in the book in this way, with Anna aware that her letters are being used as a cover to take intelligence to Elizabeth from her secret supporters at court. One of the reasons I think Anna may well have been aware of this is because of another suspected involvement in a plot; that of the escape of Katherine Willoughby and her family from Mary's England. There is, again, no true evidence that Anna was involved in their escape and the fact they made straight for Cleves might well be a coincidence, but considering Katherine and Anna were good friends and considering Cleves was the country Katherine Willoughby ran to first, I think Anna was involved. I believe she did what she could to aid her friend in escaping England, and she would likewise have done what she could to aid Elizabeth. That there is little evidence of her involvement, I think simply speaks to how careful she was.

If Mary had found she was involved in either of these affairs, Anna would surely have been arrested.

Lastly, the influence Anna has on Elizabeth in this book is striking, and I have no evidence that Anna influenced Elizabeth's approach to religion as is presented in this book, but I wanted to make a point. Many historians are quick and keen to point out that Katherine Parr had a large effect on Elizabeth, and I do not deny she did, but I agree with Heather R. Darsie (author of two marvellous books on Anna of Cleves) and I believe that Anna did too. Elizabeth's choice to remain unmarried may have come to her after witnessing the many marital disasters of her father and I think Mary's marriage and Katherine Parr's too may also have set Elizabeth against the notion. She first stated that she would not marry after Catherine Howard was executed, and I believe the death of that young girl, who also was her kinswoman, probably had a great and lasting influence on her, reminding her of the circumstances of her mother's death. Yet along with all the potential danger of marriage, which might well have put Elizabeth off, as well as the fact she would have had to at least share power with a husband even if he became her consort, there is another fact to take into account. There were obviously negative reasons to avoid marriage, but there were positive ones too. Elizabeth had the example of a woman before her who had remained single, at least mostly free, rich and independent for most of her life. Anna may have encountered problems with money and her houses being taken from her, but for the most part her life was freer than many women could boast, she experienced love and satisfaction in her friends and household, and perhaps, to a young Elizabeth looking for inspiration as to how a life could be lived, Anna became that inspiration. Through Anna Elizabeth saw how a woman could live successfully as an independent agent, not relying on marriage or children in order to be happy. In linking Anna's religious beliefs to Elizabeth's, I was simply trying to show that Anna of Cleves might well have influenced Elizabeth of England a great deal more than most people think.

I would note here, Anna's religious beliefs in this book are my invention. Certainly, she never seems to emerge as a fanatic of either the traditional or reformed faith. I based my notion of her beliefs, that there was spare difference between the two sides of the Christian coin emerging at this time, on the basis that she seemed happy to worship in whatever way the ruling monarch decided, and on her upbringing in Cleves, which was Catholic, yet notions of reform were indulged. That both her sisters became ardent Protestants and yet her faith appears more fluid I think speaks to a kind of religious pragmatism but also potentially to a belief in a "middle way" much as she speaks of in the book. Her father and brother were tolerant in terms of religion, it is possible Anna was too.

Lastly, I would like to note that Anna died quite suddenly. She had been ill, but her last illness seems to claim her life swiftly. I tried to emphasise this in the book by her sickness and death being abrupt, as if her story suddenly was cut short, which, sadly, is the way for many people. Just as they think a new time is emerging, their time ends. I have read some theories of poison, but there is small evidence for this, although it is possible, especially if it was thought she was conspiring with Elizabeth, Katherine Willoughby, and other Protestants, and men of power believed they would not be able to convince Mary to arrest her. The other, and more plausible theory, is that Anna died of an infectious disease, there were many at the time, and that this claimed her life. She was buried with haste, which may well indicate she died of something infectious.

Anna was buried at Westminster Abbey on the 4th of August 1557, and Mary gave her a grand ceremony. Her tomb was positioned on the south side of the altar and therefore occupies an illustrious position. She was the only one of all of Henry VIII's wives to be buried at Westminster Abbey, where many of the kings and queens of England were laid to rest.

Sixteen months after Anna's death, Elizabeth became Queen and was crowned at Westminster Abbey. Elizabeth and Mary are also buried there, being placed in the same vault by James I.

I believe Anna of Cleves was a far more subtle and intelligent woman than history has given her credit for, as despite the fact that we all know now the flaws and faults of Henry VIII she continues to be vilified in our minds for simply being the wife he didn't want. That he rejected her has caused her to gain a reputation I feel is undeserved, and in this series of books I hope I have presented the Anna I see when reading about her, a woman of grace, intelligence, understanding and subtlety so great that her true character has managed to elude many, and yet she is a woman who deserves to be better remembered. I hope I have done her justice.

Thank You

...to so many people for helping me make this book possible... to my proofreader, Julia Gibbs, who gave me her time, her wonderful guidance and also her encouragement. To my family for their ongoing love and support. To my friend Petra. To my friend Nessa for her support and affection, and to another friend, Anne, who has done so much for me. To Sue and Annette, more friends who read my books and cheer me on. To Terry for getting me into writing and indie publishing in the first place. To Katie and Jooles, Macer, Pip, Linda, Fe, Pete and Heather, people there in times of trial. And to all my wonderful readers, who took a chance on an unknown author, and have followed my career and books since.

To those who have left reviews or contacted me by email or on social media, I give great thanks, as you have shown support for my career as an author and enabled me to continue writing. Thank you for allowing me to live my dream.

Thank you to all of you; you'll never know how much you've helped me, but I know what I owe to you.

Gemma Lawrence
Wales
2025

About The Author

I find people talking about themselves in the third person to be entirely unsettling, so, since this section is written by me, I will use my own voice rather than try to make you believe that another person is writing about me in order to make me sound terribly important.

I am an independent author, publishing my books by myself, with the help of my lovely proofreader. I left my day job in 2016 and am now a fully-fledged, full-time author, and proud to be so.

My passion for history began early in life. As a child I lived in Croydon, near London, and my schools were lucky enough to be close to such glorious places as Hampton Court and the Tower of London, allowing field trips to take us to those castles. I write historical fiction for the main part, but I also have a fascination with ghost stories and fantasy, and I hope this book was one you enjoyed. I want to divert you as readers, to please you with my writing and to have you join me on these adventures.

A book is nothing without a reader.

As to the rest of me, I am in my forties and live in Wales with a rescued cat (who often sits on my lap when I write, which can make typing more of a challenge). I studied Literature at University after I fell in love with books as a small child. When I was little, I could often be found nestled halfway up the stairs with a pile of books in my lap and my head lost in another world. There is nothing more satisfying to me than finding a new book I adore, to place next to the multitudes I own and love... and nothing more disappointing to me to find a book I am willing to never open again. I do hope that this book was not a disappointment to you. I loved writing it and I hope that showed through the pages.

If you would like to contact me, please do so. I can be found in quite a few places!

On Twitter, (I am not calling it X) I am @TudorTweep.

You can also find me on Instagram as tudorgram1500, on Mastodon as G. Lawrence Tudor Tooter, @TudorTweep@mastodonapp.uk, and Counter Social as TudorSocial1500.

On Facebook my page is just simply G. Lawrence, and on TikTok and Threads I am tudorgram1500, the same as Instagram. I've joined Bluesky as G. Lawrence too. Often, I have a picture of the young Elizabeth I as my avatar, or there's me leaning up against a wall in Pembroke Castle.

I publish on Substack, where my account is called G. Lawrence in the Book Nook. On there I publish articles, reviews, poetry, advice for other writers and I'm publishing a book there chapter by chapter each week. Join me there!

Via email, I am tudortweep@gmail.com a dedicated email account for my readers to reach me on. I'll try and reply within a few days.

Thank you for taking a risk with an unknown author and reading my book. I do hope now that you've read one, you'll want to read more. If you'd like to leave me a review, that would be very much appreciated also!

Gemma Lawrence
Wales
2025

Select Bibliography for the Series

Ackroyd, Peter, *The Life of Thomas More*

Arnopp, Judith, *How to Dress like a Tudor*

Baldwin, David, *Henry VIII's Last Love: The Extraordinary Life of Katherine Willoughby, Lady-in-Waiting to the Tudors*

Baldwin-Smith, Lacey, *Anne Boleyn: Queen of Controversy*

Bernard, G.W, *Anne Boleyn: Fatal Attractions*

Bordo, Susan, *The Creation of Anne Boleyn*

Borman, Tracy, *Thomas Cromwell, Elizabeth's Women, The Private Lives of the Tudors*

Brigden, Susan, *Thomas Wyatt: The Heart's Forest*

Brears, Peter, *Cooking and Dining in Medieval England, All the King's Cooks*

Breverton, Terry, *The Tudor Kitchen*

Castiglione, Baldesar, *The Book of the Courtier*

Chapman, Lissa, *Anne Boleyn in London*

Childs, Jessie, *Terror and Faith in Elizabethan England*

Cummings, John, *The Hound and the Hawk: The Art of Medieval Hunting*

Darsie, Heather. R, *Anna, Duchess of Cleves, the King's Beloved Sister. Children of the House of Cleves: Anna and her Siblings*

Denny, Joanna, *Anne Boleyn: A New Life of England's Most Tragic Queen, Katherine Howard: A Tudor Conspiracy.*

Doran, Susan, *Elizabeth I and her Circle*

Duffy, Eamon, *The Stripping of the Altars*

Evans, Jennifer and Read, Sarah, *Maladies and Medicines*

Fletcher, Catherine, *The Divorce of Henry VIII: The Untold Story*

Fletcher, Stella, *Cardinal Wolsey: a Life in Renaissance Europe*

Fox, Julia, *Jane Boleyn: The Infamous Lady Rochford, Sister Queens: Katherine of Aragon and Juana, Queen of Castile*

Friedmann, P, *Anne Boleyn*

Fraser, Antonia, *The Six Wives of Henry VIII*

Gelis, Jacques, *History of Childbirth*

Goodison, Natalie Jayne, *Introducing the Medieval Swan*

Goodman, Ruth, *How to be a Tudor*

Gunn, Steven, *Charles Brandon*

Green, Monica (editor and translator), *The Trotula: An English Translation of the Medieval Compendium of Women's Medicine*

Gristwood, Sarah, *The Tudors in Love*

Grueninger, Natalie, *Discovering Tudor London*

Gwyn, Peter, *The King's Cardinal: The Rise and Fall of Thomas Wolsey*

Hammond, Peter, *Food and Feast in Medieval England*

Hart, Kelly, *The Mistresses of Henry VIII*

Haynes, Alan, *Sex in Elizabethan England*

Hayward, Maria, *Rich Apparel: Clothing and the Law in Henry VIII's England*

Hieatt, Constance and Butler, Sharon, (editors), *Curye on Inglysch*

Higgenbotham, Susan, *Margaret Pole: The Countess in the Tower*

Hutchinson, Robert, *Thomas Cromwell*

Ives, Eric, *The Life and Death of Anne Boleyn*

James, Susan, *Catherine Parr: Henry VIII's Last Love*

Jones, Philippa, *The Other Tudors*

Knecht, R.J, *Renaissance Prince and Warrior: The Reign of Francis I*

Licence, Amy, *Catherine of Aragon, Anne Boleyn: Adultery, Heresy, Desire, The Tudors, The Six Wives and Many Mistresses of Henry VIII: The Women's Stories, Woodsmoke and Sage: The Five Senses 1485-1603, In Bed with the Tudors.*

Lipscomb, Suzannah, *A Visitor's Companion to Tudor England, 1536: The Year that Changed Henry VIII.*

Loades, David, *Jane Seymour: Henry VIII's Favourite Wife, The Seymours of Wolf Hall, The Six Wives of Henry VIII, The Boleyns, Catherine Howard: the adulterous wife of Henry VIII, Bastard Prince: Henry VIII's Lost Son.*

Lofts, Norah, *Anne Boleyn*

Maddocks, Fiona, *Hildegard of Bingen: The Woman of her Age*

Machiavelli, Niccolo, *The Prince*

Mackay, Lauren, *Inside the Tudor Court*

MacCulloch, Diarmaid, *Reformation: Europe's House Divided, 1490-1700, Thomas Cranmer*

Markham, Gervase, *The English Housewife*

Matusiak, John, *Wolsey: The Life of Henry VIII's Cardinal*

Martienssen, Anthony, *Queen Katherine Parr*

Moorhouse, Geoffrey, *Great Harry's Navy*

Morris, Sarah and Grueninger, Natalie, *In the Footsteps of Anne Boleyn*

Moynahan, Brian, *Book of Fire*

Murphy, Beverley, *Bastard Prince: Henry VIII's Lost Son*

Navarre, Marguerite of, *The Heptameron, The Glass of the Sinful Soul*

Norton, Elizabeth, *Jane Seymour, The Lives of Tudor Women, Anne Boleyn: Henry VIII's Obsession, Anne Boleyn: In her own words and those of who knew her, The Boleyn Women, Anne of Cleves: Henry VIII's Discarded Bride.*

Norris, Herbert, *Tudor Costume and Fashions*

Parker, Geoffrey, *Emperor: a New Life of Charles V*

Perry, Maria, *Sisters to the King*

Plat, Hugh, *Delightes for Ladies*

Plowden, Alison, *The House of Tudor, Tudor Women: Queens and Commoners, The Young Elizabeth, Danger to Elizabeth*

Porter, Linda, *Mary Tudor, Katherine the Queen: The Remarkable life of Katherine Parr*

Power, Eileen (translator), *The Goodman of Paris*

Ridgeway, Claire, *George Boleyn, The Anne Boleyn Collection, The Anne Boleyn Papers, The Fall of Anne Boleyn*

Ridley, Jasper, *The Tudor Age*

Roud, Steve, *The English Year*

Roth, Erik, *With a Bended Bow*

Russell, Gareth, *Young, Damned and Fair: The Life and Tragedy of Catherine Howard at the Court of Henry VIII.*

Seward, Desmond, *Prince of the Renaissance*

Sharp, Jane, *The Midwives Book*

Shulman, Nicola, *Graven with Diamonds*

Sim, Alison, *The Tudor Housewife, Food and Feast in Tudor England, Pleasures and Pastimes in Tudor England,*

Siraisi, Nancy, *Medieval and Early Renaissance Medicine*

Skidmore, Chris, *Edward VI: The Lost King of England*

Smith, Lacy Baldwin, *Catherine Howard*

Soberton, Sylvia Barbara, *Medical Downfall of the Tudors*

Starkey, David, *Six Wives: The Queens of Henry VIII, The Reign of Henry VIII: Personalities and Politics, Henry: Virtuous Prince, Elizabeth.*

Thomas, Keith, *Religion and the Decline of Magic*

Tremlett, Giles, *Catherine of Aragon: Henry's Spanish Queen*

Tudor, Henry, *The Love Letters of Henry VIII, Asserto Septem Sacramentorium*

Tyndale, William, *The Obedience of a Christian Man, the Tyndale New Testament*

Van Loo, Bart, *The Burgundians: A Vanished Empire*

Watkins, Sarah-Beth, *The Tudor Brandons*

Weir, Alison, *Henry VIII, King and Court, The Lady in the Tower: The Fall of Anne Boleyn, Mary Boleyn, The Great and Infamous Whore, The Children of Henry VIII,*

Wilkinson, Josephine, *Anne Boleyn: The Young Queen To Be, The Early Loves of Anne Boleyn, Katherine Howard: The Tragic story of Henry VIII's fifth Queen.*

Williams, Patrick, *Katherine of Aragon*

Wilson, Derek, *Henry VIII: Reformer and Tyrant, Hans Holbein: Portrait of an Unknown Man*

Wyngaerde, Anthonis, *The Panorama of London circa 1544*

Printed in Great Britain
by Amazon